A
SPLENDID
RUIN

A SPLENDID RUIN

A Novel

MEGAN CHANCE

Published by Lake Union Publishing, Seattle

www.apub.com

Amazon, the Amazon logo, and Lake Union Publishing are trademarks of Amazon.com, Inc., or its affiliates.

ISBN-13: 9781542022392
ISBN-10: 1542022398

Cover design by Shasti O'Leary Soudant

Printed in the United States of America

For the cousins:
Polly, Steven, Veronica, Morgan, Shane, Evan,
Emmalee, Zia, and Ani

PART ONE:

SECRETS

SAN FRANCISCO, JULY 1904

ONE

When I arrived at the Nob Hill mansion belonging to my aunt Florence and her husband, Jonathan Sullivan, it was still more than a year from its fate as a crumbling, smoldering ruin, and I was still naive enough to believe in the welcome I found there.

My mother had died two months ago and left me abandoned and lonely. I thought I knew to trust only myself. But I underestimated the astonishment of white stone and three stories, of windows glinting in afternoon sunlight breaking through a veil of fog, of the fragrance of roses and horses and men's sweat blooming in the clammy, tangy air. Had I known what awaited me in that house, I would have done everything differently. But that day, I was too bedazzled by the men carrying chairs and boxes and crates up the marble steps and past the pillared portico to see the truth hidden by the Sullivans' money and inclusiveness.

The driver hefted my suitcase to the crushed white stone of the drive. "There'll be a footman coming for it," he said, moving back to the horses. "Au's expecting you."

Ow? I frowned, but the driver climbed aboard and drove off to the stables, leaving me standing uncertain amid the fuss.

Mama had never said anything of her family having such wealth, not once, in all our years of suffering. But then again, neither had she told me she had a sister. I should not be surprised. She'd kept so many secrets. But this . . . Why had she said nothing of *this*? Perhaps she had not known of her sister's good fortune. I told myself that had to be the reason.

I hadn't thought to see such a house in all of San Francisco, much less an entire neighborhood of them. The driver had called the area Nob Hill, and it was nothing but mansions, Gothic style and Beaux-Arts, turreted and terraced, gimcracked with all the embellishments money could buy—and each probably holding more rooms than the sum of those on my entire street in Brooklyn.

In the twenty-three years of my life, I'd dreamed of such houses, drawing their contents and imagining myself within them, but I'd never, never expected anything like this when I received the letter from the woman claiming to be my aunt Florence, expressing her sorrow over Mama's death, and inviting me to come live with her family in San Francisco. *I cannot bear the thought of Charlotte's daughter alone in that terrible city. Please. You must come.*

The train ticket had been enclosed as if there was no question that I would agree. Which I did; I had nothing to leave behind but a job as a shopgirl selling gewgaws at Mrs. Beard's Shoppe for Ladies, and a boardinghouse smelling of talc and mutton, where I'd shared a room with my mother that I could not afford on my own. I'd been days from having to find another establishment, and fearing an uncertain future.

On the train to San Francisco, I had envisioned a hundred different things: another boardinghouse, a flat perhaps, or, in my most elaborate scenarios, a small house or a brownstone. And now, here I was, and none of this felt the least bit real.

Nervously, uncomfortably, I made my way through the moving men, past pillars carved with cupids embracing a coat of arms. I paused at the open door.

"Excuse me, miss." A burly man pushed past with a crate of white roses. Their perfume engulfed me as I followed him into a foyer laid with rhomboid tiles in green and brown, pink and white. The ceiling reached two stories into a dome painted with angels. Unbelievable. The foyer, too, bustled with men unloading boxes and maids scurrying about.

A huge golden-framed mirror with a velvet banquette was to my left. Beside it stood a gold and marble table where a filigreed, claw-footed silver telephone crouched amid a riot of vases and salvers. I'd never seen a telephone so decorated. I'd no idea such a thing existed. It shuddered to life with a raucous ringing, and I jumped, startled.

A harried-looking Chinese man wearing a formal suit rushed into the foyer. He picked up the wooden-handled receiver and barked into it, "Sullivan residence."

It surprised me. There had been no Chinese in my old neighborhood, and the last thing I'd expected was to find one answering the phone in my aunt's house. The domestics I knew in Brooklyn were almost always Irish. I'd never heard of anyone having a Chinese butler. When I stepped back, he noticed me and motioned for me to wait. "No, no," he barked into the telephone. "The order was for ten, not four." At the finish of the short conversation, he put the receiver into its cradle. "You are Miss Kimble?"

His briskness and authority surprised me again. I nodded.

"The family has been expecting you. This way, miss." He turned on his heel so sharply that the braid trailing between his shoulder blades jumped. He led me past a curving set of stairs and down a hallway that branched every few feet in what seemed a dozen different directions before he stopped at an open doorway and announced, "Miss Kimble has arrived."

"Excellent!" pronounced an enthusiastic male voice.

I stepped into a relentlessly lavish drawing room as a tall, slender man dressed in a well-tailored suit rose to meet me. His close-cropped beard was the same red gold as his oiled hair. Every bit of him was expertly turned out, so much so that I might have found him intimidating if not for the warmth in his protuberant pale eyes, and his hands outstretched in greeting. "Miss Kimble, I'm Jonathan Sullivan, your uncle Jonny. How pleased we are that you're here at last." He clasped my hands with a smile that further eased my nerves. "We were so sorry to hear of your mother's passing. No one can replace her, of course, but I do hope we can help to ease her absence."

"I'm grateful that you sent for me, Uncle. And you must call me May. Please."

"May, you'll want to meet your cousin." He stepped back, gesturing to a young woman almost hidden amid the gold-flocked wallpaper, ornate woodwork, and bibelots crowding every surface.

When I saw her, there was no noticing anything else.

"I'm Goldie." She got to her feet with a grace and poise I envied. From that first moment, I was dangerously spellbound. Her smile made me forget I'd ever been lonely.

I had never met anyone who matched a name as perfectly as did my cousin. Her blue tea gown was the color of her eyes and cut to show off her fashionable hourglass figure. Her blond hair was artfully pompadoured in the style featured in all the latest magazines. The electric light glaring off the wallpaper haloed her, making her an angel to match the hordes of painted and porcelain ones decorating the house.

Uncle Jonny said, "Why, look at the two of you! A perfect match! I've no doubt at all that you will become fast friends."

Goldie enfolded me in a jasmine-scented embrace. "How wonderful that we've found you. You look so like family that I think I would have known you on the street."

It was an exaggeration, but a kind one. Goldie was about my age, or perhaps a bit younger, but there any similarities ended. My cousin looked more like my mother than did I. Mama had been beautiful, too, and I'd often despaired at my unremarkable brown eyes and hair and sallow skin.

Now, I felt my lack even more, and it didn't help that I was dust and travel stained, or that my sleepless nights must be reflected on my face. I looked around for the woman I'd come three thousand miles to meet. "And Aunt Florence?"

My uncle and cousin exchanged a quick glance. Uncle Jonny said, "She wished to be here to meet you, but I'm afraid that—"

"She has a headache," Goldie put in.

"Oh." I tried not to betray my disappointment. I had so many questions for this aunt I'd never met. My mother's secrets, the mysteries of her life, of mine . . . But that afternoon, I believed there was plenty of time to discover those things. I'd only just arrived.

Goldie took my arm in a flurry of animation. "You must be dying to change out of those clothes. The train is so awful, isn't it? I swear it's impossible to travel in anything nice at all."

This morning, I had changed into my best suit, wanting to impress my relatives. I knew Goldie could not see the mend in the shirtwaist—it was at the back, hidden by the smart jacket Mama and I had sewn to match my brown skirt—but it seemed suddenly horribly visible.

My cousin rushed on before I had time to register my humiliation. "We shall have so much fun! I'm simply dying to introduce you to everyone."

"Everyone?"

"They're all so excited to meet you. The talk has been wild for days. You were even mentioned in the Arrivals column of the *Bulletin*!"

Uncle Jonny made a face.

"It shows we are people of note," Goldie said pertly to her father. "It's of course why Mrs. Hoffman is coming."

"You're confusing May, my darling," Uncle Jonny said kindly, and then, to me, "I do hope you're not too tired from travel. Goldie insisted you wouldn't be."

"No woman is too tired for a party, Papa," Goldie said.

"A party?" I asked.

My uncle explained, "In your honor. I hope you don't mind. We felt it the best way to welcome you and show you off to our friends."

Goldie said, "Why else do you think all these servants are underfoot? I ordered fifty dozen roses and enough candles to light the entire street."

Uncle Jonny winced.

"Oh hush, Papa. It will look beautiful, and it will smell divine, and isn't it worth it to welcome my long-lost cousin? Are you all right, May? Oh, please don't tell me you *are* too tired!"

"Perhaps she's a trifle overwhelmed, my dear," Uncle Jonny suggested with an understanding glance to me.

A trifle? Much more than that. *"Never give Them a reason to think you don't belong,"* Mama had always said. She had meant Society. This was the life for which I'd been trained, though I'd never expected to need Mama's lessons. I was a shopgirl in Brooklyn, and at best, I'd thought Mama's teaching would help me get a job at one of the bigger department stores, where my perfect manners might impress a customer into buying a more expensive brooch.

I composed myself quickly and smiled. "I'm delighted. You are both so very kind."

Uncle Jonny said, "We could do no less. You are family, after all. Why don't you show May to her room, my dear? Are you hungry, May? I'll have tea sent up."

"Before a party, Papa? No woman wants tea before dancing." Goldie dragged me from the drawing room and again into the vast and bustling foyer, expertly angling past the activity. She took me up the stairs, which were laid with a murky green runner the hue of algae skimming a stagnant pond.

"Papa's asked Mr. Sotheby to perform tonight." Goldie gave me an expectant look.

It was obvious that I was supposed to know the name and be delighted. "What a treat."

"I expect everyone who matters in San Francisco will be here. I sent Alphonse Bandersnitch an invitation, so it will undoubtedly be written up in the *Bulletin*."

"Alphonse Bandersnitch?"

"He writes the best society column in town."

We reached the next floor, the green runner abruptly ending at a carpet of orange and red and gold flowers. The pale blue walls wore stucco flourishes, and mirrors in gilded frames ran the full hall, bouncing reflections back and forth, endless Mays walking with endless Goldies. A hall table teemed with more china angels and gold-spotted fawns worshipping a large marble cupid with a harp.

Goldie stopped at a door. "This is your room. Mine is just on the other side of the bath. I decorated it, so I do hope you like it. Papa is hopeless. You would have had boring gold stripes if it were up to him."

Which might have been more restful than the mauve wallpaper blooming with pink and red roses and bluebirds making nests in tangled green vines. Pink cabbage roses clustered the carpet. Two sets of pink curtains, one lace and one velvet, opened to reveal a view of fog peppered with the tops of buildings and ships' masts. The room was also as full of *things* as had been the drawing room. Perfume bottles and gilded lamps, enameled boxes and glass bowls and porcelain cherubs in all manner of poses. I could only stare at the almost aggressive profusion.

Idly, Goldie picked up one of the cherubs, stroking its gilded hair. "I suppose you couldn't go to many parties while your mother was ill. Was she sick for a long time?"

Her question distracted from the decor. "No. She wasn't ill. Her death was very sudden. Her heart—"

"Oh? But her letter made it sound quite expected."

Even more confusing. "She wrote to you?"

"To Mother. How else do you think we found you? Mother had never mentioned you at all."

How had I known nothing of this? Nothing of a family. Nothing of a letter. The questions that had bedeviled me since I'd received my aunt's summons returned, along with a familiar flicker of anger. "But why? Why did they not speak of one another?"

Goldie shrugged. "Who knows?"

"You never asked?"

"No."

"Did she say anything in the letter about my father?"

"Your father? No, not at all." Goldie glanced away. "Well, I'll leave you to get ready."

It was an obvious evasion. I'd had enough experience with Mama to recognize a deliberate change of subject. Perhaps I'd been too eager. That I had family at all was such recent news that I still had trouble believing it. One sister in San Francisco, the other in New York. The distance would have been enough excuse for a lack of knowledge once. But distance was nothing now. A train could bridge the gap in days. A telegraph in no time. If Mama had sent a letter, then she'd clearly known about her sister's location, as well as her wealth. Why, then, had she never mentioned my aunt?

So many, many secrets. A lifetime of them. *"I made a promise to your father, May,"* she'd told me, *"and what are we if we cannot keep our promises? He will not forget his debt to me, or to you. He was a good and honorable man."* Honorable? Honorable to whom? Certainly not to us.

And what had Mama promised in return? Had it something to do with why we'd been so poor? Mama had refused to answer my questions, telling me only that he was a member of New York City society, one of Mrs. Astor's famous Four Hundred families, the social elite, and that *"he would love you if he knew you."* Why, then, did he not know me?

What I saw was that Mama refused to ask him for help, and he didn't care enough to find us, and I wore boots with cardboard soles that dissolved in the winter slush and threadbare coats donated from charity organizations managed by sanctimonious women of my father's class. But Mama never wavered in her conviction that he would keep his end of their bargain, whatever it had been. Oh, how she believed and believed and believed. She would not hear a single word against him, and I soon learned to keep my criticisms to myself. I thought that he'd lied to her and abandoned us both, and I had long since grown tired of waiting for whatever he'd promised—and impatient and angry with my mother's faith in an obviously faithless man.

At twelve I'd insisted upon being taken out of school so I could work. Every spare hour we had together, Mama had schooled me in etiquette and French, dancing, and watercolors. I had always been poised between two lives: the one I lived daily in Brooklyn, and the one my mother had promised me, *"One day you'll want for nothing. You don't belong here. You are meant for something finer than this."*

But no rich society father had materialized upon her death. Perhaps this was the life she'd been promising instead, with my relatives. Perhaps her promises to my father had something to do with Aunt Florence and San Francisco. But, then, why never mention the Sullivans? What had she written to them? When? I'd never known anything about an illness.

The answers had gone to the grave with my mother, and I told myself, once again, to be patient. No doubt my aunt knew. For now, I wanted to enjoy everything. So I ignored the twitchy prick of discomfort that this was all some terrible mistake. I was to go to my first ball tonight. My life had so suddenly changed for the better that I didn't want to ruin it with old dissatisfactions.

I had no ball gown, of course. My Sunday best would have to do. It was a decent fawn-colored mousseline, and I'd been complimented on it many times in church and knew it became me. Still, when I put the dress on, the room itself seemed to mock me. I had no jewelry, but Mama had always said that a proper lady did not depend upon ornamentation. Yet my poverty had never been so evident. I looked a poor church mouse in a gilded, bejeweled box.

Then, there was a knock on my door. Before I could answer, Goldie rushed in with an armful of billowing pink silk. "I knew it." She dumped the silk carelessly on the bed. "Nick said your trunks must be delayed. You really cannot trust the trains these days! I knew no ball gown could fit in that tiny case of yours, so I thought . . . if you wished it, well, why not borrow something of mine? No one's seen me in this in ages."

I had no trunks. I did not know how to say that, nor how to tell Goldie that I had not lived the life she obviously thought I had. Not only that, but I was at least two inches taller than my cousin, and I could not come close to approaching her perfect figure. Yet I would have worn that dress for the rest of my life out of sheer gratitude.

"Thank you for thinking of it. I didn't wish to embarrass any of you."

She waved that away. "I shall send a complaint to the station on your behalf."

She blew me a kiss and left me alone with the gown, which was beautiful, and finer than anything I'd ever possessed, but yes, it would have taken a magic corset to give me my cousin's bosom, and the décolletage sagged horribly and far too low until I tucked an old lace fichu of my mother's about my shoulders. It was ancient and tattered at the edges, but if I arranged it just so, the ragged parts were hidden. The gown was too short as well, but it was more elegant and beautiful than the fawn, and the pink did put color in my pale cheeks, and at least I looked dressed for a party rather than a sermon.

I spent a great deal of time on my hair, which was frizzy and unmanageable at the best of times, trying to coax it into something approximating Goldie's stylish coiffure. I strained for the sounds of guests arriving, but I heard nothing. It was as if the bustle I'd witnessed earlier had completely vanished. I spent an hour deciding which of the many perfumes to wear, finally choosing the orange blossom.

I was starving, and I wished Goldie had not refused tea, but surely there would be food at the ball. I waited for someone to come for me. A knock on the door. A maid. Goldie or my uncle to tell me the party had begun. I went to the window and watched the carriages arrive through the densening fog, the nimbi of their lamps floating disembodied in the mist. Still, no one came. I wondered if there was some protocol for the guest of honor that I didn't know. Should I arrive on time? Late? Did I make a grand appearance? In all my mother's lessons, we had not discussed this scenario.

I opened the bedroom door and stood in the hallway—far too bright now, electric lights blazing, and soundless. How very strange. I would have thought there was no party at all had I not seen the guests arriving. I knocked on Goldie's door, but there was no answer, and when I opened it to a waft of jasmine and a glimpse of gold and white, there was no one inside. She must already be downstairs. They were waiting.

I went to the top of the stairs and grasped the rail. I was holding up everything. The guests would be impatient. I closed my eyes, thinking of my mother taking my hand in the sitting room as she taught me the waltz. *"The grandest dance of them all. A woman can charm anyone in the waltz, if she does it correctly."* That wistful smile.

"Remember who you are, May." The balm of my mother's oft-repeated words and the softness of memory banished my unease. I flew down the stairs to the party.

TWO

I was indeed late. The ballroom swarmed with more people than I'd met in my entire life. Many milled around a tall gilded statue of a lithesome—*naked*—woman in the middle of the room, but it was too crowded for me to get a good look. A small orchestra performed between pillars at the far end. Clouds of smoke obscured the gilded stucco decorations on the walls and hovered about the chandeliers, making a bright haze of the candlelight. Goldie had been right when she'd said she'd bought enough candles to light the street. Swaths of flame from tall candelabras and golden stands flashed on the studs in men's shirt fronts, glittered on their watch chains, and sent sparkles onto the ears and throats and wrists of the women. Bouquets of white roses softened every surface, their perfume so thick one could almost drink it.

I had imagined such a scene a hundred times, but the reality was much different. I felt like the outsider I'd been all those times I'd stood on the street with other onlookers to watch the guests arrive at a Vanderbilt or Belmont party, angling for the glimpse of a gown or a famous necklace. I could not possibly belong here, whatever my mother had said. But at the same time, the excitement of being among them, one of them, made my fingers itch with the desire to claim the moment, to translate those colors, those lights, into something I could keep.

I was also hideously aware of the shortness of my gown. It seemed that everyone glanced at the hem, and the fichu was too old-fashioned. A waiter went by with a tray, and I recognized champagne. I'd had it once before. Mrs. Beard's brother had brought a bottle one afternoon to celebrate the birth of his son, and I remembered the hot tickle of the bubbles in my throat and my wavering walk home and how I'd flirted with Michael Kilpatrick next door before Mama caught sight of me and ordered me inside. How at ease with the world I'd felt.

I wanted that feeling again now. I grabbed a glass and sipped with as much nonchalance as I could muster, trying to swallow my anxiety with it. My mother's advice to remember that I belonged to this society fluttered uselessly at my ears. Goldie appeared at my side just as I finished the glass and gave it to a passing waiter.

"There you are! Where have you been? We've been looking all over for you. You should be in the receiving line with me and Papa." Her scold was light, but loud enough that those nearby turned to look. She held two glasses of punch, handed me one, and led me to the door where my uncle greeted his guests. I had managed to miss the arrival of most of them.

"I'm so sorry," I whispered to my cousin.

Goldie whispered back, "Never mind that now," and turned to greet a woman swathed in silk with lace and fur trim.

It soon became obvious that my aunt was not present, either. Almost everyone asked about her—"And how is dear Florence?" "She missed our last two luncheons! I do hope she's better soon."

So she'd been ill for a little while, but there was no time to wonder; I was too busy responding to a dozen choruses of "Welcome to San

Francisco!" and *"How do you find our fair city?"* The punch, sweet and potent and seemingly bottomless, made it all much easier, but by the time Uncle Jonny said, "Why don't we join our guests?" I was unsteady on my feet and all too aware that I had not eaten since the train.

"Where is Mrs. Hoffman, Papa?" Goldie asked.

"Oh well, as to that"—Uncle Jonny cleared his throat—"I'm afraid she's sent her regrets."

"Her regrets? When?" Goldie's voice was sharp.

"A few hours ago. I'm sorry. I know you were looking forward to seeing her, but there's no help for it."

Goldie tightened her lips in obvious vexation.

It was equally obvious by my uncle's uncomfortable smile that he disliked displeasing her. Placatingly, he said, "My darling, why don't you take May about? She is the guest of honor."

"Of course." Goldie took my arm, muttering beneath her breath, "She sent her regrets. Yes, no doubt she did."

I offered, "Perhaps she was feeling unwell—"

"She was shopping just this morning. I saw her myself."

I had nothing to say to that. I didn't know who Mrs. Hoffman was, or why Goldie would be upset at her absence. Goldie snagged two more glasses of punch. She gestured toward the statue. Now I could see that the golden maiden leaned languorously on a staff that some tiny gilded putto crawled up. "Don't you just love it?" Goldie asked. "It's French. A bacchante. It's a copy of a Gérôme."

"It's very nice." Like everything in the house, the statue seemed too much, this time rather obscenely so.

But Goldie was done with the bacchante. In a low voice, she said, "Have you seen Mr. Bandersnitch anywhere?"

It took me a moment to remember that he was the *Bulletin* society columnist. "What does he look like?"

"No one knows. He's very anonymous."

"Then how should I know if I've seen him?"

She scanned the crowd as if she might somehow divine his presence. "Of course he must be here. He simply must. Where else would he be? It's the party of the night, even without Mrs. Hoffman." Goldie's face fell, then snapped into joy again. "Oh, there's Linette, thank God." She hurried off toward a young woman laughing with two men. I knew I should follow—the key to being comfortable was feigning it—but my light-headedness had become nausea, and I could not negotiate another introduction. I put aside my empty punch cup and took a toast spread with something pale and unappetizing from a passing waiter, but the smell of whatever it was only made my nausea worse, and I abandoned it on a candlelit gold salver and headed for the garden door, suddenly desperate for a breath of air.

The garden was no relief. I was immediately disoriented as I stepped out. I'd had far too much punch. Here, too, dozens of candles flickered inside their glass lamps, creating a maze of the stone benches and statues—so many statues that twice I stumbled right up to people, thinking they were made of marble, interrupting those who had escaped the ballroom looking for privacy. I walked along the wall until I found another set of French doors, which opened into a darkened room. I hurried inside with relief, relishing the coolness. I could no longer hear anything from the ballroom.

I'd come into a small sitting room, one crowded with shadows. Light from the garden glanced upon the mantelpiece—two eyes flashed at me, and then another two, small, like those of mice. I tensed, but they were only jeweled eyes, a glass menagerie stalking across the mantel, some glowing red, others blue, others in prism. The room reeked of patchouli. This must be my aunt's private parlor. Or Goldie's. But no, Goldie's would have smelled of jasmine, as did her room, as did her entire self.

Almost the moment I had the thought, the room became suddenly oppressive; I wanted only to be out. I didn't want to go back into the garden, so I crossed the room, avoiding the shadows as best I could, and opened the door, not into a bright hallway, as I'd expected, but a dark and eerily silent one. Had I not known that the ballroom just now held a hundred people or more, I would have thought the house empty. I half expected to run across dusty cobwebs, to hear my footsteps echo, but then, no—it wasn't desertion I sensed, but something else, something more unsettling. I couldn't help shivering.

There were no tables in this hallway, no mirrors or paintings, no decoration at all. I had no idea where I was. Anxiously I remembered the many hallways I'd noted earlier branching off one another. How many rooms were in this mansion? Thirty? Fifty? More?

Softly, I knocked upon one closed door. There was no answer, cautiously I opened it. The curtains were drawn, but the candlelight from the window seeped inside, shifting across a bare wooden floor, reflecting off the crystals of a hanging chandelier. Otherwise, the room was completely empty.

As was the room beside it. And the one beside that. After the over-decoration of the other rooms, it was disquieting that these were so barren. I could not rid myself of a creeping unease.

I'd opened three doors before I came upon one with any furniture, and even then, it was only books piled every which way, awaiting shelves, which were only planks leaning against a wall.

There was no puzzle in this, only unfinished rooms. This was obviously to be a library, and the other empty rooms were only awaiting their assignments. The house was newer than I'd thought. I should have known it, given the construction I'd seen elsewhere on the hill, mansions and a large hotel looming unfinished in the fog. I wondered how long the Sullivans had lived here. I'd asked not a single question of them beyond my aunt's health. I had no idea if they were new to San Francisco, or where their wealth came from, or even what my uncle did for a living. Of course, my mother would roll over in her grave if I were ever so crass as to ask such questions.

There was plenty of time to discover these things. I'd only been here a day. Less than that.

They would be missing me. But as much as I didn't want to be in these empty, creepy halls, I didn't want to go back to the party—*my party*—where I felt so out of place. Yet this was where I belonged now. It was where I must belong. I had no desire to return to my old life.

It was only that it had been a very long day, and I was thoroughly lost. But as I made my way back, my discomfort didn't settle. I might still be wandering the halls if I hadn't happened upon a Chinese maid with a heart-shaped face who stared at me as if I were a ghost. Hardly surprising, given the way I'd emerged from the darkness.

"I'm afraid I'm lost. How does anyone find their way in here?"

"The ballroom is that way, miss."

When I found it again, Goldie fell upon me. "Where did you go off to? I wanted you to meet my friends."

We'd barely approached the group—the woman Goldie had called Linette, and the two men with her—when Uncle Jonny announced that Benjamin Sotheby was going to grace us with his rendition of *Hamlet*. By the time the portly, balding man dressed extravagantly in a burgundy velvet coat and gaudily patterned vest finished the soliloquy, I had forgotten entirely that I had been anywhere but in this room. My time alone in the empty hallways felt to be an interlude from a dream, my former disquiet only a ridiculous fancy.

Goldie yawned. She did even that elegantly, with a little flutter of her hand. "That went well, I think, don't you?"

"It was perfect."

I swallowed the last of my oysters and set aside the shell, having eaten my fill of the delicious things at last. Mama had been right. The rich ate well. A few of Uncle Jonny's cronies had gone with him to his study to end the evening—which was approaching morning—with a last drink and smoke. The ballroom was empty but for the maids and footmen and that alarming statue, the gleaming woman with the grotesque little putto grinning in a way that made the lingering scents of spilled punch and champagne, overbloomed roses, smoke, and muddled perfumes uncomfortably decadent.

"We'll go to the Emporium in the morning—or no, probably the afternoon. Do you mind? I could sleep for a year."

Once again, I struggled with how to tell her I had no money, nor even the promise of it.

"Papa instructed me to buy you whatever you need," she said airily.

I struggled with pride and want and chagrin. Finally, I said quietly, "Thank you."

"You're a Sullivan now, May. You belong to us."

She knew so well how to snare me. From the very beginning, she knew.

Goldie headed for the door. "Good God, if I'm falling asleep on my feet, you must be ready to collapse. Good night!"

She was right. But the emotions of the day and the evening roiled, and after Goldie left, I watched the flurry in the ballroom until the maids began to frown and trade glances, and the butler—Au—asked, "Might I show you to your room, miss?" and I realized I was in the way. Another awkward mistake. Again I was acutely aware of the gaps in my education. Mama's lessons had not taught me everything I needed to know of this world.

I went upstairs. Once again, as in the unfinished hallway, I felt the house's quiet. How could that be, when the maids and the footmen were still cleaning up from the party? And yet, it was so.

It had never been quiet in the boardinghouse. Always women chattering, groaning, creaking, and sighing. Always the timbers of the house answering with their own settlings. The gaslight had hissed contentedly. Noise rumbled from the streets at all hours. Even in my loneliness, I'd felt the presence of others. But here . . .

I stepped into my room. A push of a button, and light blazed from onyx and gold lamps, blasting off the walls so that I walked into a maw of pink. The bluebirds on the wallpaper fluttered nauseatingly before me. I was exhausted.

I'd just laid aside the fichu and taken the pins from my hair when I heard a sound—a light tap, almost indiscernible. I turned just as my door opened and a woman stepped inside.

Mama.

I froze in shock. My mother, alive, her blond hair in a braid down her back, her nightgown unbuttoned at the throat as she preferred it. But almost in the same moment, I knew it was not her. "Aunt Florence."

"Who are you?" she asked in a hoarse whisper.

"I'm May. Your niece."

"My niece is dead." My aunt frowned. "They told me she was dead."

She was not awake. I recognized that blank stare. There had been a woman in the boardinghouse like this. Old Mrs. Welling disturbed the rest of us with her sleepwalking so often they'd had to lock her in her room. I spoke gently, "No, it's my mother who died. Your sister, Charlotte."

"May." Aunt Florence spoke my name as if it were foreign. "Oh May, oh May! It can't be. Why are you here? Oh, why have you come?"

"You invited me. You asked me to come."

"No, no." She shook her head, backing away. "No, you must go now. I told them not to. I told them."

"I—I don't understand. Told who?"

"You must go!" she shouted. "You don't belong here!"

Now it was my turn to back away. She was asleep. She had no idea what she was saying. Still, the force of her rejection shook me.

But I had her letter of invitation. The paid train ticket. That was what mattered.

"Mother!" Goldie marched through the door in her dressing gown, impatient and exasperated. "Mother, what are you doing here?"

21

Aunt Florence's hands dropped to her sides.

"I'm so sorry, May." Goldie went to her mother. "Come now, back to bed with you."

I said, "If she's sleepwalking—"

"It's nothing for you to worry about. I'll take care of it." Goldie tugged Aunt Florence to the door the way one might an ill-behaved child.

I followed them to the hallway, feeling helpless and stupid. "Do you need my help? Is there anything I can do?"

Goldie didn't answer. She took her mother into the bedroom at the end of the hall, shutting the door firmly, and the house swallowed them in silence.

THREE

I'd forgotten to draw the curtains, and I woke to a blanket of bright fog outside the window obscuring all else, and the hauntingly disorienting sense that the world had slipped away and I was suspended, imprisoned in a vast nothingness.

Some of that feeling had to do with my aunt's strange visit last night, but my dreams too had chased uncertainty and dread into the morning, though I could not remember what they'd been. Full of questions, certainly.

I listened for something to tell me that the household had thrown off sleep, but I heard nothing, not a maid, nor my aunt or uncle, nor, unsurprisingly, Goldie. Only, again, that spooky silence, accented now by the suffocating sequester of the fog. I wondered if I would make too much noise if I went to the bath. Should I dress? Should I go downstairs or wait for a maid to come? My questions only emphasized that, while I was not quite a guest, neither would I be a member of the family until

I'd mastered these details of day-to-day living. Strange, wasn't it, how such things were hardly worth thinking about until one did not know them?

I crept to the bath with its blue delft sink and tub and an embellished toilet that looked carved from marble. What a miracle, to turn a faucet and have water—hot water, too, no less. A bath in the boardinghouse had meant buckets of water heated on the stove, half grown cold before the tub was full. I might have spent all day luxuriating in this bathroom, had not the wallpaper been so intimidating. It was bright and garish, with animal faces peering from between jungle leaves. They seemed to be watching my every move, and I was glad to hurry out again.

I'd seen no sign that anyone was awake, and so I pulled my sketchbook in its leather case from my valise, along with the set of drawing pencils. The pencils had been an extravagance, and I still felt guilty when I used them. But Mama had insisted. *"I don't know where you got such talent. Not from me, certainly, and your father, well . . ."* She'd become lost in a memory, then shaken it loose with a smile and a small laugh, and when I'd begged her to share it, had only said, *"Just remember, my dear, not to judge so harshly. There are two sides to every story."*

It did no good to ask anything more; the promise my mother had made to my father, whatever it was, was as binding as her love for me. In the beginning, I'd buried my questions in imaginings about my father where I gave him a hundred excuses for being away. He was lost at sea. He'd been kidnapped. He was an explorer in the Arctic desperate to find his way home to us. As I grew older, those stories no longer satisfied; I became frustrated with everything I didn't know, frustrated with our poverty, with the everyday evidence of our want. Our rooms where nothing belonged to us, not the furniture, not the rugs, not the cheap chromolithographs on the walls. Only a few things here and there: a commemorative candy jar from the Centennial Exposition, an empty perfume bottle that still held a lingering scent of something complex and fascinating—*"French perfume,"* Mama would say, waving it entic-ingly past my nose—a few books, our clothing, the drawings I made sometimes, when there was spare paper about, of fantasy lands where my father was held prisoner, though I didn't tell my mother that's what they were. The only time I had, her sorrow had made me sick with myself.

Then one day, I'd lost my temper over something small—I don't remember now what it was—and kicked the table, which rocked so the Centennial candy jar fell to the ground and shattered, and I began to cry. To think of it now, my mother's horror at my misery, the things I said . . . *"Why must we live like this if he's so rich? Why doesn't he come for us? Why does he want us to be poor?"*

I was young; it embarrasses me now to think of it. It embarrasses me to think of the look in Mama's eyes—though what did she imagine, when she planted in my head such stories of riches and what my life should have been and would one day be?

As I raged, she tugged one of my drawings from the wall and turned it over, then shoved it into my hands. *"What would you rather our rooms looked like? Draw them for me, May. Show me what you dream about."*

That was how it started. My railing at circumstance transformed my world, if only on paper. There, I drew a fantasy for us both, rooms to escape the cheap meanness of our lives, safe harbors of beauty and peace, the places Mama told me I belonged. Her hopes for my life—wealth, comfort, society, with nothing to do but spend my hours going to balls and suppers and making my home beautiful—became my own. Those scrap pages gave way to sketchbooks, bought with hoarded pennies for my birthday, for Christmas, and then one day, a leather case with my initials stamped into the corner in gold leaf. I slipped each new sketchbook into it. I don't know how Mama afforded it, and she only smiled when I asked her and told me it was a reminder that these designs belonged to me. *"Be sure to sign each drawing, May. They are so beautiful you must claim them as your own."*

I'd taken such pride in her delighted joy when one of my ballrooms made her smile. *"It makes me think of a moonlit night."* Or an orangery brought a sigh. *"One can imagine falling in love here."* I drew rooms to please her, to elicit that faraway look when I knew she was thinking of my father, hoping always that she might reveal some snippet, some clue, and whenever she did—*"He would love this bedroom, May"*—I'd go over every detail of the drawing as if I could somehow divine what it was he would have loved, what of him I had captured, what of him was in me, that I could access this part of him so unknowingly. She revealed nothing of him, and yet, my anger with him faded a bit with every room she told me he would like.

Those hours with Mama were our best, and now the memory brought a tightness of grief that almost made me put the sketchbook down again. But no, she would be so disappointed if I let sorrow and loneliness triumph over the joy I took in this.

I crawled back into bed and opened the sketchbook to the most recent page, which I'd drawn on the train, and lost myself in the decorations, which were beautiful and harmonious, and had no clashing colors, designs, or patterns, no surfaces so crowded with ostentatious demonstrations of wealth that taste had played no part in their selection. It was a relief to draw a room where china cupids did not form a celestial army that kept one awake in fear of being battered by tiny wings.

There was a light tapping on my door, and I remembered last night with a mix of dismay and anticipation. But this time, it was not Aunt Florence who cracked open my door, but Goldie. She peeked around the edge. "You're awake? What are you doing? Reading? Is it a novel?"

"No, it's nothing. A sketchbook." I tried to put it aside.

"You can draw?"

"A bit."

"You must let me see."

She was so insistent that I put the book into her hands. Only Mama had ever seen my drawings, and I couldn't deny that I hungered for a compliment from my cousin and hoped that my mother's were not just out of fondness. And perhaps too, I hoped that Goldie might become the admirer, the friend, my mother had been.

Goldie leafed through the pages rapidly at first—*no, too quickly, she was hardly looking*—but then she slowed, suddenly attentive, and I felt a tense little anticipation.

She stilled. "They're all rooms."

Patience, I counseled myself. "Yes. I've always drawn them. When I was young, Mama thought it would—"

I'd meant to tell her the story, but I stopped at the look on her face, a careful consideration that changed to something I couldn't define. "Why, these are perfect!"

"Perfect? Thank you, but I—"

"But I've never heard of a woman interior architect."

She'd put a name to what I'd been doing with my drawings. Something I'd never thought about. That's what it was called. *Interior architect.* It had an interesting sound, even alluring, but her skepticism at the word *woman* dampened my pleasure at her praise. I reached for the sketchbook. "It's hardly as if I'm planning to be one."

Goldie held the sketchbook beyond my reach. "No, of course you aren't. That would be absurd." She flipped to a sketch of a library with arched ceilings and a squared pillar in the center with desks positioned all around it. "You could put in a few statues."

"The books are the decoration. Imagine their colors. Calfskin bindings and morocco and gold-leaf—"

"All with uncut pages, no doubt. What's the point of a book if no one reads it? Are there any paper covers on those shelves?" Goldie handed it back. "You need a new case too, one with a better leather. Look, all the gold is flaking off. Anyway, I've come to tell you to get dressed. We're going shopping."

I felt a vague disappointment, though I wasn't certain why. She'd been complimentary, hadn't she? Why then did I feel so disgruntled?

"How is your mother this morning?" I asked.

Goldie sighed. "I am sorry about last night, May. Sometimes the laudanum gives her nightmares."

"Laudanum?"

Goldie hesitated.

"If I'm to live here, you must tell me," I urged. "I heard everyone last night, you know. How long has she been ill?"

"Only a few months. It began with headaches, and the doctor gave her laudanum, which made them better, but honestly she's become more and more difficult without it. She's taken to her bed. It's best not to expect her to do, well, anything. Or to be anywhere. She probably won't remember last night. Half the time she makes no sense at all. Just ignore her."

"But I have so many questions."

"She won't be able to answer them, May, and it just confuses her more if you try to speak with her. Believe me, it's best for everyone if you don't try." She went to the door. "Don't be long."

Goldie left, and I stared after her in dismay. I had not wanted to give any credence to my fear that my aunt was unbalanced. *Half the time she makes no sense...* Yes, but what of the other half? I didn't want to confuse or upset her, yet there must be something she remembered of my mother, of the past. Also, which half had invited me here to San Francisco? Aunt Florence had been ill a few months, Goldie had said. I'd received her letter two weeks ago. But no one was surprised that I was here, and I'd been so warmly welcomed. I didn't think I needed to worry on that score, at least.

Another knock on my door, and a young Chinese woman came inside. I recognized her as the maid with the heart-shaped face who had directed me back to the ballroom last night. She wore a simple shirtwaist and skirt, and her glossy black hair was in a perfect chignon, which only accented the wideness of her face at the temples and the delicacy of her chin. Her brows were straight, her eyes dark, and her smile slight but not unfriendly as she set the tray she carried on the dressing table. "Good morning, miss. I'm Shin. I'm here to help you dress."

Her voice was accented, but her English was perfect. Goldie had said nothing about a maid, and I had no idea what to do with her, or even how to address her. "Oh. Goldie didn't tell me. I didn't expect—"

"Of course you must have a maid," she said firmly.

I felt immediately stupid, and said only, "Yes." I set my sketchbook beside the tray, which held a steaming pot of coffee, a stack of buttered toast, and a small dish of apricot jam. "It's nice to meet you, Shin, and thank you for bringing breakfast. But I don't need help dressing."

I waited for her to leave. She said nothing, but stood as if waiting for some instruction that I had no idea how to give, or even what it should be. Finally she said, "Have you unpacked, miss?"

"Oh. Oh no, there's been no time."

She was already at the foot of the bed, opening my suitcase. She took out a faded, rust-striped shirtwaist, a brown skirt, and my unmentionables. No fashionable combination underwear for me, but only a frayed chemise and drawers. Shin's clothing was of better quality than any of mine, and I could only imagine what she must think of my plain petticoats, the pink corset cover that had been washed to beige, and the oft-mended stockings. It was all I could do to keep from crawling beneath the bed in shame.

But Shin was insistent in a quiet and determined way as she began to divest me of my nightgown, and it seemed easier to give in than to resist. I supposed I should get used to this. Still, my skin goosepimpled; I could not meet her eyes. I had no idea where to put my hands, my arms, how to ignore her or even if I should, and in my attempts to avoid embarrassment, my gaze landed on her right hand, which was missing an index finger.

I gasped.

She paused. "Miss?"

Flustered and more embarrassed than ever—one could not ask about such a thing—I said, "Nothing. Nothing."

It was a relief when I was properly dressed again.

"Your hair, miss," Shin said, indicating the padded bench at the dressing table.

I sat helplessly. She poured my coffee, and then unplaited my braid while I ate and tried to keep from looking at that missing finger. It called to me like a ghost, always in my periphery. How well she managed without it. How deft she was as she began to brush my hair. I could not help closing my eyes at her steady, soothing hand. *Like Mama's.*

To distract myself from the sudden urge to cry, I opened the sketchbook. I'd gone through four or five designs when I glanced into the mirror to find Shin staring at the pages. When I caught her, she glanced quickly away.

"They're really very rough." I closed the book again.

"They're pretty, miss."

She wound my tresses skillfully about her remaining fingers. I had to force my stare away. I wondered if she noticed. "Please, I would like it if you called me May."

"Yes, Miss May."

It was probably the best I would be able to do. "I wonder if I could ask a favor, Shin. If I do something wrong or inappropriate, would you please tell me? Don't worry about my feelings. I want the Sullivans to be glad they brought me here. I want to fit in."

Shin regarded me solemnly. "Of course, Miss May."

I did not mistake her quiet censure. I had been wrong to ask. But I smiled as if I were satisfied, and when Shin had finished with my hair— doing it far more expertly than I could, even with her deformity—and held out my coat and my hat for me to put on, I thanked her, and went into the hall to wait for Goldie. Idly I counted the fawns and cupids on the table—where was the angel with the harp they'd gathered so reverently round yesterday? Perhaps it had heard my thoughts and whisked itself away. Its absence was notable, given that now all the little worshippers were praying to nothing.

Goldie came out of her room, shoving a jeweled hatpin into the crown of her hat, which had a brim nearly the width of her shoulders. It was lavishly decorated with ribbons and bows in several shades of yellow to match the short jacket she wore. She glanced at my hat, not so wide, much less fashionable, and with ribbons pinned into place so they were interchangeable and thus one hat could serve for a dozen.

"Your hair looks very fine this morning," she said. "Oh, I didn't mean—"

I laughed. "Shin worked a miracle. Thank you for sending her."

Goldie looked surprised, but then she leaned close and lowered her voice. "Mind her, May. The Chinese are the best servants we can get, but they have their faults. For one thing, you can't believe anything they say. They're terrible liars. Everyone knows it. Even the police don't believe them unless they're in a cemetery. They won't lie in front of their ancestors, you know."

"No, I didn't. She's—her finger—"

Goldie made a face and shuddered. "I know. It's horrible, isn't it? Does it trouble you? I'll have her sent away immediately. You needn't look at her again."

"Oh, no, no." I didn't know whether to be grateful for Goldie's quickness in easing my discomfort or alarmed at it for Shin's sake. "That's not what I meant. I just wondered how it happened."

"She came to us that way. Papa says she probably lost it in some factory, but I think she must have been a tong girl."

"What's a tong?"

"A Chinese gang. They're everywhere in Chinatown. There's something insolent about her, don't you think? Either she never really looks at you, or she looks too intently."

I couldn't say, having done my best not to look at *her*.

"I think she got into a fight with another tong girl and"—Goldie shrugged—"well, you know."

"I don't really. I've never known any Chinese," I confessed.

"You don't want to know any here, either, if you understand me. But never fear, I'm here to tell you everything you need." Goldie patted my arm reassuringly. She started down the stairs.

I touched her elbow to stop her, and when she looked back at me, I said, "Please do. Teach me everything important, I mean. This is all so new, and I don't wish to embarrass you, or your parents. I want to make you proud."

She smiled. "I will never lead you astray. We'll be seen everywhere together, after all. I'm certain we'll become the best of friends."

It was her special talent to know the perfect thing to say. I had not had many friends in Brooklyn; I was the only one at the shop beyond Mrs. Beard herself, my mother had quickly ended whatever relationships I'd managed in our neighborhood, and the other ladies in the boardinghouse had been much older, more kindly aunts than friends. Now here was beautiful, vibrant Goldie, saying that we would be the best of friends, and I was foolish enough to think it was what I wanted above all else.

Downstairs, Goldie paused, glancing over the telephone table with a frown. "Where is it, Au?" she called, though the butler was nowhere in sight. "Don't tell me it's not here yet."

Like magic, the butler appeared. He had a newspaper in his hand, and he handed it to her without a word, and then disappeared again rather quickly.

Goldie opened the *San Francisco Bulletin* excitedly. "Oh, I wonder what he said." Her bright blue eyes scanned the page, and her smile sank. "There's nothing about us! Nothing at all! How can that be? It was *the* party. Everyone was here."

Not everyone, I thought, remembering Goldie's disappointment over the mysterious but obviously important Mrs. Hoffman.

Goldie gave the paper to me. "Perhaps I'm missing it."

I glanced down the page until I found the headline Society News, by Alphonse Bandersnitch: The Friday Night Cotillion Club Hosts a Dozen Debutantes at Odd Fellows Hall.

I skimmed the story below:

> The popular Strozynski was booked to the very last hour preparing society "hair"esses for Friday night's ball . . . Gossip and scandal (including, one assumes, those of city politics and impending out-of-town guests) have no place at the Greenway Cotillions, Ned Greenway is oft heard to say . . . Champagne was in attendance and no doubt played the grandest of parts in Miss Hannah Brookner's recitation of "Little Orphant Annie," and her particularly inspired "An' the Gobbleuns 'at gits you Ef you Don't Watch Out!"

I burst into laughter.

"What?" Goldie asked. "Did I miss it? Is it there?"

"No, it's just this bit about 'Little Orphant Annie.' Did she really recite that at a ball?"

Goldie gave me an odd look. "He's just being clever. That's what makes his columns the best."

"You mean it didn't happen?"

"Oh, I'm certain it did. Hannah will be furious because he's made it obvious she was drunk, and her father will no doubt ask for an apology. Mr. Bandersnitch always presses too close to the unacceptable. That's why everyone reads him. One day the *Bulletin* will fire him for it. But what about us? Are we mentioned anywhere?"

"There's nothing in the column from last night, Goldie. Probably it just hasn't been written yet."

Goldie considered. "Perhaps you're right." She adjusted her hat in the elaborate foyer mirror. "Yes, of course you're right."

We went to the waiting brougham. I climbed inside while Goldie instructed the driver to take us to the Emporium, and then we were off, and I had the first true glimpse of the city that was to be my home.

That morning's fog had retreated to the hollows, on the run from a watery sun. On my arrival yesterday, the fog had been too heavy for me to make out more than the ghostly shades of buildings, though I'd marveled that it was cobblestones that the carriage bounced along, not muddy ruts. Even now, knowing that mansions existed, it was hard to put aside the vivid impressions I'd had from the magazines passed around by the ladies in the boardinghouse. Bret Harte's tales of camp-fires and mining towns.

From the top of the hill, we quickly passed into a neighborhood of wooden buildings, many decorated with unusual designs. Signs and windows advertised businesses in Chinese writing; women carried baskets and bunches of produce from stands lining the narrow streets where children played and men with single braids like Au's gathered, all wearing flat shoes and dark tunics and trousers and hats.

Goldie said, "Chinatown."

It was like nothing I'd seen before, and I was curious about it, but then I remembered Goldie's talk of tongs.

She went on, "It's perfectly safe in the daytime, but you should not come here at night."

As quickly as we passed into Chinatown, we were out again, crowded now by houses with bay windows and others with ginger-bread trim. We went into downtown, with its wires stretching from the many telephone and telegraph poles webbed above the sidewalks and its many-globed gas streetlamps decorating filthy streets scrimmed with urine and manure, and I was reminded of home. Crowds of peddlers and carts placidly ignored carriages and horses and wagons and automobiles, and people barely avoided disaster as they raced across the cable car tracks that ran down the center of the street. A man with a dozen dead rabbits and just as many birds slung from his belt called out, "Wild rabbits! Ducks! Get your game here!"

It was not New York, but it had that same deep city throb that reverberated from the ground into my heart, a pulse born of shouts and the rumble of iron rims on cobblestones, clanging cable cars, groups of men talking in the streets, men on bicycles calling out warnings as they swerved and changed direction as quickly as houseflies, stray dogs barking, and newsboys hawking headlines. Yet it was also unfamiliar, and it was more than just the tang of the sea in the air instead of the green rot of oily rivers that made it so, or the streets so steep that everything must pause halfway up to rest. San Francisco breathed expansiveness and change. It was unsettling, but exciting too, and something in me stirred and stretched, the thrill of starting anew.

The carriage stopped before a giant stone building of Beaux-Arts design with a huge arched entranceway and windows lining the front.

"The Emporium. I imagine you've never seen a store like this," Goldie said.

"We have stores in New York."

"Not like this," she said smugly. "We can get nearly everything you need here, and the rest at the City of Paris."

It was true that the store felt different than those in New York. Not because of its size, but because for me the department stores in New York had been places only to daydream, and even then, those dreams had been about working there as a salesgirl, walking crisply down those aisles, taking orders. I'd never thought to covet anything inside, because I'd never been able to afford any of the things they sold.

Goldie said, "We'll probably have to throw your clothes out once your trunks arrive. I'm sure you've nothing that's right for San Francisco. The weather is completely different, for one thing. You'll never need anything heavier than a wool coat." She tossed scarves around my neck and trailed gloves over my arms until I felt like a bedecked maypole while the salesman trailed after us with bobbing steps and an obsequious "That color is lovely as well, miss."

There was so much that she insisted I needed: cartwheel hats blooming with flowers, patterned shirtwaists, skirts and walking suits, tea gowns and shoes. Goldie preferred bolder colors, and pooh-poohed my every suggestion of anything more sedate. "I told you, you're in San Francisco now, May." I would have preferred more subtlety, but Goldie lived in society; I'd only watched it from afar, and so how should I know that owls on hats were in vogue and that white gloves were on the wane and bright colors much more the thing?

I stood in the alterations room while a dressmaker measured and pinned and Goldie circled with a finger pressed to her full lower lip, saying, "I don't like the way that drapes. You can cut that bodice a bit lower. Yes, to there."

"Goldie, do you really think . . . That's very low."

Goldie said, "Do you want to be like Mabel Byrnes?"

"Who's Mabel Byrnes?"

"The most old-fashioned girl in San Francisco. She's hardly older than you and you'd think she was on the shelf already, the way she dresses. Like a dowdy matron. She'll never attract a husband that way."

As far as husband hunting went, I had not thought of that for some time. There had been too many other things in the way—chiefly, no money and my mother's disdain for the tenor of our neighborhood. Now, the future was a new thing altogether. Who knew what it would bring? "I don't want to be old-fashioned."

"Leave it to me," Goldie assured me.

How I trusted her from the start. How wholly I gave myself over to my cousin. The lure of beautiful things, of a friend . . . I was vulnerable without knowing it, having never had either. Who wouldn't want a dress with that blue-and-white lace trim? Goldie was right, the pink was not too bright. Nor was that ivory lace ball gown too revealing. There were shirtwaists and skirts and jackets to match, plaids and stripes that the most fashionable women wore together, and oh, a gown of silk that fell like water through my fingers, the way the light gleamed upon it . . . In the end, I would have let Goldie cut the décolletage to my knees just for the privilege of wearing it.

And then the City of Paris, where we bought lace- and ribbon-festooned combinations—at last I was to have proper, fashionable underwear—embroidered corset covers and nightgowns and sheer silk stockings, and handkerchiefs and scarves. Everything was to be sent to the house when the alterations were done. I was a little sick at the money we'd spent, though Goldie only shrugged off my protests.

She told our driver, Nick, to follow us. "I want to take May somewhere."

He scowled, but nodded, and she took my arm and we started off on foot.

The afternoon was advanced, casting shadows, and the chill breeze from the water tunneled briskly through the city. A large building with a giant clock tower at the end of the street blocked the view of the harbor. "That's the ferry building," Goldie told me, "where you catch the boat to Oakland. Now, hurry."

"Is that where we're going? Oakland?"

"Why would we go there? It's *nowhere.*" Goldie grabbed her hat at an especially strong gust and walked so quickly that even with my long legs I had trouble keeping up. The street grew crowded with suited men gathering and talking sociably. As quickly as stinking clouds of cigar smoke dissipated in the breeze, new ones took their place.

"Where did everyone come from?" I asked.

"Cocktail hour." Again, Goldie's hand went to her hat. "Be ready! We're going 'round the Horn!"

She swept around the corner. I followed—and was whipped and buffeted by a breeze so strong it exposed my petticoat and tried to yank the hat from my head. I grabbed desperately at both.

Someone shouted, someone else whistled. Goldie waved at one of the groups of men leaning against a large cast-iron fountain and watching women battle their clothing. Obviously, it was the sole reason they loitered here in the triangle between streets.

"Hey, Goldie, is that the cousin we've heard so much about?" called a young man standing beneath a nearby awning.

I waited for Goldie to turn up her nose or offer a chilling set down at his familiarity, but she didn't, and I began to understand that these ogling men were what she wanted to show me. She only laughed. "It is indeed! Don't ask me why she insisted on coming down to see all you derelicts. I told her you weren't worth our time."

He waggled his eyebrows. "Why don't you two come over here and I'll make it worth it."

"We're far too busy, much to your disappointment, I'm sure!"

"Goldie!" I whispered.

"Come on, now. Don't make me beg!" the man pleaded.

"Wouldn't that be a pretty sight? My cousin says she'd like to see it. Down on your knees!"

I was stunned at such open flirting, and everyone watching.

Goldie said to me in a loud whisper, "Thank God you're not tiresome. I'd been so afraid you would be like Mabel after all."

"No. No, of course not." This was not the behavior Mama had taught me, and in Brooklyn it would have brought nothing but trouble. But such was Goldie's power that I ignored my own instincts; she convinced me that here in San Francisco, women could be daring without consequence. I had no other example to follow. My aunt was an invalid; I was far from everything I knew. I glanced over my shoulder, reassured at the sight of Nick following in the Sullivan carriage.

A man sucking on a cheroot called, "Hey, Goldie! I saw your pa at the Palace."

Goldie veered sharply over to him. "What exactly do you mean by that, sir?"

He exhaled smoke in a noxious cloud, grinning when Goldie batted it away. "Just that he's in the bar getting all cozy with Abe Ruef and Mrs. Dennehy. I guess those government contracts make a pretty penny, especially when everyone's getting paid not to watch things too closely."

"I'm sure I don't know." Goldie spun me away in the wake of his soft chuckle.

We were well down the street when I ventured, "What did he mean by that?"

"Nothing. Politics and rumors. No one cares." Goldie stopped short, gripping my arm almost painfully. "How would you like to see the Palace Hotel? It's the finest in the city. We'll go there for tea."

The gleam in her eyes told me that whatever she wanted to do was going to be as daring as flirting with young men in public. But again, perhaps it was not; I didn't want to be a Mabel. I smiled. "That sounds perfect."

Her answering smile made me glad I'd decided not to protest.

The Palace Hotel had six upper stories of bay windows and a facade of brick that had once been white, but was now patinaed by coal smoke to a drab gray. The gilded ornaments of the edifice tried vainly to sparkle through the soot. A doorman—Chinese, again—in maroon livery held the door. I followed my cousin inside, and was immediately overwhelmed by the Palace's splendor: oak floors, white pillars, redwood paneling, and great brass cuspidors. The footman said, "The Ladies' Grill is this way—"

"I know where it is. Haven't I been here a hundred times?" Goldie snapped.

Whatever he saw in Goldie's expression made him step back hastily. I followed my cousin to a bar bounded by a brass footrail.

Shafts of sunlight glowed through a room fogged with cigar smoke and swirling with the scents of tobacco, seafood, and roasted meat. Goldie paused, no doubt searching for her father through the throng of palms and men.

I caught sight of him first. My uncle sat at a table in the center of the room, his back to us. Beside him was an excitedly gesturing man with a bushy mustache and short, dark curling hair receding from a shining forehead. On my uncle's right was an auburn-haired woman, gowned elegantly in deep plum and black lace. She was not the only woman in the Palace Bar, but she stood out among the few. She was striking, with a face that in profile was sharply defined, large heavily lidded eyes, a long nose that, while dominating, was somehow regal, a small chin, and a jawline that accented the dangling pearl at her ear. Her neck was impossibly slender. More impossibly, she too smoked a cigar, and had a glass of whiskey before her. She sat very close to Uncle Jonny, whose red-gold hair shone in the sun-smoke and the light of the chandeliers. He said something, and she laughed, reaching over his arm to tap her ash. Too intimate. He turned to her with a smile, a word. I couldn't see his expression, but he was obviously intent, focused in a way that made me think uncomfortably of my aunt. The woman laughed. The curly-haired man's expression froze in impatience. He did not like dealing with my uncle's momentary distraction, I thought. I had the sense that he was a man who expected devotion and undivided attention.

Goldie cursed beneath her breath. I felt her determination deflate into resignation.

"You see that man talking with Papa?" she whispered, inclining her head toward the other man at the table. "That's Abe Ruef. Papa says nothing in this city gets done without him."

It did not surprise me. He reminded me of Mrs. Beard's brother—those same eyes that seemed to take in everything, that way he leaned back in his chair as if the room were his to command. "Then I imagine it's a good thing he's a friend of Uncle Jonny's."

Goldie laughed shortly. "A good thing. Yes, I suppose."

The woman exhaled a thin and almost elegant stream of smoke, and then whispered something in Uncle Jonny's ear. Goldie stiffened.

"Who is she?" I asked.

"Mrs. Edward Dennehy. Alma." There was no mistaking Goldie's scorn. "She's widow. Her husband worked at United Railroads. I don't remember what he did, but he was important. She's very clever. Very clever indeed."

It did not sound a compliment. "Is your father investing in United Railroads?"

"Ha. He's investing in *her*. She's Papa's mistress."

It explained the intimacy and my discomfort, but it was another disparity, another thing to question. My uncle with his mistress in such a public place, talking investments with the man who ran San Francisco. Everything I'd learned today made my mother's lessons obsolete. Either that, or San Francisco was truly nothing like New York. "Aunt Florence must be mortified."

"She doesn't know." Goldie fixed me with a searing, pointed gaze. "And she won't. The widow lives in a suite here, for which my father undoubtedly pays a great deal. Good God, that diamond she's wearing is huge—do you see? I wonder when he bought her that?"

It was hard to miss. Its flash competed with that of the crystal drops on the chandeliers—and won handily.

Goldie said sharply, "Let's go."

We were both quiet as we left. The carriage waited outside. I touched her arm gently. "I'm sorry."

"For what?" she asked.

"For your father. I imagine it's very hard to see."

Goldie's gaze was long and lingering. "You are not what I expected at all."

Compliment or curse? I didn't know. When I frowned in confusion, she smiled.

Even as I noted that it did not reach her eyes, she said, "You're more than I hoped for, May. Truly you are."

So I ignored the rest. I ignored everything that told me nothing was as I'd believed. That was my first mistake.

FOUR

On the way home, it was as if Goldie had forgotten I was there. She stared silently out the carriage window, and when we arrived, my cousin hurried up the stairs, leaving me alone in the foyer.

"May, is that you?" My aunt stepped into the hall. She looked drawn and frail, but awake, and alert. She smiled tremulously, as if afraid of her reception. "I'm your Aunt Florence. Forgive me for being unable to meet you sooner."

It was obvious that, as Goldie had warned me, my aunt had no recollection of coming to my room last night. But Goldie had made her out to be half-mad as well, and I saw no evidence of that. I was so relieved that I burst out, "I'm so very glad to meet you at last, Aunt Florence," and hugged her. She was stiff at first, but then she put her arms around me.

When I stepped back, there were tears in her eyes. She retrieved her handkerchief and blotted them away. "Where's Goldie?"

"She went to her room. I can fetch her—"

"No, no. Please." She gave me again that shaky smile. "Let's not disturb her. I'd like to get to know you. Just the two of us. Will you take tea with me, my dear May?"

"I would like that."

She led me down the hall, to the left, to the right again, until we were in the empty hallway I'd stumbled upon last night. The furnished room was indeed her sitting room; why was it located here, in a nearly empty wing? Once again, I was greeted by a cloud of patchouli and the jeweled eyes of the menagerie parading across the mantel. Last night's shadows became a casual clutter in the electric light. There was no hint today of the oppressiveness I'd felt here.

When Aunt Florence gestured for me to sit, I did so eagerly. There was already a pot of tea, along with a tray of delicate sandwiches, and another of cakes. It looked delicious, but they'd fed us a light meal at the Emporium, and Goldie's distress had stolen any incipient hunger.

The Palace Bar intruded, Mrs. Dennehy leaning over Uncle Jonny's arm. Goldie saying, *"She doesn't know . . . And she won't."* Uncomfortably, I pushed it all away.

My aunt took the chair across. "Would you mind pouring? My hands are a bit trembly this afternoon."

In fact, all of her seemed trembly. She was a mass of fluttering sighs and rolling ankles and hands that could not settle, and she kept glancing toward the closed door as if she expected an interruption. Aunt Florence seemed uncomfortable in her own skin.

I smiled reassuringly and poured the tea. My aunt waved away sugar and cream. I took mine black as well, but when I sipped it, it was cold and bitter as if it had sat there, forgotten and steeping, for hours. Again, I remembered last night, Goldie's hint about madness. How long had Aunt Florence been waiting here for our return?

My aunt blew into her cup to cool what was not the least bit warm, sipped it, and then blew into it again. She said nothing, only smiled vaguely and drank her tea as if unaware of the expectant silence between us. My questions crowded, but I was troubled by the cold tea and whatever it implied, and I looked about the room, trying to think about how best to bring up my mother. The clutter suggested a restless mind: unfinished needlework, a half-crocheted doily, a flower press with discolored, forgotten blooms scattered about it.

Then I saw the candy jar on the table, partially hidden among a mess of embroidery threads, and for a moment I was transported back in time, my tantrum and a jar just like this one tumbling from the table to smash against the floor, scattering into pieces that could not be put back together. The shards of thick glass glimmering in the lamplight.

This one was not broken, of course. It too was shaped like the famous Liberty Bell, a souvenir of the Centennial Exposition in Philadelphia. I saw the molded crack, the lettering I knew by heart, by feel. *PROCLAIM LIBERTY THROUGHOUT ALL THE LAND*, and *1776 Centennial Exposition 1876.* How often I'd run my fingers over that lettering, imagining the candy it had once held. *"Chocolate dragées. Delicious! Though I only had one or two."* My question, *"What happened to the rest?"* And the thoughtfulness on Mama's face, her quiet, *"I gave them to someone to keep them safe—I didn't want to eat all of them at once, you see, I wanted to savor them. But then they were gone."*

It had seemed a tragedy to me. *"What do you mean, 'they were gone'?"*

"She ate them . . . I gave them to someone . . ." To her sister? Here it was, the opening I'd been searching for. "That candy jar. It's from the Centennial Exposition, isn't it? My mother had one too."

"We each had one," my aunt said.

"It came filled with candy," I prompted.

"Did it?" Aunt Florence sipped her tea, tilting her head as if searching for the memory. Then, "Ah yes. I remember now. Charlotte didn't like them and she gave hers to me and then cried when I ate them as well. Can you imagine? She only wanted them after I ate them all. She raised such a terrible fuss that Mother sent me to bed without dinner.

I was so angry with her—you know, you don't look as I imagined, but you have the Kimble mouth."

Her words bounced like a ball among jacks, hitting here and there, scattering. It was not the story I knew. I tried to follow, but was too distracted by the rest. The Kimble mouth?

"I've thought that perhaps I look like my father—"

"Your father?" Her frown involved her entire face, forehead to chin. "Oh no, no."

"No? You know what he looked like. You know who he—"

"I hardly remember him. He was one of her passing fancies."

I went quiet in surprise. Whatever I'd expected, this was not it. This was also not my mother's story. Then again, had she told me how she and my father had met, or how long they'd been together? No, never. He could have been a passing fancy, but I had assumed he'd been her great love. She'd never married. She'd never even talked about another man. This confused everything. I scrambled to think; before I could say anything, Aunt Florence said, "People used to mistake us for twins now and again. Charlotte and I were so close."

Another distraction. *So close.* Yet not close enough that either had mentioned the other to her family—even to the point that my mother had not included her sister in her story of the Exposition. My mind could not keep straight. I thought it best to follow my aunt's. Softly I said, "What happened between the two of you, Aunt Florence?"

Her gaze lit on me with startling intensity. "I have missed my sister. It is good to have her child by my side. Now that you are here we must have tea together often. At least once a week. We simply must."

It was, of course, what I wanted. A chance to set things straight, to discover the truth. But I was frustrated, too, at the many turns of the conversation. "I'd be happy to do that, Aunt."

"You can trust me, I promise."

"Yes of course."

"I won't disappoint my sister."

Such fraught words. I didn't understand them at all. But again, I thought there would be time to work it all out. I thought there would be other teas, and so when came the perfunctory knock on the door, I bit back impatience and frustration and let my questions fall away as the maid entered. Shin, once more. At the time, I didn't know enough of maids to find it odd that she served all three of us: Goldie, me, and my aunt. "You rang for me, ma'am?"

Aunt Florence frowned. "Did I? I don't remember that."

"It's time for your medicine, ma'am." Shin took a bottle from her pocket. "In your tea will be best."

Aunt Florence drew her teacup close, folding her other hand over it. "No. I don't want it. Not yet. I must speak to May."

"Now, ma'am, you know you must. The doctor says."

"The doctor." Aunt Florence sounded uncertain. Her trembling increased.

I turned to Shin. "Perhaps you could leave it with me, and I'll make certain she takes it."

"It's time now," she insisted.

"Oh, but . . ."

"Come, ma'am." Shin held out her hand. Again, my gaze was drawn to that awful missing finger. "Mr. Sullivan will know if you don't."

Aunt Florence's whole manner changed. "Of course. Thank you." She was like a child as she handed over her cup and saucer. The maid measured out the medicine—laudanum, I assumed. I remembered Goldie had said Aunt Florence was taking it.

She handed the cup back to my aunt and said kindly, "It will help you to feel better."

Obediently, Aunt Florence drank. She closed her eyes briefly. I waited impatiently for Shin to go. Instead, she stepped back to wait by the mantel, a silent but obvious presence. The hairs on the back of my neck stirred. *She never really looks at you, or she looks too intently.*

My aunt took another sip of tea. "Will you have a sandwich—or a cake, my dear? I can't think why Cook made so much for just the two of us."

But had it been just for the two of us? She could not have known that Goldie would not be joining us, could she? Had she planned it that way? I took a sandwich to please her and had a bite. A very good egg salad.

Aunt Florence drank more tea. Her hands steadied. A slow, dreamy smile curved her lips. "Nick will take you around San Francisco this afternoon, so you can see the city."

I glanced at the clock. The afternoon was gone; it was after six.

"That's very kind, but already . . . I mean to say . . . Goldie took me about today. We went shopping."

"Shopping?" A shadow crossed Aunt Florence's eyes. "But I thought . . . Jonny said . . . Did Charlotte approve?"

Perhaps it was the laudanum. Or perhaps the confusion Goldie had mentioned. I set the sandwich aside in concern and sympathy, and yes, disappointment too. Gently, I said, "She's gone, Aunt."

"She's left for Newport already?"

As far as I knew, my mother had never set foot in Newport, where the rich of New York City took the summer. "No, Aunt Florence. Mama died two months ago, do you remember? I've come to stay with you now."

A confused frown. Then she licked her lips. "Oh. Yes. Yes, I remember. How was her . . . her . . . end? It was peaceful, I hope."

I had no idea of my mother's last moments. Her heart had failed as she'd returned home after picking up piecework. She'd collapsed on the street and been attended to by passersby. The doctor had not been able to give me any answers. *"I can only guess, Miss Kimble. Tell yourself it was quick, if it comforts you. It may have been. I cannot say it wasn't."*

"Yes," I said. "It was peaceful. Goldie says Mama wrote you a letter before—"

"I do worry so for Charlotte. She has never been strong."

48

One more thing to disconcert, a version of my mother opposite to my experience. Mama had been immoveable, determined, unwavering in her convictions, the strongest of which was her belief in the virtue of others. I'd never thought myself inclined to such a belief, but then, we so seldom see ourselves clearly.

"I have always been her support," Aunt Florence went on, musing almost to herself. "She relies on me so. Sometimes it is quite wearying. Someone is taking care of her while you're away, of course?" She blinked slowly, as if trying to keep her train of thought.

I felt sorry for her, and sad. Sad also for myself as it became obvious I would get no answers to my questions today. Kindly, I said, "Yes." It wasn't untrue, really. Mama was in God's hands now.

"When do you return?"

"I thought I might stay here for a time, if that pleases you."

Aunt Florence set her cup and saucer aside. There was no evidence of her nervousness from before. Now she was all languor and drowsiness. "This has been so pleasant, Charlotte. But I fear I really must lie down. Will you help me to my room? I am so very tired."

I helped her to her feet, and she sagged into me, trusting completely to my ministrations. Her soft eyes pierced with a longing and gratitude that discomfited, even after she'd closed them and rested her head on my shoulder.

I was glad now that Shin had stayed. Together, we took Aunt Florence from the sitting room and into that forlorn hallway. She seemed in a dream as we brought her upstairs to her bedroom. Though it was July and still bright daylight, the curtains were drawn and the room lit only by a dim oil lamp that glimmered faintly on the gilt-framed pictures and sent shadows jumping over the blue velvet-brocaded wall. It was strangely still, as if the room were a held breath. She sank onto a chaise by the window with a sigh. Before I could step away, she grabbed my hand, squeezing tight. "We'll have tea again. Don't forget."

"I won't," I promised.

Shin put a crocheted blanket over her and said to me, "I will stay with her now, miss."

In the hall, I was startled out of my sadness and dismay by my own reflection in one of the many mirrors. How tired I looked, as drawn as my aunt. I glanced away, only to catch myself again in the mirror opposite, a double, a triple, endless and infinite May Kimbles . . .

I frowned and looked more closely. There, something familiar. I erased my frown, smoothing my face into a semblance of what it had been before, a slight startle, raised eyebrows, and then, yes, there it was. I saw Aunt Florence where I'd never seen my mother, and it was not for lack of trying. My aunt said that I had the Kimble mouth, but Mama had never told me such a thing. I knew well the contours of my bones, my skin, every bump and flaw. I'd so often searched for something to tell me who I was, where I belonged. There had been times when I'd wondered if I was related to my mother at all.

But now I saw what I had never seen before—a family resemblance. How funny, to find a part of myself three thousand miles from where I'd started.

"I won't disappoint my sister." What a strange thing to say, especially given that Florence had dropped so completely from Mama's life. Which of them had left the other first? Where had the Kimble sisters begun, and why had they so completely lost one another?

The clues Aunt Florence had given me chased themselves. *"He was one of her passing fancies . . . Charlotte and I were so close . . . She has never been strong . . ."*

What was the story? What had happened? How was I to discover it?

A door opening sprang me from my thoughts. It was Goldie's. "I thought I heard something. What are you doing?"

"I just had tea with your mother."

Goldie's surprise was almost comical. "You what?"

"She was waiting downstairs. I told her I would fetch you, but she—"

"What did she say?" Goldie motioned for me to come into her bedroom, blinding with white furniture, gold wallpaper twined with green vines and tiny white birds, white lamps thick with golden fringe. It was hard to breathe within the overpowering cloud of jasmine.

"Tell me everything," Goldie said.

"She wants me to have tea with her once a week. I said I would."

"She said that?" Goldie frowned. "She'll have forgotten that already."

"I imagine so. Shin came in to give her laudanum."

My cousin sighed. "Thank God. She is much better with it."

"Don't you wonder what happened, Goldie?"

"What happened to what?"

"To our family. Aunt Florence just told me that she and my mother were close. Like twins, she said. And then she said . . . Well, she said something that didn't sound like Mama at all—"

"Exactly," Goldie said. "You can't believe her about anything, May. She doesn't know what she's talking about."

"I did promise her we'd have tea again."

"She won't remember, and, to be honest, I think you should ask me or Papa the next time she asks you to tea. We can tell you if it's a good idea that day or not. You don't want to make her worse."

I nodded. "No, of course not."

"Now, if you don't mind, May, I really think I should have a nap."

A nap so late? That seemed odd, but perhaps that was Goldie's habit. I went back to my room to wait for dinner. How different it was from that morning, when the fog had locked me inside so completely. Now the view was expansive, the city spreading below to the harbor, ships and steamers and tiny fishing boats with strangely shaped sails and brown hills ringing it all.

I picked up my sketchbook. I began to draw, letting my pencil take me where it would, and the comfort and certainty of draperies and wall coverings made stories about candy jars and passing fancies and impressions that made no sense to me fade, while the memories of my mother strengthened with every decoration I drew, the things I knew of her, the stories I had always trusted.

No one called me to dinner, and I don't know how much time passed. A few hours at least, because the sun had gone down when I heard the step in the hall; I was drawing in the twilight. Another footstep. I tensed, remembering my aunt's sleepwalking, but this time there was no knock on my door. More quiet steps down the hall, and suddenly I was thinking of Aunt Florence as I'd left her, how Shin and I had nearly dragged her up the stairs. She should not be walking about alone.

I put aside my sketch and cracked my door quietly, not wanting to disturb if it was nothing, and was surprised to see not my aunt, but Goldie. Goldie wearing a low-brimmed hat and a dark coat, moving quietly to the stairs. She'd said nothing about an entertainment tonight, and she wasn't dressed for a party or a ball—where could she be going?

I started to call out, then bit it back. How furtive she was. It was obvious she didn't wish to be heard or seen.

I waited until she disappeared down the stairs, and then I crept into the hall. I heard the soft tap of her boots on the tiles below, and then the quiet—oh-so-quiet—opening of the front door.

Leave it alone, I told myself. *Ask her about it tomorrow.*

I went back to my room. I sat again on the chaise and picked up my sketchbook, but now my curiosity was such that I could not distract myself by drawing. Instead, I sat listening so hard to the evening that the tiniest sound became amplified, and the strain of it made my head ache. I closed my eyes, and then the day ran over me like a train, images jumbling together—Chinatown and the wind blowing my hat from my head while the men watched and the Palace Hotel and Aunt Florence saying, *"You can trust me,"* and the next thing I knew, I was opening my eyes to gloomy gray fog, and the morning.

FIVE

When I tried my cousin's door the next morning, it was locked, and there was no reply to my quiet knock, my whispered, "Goldie, are you awake?"

She was probably asleep. She would make an appearance soon, and I was starving.

I followed the smell of food to the dining room, which was empty but for Uncle Jonny, who was at a huge mahogany table that must seat twenty. He was again impeccably dressed, this time in a charcoal suit. A gold watch chain draped across his chest with such studied perfection I wondered if it were glued in place. He read the *San Francisco Chronicle* as he sipped coffee. Beyond him, a footman stood against a pale gray wall painted to look like stone. I stared at the horns protruding from his head until I realized that behind him was one of several animal skulls mounted on wooden plaques, horned animals all.

Presumably they were meant to make the room look like an old hunting lodge. Skulls, not trophy heads, which would have been bad enough.

My uncle lowered the paper. "Well, it seems that at least one of my family has deigned to make an appearance. Good morning, May."

I could not help thinking of him at that table in the Palace Bar, with his mistress beside him while Aunt Florence waited in her sitting room with cold tea. But I knew nothing of their relationship, and here was my uncle smiling up at me, and I should not judge, especially when he'd been so kind.

"Good morning, Uncle Jonny. I'm sorry I missed dinner last night. I fell asleep."

"Dinner?" He seemed surprised at my apology. "Oh, well, no harm. No harm at all. I'm afraid I wasn't here."

Again came the image of Mrs. Dennehy smoking her cigar, the flashing diamond. I searched for something to say that wasn't about that. "You're not reading the *Bulletin*? Goldie will be disappointed. She's hoping the ball was mentioned on the society page."

I'd been half joking, but my uncle laughed with a scorn that took me aback, a bitterness that clashed with the good nature he'd previously shown me. "The *Bulletin*? I leave that trash for my daughter."

"Oh. Oh, I see . . . I . . ."

His smile came quickly, reassuring. "It's all right, my dear. It's not the society page I despise. It's the paper's editor. Please, get something to eat. Sit down. Let us get to know one another."

I went to the sideboard, which was laden with more food than I'd ever seen in one place. Eggs, both scrambled and poached, a carved breast of turkey, steaks and bacon, roasted potatoes and tomatoes. I had no idea how my uncle stayed so trim presented with this bounty each morning.

"Has the *Bulletin* editor offended you in some way?"

"My dear May, it's very good of you to pretend to be interested, but I know young women aren't much for business. No one really wants to listen to me drone on about Fremont Older."

Earnestly, I said, "But I *am* interested. I know so little about the city. I wish to truly be part of the family, Uncle. I want to know everything about you."

He chuckled. "Well, perhaps not everything. Young ladies should not be saddled with such worries."

I took eggs and tomatoes, but the staring skulls on the walls made the thought of meat suddenly distasteful. "What worries are those?"

Uncle Jonny studied me as he rose to pull out my chair. "Why, you're quite serious, aren't you? It's nothing for you to concern yourself with, I assure you. The usual business things."

I sat. "It's only that, with my mother . . . I'm afraid I've grown used to worrying."

"Well, we'll have no more of that." He took his seat again with a dramatic flair, a trait reflected, more boldly, in his daughter. "I'm here to see that those days are over."

I took a bite of the eggs, which were buttery and soft and so delicious it was all I could do not to shovel them into my mouth. When I'd swallowed, I said, "What is your business, Uncle Jonny?"

"Construction. Sullivan Building, to be precise. We've built several of the buildings you've seen downtown. Many office buildings. A few stores."

"Government buildings?"

His brow furrowed. "We built city hall, yes. Why?"

"Someone mentioned it yesterday when Goldie and I were in town."

He seemed honestly perplexed. "Who? What did they say?"

"Some man on the street. Nothing really. Something about contracts." All I could see was how my explanation would lead to the Palace Bar, and my instincts, as well as Goldie's reaction yesterday, told me to change the subject. Quickly, I said, "You were telling me why you disliked Mr. Older of the *Bulletin*."

My uncle paused. Those pale eyes of his were a little too probing, and I looked down at my food and busily stirred my eggs with my fork.

"Yes," he said slowly. "Yes, of course. Mostly I dislike him because Older is an enemy of our good mayor Schmitz and Schmitz's right-hand man, Abe Ruef."

Again I remembered yesterday, the man at my uncle's table. Abe Ruef, Goldie had said. *"Nothing in this city gets done without him."*

"I see."

"Older has been trying to rile up public sentiment to investigate this fairy tale he imagines of corruption in city government, but no one wants such a thing. The mayor gets things done, and Ruef too. The city is growing; we don't need a bunch of blown-up scandals and investigations and trials slowing things down."

Uncle Jonny's words came quickly, clipped. I had the impression that, in his enthusiasm, he'd forgotten he was speaking to me. "Older's not pro-business, and we need someone who is. Not someone who thinks a city beautification plan drawn by some garden planner out of Chicago is the best thing for San Francisco. We can be the queen of the West without all that. Who's going to stop us? *Seattle?* Ha! Putting in all those boulevards and statues will only slow us down. The only good thing the plan does is get rid of Chinatown."

I perked up, remembering the Chinese writing on the shop windows, the embroidered silks reflecting the light. "What happens to it?"

Uncle Jonny shrugged. "Who cares? It's taking up valuable land. The best locations in town. Imagine what could be there if it was gone. Hotels like the Fairmont for one—you've seen it, haven't you, going up just down the street?"

I nodded.

"If we could get the Chinese out . . . Well, just think of it! We're running out of good building sites. Prime rental properties. There's money to be made, no doubt about it." He cleared his throat. "The city should give it to the rest of us, for the good of everyone. I've got a new project myself, on one of the last good lots left—or I will have, as soon as the architect accepts my commission. But no, proper city growth isn't what Older wants to talk about. All he cares about are his graft hobgoblins."

My uncle cleared his throat. "Pardon me, my dear, I do tend to get carried away. You've just arrived; you can't know any of these people. As you may guess, it's somewhat of an important topic for me."

"I'm interested, truly. If San Francisco is to be my home, I think I should know about it."

"Such complications are best left to men." His voice changed from businesslike to regretful as he raised another subject. "I am sorry you've not yet had an opportunity to meet your aunt. She is often poorly. I'm sure Goldie has told you."

"Oh, but I have met her. Yesterday. We had tea together."

Uncle Jonny's eyebrows rose in surprise. "Tea?"

"When Goldie and I came back from shopping."

"Goldie was there as well?"

"She'd already gone upstairs. It was only me and Aunt Florence, at least until Shin came with the laudanum."

My uncle sat back in his chair, looking oddly stumped. "I heard nothing of this."

I buttered a piece of toast and dipped it into a pool of sagging tomato. "We had a very pleasant time."

"Did you? What did you talk about?"

"Mama, mostly. Has she told you anything about my mother?"

Uncle Jonny shook his head. "When we met, she told me her parents were dead. She said nothing about a sister. I was very surprised to find she had one."

"You only discovered it when my mother sent the letter?"

He frowned. "The letter?"

"Goldie said Mama had sent one and that was how you knew I existed."

"Oh. Oh, yes of course. The letter." My uncle tapped his well-manicured fingers on the newspaper as if the action aided his recollection. "It was addressed to your aunt, and she told me what was in it and that she wished to send for you. I'd forgotten all about it."

"Do you think I might look at it?"

"If it can be found. I've no idea where it is. No doubt your aunt has it somewhere."

"Perhaps she'll remember where she put it." I was not at all confident in my aunt's memory. "I'll ask her the next time we have tea."

"The next time?"

I nodded. "She's asked me to take tea with her once a week."

Now he sighed heavily.

Quickly, I added, "I promised Goldie I wouldn't do so without talking to one of you first. I'd hoped, since neither you nor Goldie know anything about her family"—*or my father*—"that I might ask her some questions."

He waggled his head, visibly weighing his uncertainty, and I thought how deliberate seemed his actions, his way of dressing, as if he were aware of observation at every moment. "I think it best that I consult with Dr. Browne before I allow such a thing. She is so easily confused. Did she seem lucid to you?"

"Somewhat, at first."

"Then you were very lucky. You witnessed a rare event." My uncle pushed his plate away and leaned forward, his elbows on the table. "Let me save you from a painful lesson, May. Flossie's moments of clearmindedness are few and far between, with or without the laudanum. Your aunt is a hysteric, unfortunately. Obviously this is a private matter, and not for society gossip."

58

"Of course." I had hoped he might tell me something different from what Goldie had said, or what I'd seen myself. "Goldie says she's been this way since her headaches began?"

Another sigh. "There were aspects before then, I'm afraid, but yes."

Uneasily I addressed the fact of my invitation here, just to be certain. "I do hope my arrival was not a surprise to you. I don't wish to be a burden—"

"Oh good God, no! When Flossie told me of your circumstance, I was the first one to say you must come."

I was relieved.

"But your aunt is ill, and in fact, I think you can help her best by following the doctor's orders, as do we all. He suggests we keep her on a steady regimen of laudanum, and I believe he knows best in this. She is less restless, more at peace." His pale eyes came to mine; I did not miss the grief in them. It made me forget about his mistress and believe in him. "I wish it were otherwise, May. I wish it with my whole heart. Your aunt has been everything to me. If not for her help, I would have none of this." He waved at the room. "She has been a good wife and I want only the best for her. Do you know where I started, May?"

I shook my head.

"My father was a forty-niner. He came over from Ireland to strike gold, but he never found more than a few flakes of it. He saved it, and when he died, he left it to me. He had no genius for money, he told me, but he thought I did, and he wished me to make something of myself."

"No doubt he would be proud now," I offered.

"He was a liar and a thief, but I have him to thank for your aunt. One day I saw her coming from the City of Paris. My father told me she was so far above me in class that I had no chance with her. So I went up to her, just to prove him wrong, and do you know what, May? If I had a genius for money, your aunt was my equal. Together, we made our fortune." He went quiet, lost in his own thoughts, and I waited for him to elaborate, the questions loud in my head—what talent had my aunt? What had she been doing in the City of Paris? Had she money of her own before she met my uncle? Had my mother been here with her? But when he spoke again, my uncle said only, "What do you think of San Francisco so far? Are you enjoying yourself?"

I tried to gather myself at the abrupt change of subject. "Yes. Very much."

"You have nothing of which to complain? You don't miss home?"

"Not at all." That was honest. "San Francisco is very different, but it's invigorating."

"It is a good place to start fresh. San Francisco doesn't hold your mistakes against you. There are always opportunities. Always. You just have to take advantage of them when you see them." Again, that studied gaze. "I do hope you understand."

So it had not really been a change of subject at all. Still, I was bemused. "I—I think so."

"There are many opportunities in a life. It's not a failing to take whatever comes one's way. In fact, I rather think it a strength."

Sometimes people tell you exactly who they are, but I was not listening, distracted as I was by his story about my aunt, and my own questions.

"Now, if you'll excuse me, the office awaits." My uncle folded the newspaper and got to his feet. "You'll wait until I speak with Dr. Browne before you take tea with your aunt again? Perhaps I can arrange a meeting, and you can ask him any questions you have."

"That's not necessary. But I would very much like to see my mother's letter."

"I'll make inquiries."

"Thank you."

He smiled and put his hand on my shoulder. "One last thing, May. If you're in need of anything, anything at all, you mustn't be afraid to ask. You're part of the family now. I wish for you never to forget it. You're a Sullivan in everything but name."

Such generosity. "You're so very good to me, Uncle Jonny. All of you."

He patted my shoulder reassuringly. "Here comes your cousin. I'll leave the two of you to your gossip."

I glanced toward the doorway to see Goldie, dressed in a green-striped shirtwaist and deep green skirt. She offered a cheek for her father to kiss, which he did before he whispered something to her and left the room. She meandered to the sideboard; when she came to the table, she had only toast and a few strips of bacon.

She looked tired. Not so fresh faced as usual. I could not help my curiosity, and given her talk about friends and how she'd confided in me about Mrs. Dennehy yesterday, I didn't think she'd mind my questions.

"I'm surprised you're still not abed, given how late you must have been out."

Goldie sat across from me and poured a cup of coffee. "Late? I came home when you did, remember?"

"I meant after that." I lowered my voice. "I saw you go out again later. Where did you go?"

Goldie lifted her brow. "I've no idea what you're talking about. I went to bed and didn't move the entire night."

"But I saw you—"

"You must have been dreaming."

"You were wearing a dark coat and a hat, and—"

"Do we need to call a doctor?" My cousin peered at me as if she could not decide whether to be worried or amused. "Do I see—ah, yes, perhaps I do. Absolutely. Definite signs of lunacy."

She laughed, teasing, and I smiled wanly. "Well, I—"

"Friends trust each other, don't they, May?"

"I suppose they do."

"You don't sound certain."

"I've never really had a friend."

"Never? I don't believe that."

"Mama didn't allow it." My isolation and loneliness were hard things to admit. I had spent so much time trying to pretend that they didn't exist, that I didn't need the friendships I'd read about in novels, or that the people I watched from the windows didn't inspire envy. I had rebelled now and again—what child didn't?—but my mother's anger and disappointment had not been worth it in the end, and it was easier to do as she asked. When she died, the hardest thing to face was the fact that now that I was free to do whatever I wanted, I had no friend to turn to. "The neighborhood where we lived wasn't of our class. It was mostly immigrants. She didn't like me to have anything to do with them."

"You can't mean it," Goldie said.

"She meant well. She didn't want me to tarnish my pedigree." I laughed a little bitterly.

Slowly, Goldie put down her coffee. "Your pedigree? I thought— Papa said you were—"

"A bastard? Yes. I never knew my father. I still don't. He could be William Vanderbilt, for all I know."

"You don't mean it. Really? Vanderbilt?"

Another difficult-to-make admission. But if I meant to have honesty from Goldie, I must offer mine in return. "Mama said he was from one of the oldest families in New York, and very rich."

"She lied?"

"I don't know. I think . . . well, honestly, I think she trusted him too well. She said that one day I would have the life I was born for. She made some kind of bargain with him. I never knew what it was. Whatever promise he made, he never kept, at least not that I know. We lived in a boardinghouse. Mama did piecework. I worked in a shop. I asked Mama a hundred questions. She would never answer them. She refused to tell me anything about him or her life before I was born, or her family. When she died, I gave him one last chance. I put the notice of her death in the newspaper. It was a waste of time and money. He never appeared or sent any word at all."

Goldie stared at me as if I were telling her some incredible tale. "I had no idea. I suppose I should have known by your clothes. There are no trunks coming, are there?"

I shook my head.

"But your manners are so good and you speak so well, and—" She cut herself off. "Well, your mother sounds quite mad. Like mine. Perhaps it was all a fantasy."

An easy explanation, but I shook my head. "No, I never saw that. I think he lied to her. She believed in him. She died believing in him. She never loved anyone else."

"You really have no idea who your father was?" Goldie asked.

"None, and I've considered everyone. I used to study the pictures in the society pages and magazines to see if anyone had my nose, or my eyes. A hundred times, I imagined someone did, and I'd dream of it that night, and when I woke in the morning I'd see that I was fooling myself."

"Well, you don't need a father. Not when you have us." Goldie jumped to her feet. "Starting right now, I appoint myself your official guide to a new life and to new friends. We will keep you so busy, you won't have time to remember New York at all. Come now, stand up! First, we'll go skating at the Pavilion—have you ever tried it? It's fabulously difficult, but so much fun. The rink is right across the street from city hall. It's the most beautiful building in San Francisco—Papa's company built it. Then we'll go to Golden Gate Park. We've already two suppers to attend this week. Do you like opera?"

"I—I don't know."

"You'll love it, I know! Come, come, we must hurry! There's so much to do!" She came to me, laughing, urging me from my chair, and pulling me into an impromptu dance, whirling me about the room until I was giddy with joy.

SIX

Goldie was as good as her word. She threw me into the life I'd been promised, the one of which I'd dreamed. We attended more dances and dinners, operas and theater than I'd thought possible. We went to church on Sundays and promenaded after. We went on carriage rides, shopped and lunched and made calls in the afternoons. We roller-skated, and Goldie took me on a tour of the impressive city hall, with its grandiose pillars and its dome reaching over three hundred feet from the curb to Freedom's torch at the top. She was as proud of it as if she'd built it herself, and made me proud too of Sullivan Building's achievement.

These were the activities my mother had taught me to long for. These were the glittering, wine- and laughter-chased conversations and entertainments I'd imagined, lasting well into the night, until one collapsed exhausted into bed, sleeping away the morning until it was time to wake and do it all again. My sketchbook and pencils admonished me from my bedside table, unopened, ignored. There was no time.

The weeks passed in a whirlwind, then the months, one and then two and then a third. There were days when I was home only long enough to sleep. Days when I didn't lay eyes on my uncle except for Sunday service, or when the only news of my aunt was Shin's "She is just the same, Miss May." There was no more mention of my mother's letter. Goldie shrugged away the subject with, "Does it matter? You're here now, where you belong."

And yet . . . after all my longing for this life, it felt strangely empty, beautiful but hollow. I did not want to admit that I found it boring, or that I was floundering in its shallows. How little they thought about anything but their own amusement. Their lives were so easy, so full of beauty and money. How much they could *do* with it, and how disappointing to find them so vacant.

I missed my drawing with a startling intensity. I missed things I never expected to think about again. At the boardinghouse in Brooklyn, my mother and I had gathered every night for dinner with the other boarders. It had been one of my favorite times of the day—in spite of the food, which had been cheap and tasteless, if filling—because of the warmth of real companionship, even if it had only been for an hour. But whenever I suggested to Goldie that we might go home to have dinner as a family, she seemed confused by the very notion. *"That's so old-fashioned, May. Who does that anymore? It's almost . . . vulgar."*

The truth was that what I enjoyed the most were the society columns in the *Bulletin*. As I sat through another boring conversation about so-and-so's new bay gelding that was entered in the third race at Ingleside, I would amuse myself remembering how Alphonse Bandersnitch—which could not possibly be his real name; it must all be part of his anonymity—had made mention of the racetrack.

Wednesday night's theme at the Literary Club dinner was "What Do Women Need?" The answer, apparently, was not Miss Lucille Traynor, who was given the cut direct early in the evening by Miss Sarah Pastor, in spite of the fact that just last week, the same two ladies were seen arm in arm, pushing against the fence at Ingleside, screaming for their favorites and waving their betting tickets like the veriest hoi polloi. One wonders if Miss Traynor's rumored friendship with jockey Robert Rudford skewed the betting pool to Miss Pastor's detriment? On Friday the Traynors departed on a "long-planned" trip to the Continent. Now that Miss Pastor is deprived of her racetrack partner, one hopes she does not take to visiting the gambling hells incognito like the rest of society.

The day after I'd attended Celeste Johnson's reception with Goldie, I laughed so hard at the columnist's irony that I nearly snorted coffee from my nose.

At Miss Celeste Johnson's reception at her new home in Pine Street, she shared photographs and brochures from her visit to the Exposition. She was most anxious to tell everyone of her experiences with the tattooed and obscene savages in the Igorot exhibit, and the ferocious Congolese Pygmy with his pointed teeth, whom she declares "the most frightening cannibal I've ever known!" Which of course makes one wonder who in our fair city is hiding a terrible secret.

Goldie had been mystified by my laughter. "What's so funny?"

It wasn't the first time she'd missed his jabs. Her friends often seemed equally dense. He was making fun of them, how could they not see it? But either they didn't, or they were so glad to be mentioned in his pages that they didn't care. I began to think of Mr. Bandersnitch as belonging to me, somehow, a confidant. Someone only I understood. I was never at an entertainment where I didn't wonder if he was there too, though I had no idea what he looked like, and no one else seemed to know, either. He was either a master of disguise, or he was a member of society slumming as a reporter, and there was a great deal of speculation either way.

I personally leaned toward the member-of-society theory. I imagined him as rather short. Portly, with a love of sherry and cream puffs. Blond, perhaps, well dressed, educated, and with a sense of humor and an eye for absurdity. No one I'd met matched that description, but I thought of what I might do if I found him, how the two of us would stand back in a corner and watch and comment, amusing ourselves all night long with our asides . . . Oh, but that too was a fantasy, and I resigned myself to spending my hours pretending this was exactly what I'd always wanted and trying not to disappoint Goldie. I didn't want her to accuse me of being a Mabel. My ever-present loneliness only grew worse. How could I complain? I'd come from nothing. I was the luckiest girl in the world. I had a family now. How ungrateful I was, to want anything more.

And now, this beautiful October day, Goldie had whisked me away on a safety bicycle ride along the oceanside highway.

The view was magnificent. Twice I'd stopped pedaling to stare at waves crashing on a sandy beach and huge rocks dotted with black and shining seals. The fog that had cloaked the morning was now only spun sugar clouds in a blue sky, shifting with the salty, sweet breeze.

"Come on!" Goldie shouted from ahead. The front wheel of her bicycle wobbled as she slowed. "You'll have plenty of time to look from the restaurant!" Then she turned back again, pedaling fast.

I caught up with her and Thomas O'Keefe, Jerome Belden, and Linette Wall—the group of Goldie's closest friends I'd met the night of my arrival—just as we reached the Cliff House, a red-roofed, Bavarian-styled resort with turrets and a profusion of spires perched on the very edge of the cliff like an elegant steamer come ashore. The barking seals on the rocks below sounded like a pack of dogs. There had to be dozens of them, and just as many people populated the railed pathway sweeping to the beach, more promenading and picnicking on the sand, some even daring the water.

I came up beside my cousin just as Goldie dismounted. Her skirt caught on the pedal, and she nearly lost her balance. Fortunately, Thomas was right there to catch her. He was sandy haired and long faced and very patrician, with spectacles that made him look the perfect scholar, though his only studies were yachting and polo.

Goldie batted him away with a flirtatious smile. "The next time, I'm going to wear knickers like you and Jerry."

"Knickers, ha! The next time, we'll wear bloomers." Linette, who had been Goldie's best friend in finishing school, dumped her bicycle on the grass and delicately patted her pinkly glowing cheeks with her handkerchief. Beneath her tam her chestnut hair shone like copper in the sun.

Jerome, who at twenty-five was our senior, made a face and smoothed his dark beard. "Bloomers? Good God, no. I'm afraid I cannot be seen with any woman who wears bloomers."

"And we should never wear anything of which you don't approve, no matter how inconvenient," Goldie said dryly.

"Even beauty can't keep some things from looking ridiculous." Thomas freed Goldie's divided skirt from the pedal.

She gave him a grateful smile and said to me, "It took you forever to catch up."

"I thought I did well, especially since it's been ages since I've ridden. Not since grade school."

"I told you, they say one never forgets."

Jerome pulled at the high neck of his jersey. "Let's go in. I'm starving."

"You're always starving," Goldie teased.

"You make me ravenous, darling," he teased back, taking Linette's arm.

It seemed that nearly everyone in San Francisco had the idea to go to the Cliff House that Sunday—or to the enormous, Grecian-styled Sutro Baths nearby. The oceanside highway had been lively with horses and carriages, other bicyclists, and automobiles, and now they crowded the entrance. Men in their driving and bicycling caps dallied on the huge porch, women with colorful parasols and scarves and tams and, yes, one or two in bloomers.

"We need a table at the west windows," Goldie said as we went inside. "I want May to see the view."

The hall was long, the woodwork gleaming, the decor elegant, beautiful, and soothing. Places like this accentuated how truly the Sullivan house unsettled, that a resort should feel more like home.

Pillars punctuated the dining room, which was tastefully ornamented with palms and ferns and hanging lamps. It was indeed crowded, but we were seated promptly at a white-clothed table next to a window overlooking a veranda and the Pacific Ocean. Talk, silver clinking against plate, and the wonderful smells of food and smoke and that underlying, ever-present scent of the sea only added to the stunning view.

"Don't you love it, May?" Goldie asked. "Aren't you glad you're here instead of gloomy old Brooklyn?"

"You know I am. How many times must I say it?"

"If we don't eat soon, I'm going to collapse," Jerome said.

"The ride a bit too much for you, was it?" Thomas teased. "I thought I saw you lagging."

"I wasn't lagging," Jerome said in indignation. "I was distracted."

"By what?" Linette asked.

"By the sight of your lovely ankle." Jerome threw an annoyed glance over his shoulder. "That woman's hat keeps hitting the back of my head.

Why the hell do they need to be so big? They're devilishly annoying. Not only that, but they get in the way at the theater."

"Only last night I had to watch a play through the flock of birds in front of me," Thomas agreed. "Though, I have to admit it amused me to imagine them pecking the villain to death."

I smiled, though I was weary of the talk already. Fortunately, the view was worth the boredom I anticipated.

Jerome brought his chair closer to the table, away from the offending hat. "Well, what shall it be, ladies?"

"I'm partial to the baked oysters," Linette said.

The suited waiter came to take our order. Jerome and Thomas talked over one another to be the one who gave it. "No, let me," Jerome said finally. "There's something special I want May to try."

I glanced up from the menu. "How do you know I'll like it?"

"Because I know just by looking at you. Trust me, I'm very good at this."

"You're horrible at this," Linette disagreed. "You ordered snails for me once and swore I'd like them!"

"You told me you liked escargot."

"I was trying to impress you. Yes, I know, silly of me, wasn't it? Anyway, it sounded very French."

"It is very French."

"For *snails*."

The waiter hovered politely, but I sensed his impatience.

Jerome studied me in a way that made me shy again. I was still not quite used to their flirting, or the fact that it meant nothing. "Let me see—ah, I have it! You're a very serious girl, therefore nothing too decadent. Something like the Chicken Mayonnaise."

Goldie sighed heavily. "She already has a tendency to be boring. You'll only make her more so. We'll start with the caviar."

"And champagne," Thomas said to the waiter. "Sir, we will indeed need plenty of champagne."

The waiter departed with what seemed to be relief.

Jerome glanced toward the far end of the room. "My God, Ellis Farge is here."

I looked to where a dark-haired man sat alone at a table, toying with a glass of wine. He was very pale, his face chiseled, almost gaunt. He huddled in a heavy coat as if he were cold, though the day was fine and the sun poured warmly through the windows. "Who's Ellis Farge?"

"Only the most sought-after architect in San Francisco," Jerome explained.

Linette leaned forward, lowering her voice. "I've heard he's been refusing all commissions."

"Well, he can't take them all, can he?" Jerome asked reasonably. "Everyone wants him. He'd be swamped."

"But to turn them *all* down!"

"I doubt that," Goldie said firmly. "Why, my father has asked him and I don't imagine even someone as famous as Mr. Farge will refuse Sullivan Building."

"No, no one refuses Sullivan Building," Thomas murmured, so low that I didn't think Goldie heard him.

"I'm surprised to see him here. I heard he was at Del Monte," Linette said.

Goldie glanced up from her menu and gave Mr. Farge a casual look. "He's been back for days now."

They all looked at her in surprise.

"Don't you ever read the society page? He was in the Arrivals column just last week." Then she grinned and nudged me. "Perhaps you should go over and introduce yourself."

For a moment I thought she was serious. Then I decided she must be joking, and I laughed. "Yes, of course. It's not the least bit brazen, is it? He wouldn't think me fast at all."

She whispered in my ear, "I don't mean that. I mean you could tell him about your sketches." Suddenly she stiffened and murmured, "Oh, dear God."

I had never seen my cousin wear that expression. Dread—or perhaps even fear. I hadn't thought Goldie feared anything. "What?" I asked in alarm. "What is it?"

Jerome glanced over his shoulder.

"Don't look!" Goldie reached over the table to slap his hand.

"Who is it?" Linette whispered.

"Ah, I'd recognize those feathers anywhere." Thomas whistled quietly. "My, my, how interesting."

"What's interesting?" Linette demanded. "If you don't tell me, I'll look for myself."

But Goldie looked as if she might be sick. She grabbed the napkin from the table, pulling it to her lap, crumpling it in her fingers.

"Goldie, what is it?" I asked again.

The words had barely left my lips before a tall, aristocratic man with dark, oiled hair wearing a checkered scarf about his neck and a much older woman with black and gray feathers bobbing on her hat approached our table.

"Miss Sullivan. You're well, I hope," the man said with a tiny smile. Then his gaze came to me. "I'd heard your cousin was visiting. It's all the talk."

Goldie said nothing. In fact, she looked as if she were incapable of speech.

Another thing I'd never seen: Goldie at a loss for words. Not only that, but the others looked startled into silence as well. The man waited. Politely, I said, "Hello. I'm May Kimble."

The man tipped his hat. "I'm very glad to make your acquaintance, Miss Kimble. Allow me to present Mrs. James Hoffman. I'm Stephen Oelrichs."

72

Mrs. Hoffman. *The* Mrs. Hoffman? The Mrs. Hoffman who had sent her regrets to my welcoming party? The Mrs. Hoffman who seemed to matter so much to Goldie? I threw a quick glance at my cousin, whose expression had set mutinously.

Mrs. Hoffman said, "You're from New York, I understand, Miss Kimble? Will you be in our city long?"

I wondered what about this woman had so silenced my cousin. "It's my home now."

"Really?" Stephen Oelrichs spoke to me, but he looked at Goldie, again with that tiny smile. "Well then, I wish you luck, Miss Kimble. Good afternoon."

The encounter had lasted less than two minutes, and yet it set a pall over our party. The waiter arrived immediately after with the champagne. None of us said a word as he opened it with a flourish. Goldie had twisted her napkin into a coil, and she looked ready to cry—or to destroy something.

The waiter poured the champagne and left.

Jerome said, "Well," and lifted his glass.

Goldie lurched to her feet. "Excuse me." She pushed past Thomas and me.

Thomas looked after her in concern. "I suppose I should go after her."

"No, I'll go." Apparently I was not to be bored after all. This was so out of character for my cousin that I had to know the reason. So I did exactly what Goldie wished for me to do—I hurried off in search of her. She was walking so quickly that she was already gone by the time I stepped from the dining room. I saw no sign of her until I went out onto the porch, and spotted her striding down the pathway to the beach.

I ran after her. "Goldie, what is it?"

Goldie shrugged my hand from her shoulder and kept walking. She was crying. "I'm fine. Truly."

I had not known my cousin long, that was true. But to see her this way, so discomposed, affected me more than I expected. I had no idea what to do, or what to say. All I could do was accompany her and give her my handkerchief. Goldie took it, but only clenched it in her fist.

Warily, I said, "Why does she matter to you? What did she do?"

Goldie frowned at me. "Who?"

"Mrs. Hoffman. I don't understand. She seemed perfectly polite. I know she didn't come to my party, but—"

"Mrs. Hoffman?" she repeated dully. "Oh, you perfect idiot, May. It isn't about Mrs. Hoffman, at least not today."

"It was him then? That man?"

She stared out over the water at a passing steamer, and then without a word, walked on through the dry and shifting sand and sat.

I hesitated. My skirt was new, one of those we'd bought at the Emporium, and I had not yet gained my cousin's habit of heedlessness. But I was no longer poor May who had to do her own laundry, and when I sat beside Goldie, there was a certain satisfaction in being so heedless myself.

Goldie wrapped her arms about her knees. "I was engaged to him."

"You were engaged? When?"

"A year ago. I was nineteen. He's quite a catch. His family is one of the most prominent in San Francisco. His father came from New York and made his fortune in the gold mines. Stephen's a lawyer and he's handsome and rich, everything a girl could want."

"You can tell that he knows it."

Goldie's laugh was very small and short. "Oh yes."

"What was he doing with Mrs. Hoffman?"

"His mother and Mrs. Hoffman cochair the Ladies' Aid. No doubt it's something to do with their annual charity ball, or the Friday Night Cotillion Club. He's a friend of Ned Greenway."

"Who's Ned Greenway?"

"You remember—you read about him in the society column. He runs the Cotillion Club. Everyone wants to get in but no one joins it without Ned Greenway's approval. When Stephen and I were engaged, I was all set to be a member. I had my gown and everything. But then, well . . ."

"The engagement was off," I put in.

Goldie scowled. "I even met with Mr. Greenway *personally* to convince him that I didn't need to be Mrs. Oelrichs to belong, but he's really such a precious little snob."

"So this Cotillion Club is important?"

"Oh, I thought it was then, but it's really just a stupid dance club. Very staid and boring. I don't know why anyone wants to spend their Fridays drinking lemonade and following Ned Greenway's silly rules when there are so many more interesting things to do. Don't ask me how he got to be so important. He's just a stupid champagne salesman."

"Everyone likes champagne," I offered.

"It's not that. He's very clever. He managed to do favors for Mr. Hoffman and after that it was just a hop and a skip to his wife. Stephen's mother too. Mrs. Oelrichs organized the best-attended charity ball three years ago. Mother was on the committee then."

I tried to imagine my aunt on such a committee and couldn't. "Did Aunt Florence do a great deal of charity work?"

Goldie rolled her eyes. "She used to say that she liked to feel needed."

I filed that away. Being needed sounded at least interesting, something of purpose to fill the wasted hours.

"But that's how I was introduced to Stephen, and that's what Mother really wanted," Goldie went on. "Old San Francisco money. The Oelrichs name. Their house is one of those old and creaking places on Van Ness."

I didn't understand how important that was. "Not Nob Hill?"

"Oh no. They'd never build there." She laughed shortly. "They're such hypocrites."

"What do you mean?"

"They sneer at everything that hasn't been in San Francisco a hundred years—as if anyone has but the Californios! But really it's that they don't have the money to build a house like ours, so they pretend they don't want to. I'll bet talk of today has already reached Mr. Bandersnitch. Another chance for Stephen to humiliate me. I swear it's his favorite thing to do."

"How can he humiliate you? Why would he? Is he angry that you ended the engagement?"

Goldie dug her fingers into the sand, lifting a palmful, letting it fall like water. "I didn't end it. He did."

Of all the things Goldie could have said, that was what I'd least expected. "You're joking."

"Not at all."

"But why?"

"Stephen gambles. Everyone knows it. It's the bane of his family, but he doesn't often lose."

"How lucky for him."

"I'd never even held cards before he taught me how to play. He took me to Ingleside too, so we could bet on the horses. I had no idea what I was doing, of course, but Stephen likes games. I didn't realize that . . ." Goldie stared off again at the ocean.

I waited. Finally, I prodded, "What didn't you realize, Goldie?"

She followed a coasting seagull with her gaze. "He liked the adventure of it. He liked it when we gambled together. It was all very risky and exciting. But it turned out that he didn't want it in a wife. He's so old-fashioned. The world has changed, but he couldn't see it. I swear he would have kept me as some . . . some obedient little broodmare."

"I doubt you would have let him."

Goldie snorted. Even that was elegant. "He can't resist making everyone think I'm the one at fault! They all think I turned down the perfect Stephen Oelrichs. That's what he's told everyone, because he can't bear to look bad. When he came over to our table today he meant only to show Mrs. Hoffman how *valiant* he is, and how nasty I am to ignore him."

"Why didn't you tell everyone the truth?"

She gave me a horrified look. "A girl doesn't tattle about a man like that, May. What would Mr. Greenway and Mrs. Hoffman think of me then?" She reached for my hands and gripped them tightly. "You will stay away from Stephen, May, for my sake?"

"Yes of course. I don't want anything to do with him."

"You mustn't believe anything he says. Promise me you won't."

"Why would I listen to him? I'm your family."

"Yes, we're family." Goldie squeezed my hands again, smiling in that way I could not help but answer. That smile of hers was her most potent weapon—it distracted and disguised, and I was its best victim. It swept away whatever questions I might have had about Stephen or her story.

Goldie let out her breath. "Well, that's that. I suppose we should go back. I hope they haven't finished all the champagne without us."

"If they have, they'll be very drunk."

"On one bottle?" Goldie laughed again and pulled me to my feet. "Oh, my dear cousin, you have so much to learn!"

The foyer wavered. Only Goldie's arm around my waist saved me from falling.

"Too much champagne." My voice did not sound like mine. For one thing, my lips did not want to form the right words. For another, it echoed strangely, as did every noise in this house. I stumbled back, expecting to land on the padded banquette of the hallway mirror, which was most unexpectedly not there. I fell to the floor, pulling Goldie with me. "Where is it?"

"Where is what?"

"The mirror?"

"Out to be regilded, I suppose. Come on—shhh, don't wake anyone!" Goldie pulled me up, then grabbed the table to keep us both upright.

"No one's even here. Where are they?"

"Oh, who knows? The servants are probably out having a picnic."

The vision of Au lounging on the grass in his formal suit made me laugh so I nearly choked.

Goldie staggered to the stairs. She gripped the newel post, where she paused, wavering, spinning in circles—or no, it wasn't Goldie spinning. It was the hall itself.

"I have to go to bed or die," Goldie said dramatically.

It seemed to take me forever to follow her up. When finally I opened my door, it was so smooth, and the squeak was gone. Someone in the boardinghouse must have oiled the hinge at last—oh, but wait, no . . . the door here had never squeaked and everything was perfectly pink. Pink, pink, pink. My stomach flipped, a wave of nausea had me racing to the bed. I closed my eyes tight, trying to ignore the spinning room, thinking instead of the day, the champagne . . . oh, the champagne. Jerome's cousin had been at the Cliff House, and he'd tied the bicycles to his carriage and brought us all back because riding was impossible. It had been stuffy with all of us piled inside, sitting on each other, and the carriage swaying, and—

I ran for the bathroom.

Afterward, I felt marginally better, but the room remained shaky and my head began to pound, and the only thing to do was to lie very, very still, and to think of nothing.

I heard a sound, a squeak. Mice. I closed my eyes again, but then I remembered I wasn't in the boardinghouse; there were no mice here, and there was the sound again, a hush, the quiet click of a door. Aunt Florence, sleepwalking again. Or Goldie, sneaking out as she had the last time, disappearing into the night, dark coated, a waft of jasmine . . . Oh, but even my curiosity was not enough to prod me into rising. I heard footsteps down the hall—or I thought I heard footsteps. It could have been a dream. It was a dream. Only a dream.

SEVEN

When I woke, it was late morning, and I was cloaked in sweat and faintly nauseated. I'd fallen onto the bed without even removing my boots. My tam flipped into my face, and I tore the hat from my head without a care for the pins that came with it. Half of my hair tumbled loose. I managed to take off my boots, and staggered to the dressing table, where I saw in the mirror that the chenille bedcover had imprinted itself upon my cheek.

I rubbed, trying to make it disappear, and then I noted the circles beneath my eyes and my rat's nest of hair. "There's no hope for you, May Kimble," I muttered.

At the knock on my door, I said, "Come in," and thought grimly that I would stab myself with a hatpin if my cousin came inside showing no ill effects—which of course she would, because she was Goldie Sullivan, and I was . . . me.

But it wasn't Goldie. It was Shin, bearing a tray with what smelled like coffee.

"Bless you!" I grabbed the cup nearly before she'd had the chance to set it down. There was bacon too, and a pastry of some kind, neither of which looked appetizing this morning.

Shin looked at me critically, but all she said was, "Would you like to bathe, miss?"

I felt stupid and embarrassed. What must she think? But I was grateful for the suggestion, and by the time I was bathed and dressed and sitting in front of the mirror while she attacked the knots of my hair, I felt more myself. I watched as she tamed the tangle into a sleek smoothness that I had never, ever managed, even with all my digits, and tried not to reveal my continued fascination with the nub of her index finger. "Is Goldie still asleep?"

"She has gone out, miss."

"Out? Where?"

"I don't know, miss," Shin said.

"She said nothing at all?"

The maid only shook her head as she went after another tangle. I sipped my coffee and told myself it was nothing. No doubt Goldie knew I felt terrible and didn't wish to wake me. Still, the idea that she'd gone out without leaving any kind of word . . . "It isn't like her," I murmured.

I felt Shin pause, and I glanced at her in the mirror. She looked as if she might say something, then tightened her lips and continued with my hair, and there was something about that pause, something about her expression that made me remember last night, the footsteps in the hall.

Shin wrapped a curl around her fingers and pinned it in place.

Another curl, another pin. Shin put her fingers gently at my temples, turning my head in the mirror to admire her handiwork. She said—so quietly that I wasn't certain I heard at first—"Be careful, Miss May."

I tried to catch her gaze in the mirror.

She avoided mine neatly, placed the last pin, and said, "Will you wear the blue skirt today, miss?"

I should have questioned her; instead I assumed that I'd misstepped again. I took her words to mean one did not ask about others in the house, and I'd crossed some tacit boundary. I had asked Shin for her help; I should not feel ashamed or embarrassed when she gave it to me.

But I felt both. Where was Goldie? Where had she gone in the middle of the night? Why?

"Thank you, Shin," I said, pretending that I was everything I'd been taught to be. "Yes, the blue will be fine."

The house was empty. No Goldie, no Uncle Jonny. Even with the maids and the footmen who moved from room to room like shadows, I felt alone and restless, and worse, without purpose. The thought of a life spent this way . . . I could not fathom it. With no money of my own and no pedigree, I was not a good candidate for marriage. But I could not be a poor relation dependent on my aunt and uncle forever.

What was I to do with myself?

I remembered what Goldie had said yesterday about Aunt Florence on a charity committee, about the other women, Mrs. Oelrichs and Mrs. Hoffman, arranging charity balls. It was another thing I would have liked to ask my aunt about, and whether she'd found it interesting or satisfying, but there were my uncle's warnings to consider, and I didn't want to upset her. She held the key to so many riddles, and today, with nothing to distract for once, those riddles beckoned. I couldn't go to Aunt Florence without permission, but I remembered the Liberty Bell candy jar in her sitting room, the souvenir of her life before this one. She must have other things as well. Scrapbooks or . . . or perhaps

I might find the letter my mother had sent. Surely it wouldn't hurt to do a little exploring on my own?

I wandered from my bedroom and into the hallway. The *Bulletin* was on the table there, among the china fawns, awaiting Goldie, and I picked it up. It was already turned to the society page; how well everyone in the household anticipated Goldie's every need.

> At last night's Bohemian Club Hi-Jinx, there was much talk about the mysteries of Chinatown, though everyone seems to know every detail of the opium dens there. Professional guides will tell you of dank cellars reached by the twisting tunnels beneath the joss houses and gambling hells, but the real thing is only small back rooms full of pallets where devotees of the long pipe dream away their afternoons. That many of those devotees are oft mentioned in the society news is an open secret. That debutante (everyone knows her name) shopping for the silks and embroidered slippers in the Chinese store windows? The men-about-town playing flaneur (notable architect and favorite sitting judge among them)? And what about the matrons who have given up their Tuesday calling days to take a sudden interest in the Chinatown markets?

Always so intriguing. How did he know all this? And what debutante would dare an opium den? No doubt she too was nearly prostrate with ennui.

> Notable sighting of the week: Miss May Kimble and her cousin, the popular Miss Goldie Sullivan, were conspicuously festive at the Cliff House yesterday with Mr. Jerome Belden, Mr. Thomas O'Keefe, and Miss

Linette Wall. All were enjoying the best champagne
the resort has to offer. As usual, Miss May Kimble was
the talk of the town. Mr. Edward Hertford escorted the
very jovial party home.

As usual, the talk of the town? There was nothing overtly censori-
ous about the mention, but I was horrified. I'd had no idea that *the*
Alphonse Bandersnitch was even at the Cliff House. Why should he
be? And surely . . . *conspicuously festive* and *very jovial* did not mean
drunk, did they?

My liking for the reporter chilled. Not so very amusing when it was
me he turned that sharp wit to, was it? At least there was no mention of
Stephen Oelrichs, as Goldie had feared. But what was to be done about
this mention, if anything? Goldie would certainly know—

A door opened at the end of the hall. I looked up to see my aunt
Florence.

"May." She whispered my name, then looked quickly behind her
as if afraid. She gestured furtively. "Come. Hurry. We've so little time."

I hesitated. I'd promised both my uncle and my cousin not to
visit her again without approval. But how could I refuse a direct
request? Not only that, she looked so distraught, and no one else
was around.

Once again, my aunt motioned. I followed her to her bedroom.
She drew back into the darkness beyond her door to allow me to slip
inside, then closed the door. Again, the curtains were drawn. The flame
of a very small lamp struggled against soot-covered glass that looked
as if no one had seen to it for a year. Again, that sense of being stifled,
cloistered, removed from the world and locked away.

"Did they follow you?" my aunt asked, fumbling with the doorknob.

"Did who follow me?"

"Anyone. Are they listening?"

I frowned. "No. No, we're quite alone."

She opened the door, glanced out, shut it again. "They must not hear, do you understand? They must not know."

"Know what? Hear what? Are you all right, Aunt Florence? Is there something wrong? Something I can help you with?"

"You don't know what they'll do." She moved agitatedly from the door, jerking movements, darting eyes. "I promised Charlotte."

"My mother?" I grasped the one thing I understood. "What about my mother?"

She stopped and turned to me, frowning. "Charlotte."

In relief, I said, "Yes, Charlotte. My mother."

My aunt flailed for a nearby chair, and I hurried to help her sit. "Charlotte is dead."

"Yes." I could offer nothing beyond that.

"She asked me . . ." She stared, mesmerized, at the shadow of the lamp jumping on the wall. "She asked me to care for her baby."

She twitched, lost in the past. *I* was that baby, grown up now. "That was long ago, Aunt Florence. She sent another letter. Only a few months ago. Do you remember? Do you have it here?"

"The letter," she murmured. "I said no."

"Do you have it?" I asked again. I went to her bureau and glanced over the cluttered top. No letter, only crocheted doilies, medicine bottles, hairpins. "Is it in here?"

I turned to her, and she said nothing. I took it for permission. I was desperate; I wanted only to know something, anything, and I opened the first drawer. I'd no sooner done it than she cried out, "I said no! I promise I did. I said no!"

Dismayed, I hurried to her. I touched her arm, wanting to comfort her, trying to understand.

My touch only seemed to distress her more. She half rose from the chair, gripping my arms, those slender fingers like claws.

"You don't understand! She trusted me!" Her nails bit. She was stronger than she looked. "You should not have come. I want you to go home. Go home!"

She threw the words at me. Her eyes were black with anger and desperation and horror. I felt she could suck me up by sheer force of will, and she meant to. I tried to step away, unable to stem a growing panic.

"Please, Aunt Florence. Please!" Too loud. I heard my own fear and desperation.

The door burst open. Shin hurried to my aunt, taking her shoulders, easing her, and I went weak with relief and shame. "Now, now, Mrs. Sullivan. I have your medicine. That's right. This way."

Aunt Florence let the maid direct her. She collapsed again into the chair, and began to sob.

"Now, now," Shin soothed, taking the laudanum from her pocket. Then her gaze slipped to the bureau drawer, still opened, and I knew by the way she looked at me that she understood what I'd done.

My shame turned hot. I left quickly, jittery, devastated. I'd never heard anyone cry that way, so brokenheartedly. I did not know what to do, how to make things better, or how I would explain myself to my uncle, or to Goldie, when Shin told them that I'd upset my aunt going through her things, and, as if in response to my thought, there was Goldie, coming up the stairs.

She had been gone, I remembered. "There you are!" Guilt and fear and worry made me overly hearty. "Where have you been?"

Her head jerked up; something flashed through her eyes—irritation?—but then she smiled, and it was gone. "Oh, hello." There was an odd lilt to her voice.

"Where have you been?" I asked again.

"I went for ice cream. I had a craving for it, and I didn't want to wake you up. You were sleeping so soundly."

Ice cream? It was nearly two in the afternoon now; and she'd been gone for hours and hours. And who went for ice cream in the middle of the night? What confectioners would even be open?

But I saw no lie in her face, and there were plenty of reasons to doubt myself. All that champagne, my headache . . . Had I really heard anything last night, or had it all been the dream I'd thought it then?

"What's wrong with Mother?"

Aunt Florence's crying had quieted, but it was still audible. "I'm so sorry. I know I shouldn't have, but she wished to speak to me, and I—"

"You didn't. May, I told you!" Goldie pushed past me.

"Shin is with her—"

I started to follow Goldie into her mother's room, but she closed the door in my face. Well, of course. I deserved that, though it hurt. I heard her low and furious murmur, Shin's reply. I imagined what the maid must be telling her, and that was enough to send me to my bedroom, where I picked up my sketchbook. But I could only stare blankly at the pages, and the pencil felt foreign in my hand. I could think of nothing to draw.

Not long after, my aunt's door opened and closed, and my cousin appeared at mine, which I'd left open in resigned expectation. "A word, May, if you don't mind?"

She did not sound angry, which was a relief. She did not seem angry, either, only tired. There was a part of me that was reassured that her looks could suffer even as I braced myself for her scolding. "I'm so sorry. I promise it isn't what it looks like—"

"What did she say to you?" Goldie stepped inside and closed the door behind her.

"I hardly know. She made no sense at all." Except for the *"I want you to go . . ."* That had made perfect sense.

"You said she wished to speak with you."

"It was all nonsense, Goldie. You were right. I should have listened to you and Uncle Jonny. I should have refused her."

Goldie nodded thoughtfully. "What did you say to make her cry?"

I winced. "I'm sorry."

"Never mind that. Why is she crying?"

"I don't know. I—" I tried to remember something beyond that horror in her stare, that hard grip, the pinch of her nails. "I asked her about the letter. I—I thought she must have it, which is why I—why her—"

"What letter?" Goldie looked confused. Obviously she hadn't seen the opened drawer, or Shin had said nothing of my intrusion.

"The one you told me my mother sent. The one that told you where I was. I'd hoped to read it. I hoped it might hold some answers—"

"About your father, you mean?"

"About *anything*," I corrected with a short laugh.

"I don't think the letter would help you, May. It was just 'I'm ill and I'm worried about my daughter, and could you help her?' There was nothing more, I don't think. I never read it. She told us of it."

"But Mama did say she was ill?"

Goldie nodded.

"Even that she didn't tell me." I took a deep breath. "Anyway, I'm sorry. Uncle Jonny promised to ask about the letter for me, and I should have just waited for him. I am impatient sometimes."

"She's resting now. The laudanum is really quite a miracle."

"I'm glad."

Silence fell between us. It felt awkward, as silence hadn't in the time I'd known her.

I said, "How was the ice cream?"

"The ice cream?" She looked blank for a moment, and then laughed as if there were a joke in there somewhere I couldn't see. "Oh yes, delicious, of course. Too bad you were sleeping."

"You could have awakened me. I wouldn't have complained."

"Well, you were really quite drunk yesterday."

Which only reminded me of the gossip in the *Bulletin*.

"Did you see the society news today?"

Goldie shook her head. "Why?"

"It mentions us at the Cliff House."

Goldie squealed. "It does? Where is it?"

"It's not very complimentary. It says we drank a lot of champagne and were a 'jovial' company."

"Which is true."

"And it also says that I'm the talk of the town 'as usual.'"

"It does?" She raised a brow. "Well, well."

"What should we do?"

"Do? What do you mean, 'do'?"

"He said we were 'conspicuously festive.' Surely we can't let him gossip about us in such a derogatory way."

Goldie laughed. "Oh my dear May, tell me you're joking. We've been mentioned in the *Bulletin* society news. Do you know how many people would do anything for that? It's a triumph! Please don't be a Mabel."

She did seem truly happy about it. I told myself that I was, once again, too behind the times. Mama had always opined that real ladies were not gossiped about in the newspaper, but Mama had been from a different time and place, and so I allowed Goldie's joy over the mention to erase my misgivings.

"If you make a fuss, you'll just be telling everyone that you don't belong," Goldie said. "Is that what you want?"

It was most assuredly not. *Remember who you are.* "Well, I guess it's something to celebrate then. Shall we?"

My cousin put a hand to her eyes. "Perhaps later. I've a ravishing headache."

As she started to the door, I said, "Goldie, I am so very sorry about your mother. Not only because I upset her, but because she is . . . that way. I really am so sorry."

"Well." She took a deep breath. "Don't let it trouble you too much. She's far away now in dreamland, where she likes best to be. Nothing can touch her there."

EIGHT

The next morning, as Goldie and I promenaded the paths circling the trimmed lawns of Union Square, the St. Francis Hotel looming just beyond, my cousin grabbed my arm and jerked me behind the pedestal of the statue of Winged Victory. Silently, she nodded toward a couple also walking—my uncle, and his mistress, Alma Dennehy.

They were arm in arm, her hatted head nearly resting on his shoulder. A cloud of smoke—his cigar, hers—enveloped them. They were so very public. I wondered why they were not the topic of every conversation. It seemed such a scandal. "Why does he never write about them?"

"Who?"

"Mr. Bandersnitch."

"He will soon enough," Goldie's voice dragged with resignation.

"How long has it been going on?"

"Her late husband introduced Papa to Abe Ruef. That was three or four years ago. But this"—a shrug—"who knows really? Perhaps a few months? All I know is that he's been squiring her about in public lately and he doesn't seem to care what anyone thinks."

"He might care if it's in the *Bulletin*."

"He hates the *Bulletin*. And anyway, she has Mr. Ruef's ear. Papa's been lavishing money on her too—is she wearing any new jewelry? Can you see?"

"How would I know if it were new?"

Goldie sighed.

"Are you certain Aunt Florence doesn't know?" I asked. "This isn't—it couldn't be the reason for her headaches?"

Goldie studied me as if I'd just said something surprising. "Her headaches?"

"Perhaps she discovered it, and the strain . . . you know."

"Ah." Goldie considered. "Yes, perhaps. How clever of you to think of it, May. Perhaps that explains everything."

My cousin looked satisfied, and I was pleased that I'd provided an answer to at least one mystery, though I wondered that Goldie hadn't thought of this herself—it seemed such an obvious conclusion. Nor did the idea seem to pain her as it did me. But then, I was troubled and disconsolate over my visit with my aunt yesterday, and that made it easy to look for someone else to blame.

We waited until my uncle and his mistress walked from the park, and then another five minutes to be certain before Goldie let us emerge from behind Winged Victory. When we returned home some hours later, I went to the garden with my pencils and sketchbook in its worn leather case, hoping to forget my uncle and Mrs. Dennehy, as well as my own guilt, and find solace.

But in drawing, I was out of practice, and the garden was no refuge; like the rest of the house, it was both overcrowded and strangely deserted. The white stone path meandered through rose-filled parterres guarded by platoons of statues. Against one of the many bas-relief-decorated walls, a fountain of nymphs poured water from large urns.

There was no peace for the eye, but at least there was no confining roof, and the bright October sky stretched blue and far above.

When I saw my uncle approaching, I tensed, thinking not only of how I'd seen him this morning, arm in arm with his mistress, but also knowing why he'd searched me out. I'd had all night to think of what excuse I could make for my encounter with Aunt Florence, and I had none. I'd been warned. I'd allowed my curiosity to get the best of me. I would be lucky if he didn't ask me to leave.

"There you are." Intimidatingly perfect, as usual. He gestured to the bench. "Do you mind?"

"Please." I moved to give him room.

He craned his neck to look at the open pages. "Goldie said you liked to draw. She was right. You're quite good. May I?" He reached for the book, and, unable to find a graceful way to refuse, I handed it to him. He gave the sketches honest attention. "Perhaps I should let you design my building, given how much trouble I've had getting the architect I want."

I blinked in surprise. "You're joking, of course."

He sighed. "You've a good eye. Though I would insist on more angels."

"You seem to have a special fondness for them."

"I've been blessed," he said simply, giving me the book again. "I like to pay tribute to the Lord when I can."

There might be better ways than buying grosses of porcelain cupids. Wisely, I kept that to myself. While we went to church every Sunday, my uncle spent more time socializing than listening to the sermon. In fact, it was all I could do not to think of all the ways my uncle was *not* paying tribute to the Lord. "Who is the architect?"

"Ellis Farge—ah, I see you've heard of him?"

"He was at the Cliff House the other day. Goldie pointed him out." I remembered, too, Thomas's quiet comment about no one refusing Sullivan Building. It seemed someone had after all.

"He was? How odd. He's been a bit of a recluse lately, I understand. Commissioning him would be quite a coup, but he's been tiresome— ah, but that's nothing to do with you, my dear." He sighed. There was a wealth of disappointment in the sound. "There was something else I wanted to speak to you about. I understand there was a situation with Flossie yesterday."

"I'm sorry," I rushed in. "Truly. She asked me to visit with her, and I should have refused, but—"

He put up his hand to stop me. "Dr. Browne is looking in on her now. I think you should have a talk with him."

He spoke to me as if I were a small child, and I felt myself flush. "I've learned my lesson, Uncle Jonny."

"Perhaps. But it would ease my mind. Perhaps he can better put things into perspective for you." My uncle rose and offered his hand. I tucked my sketchbook beneath my arm and went with him into the parlor to wait for the doctor.

My remorse was already overwhelming; in the crowded parlor, it paralyzed me. I sat nervously while Uncle Jonny smoked. Soon the room was as foggy as the harbor. When Dr. Browne finally arrived, I thought I might be ill.

He peered down at me from a height. His deep-set brown eyes were faintly hostile. "Surely you must be familiar with your aunt's condition, given your own experience."

"My experience?"

"I understand there's a history of madness in your family."

I stared, uncomprehending.

"Your mother?" he prompted. "Was she not troubled by delusions and fantasies?"

"Oh. No. No, I never—"

"Perhaps you did not allow yourself to consider it. We often try very hard to excuse the behavior of those we love." Dr. Browne looked sympathetic. "Madness often runs in families. It would not be surprising for sisters to be equally afflicted."

I was so stunned at his implication that I barely heard the rest, which was all about the best way to manage my aunt—laudanum and calm—everything I already knew. When he finally left, I was relieved. I didn't like Dr. Browne or his assumptions, which were ridiculous.

My uncle asked, "Are you quite all right, May? I hope you did not find that too distressing."

"No, of course not. I just wish there was something I could do to help."

"It's nothing for you to fret about. You should be out with Goldie, playing about the city." He made a fluttering gesture with his hand. "One is only young once, after all."

I tried to smile. "I think I'm not much for playing, Uncle Jonny. I feel rather useless."

"Useless?"

"I've been here for three months now, and I feel I must find something to do with myself."

"Do?" My uncle spoke the word as if it were distasteful. "Do? Why, what is there to do except for what you're doing?"

"I should find a job. Perhaps I could become a governess, or . . . or something. I could take up charity work. I feel I'm taking advantage of your generosity."

Uncle Jonny laughed. "I think of you as another daughter, May. Please, no more of this talk of doing things, or taking advantage. What would people say if I let my niece *work* for a living? Good God, no, you will do nothing of the sort. I wish you to do just as your cousin does, be frivolous and gay. It does me good to see it."

My heart sank even as I tried to return his smile. "Still, Uncle. Aunt Florence did serve on some charitable committees."

"It was a terrible strain. I believe it led directly to her affliction now."

That? *Or Alma Dennehy?*

"Truly, May, I don't wish you to end up like your aunt. You heard what the doctor said—it runs in families."

"My mother was not—"

"Young women should not strain their minds or their bodies with too much work," he said affectionately. "I'll hear no more of it. In fact, I believe Goldie has a treat for you today. I hereby order you to stop thinking of these absurdities and enjoy yourself thoroughly. Am I understood?"

I nodded reluctantly. "Yes, Uncle."

"Excellent!" He clasped my shoulder and squeezed lightly. "Your old life is in the past, May. You have had too many years of worry. Now it is time for pleasure."

He made my concerns sound so unreasonable—truly, who would wish for purpose when they had the choice of ease?—and yet a heaviness set upon me that I could not shake, and when Goldie came to me in my bedroom later, I was no better.

"Papa thinks you need a distraction, and so do I."

"Goldie, I—"

"I won't take no for an answer. Come along. We're going on an adventure."

"To where?"

"It's a surprise." There was that mischievous gleam in my cousin's eyes again, that sly smile. "But I promise you will love it."

Which is how I found myself with Goldie on a crowded streetcar on Clement. There were few businessmen on the trolley; it was mostly families, mothers and children, and young men who looked dressed for an outing. The clanging and screeching of the wheels and the steel cables and the excited talk coming from those clearly anticipating fun raised my spirits somewhat.

Goldie would not say where we were going. Neither would she tell me what she carried in the large carpetbag on her lap.

"You'll see," she said. "Now stop asking questions."

Then, with a screech of brakes and a throng of racing children and mothers calling out for them to wait and boys jostling each other to disembark, we came out of the streetcar depot to Sutro Baths.

I had seen it from the Cliff House, but I'd not yet been inside. It was huge, a three-acre natatorium, a glass-topped, cupola-embellished, mammoth structure stretching just above the beach.

"We're going swimming?" I asked Goldie.

"Have you ever been?"

"Not ever." There'd been no money for it. Even Coney Island had been out of reach. "Goldie, I can't swim. I don't even have a bathing costume."

"There are shallow ends just for splashing. And as for the rest"—she patted the bag—"I've planned for everything."

She led the way into the Grecian temple entrance, then down a broad stairway several flights to the swimming tanks, ringed on each level by promenades and stadium observation decks. A domed glass ceiling and walls of windows fronting the oceanside blasted sunlight. Tropical plants and arching palms decorated the staircase and restaurant verandas. It was warm and humid, smelling of salt water and fried food and hair oil, echoing with children's squeals and people talking as they meandered the promenades.

Goldie took me to the ladies' dressing rooms and pulled from her bag two parcels wrapped in paper.

"Here's your bathing costume, as I promised." She was vibrating in a way that reminded me of Aunt Florence at tea, that barely suppressed tension, though in Goldie it wasn't tension but excitement. "Now, don't scold."

I took the package. "Why should I scold?"

"Just open it."

I tore away the paper. Inside was folded white fabric instead of the black or gray I'd expected. I shook it out. At first, I thought she'd brought the wrong package. It looked more like an undergarment. It was skirted, with short bloomers beneath, the bodice cut in a deep V to a belted waist, the V filled in with black-and-white-striped fabric that repeated at the hem of the skirt and decorated the short sleeves.

I gaped at my cousin. "What is this?"

"Your bathing costume, of course."

"This is a bathing costume? It's no bigger than a handkerchief!"

"Don't be silly. It's much larger than that." Goldie held hers—which matched mine, but in black—against her body.

"Where are the stockings?"

"There are no stockings, Mabel."

"But our legs will be showing."

"I know." Goldie grinned and widened her eyes in mockery. "Isn't it wonderful? Now we will actually feel the water!"

I stared at it dubiously. "This looks indecent."

"It's the very latest fashion, May. Half of the girls in there will have them on. Don't tell me you're too afraid to wear it."

"No, but—"

Goldie sighed and grabbed it from my hands. "Oh very well. Look like some old matron if you want. They've got costumes for rent, but they're those ancient wool things that make everyone look awful."

"Goldie—"

"Go on, go get one. Here." She pulled some coins from her bag and shoved them at me. "But you're ruining everything."

"Don't be silly." I pushed the coins away and grabbed the suit back. "Of course I'll wear it. I was only surprised."

She gave me the golden smile that made me her puppet. I ducked into the dressing room and changed, then tried desperately to ignore the shocking pale thinness of my legs, the exposed expanse of skin. I tugged at the skirt, hoping it might miraculously unfurl to cover at least my thighs, but it remained stubbornly short. Perhaps people would mistake my white legs for matching stockings.

I stepped out, self-conscious, barefoot, only to hear Goldie's cry of dismay.

"What is it?" I asked.

She was inside another dressing room. "Oh, I can't believe it! No, no, no!"

"What's wrong?"

"They sent the wrong size! Oh, I will scream at that salesgirl for this. I *told* her."

"Surely we can pin it in places," I suggested.

"May, it's far too small. I can't even get it over my hips. Oh, hell!"

Some of the other women in the changing rooms turned to look. I crept closer and lowered my voice, trying not to seem too relieved. "You can wear mine."

"Don't be a fool. You're a foot taller at least. It will never fit."

I was not a foot taller. Only a few inches, but it was true that my costume fit perfectly, and I saw no real way for Goldie to wear it. "There's no help for it then. We can go swimming another day."

"No, no. I don't want to ruin your fun. I'll go rent a bathing suit. You go on out. I'll meet you in the warm tank closest to the one for the women and children."

"Closest?" I asked. "You mean we aren't swimming in the women's tank?"

Goldie poked her face out. "Why would we, when we can flirt with half-dressed men? Now go. I'll meet you in a few minutes. If you aren't talking to some man by the time I get there, I'll send you back to Brooklyn!"

"I'll just wait for you here."

"You absolutely will not. Go!" She shooed me away with a laugh. "You're a Sullivan, and Sullivans go forth!"

I stepped from the dressing room, making my way to the tanks. The sun glared onto the water through the many windows and the ceiling. Swimmers scrambled over slides and springboards and bobbed in the tanks, all of them black suited, most of the women stockinged. There were only a few dressed like me.

I stood at the edge of a tank, aware that suddenly I seemed to be the focus of everyone's attention, each taking in my white suit, my indecently bare legs—I looked ridiculous.

A man dodged in front of me—"Smile, miss! It's for the *Bulletin*"—and there was a blast of light, blinding, so that I stepped back, too far, and fell with a resounding splash into the shallow end of the pool.

Goldie was nowhere to be found, and when she didn't appear after what felt like forever, I harnessed my humiliation and left the tank with what remained of my dignity. When she still hadn't appeared after I'd dried off and dressed, I went looking for her.

The baths were enormous, and there were a hundred places to look, too many restaurants and promenades and bleachers. I went back to the dressing room several times. She was not there. Neither was she where one rented bathing costumes. Perhaps we'd crossed one another, and she was swimming, so I went to the observation deck to look out over the tanks. I saw no distinctive blond head, though it was difficult to tell people apart in the ugly woolen costumes.

I stared out over the rippling water at the men diving and the children squealing as they slid down the giant slides. A prickling sense—someone watching—made me look over to where a man in a long dark coat and hat pressed against the railing. Ellis Farge. I recognized him from the Cliff House. He was alone, and he was not looking at me, though I'd felt he was. He looked out at the swimmers.

There was something odd about him, and it was not just that he was wearing a heavy winter coat in the middle of a humid, warm natatorium. His distraction was evident. He tapped the rail in an incessant rhythm; the thud of it vibrated down the rail where I stood several feet away, and his restlessness troubled the air.

Uncle Jonny had said Farge was a recluse, and only today had said he wished to commission the man. It seemed somehow fated to come upon Ellis Farge here, almost as if I'd conjured him.

Perhaps he felt me looking at him; he glanced over. Quickly, I glanced away, praying I didn't blush, though of course I could feel that I already was. I should approach him. For my uncle's sake, of course. It would be one way to repay him for his generosity to me. But I was not Goldie, and I could not be so forward.

The thudding on the rail intensified. Now, I felt it against the bottom of the rail too, his foot tapping. Impossible to ignore. I glanced over again, and there he was, staring at me, frowning, as if he were trying to make me out. That chiseled face was handsome, the face of an aesthete. Yet he was still so very pale, and there were shadows beneath his deeply blue eyes.

"Do I know you?" he asked.

"No," I said. "Oh no. No, you don't."

He slid closer. "Then why do you keep looking at me?"

My mouth went dry. "Um—you're shaking the railing."

"Oh." He stopped tapping and backed away from the rail. "Sorry. I'm just a bit . . . distracted."

"Yes, I can tell."

"Desperately so, really." His foot nudged the rail as if he could not help himself, rapping again. "Oh, sorry."

"Desperately distracted about what?"

"Seriously, I can't concentrate on a damn thing—sorry, forgive me. I'm not usually profane. I don't know why I said that. Do you think it's the weather? Ah, never mind."

"Perhaps you're too hot. It's quite warm in here."

"Is it? Well, it was raining this morning, wasn't it?"

"No."

"No?" He seemed discomfited. "You see. I've lost track of time, I think." He stared at me now, and it was compelling at first; it started a sweet little shiver over my skin just before it became uncomfortable.

I looked away, suddenly not knowing what to do or what to say. Flirting was Goldie's specialty, not mine. I was not even certain he was flirting. *Tell him your name. Tell him about your uncle.* But I could do neither, and I knew that I was going to walk away, to say goodbye, to let this chance go because I did not have the ease with the world to take it as my cousin would, and I felt a little envy at that—how did one learn such a thing?

"Please don't go," he said, as if he knew my thoughts. "I don't mean to be rude. It's only that I'm not quite myself today. Who are you? Where are you from? I promise I'm not a criminal or a kidnapper. I'm an architect."

"I know who you are," I said.

He raised a brow.

"Doesn't everyone? You're Ellis Farge."

"Ah. You have me at a disadvantage, Miss—?"

"Kimble. May Kimble."

"Kimble." He came closer and reached for my hand, which he enveloped in his. His fingers were warm and somehow electric. "I feel I should know you, given that you know me."

"You're San Francisco's most sought-after architect."

He grimaced. "Indeed."

"There you are, May!"

I looked over my shoulder to see Goldie at the top of the bleachers that overlooked the observation promenade. She waved enthusiastically.

Mr. Farge tipped his hat and said, "I'll let you get back to your friend. Good day, Miss Kimble."

Goldie hurried down the stairs, and he slipped away before I even knew he was gone, taking his restlessness with him.

"Was that *Ellis Farge*?" she asked upon reaching me.

"Yes." How had he disappeared so quickly?

"I can't believe it! Did you tell him about your sketches?"

"My sketches? Why would I?"

"Papa will be thrilled to hear you've met him."

"It was hardly a meeting," I said. "We spoke only a moment."

"Oh, did I interrupt too soon? I'm so sorry."

"I doubt he'll remember me tomorrow. Where were you, anyway?"

"Oh"—she waved that away—"I couldn't bear to wear a rental, so I just walked about a bit to give you a chance to bathe."

"You missed the spectacle I made of myself." I told her about the photographer and my misstep, and she let out a little peal of delight.

"You'll be all over the newspaper tomorrow."

"Please don't say that."

"You'll make headlines—don't cringe. You're becoming the most mentioned girl on the society page."

"If you say so."

"Anyway, you're in a better mood now."

It was true, I had to admit. Ellis Farge and his restlessness had entirely distracted me from my lack of purpose and the episode with my aunt and my questions.

Goldie and I ate sandwiches and ice cream at one of the restaurants while I tried to ignore the now-and-again glances from those who had undoubtedly seen me in the white bathing costume. More than one man tipped his hat to me with a knowing smile, and when Goldie and I walked past one of the restaurant balconies, someone catcalled and whistled.

Goldie seemed so delighted by the attention that I could not bring myself to be dismayed, but I was relieved when we started back to the streetcar depot. The bathing complex, with its expanse of glass and its twin cupolas decorating an arched roof, flared like its own sun.

Goldie stopped. She put her hand to her eyes to shield them and said, "There's Mr. Farge again."

I glanced in the direction she was looking, and yes, he was coming from the building, still in that winter coat.

"May, you must make him remember you. For Papa's sake. Promise me you will."

"How am I to do that?"

"You'll have to seek him out."

"Goldie—"

I was interrupted by the clanging bell of the streetcar as it dragged, screeching, into the depot, and Goldie and I had to run to catch it.

NINE

Of course, Goldie had not forgotten any of it. Almost the moment we sat at breakfast the next morning, she said to Uncle Jonny, "You'll never guess who May met yesterday at Sutro's."

Uncle Jonny barely glanced up from his eggs. "You're right, I never will. Who was it?"

"Ellis Farge!" she announced.

A suddenly intense interest replaced my uncle's inattention. "Ellis Farge?"

"Can you believe it?"

His gaze landed on me. "How exactly did May achieve this impossible thing?"

I tried to shrug it away and took a small bite of toast. "I happened upon him."

"She *happened* upon him," Goldie mocked gently.

Uncle Jonny wiped his mouth. "He's avoiding me. I'm not alone in that, either. He's shaken off Ruef for months."

Abe Ruef. The man sitting at the Palace Bar with Uncle Jonny and the widow Dennehy. The man without whom nothing in the city got done.

"It seems like fate that May met him, doesn't it, Papa? I told her it was a perfect opportunity."

"He's my first choice for the Nance building," Uncle Jonny said thoughtfully. "We've been having trouble getting commitments. If they just could see a design . . ."

"Commitments?" I asked.

"Leases," he provided.

"Ellis Farge's design of Papa's new building is bound to be famous. If it's famous, then everyone will be rushing to lease space. If everyone's rushing to lease space, it will be a huge success." Goldie laid it out simply.

"Oh, I see."

"There's also that land in Chinatown I'm looking at." My uncle spoke as if he were thinking out loud. "It may be easier for me to buy it if I can convince the seller I'll bring in more business than anyone else. A connection with Farge could make that happen too."

"You will simply have to go to Mr. Farge's office, May," Goldie said. "Don't you think so, Papa?"

"Go to his office?" It was very forward, but I *had* approached him already, hadn't I? It wasn't as if we hadn't been introduced. In a way.

"Of course. You're an independent, modern woman, aren't you?"

Uncle Jonny cautioned, "We cannot ask such a thing of May, my darling."

"But you just said it would help, and she's already got Mr. Farge's attention."

"Well, yes." My uncle spoke with obvious reluctance. "But if it makes you uncomfortable, May, my dear, then please don't give it another thought."

I owed him so much. I owed them all so much. My meeting with Ellis Farge had been fated, as I'd thought. And I was a modern woman, as Goldie said. Why shouldn't I go to his office?

"Of course I'll call upon him. I would do anything to help, Uncle Jonny. You must know that."

Goldie settled back with a smile. "How very good you are, May. Really, you simply could not be better."

"You'll come right back? I want to hear everything." Goldie lounged on my bed an hour later, watching Shin artfully shape my hair into elegance.

"I won't delay a moment."

"Good. Do your very best, Shin. I want him unable to refuse her." Goldie got off the bed. She took my sketchbook in its leather case from the bedside table and shoved it into my bag.

"What are you doing?"

"Show him these."

"Goldie, I couldn't. They're only sketches, and he's—"

"It's a way to gain his sympathies. Ask his advice. Men can't resist a woman asking for help."

I would never have thought of it. I knew I could not ask it of him. I knew I *would* not.

"Good luck!" Goldie blew me a kiss as she left the bedroom.

It was the first time I'd been alone with Shin since the debacle with my aunt. I wanted to ask her why she'd said nothing of my going through Aunt Florence's drawers. I also wanted not to broach it. Perhaps she'd forgotten; perhaps she'd thought nothing of it. I didn't want to give her a reason to tell my uncle if she hadn't realized there was one. In the end, it seemed best to say nothing, to let her bring it up if she wished to do so. Still, I felt ashamed every time I met her eyes. I waited for her to say something about it. When she didn't, I pretended my nervousness was because of my impending visit with Ellis Farge. That was partially true, anyway. Shin tucked in the last pin and stood back to survey her handiwork. "A ribbon, Miss May?"

I shook my head. "Businesslike is best, I think. Thank you, Shin."

She helped me into my coat and pinned one of the giant cartwheel hats on my head—this one with a short veil and a bobbing owl perched in a sprawl of web-like silk branches. Shin looked as if she were about to say something, but thought better of it.

I patted the owl. "What is it? Does it look ridiculous?"

She handed over my bag. "You should not show him your drawings, Miss May."

It was one thing to know myself that a renowned architect would find my sketches juvenile. It was another to be told. Shin's words stung. That, and my guilt over Aunt Florence made my response sharper than I meant. "Of course not. I know that. I'm not an idiot."

I refused to feel sorry at her wounded surprise, though I was irritated with myself as I went out to the waiting carriage and asked Nick to drive me to the office of Farge & Partners.

With every block that passed, I grew more nervous. When we reached the Italianate-styled building that took up an entire block on Montgomery Street, I did not want to get out of the carriage. I stared up at the four floors of windows, with restaurants and shops on the street, wondering if I could go home again and pretend that Ellis Farge had not been in. But then Nick was opening the door and I was stepping out, and before I knew it, I was at the door, where a directory indicated that Farge & Partners was on the top floor.

I would have sworn every eye in the place focused on me, and that meant it was impossible to turn around again without looking like a fool. *"Remember who you are."* I adopted my most confident air as I made my way up the stairs. It wasn't only architects and bankers and lawyers who had offices here, but artists. Doors opened to show high-ceilinged, light-filled studios. Men smoking and talking and gesturing were on every landing. It smelled of plaster and clay and paint, something acrid that mixed with the earthy sweetness of garlic coming from a downstairs restaurant.

Then the door was before me. I did not have to go in. No one would know. But my family meant more to me than my nerves. I owed them everything. This was a small enough payment. I took a deep breath and opened the door into an office smelling of paper and tobacco, and a young man pounding on a typewriter. When I entered, he turned to me with a polite expression of inquiry.

"I'm here to see Mr. Farge," I told him.

"Ah. Do you have an appointment, Miss—"

"No, I don't. But if you could just tell him that Miss Kimble came to inquire after him? May Kimble."

"He's very busy, Miss Kimble. Without an appointment, I don't think he'll be able to see you."

"Please. I won't take up much of his time."

The young man sighed, but obediently went down the hall. While he was gone, I glanced at the framed pictures on the wall, photographs of buildings, some sketches. Mr. Farge had been productive for someone his age, which I'd guessed to be early thirties. All of the designs were quite interesting, if not as daring as I'd expected, given everything I'd heard. I was disappointed; I'd expected something more, but I couldn't say what really. After all, how different could a building be? I knew nothing about real architecture. Perhaps these were visionary. How would I know?

"He'll see you." The young man was back, and he seemed surprised. I was surprised myself.

He led me past a room holding a large table spread with drawings to an office at the back and Ellis Farge. He was just as handsome, but he smiled when he saw me and his blue eyes laughed as they had not yesterday. In fact, there was about him none of the restlessness I'd seen then. I wondered if I'd imagined it. Today, too, he was dressed more warmly than the day warranted, in a thick woolen suit, and the office was heated almost to discomfort.

He stood at a desk covered with unopened mail. "Well, if it isn't Miss Kimble. The *Bulletin* Girl."

"The what?" I asked.

He reached behind him for a newspaper, which he held out to me. That he had been looking at that page recently was not in doubt. There were two pictures from Sutro Baths there, the first with me looking pale and gawky in the revealing suit, and then in the next, my plunge backward into the pool. The caption read: *The daring Miss Kimble models at Sutro Baths—and proves that this latest Parisian fashion is all wet.*

I would have laughed at the caption had it been about anyone but me. Goldie must have seen it this morning, but she'd said nothing. Why hadn't she warned me? My face felt on fire. "Oh dear."

"You weren't wearing that bathing costume when I saw you at the baths."

"Thankfully I had it on for a very short time."

"You belong to the Sullivans, I understand," he said thoughtfully.

I was surprised again, that he knew it, that he'd offered me an opening so quickly, as if he'd known why I'd come. Perhaps, had those eyes been less blue, his smile less ready, I might have been suspicious. But he was attractive, and the drawing tools settled in a velvet-lined case on his desk—brass-plated compasses and rulers, thin wooden templates in triangles and curves—raised the beginnings of a hunger I didn't recognize. "You've heard of us then."

"Oh yes."

"You know who my uncle is? He certainly knows of you. He's longing to work with you. He says you're avoiding him."

"Ah, well." Farge turned to the window. "It has nothing to do with him. I'm not working much these days."

"Why not? My uncle says you're very talented."

"And you're here to beg on his behalf."

I paused. "Something like that."

He said nothing. An awkwardness fell between us, and I looked at one of the framed drawings on the wall, a building of Egyptian fashion, with geometric walls that hinted at a ziggurat and many-sided columns topped with the distinctive bundled reeds. But it was a confusing mix of styles.

"The Hartford building." He had turned from the window to watch me study it. "Finished earlier this year. What do you think?"

"It's very nice."

"Do you know what your friend at the *Bulletin* called it? 'Bewildering' and 'cramped.'"

"I don't have a friend at the *Bulletin*."

He ignored that. "Do you agree with him?"

"I'm hardly an architect—"

"You don't need to be an architect. Just tell me what you think."

There was an intensity in his question that felt like his distraction of yesterday, and that kept me from honesty. I said carefully, "Surely people wouldn't be clamoring to commission you if they thought your buildings ugly."

"But you do," he accused.

"I said no such thing."

"Would *you* commission me, Miss Kimble?"

"I—"

"When I first came to San Francisco, I thought, what a place. What a place to do something new. It breathes in a way other cities don't."

"I know exactly what you mean." I was eager to find common ground. "It feels new and exciting."

"I see you understand."

"It's theatrical and yet—"

"Trying very hard to be classic," he finished.

I laughed. "It wants to be flashy, but it wants to be respected too."

He smiled now. "You know about the Burnham Plan?"

I nodded. "The city beautification project? My uncle says that the city doesn't need it. He thinks it will hamper business."

"It will cost too much and cause too much disruption. But it's an opportunity for San Francisco to make a mark. It needs architects who aren't afraid to try something new. That's what I wanted the Hartford to be." Ellis Farge nodded to the drawing. "Well? Don't think you can get away so easily. What do you think? Not flashy enough?"

"What's it meant for?"

His brow furrowed. "It's a business building."

"Offices? Then it's trying too hard. The pyramid styling is interesting, but it does look cramped, and there are hardly any windows. It must feel like a prison inside."

He stepped up beside me, a bit too close, and I was too conscious of the space between us. "You've studied architecture?"

"Oh no, just—I draw a bit but—"

"Is that a sketchbook? In your bag?"

I had forgotten it was there, and now I was horrified. Why had I not left it in the carriage? Goldie had been so sanguine, but it was Shin's words that stayed with me, *You should not show him your drawings,"* a reminder of impending embarrassment. "Oh, no. No, it's nothing at all—"

A short, impatient gesture. "Hand it over. Let me see."

"Please, it's really so stupid—"

"No commentary please. Let me judge for myself."

I handed it over, moved more by his insistence than by any volition.

He took his time over the pages, studying them intently, no doubt finding every flaw. I would almost have preferred that he look through it quickly and decisively, putting a quick end to my nerves.

Finally he glanced up. "What's wrong?"

"I'm very nervous."

"Why should you be? These are very good. You've a fine eye. I like this one especially." He flipped to the library that Goldie had said needed statues. "And this." A dark-paneled dining room with a contrasting wooden floor laid in a radiating pattern. It had been a chromo of a winter scene that had given me the idea. I didn't remember the rest of the picture that had so captured me, only the ice-covered pond glowing against a stormy winter sky. "Really there are too many to choose from."

It didn't seem possible that he might think it. I waited for the *but*. *But* there should be more statues. *But* the wall color is wrong. *But, but, but . . .*

He said, "Where did you learn this?"

"I didn't. Well, I had a book of watercolors, so I suppose it was that."

"No book taught you how to do this. You never had a lesson in design?"

"I read the Wharton book, and a few others."

"Ah." He looked back at the page. "But mostly you've paid attention." He seemed surprised, and impressed, and my nerves melted into dizzyingly warm pride. "This is beautiful. They're all beautiful."

"Thank you. I'm flattered." An understatement.

"It's a pity that you're a woman." He closed the book. Before I could react to that—the truth of it, the unexpected disappointment of it—he tapped the cover and asked, "Have you more of these?"

"Dozens. I've been drawing them forever. It was a way to—" I stopped, surprised that I'd almost said the truth about my mother and what these drawings had meant, about the future I'd been promised, my loneliness and need.

He did not let it go, as I'd hoped. "A way to what?"

"Nothing. Nothing." I'd wanted to put a stop to his inquiries, but then I was disappointed when he only nodded.

He handed back the sketchbook. "Well, you've done what I thought was impossible, Miss Kimble. You've won my attention. Ask your uncle to call me."

"Thank you, Mr. Farge." I nearly dropped the sketchbook in the flurry of my gratitude. "I can't tell you how much I appreciate it."

He considered me again, this time quizzically. "You care very deeply for your family, don't you, Miss Kimble?"

"They're everything to me," I said simply. "They saved me, you see."

On the way home, I expected to be basking in glory. I wasn't. I'd won what my uncle had wanted, but I was not satisfied, and Farge's admiration for my work, his office, the unfamiliar tools on his desk, had spurred a surprising little ache that was not quite an ache, an excitement shivering with both hope and fear, as if the world had briefly opened to show me something I had never before allowed myself to glimpse. Possibility. Opportunity. And then disappointment. *A pity that you're a woman.* I was uncertain what I'd wanted from him, but I knew I wanted something—and that I longed for it still.

TEN

As brilliantly as the Sullivan mansion shone in the sunshine, it looked cold and austere, the windows blank and still and blind. In spite of the fact that I had good news to tell my uncle, I was unsettled now by Ellis Farge, and a yearning I could not quite put a name to, and the house only exacerbated my discomfort.

There was no one about; the place was again eerily silent. Not even the footsteps of a maid, and Au did not appear out of nowhere to take my coat and hat. Goldie must be in her room. I went upstairs, meaning to ask her why she hadn't told me about my picture in the *Bulletin*, but before I could go to my cousin, the door to my aunt's bedroom opened, and Shin motioned for me to come.

I shook my head. "Dr. Browne said I wasn't to see her without permission."

"Please, miss. She is good today. She wishes to see you."

"I cannot."

"Mr. Sullivan is gone."

I knew she meant to reassure me; it only made this more illicit. "The doctor warned me—"

"Please." How ardent she was, almost pleading.

Shin was so adamant, and she knew better than anyone the effect I had on Aunt Florence. There must be a reason for her insistence.

It was not a good idea, but I followed Shin inside. The maid was so obviously relieved that I was glad I had. My aunt reclined listlessly on the chaise. Her hand swayed to some music only she could hear. Like my mother swaying to music, humming to a waltz. The same expression. Mama's smell—a ghost of talc and wool stored in cedar—here and gone, startling and disconcerting.

I worked to right myself again, to focus on the corporeal and not the memory: a softly burning lamp, a book of Browning's poetry splayed open beside it, and beside that, a copy of the *Bulletin*, folded to the page of my poolside humiliation.

I went to sit on the edge of the chaise. "Hello, Aunt Florence."

My aunt's gaze came slowly to rest upon me, faded blue, not so vibrant as my mother's, not so beautiful. "May. Where have you been?"

"In town."

"No," Florence murmured. "No, you were somewhere else. Somewhere . . ." She glanced to the newspaper. "She took you there."

"Goldie, you mean? Yes, we were there yesterday." I reached over to close the newspaper.

She stopped me. "Indecent. She told you to wear it, didn't she?"

"It's the latest fashion, Aunt." It didn't matter if I agreed; I was not going to blame Goldie.

"No respectable young woman has her picture in the newspaper."

She sounded so like my mother that I was taken aback. "I didn't know the photographer was there."

Aunt Florence closed her eyes. "There is always one around. Remember who you are, May. Never forget that."

Another uncomfortable echo.

She went on. "You mustn't always do as Goldie says."

"It was my own decision, Aunt. I'm a modern woman."

"Those are her words, May. You are what she makes you."

I didn't understand the criticism of her own daughter, and Goldie had been so good to me that I opened my mouth to defend her. But then Shin, at the dressing table, shook her head at me, and though that too was confusing, I let my argument slip away.

Aunt Florence said, "Charlotte has never forgiven me for what happened. She has hated me for years."

A leap in thought, a connection I could not follow. I meant to let it go. I was not going to ask. I could not upset her. But Shin did not stop me this time, and so I tried, "What happened, Aunt Florence? Why did Mama hate you?"

"I was wrong. Will you tell her that? I meant to write, but I could not. I was too proud. That old saying . . . we despise most those who know us at our worst. It's true. It's so true."

I frowned, only more confused. "But she wrote you, didn't she? She sent you a letter—"

"I was wrong." My aunt gripped my hand with skeletal fingers. "You must tell her. I would make it up now. I would protect you. Do you see?"

Her lucidity was fading. Desperately, I tried to snatch from it what I could. "Protect me from what? What happened? Did you know my father? Do you know who he is?"

She leaned so close I smelled her laudanum-tainted breath, stale and unpleasant. Her hair brushed my cheek. "Shhh. They watch. Always they watch. They listen."

I could not temper my frustration. "What does this have to do with my mother?"

"I wish . . . oh, I cannot keep my . . . thoughts together. I cannot think." She hit the flat of her palm against her head. "Think!"

I took her hand away and spoke as soothingly as I could. "Perhaps you should rest—"

"No!"

A crash from the dressing table made us both jump. Shin had dropped something at my aunt's outburst.

"You must listen. It will be soon. Soon, the papers—you must hurry." This time, my aunt pressed a fist to her temple. Her skin was taut with strain, or pain, or perhaps both. "Shin!"

The maid scurried over with the bottle of laudanum, but she made no move to give the medicine. "Mrs. Sullivan, you told me to say no."

"I've changed my mind," Aunt Florence said.

Was she speaking of the laudanum, or something else?

Aunt Florence sagged back upon the chaise and stared at the drape-concealed window as if fascinated. "You must go, May." Only a whisper now, barely discernable. "Take whatever you want. Go back to New York."

"I can't. This is my home now. I don't want to go back."

Her expression stole my words. I'd never seen a face so hard, so chillingly stark, such bleak and empty eyes. Then she reached out to Shin, fingers outstretched, a demand that could not be denied.

Shin gave her the laudanum, and my aunt turned her head away from me as if I had ceased to exist. I was dismissed.

I went slowly to the door, confused and unsettled and apprehensive about nothing I could define. What memories existed of my mother were lodged so deeply in my aunt's mind that I was afraid I would never discover them. And how could I be so selfish as to keep trying? To see her this way, so much like Mama and yet not at all like her, was unbearable. Yet Shin had not stopped me from asking what had happened between my mother and my aunt. She had even helped me. It was then that I understood her silence about my snooping had been deliberate. She was my ally, but in what, exactly, I had no idea.

The next morning at breakfast, Uncle Jonny could barely contain himself. "Champagne, please, Arthur."

The footman did not even blink at the early morning request.

Goldie asked, "Are we celebrating?"

"Oh, we are indeed."

I looked up from my coddled eggs and ham. "What are we celebrating?"

"The day you came to us," Uncle Jonny said, smiling so broadly I could not help smiling in return. "Thanks to you, my dear May, Mr. Farge is at work on the Nance building."

"That's wonderful." Goldie spoke without her usual enthusiasm. She had awakened irritated. I had decided against asking her why she hadn't told me about the *Bulletin* picture. She was in a mood and I didn't want to be a Mabel and I knew already that Goldie considered any mention in the society pages to be a good thing.

Uncle Jonny didn't seem to notice her displeasure. The champagne came; Uncle Jonny toasted, "To you, May, and to the very bright future of Sullivan Building."

He had gulped his champagne before I'd taken more than a sip of my own. Then he rose. "Now, my dears, enjoy your day. I fear I must be off. Oh, and May—Farge asked that you call him this morning."

"Call him? Whatever for?"

"I believe he has something of importance to discuss with you."

He nearly bounced from the dining room.

I frowned. "What could that be?"

Goldie drank her champagne. "How should I know?"

"Is something wrong? You seem upset this morning."

"Oh, don't be ridiculous. I'm not the least bit upset," Goldie snapped. "Why don't you call Mr. Farge and find out what he needs?"

So I did. I fidgeted nervously as I placed the call and waited to be connected, idly counting the silver, gold, and glass salvers on the table—seventeen. Who needed seventeen salvers? A man said, "Hello?"

and I recognized his voice, crackly and scratchy through the line, with a small thrill.

"It's May Kimble. My uncle said you wished for me to call?"

"I did indeed. Can you meet with me this afternoon? At Coppa's, say, at five?"

I had some vague idea of that being the name of the restaurant on the bottom floor of the Montgomery Block. "Coppa's?"

"Don't worry. I'll make certain it's all perfectly respectable."

It had not occurred to me that it might not be. "Oh. All right."

"And bring your other sketchbooks. I've some news for you that I think you'll be glad to hear."

"My uncle already told me you've agreed to work with him." I glanced up to see Goldie idling in the hall, unabashedly listening.

"That's only part of what I want to tell you," he said. "Five o'clock. Coppa's."

We said our goodbyes, and I stood staring at the receiver in my hand.

"Well?" Goldie asked. "What did he want?"

"He asked me to meet him at Coppa's at five." Slowly I put the receiver in the cradle.

"Really?" Goldie lifted a perfectly arched brow. "The start of the cocktail hour. You'll be there through dinner, I'm sure. My, my. Don't tell me you have an admirer."

"I hardly think so. He said he had something to tell me."

"Probably that he's mad for you," Goldie teased, though there was an edge in her voice, that irritability again.

"Don't be absurd."

"Well, whatever it is, you should pretend to be pleased, even if you're not. I've heard he's very mercurial, May, so try to stay in his good graces, especially now." She sashayed to the stairs. "Our family fortunes are in your hands."

It was, unbeknownst to me, no exaggeration. "I won't disappoint you," I called after her as she went upstairs.

What should one wear for an appointment with an architect at Coppa's? He'd asked me to bring my sketchbooks. Perhaps he meant to offer his advice. He'd seen talent, he'd said, and I wanted to believe him. There had been no reason for him to flatter me. I'd been asking a favor. In fact, it would have made more sense for him to dismiss my drawings completely.

So what could he want? Ultimately, it didn't matter, because I couldn't suppress my excitement—and yes, the hope—at the idea of meeting him once more, or again that sense that the world was holding out its hand to offer me something I hadn't known I wanted.

ELEVEN

I dressed carefully in a gray suit and plaid waist, along with a hat banded with a red ribbon and black and gray feathers and a small brim that curled coquettishly at one side. The hallway mirror was still gone, not having returned from its cleaning or regilding or whatever, so I could not check myself head to toe, and Goldie was not there to give me final words of encouragement. She'd gone earlier to tea with Linette, and had left me with a kiss on the cheek and "It's the perfect ensemble. Don't worry. Show him you're no one to be trifled with! But remember to charm him too!"

I called the small buggy to take me to Coppa's. Goldie had already taken the brougham and Nick; Uncle Jonny usually took the trolley to his office.

In Brooklyn, the weather would have taken on a distinctive autumn chill by now, but here the weather was fine and the buggy open as we passed the mansions on Nob Hill with their gardeners still out in force, and then, a few more blocks, and Chinatown, the silk and jade in the shop windows shimmering brightly in the sun, and—

Goldie. That was Goldie, wasn't it, walking down the street? I would recognize my cousin anywhere, that distinctive sway, the golden hair, the hat with the blue ribbons, which we had bought at the City of Paris. But no, it couldn't be Goldie. Goldie was at tea with Linette. Goldie would not be walking in Chinatown, nor would she be disappearing through a door carved with Chinese characters into a windowless building that looked nothing like a shop.

I opened my mouth to tell Petey to stop, to go back, but Ellis Farge waited for me at Coppa's, and I could not be late, and it had to be an illusion anyway, some woman who only looked like Goldie. There was no reason for Goldie to be in Chinatown.

I forgot it all as we grew closer to Montgomery Street, and the restaurant, and my nervous excitement over my meeting with Ellis Farge returned. Petey pulled up before a small restaurant on the first floor corner of the Montgomery Block, where a sign in lights declared **ORIGINAL COPPA**, with **COPPA RESTAURANT** painted below.

The boy helped me from the carriage and went to wait, and I licked my dry lips and walked into the restaurant, where I was greeted by the buzz of talk, and garlic- and onion- and tobacco-scented air. An elaborately framed mirror behind the bar reflected the twenty or so tables in the narrow room. Even with the high ceilings and the tall windows at the front, the place felt close and intimate, made more so by garish red walls decorated in places with painted murals and cartoons. A frieze of faintly sinister black cats with yellow eyes stalked along the top of the walls, with the names of great men written below, among them Aristotle, Martinez, Rabelais, and . . . *Maisie?* A huge lobster stood on an island named *BOHEMIA*, as a scrolled banner above declared *You cannot argue with the choice of the soul.* Nudes straddled other mottos, and caricatures of people I did not recognize grinned and jabbered and bowed.

It was obscene and repulsive and delightful and too much to take in at once. It was also crowded and loud. Both men and women gestured and laughed, blowing cigarette smoke in clouds while waiters dodged about with bottles of wine and plates piled high with spaghetti and bread. The bustle bewildered and challenged and entranced. It was like nothing I'd ever seen before.

"Miss Kimble!" Mr. Farge rose and gestured from a table at the back of the restaurant.

I hurried toward him, aware of the curious glances from those I passed, though I pretended not to be. Mr. Farge wore a dark suit and a silk scarf wound many times about his throat, and I smiled at the sight of him. "How good it is to see you again, Mr. Farge."

"And you, Miss Kimble." He held out my chair, and I sat, and before I knew it, a bottle of wine appeared, along with two glasses.

"It comes with the meal," Mr. Farge told me. "You don't have to drink it if you don't wish."

"Everyone is drinking," I noted.

"That's the artist life for you."

"But you're an artist too, aren't you?"

He looked sheepish as he poured the wine. "If you want to call it that."

"I do." I reached into my bag, pulling out some of the sketchbooks I'd brought. "You said you wanted to see them—"

He put up a hand to stop me, glancing about. "Not here."

"Oh." Of course. Why would he wish to be seen in public poring over the drawings of an amateur designer—and one who was a woman, no less? "Forgive me."

"There's nothing to forgive. I just thought we should save business for the office. Except for one thing. I asked your uncle to let me tell you in person."

He could not have been more mysterious. "Tell me what?"

"You're to be the liaison between my office and your uncle."

There it was, the possibility I had not dared to imagine. My uncle had listened to me when I'd despaired of my lack of purpose, but to offer me this, for Ellis Farge to have agreed . . . I was astonished at the opportunity to work with an architect of Mr. Farge's renown. To show him my ideas. To perhaps design rooms for my uncle's building—oh, but I was getting ahead of myself. *Slow down.*

"Have I distressed you so much? You can say no, but I'd hoped—"

"Of course I would not say no," I burst out. "I would be mad to say no."

"Or perhaps you'd be mad to say yes."

"There's so much I could learn."

He looked uncomfortable.

I winced. "I sound like a fool."

"Only a small one," he teased, relaxing. "I'm glad you like the idea. I'd thought you might raise an objection to coming to my office. A woman alone, and all that."

"Times have changed, Mr. Farge." I sounded like Goldie. But this was San Francisco, and everything was so different than what I'd known; why shouldn't it be true?

Mr. Farge handed me a glass of wine and lifted his own. "To new opportunities."

"To opportunity." The wine was thin and sour, but I gulped it eagerly. "This is such an interesting place."

Mr. Farge's eyes were dark in the dim restaurant; the gaslight threw itself across his sharp cheekbones and his nose and tangled in the hair swept back from his high forehead. He leaned forward, lowering his voice. "So I've done a bit of research on you, Miss Kimble, and I'll admit I'm curious. You're from New York?"

I nodded, gripping my wine glass. "Well, Brooklyn, actually. My mother died and Aunt Florence invited me to come to San Francisco."

"And your father?"

It was a habit to glance away, to soften the truth. *My father is from one of the original Four Hundred families in New York City. No, I can't tell you his name just yet. It's a bit of a secret.* The same words came to me now, but the way Mr. Farge watched me, the way he listened, as if it mattered to him what I said, was hard to resist. In New York, those stories had been a way to protect myself. But here in San Francisco, what did it matter? I was a Sullivan now. The truth could not hurt me. "I don't know. He abandoned my mother when she was expecting me. I don't even know his name."

"A grand affair?" he suggested.

"The secret's gone to the grave with Mama. As far as I know, the Sullivans are my only family."

"How strange to see you here with a woman, Farge," said a man as he approached our table.

Ellis Farge made a face. "Gelett Addison, meet Miss May Kimble. Miss Kimble, here is one of the most odious creatures in the world, the art critic. Please don't let his idiocy blind you to his very few virtues."

There were two extra chairs at our table, and Gelett Addison chuckled and sat at one without invitation. He was short and plump, with a round, shining forehead and receding hair perfectly combed into place, as well as a carefully kept mustache. "Miss Kimble, I am delighted, though frankly I'm flummoxed as to why you've deigned to associate with this man. Where did you meet this charming creature, Farge? At Del Monte, where the rich while away their hours swimming naked in the ocean and dancing by the light of the moon?"

"Or something like that," Mr. Farge said.

"Come, my friend, if you tell me there are no pagan rituals among the upper crust, I shall be severely disappointed."

"They worship a small white ball, which they fling with long sticks into very small holes."

"Sounds enticing." Addison reached for Farge's wine and took a gulp, and then called out, "LaRosa! My darling Blythe! Farge has brought us a new one!"

Mr. Farge sighed. "I see it was too much to hope for privacy here. I am sorry, Miss Kimble."

The people Mr. Addison had called began to drift over, all of them holding half-full glasses of wine, but for a woman clad in a severe black walking suit and small black hat perched upon a hillock of dark, glossy hair, who had a small cup of coffee. Gelett Addison leaped to his feet, dragging over chairs and then the table they'd occupied, pushing it together with ours—no one in the restaurant even looked twice; apparently this was usual behavior. He rattled off introductions as he did so. A dapper-looking young man with a thin face and small mustache and auburn hair curling in a comma above his temple was Wenceslas Piper, whom everyone called Wence. He had fine light eyes and an insouciant air and fingers stained with colored inks and was an illustrator for the satire magazine the *Wasp*.

Mr. Addison said, "He also writes terrible poetry, perhaps you've read some?"

"I couldn't say," I said politely.

"You know the purple cow rhyme? 'I never saw a purple cow, I never hope to see one . . .'?" Then, at my nod, "He didn't write that. His are all moons and Junes—"

"And loons," joked the man introduced as Dante LaRosa. He had thick dark hair and olive skin and he smoked his cigarette and looked at me as if surprised to find me here, which made me wonder if I knew him from somewhere. But he had a distinctive face. I thought I would have remembered him.

"LaRosa's a writer too," said Addison.

"Or at least that's the rumor," Mr. Farge said.

"I told you I was sorry, Farge," LaRosa said. "I was only quoting Radisson at the opening. What was I supposed to do, make something up?"

"Don't you usually?"

I felt LaRosa bristle, but Addison swept in lightly, saying, "Now, now, boys. LaRosa writes for the *Bulletin*, Miss Kimble. Be careful around him, or he'll have you in the gossip pages by morning."

LaRosa grimaced. "It's bad enough to have to talk about society when I'm working. Must we do so here too?"

"Wait—*you're* the society page columnist for the *Bulletin*?" I asked.

Wence whistled low and mimed ducking for cover. "Oh my God, here's someone else he's offended!"

LaRosa ignored him and dragged on his cigarette. To me, he said dryly, "No flies on you."

"But . . . but you can't be."

"He is. Alphonse Bandersnitch, in the flesh," Addison said. "I told him it was a terrible name."

"It's kept me hidden well enough, hasn't it?" LaRosa asked.

"Oh, but you're not at all what I expected!" I said. He was too young, too masculine, too Italian.

"That's what everyone says," Addison put in. "I keep telling you, LaRosa, you write like a sour old woman who lives with a hundred cats."

Dante LaRosa gave him a thin smile. "Perhaps you could lend me some of your cats, Addison, so I could better fit your picture. Anyway, Older's promised to put me on the Barbary Coast beat soon."

"He promises that to everyone," said the woman in black. She introduced herself as Blythe Markowitz, the Sunday feature writer for the *Examiner*. Then, to LaRosa, "He'll say whatever you want to hear as long as it keeps you working for him. It doesn't mean he'll do it."

"This time, I believe he means it," LaRosa said glumly.

"To go from the crème de la crème to the scum of the earth—that's quite a drop even for you," said Addison.

"God knows it would be a relief to write about murderers of men instead of murderers of cotillion etiquette," LaRosa said. "Something that matters for a change."

A woman wearing a turban wandered over. "Is there a party? Why wasn't I invited?"

"Because you're wearing that ridiculous hat," said Wence.

The woman patted the patterned silk. "Don't you like it? I think it very stylish."

"Worshipping idols in Chinatown again?" asked Addison.

Blythe Markowitz sighed. "Oh, Gelly, when, when, *when* will you ever get your religions straight? Edith, come and meet our new Miss May Kimble, the mystery Ellis has brought foolishly into Coppa's. Miss Kimble, Edith Jackson."

"A painter," Mr. Addison explained.

Edith Jackson blew the smoke from her cigarette toward the ceiling in a long breath. "How mundane, Gelett. You're usually not so careless with words. I prefer 'Artist,' with a capital *A*. What do you do, Miss Kimble? Besides grace the arm of our very eligible architect?"

"Do?" I asked.

"Are you a writer? A poet? A playwright?" She gestured about the room. "Please don't tell me you paint, or I shall have to flee to Carmel, where there's less competition."

I laughed softly. "I do draw a little, but only rooms."

"Rooms?" echoed Miss Jackson.

Ellis Farge poured more wine into my glass and said, "For God's sake, enough of the inquisition."

"We don't stand on ceremony here," Wence said. "No *misses* and *misters* at this table. We must think up a suitable nickname for you. That is, if we allow you to stay. You know we shall hold our traditional vote when you're gone."

"Vote on what?" I asked.

"Whether we like you or not. You're on trial. Take care." Dante LaRosa stubbed out the last of his cigarette into his now empty wine glass and sat back, then lowered his voice to say to me privately, "Slumming, Miss Kimble?"

The conversation went on loudly around us. I glanced about, but no one seemed to notice or care that he spoke only to me. "I have no idea what you mean."

"Just that Coppa's isn't the usual haunt for society, not even the Sporting set."

"The Sporting set? Is that what I am?"

"Generally seen about Ingleside, or at drunken yacht parties, or wearing scandalous bathing costumes at Sutro's."

I flushed and tried to ignore it, to match his drollness. "Oh yes, thank you for that. Your caption was very clever. It was yours?"

He grinned. "I'm glad you enjoyed it. I wish I'd been there to see it in person."

"I'm surprised you weren't. You seem to be everywhere."

He made a face. "Not everywhere. I try to avoid the Dead Slow set. Too boring."

"The Dead Slow? Who are they?"

"Miss Sullivan hasn't enlightened you? I'm surprised. They're up there with the Conservative set, but duller. Senators' wives and such. Very old school."

I knew none of this. "And the Conservative set?"

"Hoffman, Oelrichs, the McKays . . . the top one hundred families."

"Old San Francisco families," I guessed.

"Old *money*, such as it is." He leaned closer. "Very respectable. But not that fun. Where you really want to be is the Smart set, the Ultras. Never a dull moment, and not such parvenus as your Sporting set."

Parvenus. Goldie's talk of the Hoffmans and the Oelrichses, the Cotillion Club . . . It all jangled uncomfortably in my head. I think I must have been gaping. "I had no idea."

"Your education's been lacking." He lit another cigarette. "How did you meet Farge?"

"He's working for my uncle."

"Jonathan Sullivan," LaRosa intoned. "Builder, member of the board of supervisors. Has a mistress with Very Important connections, a wife who is ill, and a beautiful daughter."

I was taken aback. "Do you always do this when you meet someone?"

"Do what?"

"List everything you know about them?"

He shrugged. "Best to have things out in the open."

I was uncertain how to take him. I had thought of the *Bulletin* columnist as belonging to me somehow, but now I realized that I had only been reading into the writer the friend I wanted to see. Humor, yes, and cleverness, and he had an arresting charisma. I had no idea how I'd never noticed him before. But his bite held a keener edge than I'd thought. "Perhaps not everything should be out in the open."

"Secrets." He exhaled the word on smoke. "My stock-in-trade. Which brings me to the mystery of you. Why are you at Coppa's instead of skating with your cousin at the Pavilion or wrapping poor Edward Hertford into knots?"

I barely remembered him. "Oh, Jerome's cousin."

"You seemed very close the other day at the Cliff House." He offered the observation with an arch grin, an *I know you better than you know yourself* glint, and I remembered the article he'd written.

"During our *jovial* party, you mean?"

"I could have said *drunken*."

"The champagne was *very* good," I said with great dignity.

He laughed. "You're no coward, Miss Kimble. I'll say that for you."

"How is it you manage to remain so anonymous, Mr. LaRosa?" I asked. "It seems frankly impossible."

"It's a skill." He blew smoke from the corner of his mouth and met my gaze. "I do hope I can rely on your discretion. I don't think you want me to write about your visit here."

I was startled. Why should his writing about my visit here matter? But it was clear that he thought it would, and his words about slumming, and society not frequenting Coppa's, and Ellis Farge assuring me in our phone conversation that he would make sure it was all respectable came together, and I realized that these were the kind of people my mother had warned me about. Of course society would not come here. *"Artists are interesting, but they are only for show, May. One must never actually consort with them, not and remain above reproach."*

Yet, Ellis Farge was here, and had brought me with him, and Goldie had not raised a brow at the mention of it.

"Come, come, LaRosa, you're monopolizing our guest," objected Gelett Addison.

"Just getting acquainted." Dante LaRosa flicked the ash from his cigarette into the glass serving as his ashtray. "Given how odd it is for our friend here to bring such a woman to Coppa's."

Ellis Farge's eyes narrowed. "What do you mean by that?"

"Just a joke."

Again that palpable tension between them. Then Wence rose and Blythe Markowitz asked, "Whence goes Wence?"

"To order some food. I'm starving."

After that, the conversation began again, and Ellis Farge relaxed. LaRosa put out his second cigarette, only half-smoked. "Well, I'm off."

"Nose to the ground, as always," said Addison. "What scent are you following today, oh, newshound? And why haven't you written a piece about us? Aren't we interesting enough?"

"If I wrote about you, people would actually read your reviews, and you'd lose your bohemian bona fides." Then Dante LaRosa said something in Italian that made Blythe laugh.

"What? What did he say?" Addison demanded. "Damn you, LaRosa! It's not fair when you speak that peasant tongue."

"A little respect please, Addison. That 'peasant tongue' once ruled the world."

"I do respect your people. I give thanks every day for spaghetti and a glass of good chianti." Addison raised his glass in salute.

"Tell us what Dante said, Blythe," urged Edith.

Blythe said, "It was quite vulgar. Something along the lines of not shitting where you eat."

"Language!" LaRosa admonished her, but he was laughing. "It was a pleasure to meet you, Miss Kimble." Then he was gone, and Edith Jackson moved to take his place.

The conversation raced along; at some point plates of spaghetti came; everyone treated them as communal dishes, and certainly there was enough on the two plates to feed a crowd. The entrée of roasted chicken, the salad, the loaf of crusty French bread—it all disappeared almost before I could do more than taste it. The play of their talk and laughter, and my excitement over my new role as my uncle's liaison with Ellis Farge, made it hard for me to pay much heed to my revelation about who they were and their place in society. This was the most engaging crowd I'd encountered since I'd been in San Francisco. I told myself my mother's warning was just another one of her old-fashioned ideas. I was vaguely aware that the crowd was waning, then waxing again, and the light outside fading, windows darkening, streetlights being lit. It only made our company feel more cozy and intimate, and I hated to see the evening end. I had enjoyed myself, which was so refreshing after the balls and entertainments I'd attended, and I didn't want to leave. Or perhaps it was only my giddiness at possibility and purpose that put such a roseate light on the gathering.

The others, one by one, were drawn away by other obligations, until only Wence and Mr. Farge and I remained at the pushed-together tables at the back of the restaurant.

"I'll order another bottle of wine," Wence said, but as he raised his hand to summon the waiter, Farge said softly, "Don't you have somewhere to be, Wence?"

Wenceslas Piper lowered his arm and glanced hastily at me. "Actually, I do, and I just realized I'm late. Good evening, May. I hope you will return."

I was alone with Ellis Farge again. He grinned. "I'm sorry for all that."

"Don't be. I had a wonderful time."

"They're scoundrels and wastrels, most of them. And they've left me with the bill, again."

"You obviously enjoy them."

"Sometimes. It's nearly nine. Let me see you to your carriage."

"Nine?" Later than I'd thought. "How quickly it went. I suppose because everyone was so interesting."

"You'll grow tired of Coppa's soon enough once we've started work on your uncle's building." Farge put money on the table to pay the bill and rose. "Do you mind leaving your sketches with me? I'll look at them tomorrow."

"Not at all. But I would like to hear your opinion."

"I'll be glad to tell you. Soon, I hope."

It wasn't until I left the table that I realized how much wine I'd drunk. Ellis Farge said goodbye at the carriage, and I watched him walk off, my bag of sketchbooks bouncing at his thigh, and the night seemed so beautiful. I wasn't tired at all, but invigorated.

And so, when the buggy began its slow way home, and we came again to the street in Chinatown where I thought I'd spotted Goldie earlier, it did not seem foolish at all to ask Petey to stop. Inspired by the evening spent with artists and a glimpse of a new future for myself—and by a bit of drunkenness too, more than a bit—I felt brave and daring enough to jump down. I ignored Petey's protest as I passed the store on the corner with its carvings and clothing in the windows, the closed market stalls, and the smiling Buddha at the neighboring joss house. I paused at the door where Goldie/not Goldie had disappeared.

I saw nothing to indicate what this place was. The door, dark and heavily carved, was just a door. It was not menacing. The woman who might have been Goldie had walked inside without a knock, without hesitation. But then again, it was hours ago that I'd seen that woman going through this door. What did I want? To learn that it was not Goldie? Or to learn that it was? What would I do once the question was answered? What did I hope for?

I heard Dante LaRosa's voice in my ear: *"You're no coward, Miss Kimble."*

Go forth, I told myself. I opened the door.

TWELVE

It opened onto stairs—one flight up, another down—and a gloom that seized my drunken bravery and flung it into dread. The haze was fragrant with incense and the stink of tobacco and something else, heavier, sweeter, nauseating. There was light above, sounds of life. Below was quiet.

I swallowed hard. I had no business here. Suddenly I remembered Goldie telling me about tongs and how Chinatown was dangerous at night, and my foreboding increased, yet even so I found myself going up those stairs, into a warehouse-like room even more heavily clouded with smoke. Everywhere were tables filled with men and women. Many were Chinese, but there were plenty of others too. There was no one I recognized. I didn't see Goldie, and I didn't know whether to be relieved or dismayed at that. At least she would have been an ally in this place. I felt my strangeness keenly as people glanced up with curiosity. Too many eyes, too little talk; clicking tiles, shuffling cards, clinking coins served as the common language.

I should not be here. Time to go, and quickly. I turned, but before I took a step, a heavy hand on my arm stopped me. A Chinese man with an angular face and a long braid—a queue, Shin called it—said in heavily accented English, "What will you play? Faro? Poker? Pick what you like."

"I'm sorry. No."

"Ah. What you want is downstairs." He pointed toward the stairs.

"No. No, thank you. I—I'm going now."

His gaze sharpened. "Who are you? Who brought you here, rich girl?"

"No one."

His frown deepened, and he raised his voice, speaking in Chinese. My mouth went dry. I wished I hadn't come. Another man, a white man this time, heavyset and squat, with a grim expression, rose in response.

"I—I was only looking for someone," I explained quickly. "I only came because—because . . . my cousin. Goldie Sullivan."

The Chinese man waved off his lackey and regarded me with interest. "Ah, Goldilocks." The nickname, his tone, raised a different kind of fear. "Yes, yes. Go downstairs. You want Joe. He knows what she likes. You will like it too."

But I liked that tone no better, and I had no wish to go downstairs into that darkness.

"Go now," he said insistently, gesturing to the squat man, who rose again.

In dread of escort, I muttered, "Thank you," and hurried off.

I was here now, after all. I would not have the courage to come back again. And if Goldie was downstairs . . . I did not want to think what she might be doing there, but I could not leave her in this place. What if she was in danger? I kept my hand to the wall, down and down to a small, battered foyer, each step raising a panic I could not swallow. *Don't let her be here. Let it all be a mistake.* A curtain blocked off a doorway. Beyond glowed a soft and rosy light.

"Hello?" I stepped to the curtain, gently pulling it aside.

The room was lit only by a lamp covered with a red scarf. Hats and coats on hooks polka-dotted the dingy walls. Pallets were strewn about haphazardly; nearly every one held someone lolling in dreams. A woman drooled onto her pillow. A rough-faced man murmured restlessly. The words of the *Bulletin* column came back to me, Alphonse Bandersnitch's—no, Dante LaRosa's words . . . *Devotees of the long pipe . . . mentioned in the society news . . . That debutante (everyone knows her name) . . .*

Goldie.

A man with a gray scarf bound about his black hair looked up from where he and another bent over a small flame and a long pipe. Their eyes glittered in the half dark. I stepped back and heard myself answer their silent question with a bare whisper. "Joe?"

The man with the scarf called something, and a curtain at the back was pushed aside. Through it came another Chinese man. I could not tell his age, not in the rosy light, which flattered everything it touched. He had the kind of sculpted face one saw on statues, chiseled cheekbones and skin stretched so tautly over them it looked as if it might split with any movement. His hair was thick and straight and he wore no queue. The man upstairs had frightened me, but this man's menace thickened the air. It was already quiet—now the room became deadly silent.

He spoke quickly to me in Chinese—that face was remarkably mobile after all—and I shook my head, trying not to appear as frightened as I was, and swallowed hard. "They told me upstairs to ask for you. Goldie. Goldie is my cousin. Where is she?"

The same remarkable change came over him that had come over the man upstairs, but his smile was more disturbing, and more possessive too—he not only knew Goldie, but knew her better than I could ever hope to. And there was more to it too, something darkly threatening. I had never before been afraid of a smile, but his was terrifying. When he said "Goldie," lingering over her name, polishing it like a smooth stone in his mouth, I knew suddenly and completely that this man had a relationship with my cousin that I did not want to understand. Involuntarily, I stepped back.

He noticed. He noticed every move, I thought, every flicker. His eyes narrowed. "Goldilocks is gone, but she will be back. She always comes back. Tell her when you see her that I expect my money this time." Again that horrible smile. His voice fell to a husky whisper. "If you remember." He gestured to me, a cupped hand, *come*, but I was done with this. My cousin wasn't here. I let my fear take me, and I shook my head and ran, racing up the stairs so quickly that I tripped on my skirts and slammed against the door.

I stumbled out into the night, taking a great, deep breath of the scented air of Chinatown, woody and fishy, stinking and sweet. I went unseeingly to the buggy. Petey took my arm.

"Are you all right, miss?" he asked.

"Take me home," I ordered.

I was still undone when I arrived. I was so desperate for a reasonable explanation, for reassurance, that I did the most stupid thing possible. I went directly to my cousin's door and knocked. Her "come in" was sleepy and soft.

She lounged on the chaise in the half light of garden lamps glowing through the windows and a lazily burning fire. The porcelain shepherdesses dancing across Goldie's marble mantel were shadows. She wore only her chemise and her dressing gown.

"There you are." Her voice was barely a murmur. "Where have you been? Oh yes. With Mr. Farge." She sat up, blinking. "How late is it? You were gone so long."

"On the way home, I stopped—"

"What time is it?"

"Goldie." I pulled a chair close to the chaise and sat. "I stopped in Chinatown afterward."

"Whatever for?"

"Because I saw you there earlier."

"Don't be silly."

"I saw you go into an opium den. I paid a visit there myself. I saw it all. I met Joe. He's awful. I don't know how you bear him."

Goldie frowned. "I don't know what you're talking about."

"Oh, Goldie, how often do you go? And he said—Joe said—that he wants his money. How much do you owe him?"

Goldie's expression shuttered.

"You must tell me the truth. I've seen you sneak out. I know it must be where you go."

"You mustn't tell Papa." She was wide awake now. "He mustn't hear a word of it. Do you understand me, May? Not a word."

"You cannot tell me he doesn't suspect—"

"Not a word, May!" Goldie lurched from the chaise. "I'll be destroyed if this gets out."

"But—" I thought of LaRosa's column. *The debutante (everyone knows her name).* "Are you certain no one knows already?"

"Of course not! I've been very careful."

She was so adamant.

"Oh, I've been such an idiot. You must promise me, May. I need you to help me. Please."

"However I can."

The glistening in her eyes became tears. Her loosened hair brushed my arm. "You must help me keep it secret."

Again, I doubted that it was as unknown as she believed, but it was obvious that Goldie had not seen herself in LaRosa's words, and I remembered how oblivious she and her friends seemed to be when it came to his jabs. I thought I should inform her, but then she said, "I'm going to stop. It's no good for me, I know. You must help me stop."

If she did stop, the column would be a fiction, and it would only distress her to think that society had suspected her predilection. And anyway, perhaps I was wrong. It could have been anyone in LaRosa's column, any debutante. Surely Goldie was not the only one with a liking for opium.

"I will," I assured her with relief, until I remembered Joe. "But you should give him the money you owe him. How much is it?"

"You mean China Joe? Oh, hardly anything. It doesn't matter."

"It seemed to matter to him. He told me to tell you to bring it next time."

"There won't be a next time," she said, lifting her chin.

"Yes, but perhaps it's best to pay him."

"Why would I do that? He's just a Chinaman. What can he do to me?"

I remembered his smile, his menace. I did not understand how she could be so glibly unconcerned, how we saw this Joe—China Joe—so differently. Goldie grabbed my arm; China Joe loomed so in my head that I jumped.

"I'm trusting you with my most important secret. You mustn't tell anyone. I have needed a friend like you for so long, May. You cannot know how hard this has been."

"You're not alone any longer, Goldie," I assured her, trying to calm my racing heart. "I'm here to help you. Always."

THIRTEEN

We had been invited to the Anderson soiree, a showcase for a newly lauded soprano, Verina Lombardi. That evening, as I dressed, I started at a shout from the hall. I met Shin's gaze in the mirror as she pinned my hair. "What was that?"

Another shout. Shin went to the bedroom door. "Mrs. Sullivan!" She ran into the hallway, and I hurried after.

My aunt's dressing gown was askew, her hair a mess, and her eyes wild and unfocused.

Shin tried to ease her back into the bedroom. "Come now, missus. You must rest."

Then my aunt caught sight of me. "Why aren't you gone? They told me you were gone!"

My heart sank. How I hated this. How I wished I knew some way to help her.

"Come back to bed, missus," Shin crooned again. "Come now."

"Aunt Florence, do as Shin says. You need to be in bed," I said soothingly.

My aunt lurched from Shin to grip my hands. "You must go. Now. You don't belong here."

Shin pried my aunt's fingers from my hand, releasing me from both my aunt's hold and her glare. "Miss, if you would please—"

"Yes, of course," I said heavily, turning back.

Now, Goldie came from her room. She looked beautiful in soft pink. The only thing marring her prettiness was her disgust. "For God's sake, what is she doing now? What are you doing, Mother? Shin, why isn't she in bed?"

"She won't come, miss."

The layers of Goldie's silk gown skipped about her ankles as she gave her mother's arm a little jerk and said, "Let go of Shin now, Mother. That's right. Back to bed with you. Really, you are making a terrible scene."

As on that first night, my aunt seemed to lose her will at Goldie's touch. She let her daughter lead her back to the bedroom.

"I wish I knew what to do," I murmured to Shin. "She always seems so alone. How often does my uncle look in on her? I've never seen them together." I could not help the snarly thought of the Dennehy woman, my uncle's mistress, nor my resentment that she was undoubtedly keeping him from my aunt's side.

Shin said, "It is better if he stays away." Then she followed Goldie and Aunt Florence.

Only Goldie and laudanum seemed able to soothe my aunt. Goldie had a way of making problems and worries disappear, to distract until one was so wrapped up in her world that one's own seemed no longer important. We were all so pliable in Goldie's hands, weren't we?

It seemed a lucky thing. I did not know how she managed it when her own worries loomed so large. Goldie came from her mother's bedroom, looking more beautiful to me than ever now that I knew her vulnerability. She smiled. "Are you quite ready, May? We don't want to be late."

The Anderson house was only a few blocks away. Italianate, with a ballroom decorated by a colonnade of classical Greek figures that put the indecent, gilded Sullivan bacchante to shame, and festooned with bunches of silk leaves in golds and reds and oranges, basket cornucopias spilling dried corn and pinecones—all very November, celebrating the coming holiday when there was no real evidence of it outside. The weather had turned damp but showed no seasonal change, not like Brooklyn. I did not miss it really, but I did warm to the decorations.

Mrs. Jeffers Anderson was as small as her house was huge, and she was plump and wore her beaded blue-and-gold Parisian Worth gown with easy elegance. It seemed everyone we knew was there, and though I smiled and tried to enjoy myself, I was bored before we arrived, already knowing that I would feel awkward and lonely, and still upset by my aunt's fit.

Goldie looked for champagne as I went to the French doors, which were opened onto a parterred garden.

The soon-to-be-famous soprano stood near a gushing fountain in the garden, surrounded by adoring fans. She was dark haired, bejeweled, and beautiful, her voluptuousness encased in shot green silk, emeralds encircling her throat and enhancing her double chin. She chattered away to her circle of admirers, and I wondered if her excitement was real, or if she too was simply playing at being engaged.

"Hard to believe she grew up selling sardines on Fisherman's Wharf, isn't it?"

The voice in my ear was familiar. I turned to see Dante LaRosa, dressed in a suit—not evening wear—and suddenly the tenor of the night changed; here was something interesting at last.

"Why, if it isn't Mr. Bandersnitch, in the flesh. What are you doing here?"

"Not so loud." He winced. "And I was invited. At least, Bandersnitch was."

"You cannot tell me that no one here suspects who you are. You stand out."

"Do I? I think it's only because we've met. You've never noticed me before. Not at the Cliff House, not anywhere."

I was flummoxed by the truth of his words. It was the most discombobulating feeling. I couldn't reconcile his charisma, or frankly, his out-of-placeness, with his apparent invisibility. I wanted to tell myself he'd simply never been to the events I'd attended. But of course he had. He'd written about them. He'd written about me.

He smiled. "People see what they want to see. They're busy trying to figure out who Bandersnitch is, but what they don't expect is someone who looks like me, so no one sees me, even when I'm right in front of them. I'm hiding in plain sight. I stay in the background mostly. It's a damnable thing, but it works. You were surprised at who I was, remember. I wasn't as you imagined me."

"No," I admitted. "I'd thought you shorter."

"An old woman with cats."

"Not exactly. A roundish blond man with a liking for cream puffs."

"You've just described Ned Greenway perfectly. I trust you'll keep my secret."

"And if I don't?"

He indicated the soprano laughing just beyond us. "Verina Lombardi's real name is Anna Russo. Not quite so fancy, is it? She used to slide around in fish blood at the market and pretend she was skating. Once, she threw a calamari in my face. She has a bad temper."

"What's a calamari?"

"A squid."

I made a face. "What did you do to offend her?"

144

"What makes you think it was my fault?"

"Wasn't it?"

"I tried to kiss her. It was a festa."

"I see."

"She was irresistible. Even back then she had this voice . . . Nothing sounds as good as Verdi sung from the fishmarket. She and Luigi Conti used to duet. He had the stall next door to her father's."

"Is he an opera singer?"

"He's a fisherman. You can hear him sing every evening when he's cleaning his nets. Along with most of the other fisherman. Now Anna—Verina—would tell you in a minute that I'm no one important. A fisherman's son. Up to my elbows in fish guts. You'd never convince her I was anything more than that. You'd never convince anyone." He was direct; there was no hint of self-deprecation.

"She'll be surprised to see you tonight, then," I said.

"She won't see me, and even if she did, she'd never acknowledge me. It would ruin the history she's written for herself." He took in my gown. "Pretty. City of Paris or Emporium?"

"Emporium."

"No Worth gown imported from Paris for you, I see."

"Well, I—"

"But she's wearing one, isn't she?" He nodded toward my cousin, who laughed and flirted with Jerome Belden.

"You have a very good eye."

"It's my job to figure out where everyone stands," he said. "Belden's father is in silver, but his mother is a gadabout. She's in London right now. Over there is Robert Krieg. Railroads. A bit of a drunk. There, Mrs. Martin Rolfe. A fortune from the gasworks, but her mother was a chorus girl. So Verina's got her foot on the next rung of the ladder, but she's not at the top yet. This is second best. Maybe third. Verina'll be disappointed. Expect her to throw a champagne bottle at some point this evening when she realizes it."

"Second or third best?" I was surprised.

"Do you see Mrs. Hoffman? Or Mrs. McKay? Oelrichs is here somewhere, but he's just slumming."

Sets and rungs. Now I understood as I hadn't before, the true worth of Goldie's engagement to Stephen Oelrichs. "Who belongs to the Cotillion Club?"

"The Conservatives. The Ultras. Some of them, anyway. The Fashionables looking for husbands or wives." A studied glance. "I'm still trying to figure out where you belong."

"What is there to wonder about? I'm one of the Sporting set. You said it yourself."

"They say you're the fast one."

"What?"

"I would have thought it by the bathing costume. You looked nice in it, by the way. But there's something about you—I don't know. I find you puzzling."

I frowned. "I'm afraid I don't take your meaning."

"No, I suppose not. How well do you know Farge?" He glanced about the ballroom. He paused, caught by something, and murmured to himself as if to remember it. It reminded me that he was a reporter.

"Is my answer going to be in the *Bulletin*?"

"Not if you don't wish it."

"I told you already. My uncle hired him to design a building."

"That's not what I asked."

"That's my answer, however. It's really none of your business, is it?"

That got his attention. A faint smile touched his full lips. "Verina won't sing for an hour yet. Not until she's done being feted. Come with me. Let's get some champagne."

"Why should I?"

"Because you wonder why I'm asking. There's a waiter over there. Grab two glasses, won't you? I don't want to call attention to myself. Hiding in plain sight, you know."

I did, and handed him one as we went into the hall, which became a gallery hung with portraits down its length. Very classic, very moneyed. The talk and the music from the ballroom were loud, and it wasn't as if we were alone; people drifted in and out, laughing, smoking, mingling.

LaRosa gestured with his champagne to one of the paintings—an unsmilingly earnest man of impressive girth. "Ten to one none of these is any relation to the Andersons."

"There's something familiar about that one. The nose, maybe." I sipped at my drink.

"And the stomach too," he said. "So maybe him. I'll bet the rest all came from Gump's. There, they've pedigrees for sale—for the right price."

Goldie had pointed out the exclusive store, where society shopped for their statues and paintings. "That's a bit cruel."

"Is it? You know where the Anderson money came from?"

I shook my head.

"Real estate speculation."

"They're no different than half of San Francisco."

"And corruption."

I wandered down the length of the gallery, taking in the bewigged and powdered women, the bearded, courtly men.

"You don't seem surprised," said LaRosa, following.

"I don't know anything about it."

"Jeffers Anderson is on the city board of supervisors. As was Edward Dennehy. You might know him better as the late husband of your uncle's mistress. Now, of course, your uncle's on the board too."

"What has that to do with anything?"

He stopped to consider one of the portraits as he drank his champagne. "You know Abe Ruef, I take it?"

The name was mentioned so often by my uncle that I could not forget the dark, curly-haired man with the receding hairline I'd seen months ago at the Palace.

Lightly, I quoted Goldie. "Nothing in this city gets done without Abe Ruef."

LaRosa lifted a brow. "You do know him."

"I know who he is."

"Has your uncle ever spoken of him?"

There was something in his voice that made me wary. I wished I hadn't been so light. "Why would he speak of him to me?"

A shrug. "I thought he might, given . . ."

"Given what?"

"Well . . . your position in the family." His expression was pleasant, but I could not help tensing.

I was reminded again that my fantasy friendship with him was only that. I hardly knew him. "What are you implying, Mr. LaRosa?"

"Dante," he corrected. "We're friends, aren't we, May? Coppa's Comrades, so to speak."

"Then why do I feel as if you're accusing me of something?"

"I'm only wondering. One minute I've never seen or heard of you, and the next you're everywhere. You're all the talk, you're always at Goldie Sullivan's side, and then you show up on the arm of Ellis Farge."

"I'm only all the talk because you've made it so."

"Touché," he said. "But you have to admit you've made it impossible to ignore you."

"Really? I'm really very ordinary. My mother died, and my aunt and uncle took me in. Goldie is my cousin, and my uncle commissioned Ellis Farge. You know all of this already."

"Why do I feel there's more to it?"

"I have no idea."

"The Sullivans are not well known for their generosity."

Now I was becoming irritated. "You don't know them at all if you think that."

"And—forgive my frankness—but you aren't Farge's type. Nothing about you makes sense, unless . . ."

He was a reporter. He was looking for stories. And not just any stories, but society secrets. He'd told me that outright. I should have listened.

He was *not* a friend, and I could not trust him.

He pressed, "I think you might have some knowledge about your uncle's involvement with Ruef and the board, and maybe, because we're friends, you'd be willing to help me find the evidence I need."

"Evidence of what?"

"Graft. Bribery. Unsavory dealings."

"Mr. LaRosa, I have no idea why you would think my uncle might be involved in any such thing."

He said nothing, but his gaze lingered on my face, and I felt the threat in it, a tacit quid pro quo. *Keep my secret, and I'll keep yours.* I remembered his article about Chinatown. The debutante who'd gone unnamed. Goldie. He knew about her, of course he did. Just as he knew about my uncle's mistress. *Tell me what I want to know, or . . . Goldie, Chinatown . . .* It was all the more powerful for being unstated. The danger of it prickled my skin.

A moment, and then two, and then his expression softened; he tapped my glass with his own as if acknowledging a stalemate, and his intensity drained away as quickly as it came. It had bound me more fiercely than I'd realized.

"Well, I'll leave you to Verina. Give her my best, won't you? No, wait—on the other hand, don't. She might throw something at you when she hears my name."

"That must be a common reaction," I said.

His mouth quirked in a half smile. "Maybe I'll see you at Coppa's." Then he turned on his heel and walked away.

I started back to the ballroom, relieved that he was gone, but so distracted by his questions and his implications that I did not see the man who stepped in front of me until I nearly ran into him.

"My pardon, Miss Kimble." He put his hands on my arms to stop my forward movement. "You seem in another world."

He was familiar, though I could not place him, and then, suddenly, I did. The Cliff House, the bouncing black feathers on Mrs. Hoffman's hat, Goldie's tears and the beach and her explanations of her failed engagement. Dante LaRosa's comment, *"Oelrichs is here somewhere . . . slumming."*

"Oh. Mr. Oelrichs, hello."

His gaze leaped over my shoulder. "If you're here, then it means Miss Sullivan must not be far behind. The two of you are in each other's pockets these days."

"We are very close," I said.

"So the gossip says."

"The gossip?" I asked, unable to help myself, and then remembered my promise to Goldie that I would not listen to anything Stephen Oelrichs had to say.

But Oelrichs looked amused. He had hoped I would ask. He'd set a trap, and I had unwittingly raced right into it. "Why, they say that you lead Miss Sullivan into all manner of indiscreet behavior."

I blinked in surprise. "Me?"

"That is what they say. You know, at the Cliff House, Mrs. Hoffman liked the look of you. She said you seemed a 'good girl,' and that perhaps you might be the one to bring Goldie Sullivan to heel at last." He tapped my chin, too intimate, too close. "But you and I know better, don't we?"

"I—I don't know what you mean."

His polite expression did not waver. Anyone watching us would have seen only a courteous encounter. "May I offer you a bit of advice? Stay away from China Joe. He's not the ignorant Chinaman he pretends to be. And he understands English perfectly well."

I struggled to hide my shock.

Oelrichs went on with a quiet lightness that belied his words, "You don't belong here, Miss Kimble. You're completely in over your head. Learn to swim, or drown. Those are your only choices when it comes to the Sullivans. Now, if you'll excuse me, I'll wish you good evening."

He left me astonished and bewildered. Given everything Goldie had said about Stephen Oelrichs, I would have discounted his comments without thought. But now, coming so soon after Dante LaRosa's, it was not so easy to do.

I went back to the ballroom to find my cousin. When she saw me, she gave me her great golden smile and said, "Where *have* you been? We've been looking everywhere!" and I let her sparkle carry me into the party, and wrapped myself once again in the jocular good natures of Linette and Thomas and Jerome. I tried not to think of what Dante had said about social tiers that we did not belong to, or about secrets and corruption, or about Abe Ruef sitting at a table in the Palace Bar with my uncle and his mistress with her Important Connections. I tried not to think of Stephen Oelrichs. *"You don't belong here . . . Learn to swim, or drown."*

FOURTEEN

The next Sunday, Uncle Jonny received a call just before we left for church. He came out to the carriage, where Goldie and I waited, with a large envelope and an apologetic smile.

"There's no help for it, I'm afraid. These papers need to be at Farge's before the afternoon."

I said, "But it's Sunday! Surely Mr. Farge will be at church as well."

"He's as caught up in deadlines as the rest of us."

Goldie warned, "We're going to be late."

"Surely Petey can deliver them," I said.

"Petey is not my liaison to Farge. You are." My uncle put the envelope into my hand as he helped me from the carriage. "Farge is at his office now. He's expecting you. You're to wait until he's gone over them, in case he has questions. I don't know how long that will take, but I'm afraid you'll have to miss the service today."

"Won't there be talk if I'm not at church?" Uneasily I remembered LaRosa's comments about my being fast—among other things—even as I had to admit that a day spent learning at Ellis Farge's side sounded far more alluring than a sermon.

"We'll smooth all the ruffled feathers," Goldie assured me. "You're festering from some dire illness and simply cannot show your face to the world."

My uncle climbed into the carriage. "Petey will have the buggy ready in a few moments."

The carriage door closed; they drove away. I did not have to wait long until the stable boy appeared with the buggy, and we were off.

I glanced at the envelope in my lap, wondering what could be inside that was so important it must be delivered on Sunday, but I didn't really care; I was just glad to be the courier. When we reached the Montgomery Block, it was as busy as the other times I'd been there—apparently I wasn't the only person skipping church.

I was sorry to see that Coppa's was closed, however, and pleasantly nervous to note that Ellis was the only one at his office. The place felt empty.

"Ellis?" I called softly.

"May, is that you?" His called answer was followed quickly by Ellis himself. He smiled brilliantly when I gave him the envelope. He slid it open, leafing through the papers inside. "Thank God. I thought I'd mislaid these."

"My uncle was determined that you should get them today. I'm to wait until you go over them. I'm missing church."

"I hope it won't imperil your immortal soul," Ellis said.

"I expect God makes allowances for emergencies. Are they very important, then?" I craned to get a look.

Ellis put the envelope on his desk. "Crucial to the project. Please, sit down."

He sat at his desk, and I took the chair across. He scrutinized the papers while I looked about his office and tried to contain my fascination with the framed plans, the photographs, the wooden case with the drawing tools nestled inside, *F. Hommel-Esser* stamped in gold on the blue velvet.

Impatiently I waited for Ellis to put the papers aside, and then could not wait another moment to say, "Have you considered the design?"

"I've been unable to without these. Now all I need is a bit of inspiration."

"Perhaps I can help. Is it to be an office building? My uncle spoke of leases, but that could be anything. I'd just like to know what it should feel like."

"What it should feel like?"

"Isn't that how you begin to plan?" I asked. "Isn't the way the building should feel the first thing to come to you?"

"The use comes first."

"Of course, but"—I struggled to explain—"but like this place. It's meant for artists, you can tell."

He gave me a puzzled look.

"The high ceilings. The windows everywhere. So much light. Of course artists would flock to it."

Ellis chuckled. "I rather think it was the cheap rents."

"Oh. I hadn't thought of that. Yes, of course."

"But yes, I suppose the light has something to do with it. They called it Halleck's Folly when it was first built. No one thought all the rooms would ever be filled. And like attracts like. You know what they call it now? The Monkey Block."

I laughed. "That seems appropriate."

He made a face. "Indeed. Nothing but monkeys here. Speaking of which, why don't we go over to Coppa's?"

"It's closed."

"Ah, it only seems that way," he said mysteriously.

154

I did not need much convincing. I had already missed the service, and my uncle and cousin would be busy with social obligations for hours yet. Not only that, but Goldie would have told everyone I was too ill to attend church, and it would not do to suddenly appear in perfect health.

I began to follow him, and then remembered the Anderson ball and stopped. "Will Dante LaRosa be there?"

"I don't know. Why?"

"I saw him the other night. At a dance. He was reporting on it." He had written nothing of me in his article on the Anderson soiree. I wasn't certain why, but I was grateful.

"I hope he didn't trouble you. He's a bottom-feeder, May. You should avoid him."

"You don't like him. Why?"

"Dante LaRosa never met a snide comment he didn't like. He's tried to destroy me more than once."

"Destroy you? Why?"

"Who knows? I suspect simply for the fun of it. He's very eager to write anyone's bad opinion of my work. Did he say anything about me at this dance?"

"He seemed more concerned about my uncle."

"What about your uncle?"

"I don't know. Something about city corruption, and bribery—"

"The same old thing. He's been talking of that for months. He's trying to find a story that isn't there," Ellis assured me. "He's desperate to move from the society beat. You heard him say it himself. What's more likely to happen is that he gets fired."

"Why do you say that?"

"Because I'm not the only one he's annoyed with his articles. Sooner or later, someone is going to go after him."

"Why haven't you exposed him? Why hasn't anyone at Coppa's? You all know who he really is."

"Who would believe me? No, I've no wish to play his petty games. Let him roll in the mud without me." Ellis glanced away, and I understood that, like me, he was afraid of what Dante LaRosa knew; Ellis Farge too had people or secrets he wished to protect. I wanted to ask what they might be, but I did not want him asking in return, and so I buried my curiosity.

Ellis went on, "Those at Coppa's love anything that snips at the status quo, and LaRosa does snip. His articles are their favorite entertainment. They'll never expose him. Come along now, before they drink all the wine."

"Wine? So early?"

"Oh, don't be so bourgeois," he teased.

Ellis ignored the CLOSED sign on Coppa's front door and rapped softly. It opened, and we were greeted by a rotund man with a long black mustache and a black skullcap. He ushered us inside quickly.

"Poppa Coppa, this is Miss May Kimble," introduced Ellis.

Coppa bowed over my hand. "Miss Kimble, welcome. Go on back, go back! Tell them I am bringing the wine and do not draw over Martinelli!"

The tables had been shoved together in the middle back of the restaurant, reminding me of the last time I'd been here. Several people were gathered there, gulping wine and making sandwiches of bread and cold cuts. Wenceslas Piper had tied back his auburn hair. He stood on a stool, drawing a caricature of Gelett Addison hunched over an enormous bottle of ink, laurel wreath slipping over his ear. Nearby, on another stool, Edith Jackson added embellishments to the words she'd already written: *Something terrible is going to happen*, and Gelett gestured at her with his wine, spattering it over the table.

"Why, it sounds a portent, Edie! Whyever would you put such a thing on these walls?"

"It's from Oscar Wilde," she retorted. "From *Salomé*."

"A wretched play. A doomed play. And now you've doomed us all!"

Wence laughed and leaned over to draw a heart over the *i* in *terrible.*
"There, I've made it all better."

Edith glared at him and scratched it out.

"Ah, there she is! Our newest freak!" Gelett called out.

"How tiresome you can be, Gelly," Blythe Markowitz said from
where she leaned beneath the painted motto, *Oh, Love! dead and your
adjectives still in you!*

Ellis led me to the table and poured wine for us both. We watched
and talked with the others and ate sandwiches until the wine and the
company combined to make me languorous and easy, and I forgot
the passing of time, or that anyone might expect me home again. But
then, as if to remind me, Dante LaRosa came through a back door.
The mist of the morning had turned to rain that spattered his hat and
the shoulders of his coat. When he saw us, he stopped; I saw his quick
recalculation, a forced smile. "Well, look who's here."

"No soirees for you to dim today?" Ellis asked.

"It's Sunday. Even the stupidest of society don't dance today."
Dante's glance came to me. "No church for the wicked, hmmm?"

"You're here, I see. I didn't know newspaper reporters painted the
walls of Coppa's," I said lightly.

"Anyone can write bad poetry." Dante took off his hat, then grabbed
wine and pulled out a chair. "Look at that opus over there." He pointed
to a large devil fishing as he roasted his cloven foot in a fire above the
words: *It is a crime.* Nearby were stanzas that began *Through the fog of
centuries . . .* and ended musing about cat soul mates.

"You see?" Dante grinned and lit a cigarette. "The bar is low." He
grabbed a piece of orange chalk from a grimy, powdery box of different
colors and rolled it across the table. "What about you? Why aren't you
drawing?"

"I don't really draw—"

"Of course you do. Rooms, isn't it? Isn't that what you said? Go on.
Show us what you can do."

"I'm not an artist."

"Neither is Wence, but he's desecrating with the best of them," Gelett joked.

"The word should be 'secrating,' without the 'de,'" Wence returned, now adding *Ars Vincit Omnia* above the caricature.

"Is 'secrating' even a word?" Dante asked.

"Only in Wence's mind," said Edith.

"I've invented it, because there is no other word that celebrates the genius that is me."

"You see, May? You'd best mark your spot before all the space is gone and the world thinks that the only genius here was Wence," Blythe said. "Otherwise no one will know you existed."

"Scream to the universe: I was here!" Edith sang out. "For long after we are gone, Coppa's will live on!"

"God knows it's the only thing worth saving in this entire city," Gelett said, pouring more wine.

Ellis threw the piece of chalk back into the box.

"You aren't going to let her mark her territory?" Dante asked.

"Go on, May, put a big *X* on Ellis's forehead," Edith said.

I could not look at any of them as they all laughed, and I knew I must be red.

"Draw us something," Dante urged.

"She needn't prove herself to you," Ellis snapped.

"This grows wearying between the two of you," Gelett said with an exaggerated sigh. "Shall we have fisticuffs at dawn instead?"

"I propose a drinking contest." Wence lifted a mostly empty bottle of wine. "Poppa! More wine!"

"More wine, more wine, more wine," came Poppa Coppa's chiding voice from the kitchen.

"We're increasing your value," Gelett called back. "Think how many tourists will come just to see the newest splat that Wence Piper put upon these sacred walls."

Dante dragged on his cigarette and exhaled a thin, steady stream of smoke, picked up his wine, then said to me, "Well? We've voted to let you stay. You might as well prove you deserve it."

It was a challenge.

Ellis said quietly, "Tell him to go to hell. Don't give him the satisfaction."

But it felt a test to me, and I suspected there was something more here too, that Dante meant not just to challenge me, and perhaps to punish me for not giving him what he'd wanted at the Anderson ball, but also to embarrass Ellis. I would not let that happen.

I took the box of chalk, and then I picked up my glass of wine and sauntered as casually as I could to a bare spot on the wall, below a satyr toasting a nude maiden with champagne. I confronted the spot as if I were a gladiator in combat—I had no idea what I would draw or what might impress them. I tossed back the rest of my wine in a gesture of bravery, and then, pretending I *was* brave, I drew the first line.

I was aware of the others talking and joking behind me, the hum of conversation and laughter, and someone refilling my wineglass so it was never empty, but all I saw was the room taking form beneath my fingers, a room of gorgeous decoration, sculpted window and door casings, a floor of colored tiles and narrow mullioned windows, a painted paradise of a domed ceiling, nymphs dancing by a spring as they looked down onto a wall mural of a ball full of glowing lanterns and gilded creatures. All smiling, all celebrating. The color and the light fantastic and strange and beautiful.

I drew and drew, losing myself to time, to talk, to everything, and when it was done, and the vision faded, I stepped back to look at what I'd done.

It was a mockery. Like the bacchante in the Sullivan ballroom, the room I'd drawn was lewd in its overabundance, grotesque, breathless and constricting and empty, and the terror of it had me setting aside my wine, putting my hand to my throat as if that might somehow help me to breathe again. The leering faces of the golden creatures, the lushness with no depth, windows that stared out onto painted walls. All facade, all vacant, enjoyment without sustenance, celebration without boundaries or purpose. It was all terrifyingly close and painfully hollow, the prison that neither I nor my mother had ever seen in the life she'd chosen for me.

Why had I drawn this nightmare?

The room buzzed all about me, but I felt as alone and alien as I had at any ball or dinner in San Francisco. Unnoticed, a ghost of myself, and with this odd sense that I had somehow locked myself inside the room I'd drawn, that I was one of those painted nymphs bending toward the spring, a smile on my face and horror behind my eyes, a lifetime of pretense—*Ah, but what have you to complain of? You've everything you've ever dreamed about.*

I had to resist the urge to erase it. I went silently back to the table, and no one said anything. They did not note me as I sat down. I think I might have walked out of Coppa's without anyone heeding.

Gelett and Blythe argued. Wence had finished his painting and was pulling out the cork of another bottle of wine. Edith sat on the floor against the wall, legs straight out, her turban askew. Ellis, however, had twisted in his chair to watch me. He was dead silent, expressionless. I could not tell if he admired or disliked what I'd done.

Behind a haze of cigarette smoke, Dante LaRosa did not look at my drawing, or at me, but only stared at Ellis, slowly, thoughtfully.

Ellis took my hand, wrapping it in his, and whispered, "I've had enough, have you?"

I nodded. Ellis pulled me to my feet. He was unsteady—too much wine, I thought, and I wondered how long we'd been here, how long I'd been drawing. He took me over to my picture and reached out to trace a line with his finger, and murmured, "Beautiful. Everything you do is beautiful," and there was a tone in his voice I could not decipher—wistfulness perhaps, or no, something sharper, harder. He didn't see the truth of the picture. I didn't know how he couldn't see what was so obvious to me. He drew back again, lost his balance, and before I could steady him, he fell against the wall. The chalk smeared, streaking his suitcoat, colors blending in a swath across the middle of the drawing.

"Look what I've done," Ellis said in horror.

"It's all right. It meant nothing." That was not true, but I was glad he'd smeared it. I wanted the horrible thing gone.

I don't think the others noticed as we left the restaurant and stepped out into the night—night, how odd was that? It had seemed to be minutes since we'd gone inside. I had no idea what time it was. I'd lost my bearings.

My carriage was just over there, Petey slumped in the seat, asleep. Ellis put his hand to his eyes and let out his breath. I felt him stiffen as if in preparation for something, and I turned to him, waiting for him to say or do whatever it was I felt him ready to do.

He dropped his hand. He wanted something from me, I knew, but I didn't know what, and I waited, taut and expectant, and was disappointed when all he did was touch my jaw, gently stroking with his thumb. "It's late. You should go home."

"Yes." But the way he looked at me. The way he glanced about, and then back, as if he wished to leave and couldn't, or as if he disliked himself, or me—yes, it was me he disliked—and his mood gripped me, puzzling, bewildering.

I didn't understand anything, not where I was or what I'd done. There was only that soft caress that spoke of—what? Regret? Desire? Shame?

He stepped away, releasing me from its spell. "Go home." He hit the edge of the carriage hard, startling the horse, startling Petey awake, and I had the sense that it had been a deliberate act, though why I didn't know.

"Miss Kimble?" asked Petey, scrambling from the seat.

Ellis helped me inside. "I'll see you soon." His expression was bemused, or perhaps it was only a smile. In the near darkness, I could not tell, and I did not realize how important it would have been to know.

The misty, sea-tinged air hid the moon but for a bit of brightness. It was chill and wet; a clock on a building we passed read nearly eleven. As we reached the drive, I told Petey to go directly to the stable; I did not want to alert anyone that I was coming in so late. I sneaked from the stable to the back door, the stone steps that led to the kitchen. As I reached for the handle, a shiver passed through me. *"A goose stepped on your grave,"* Mama would have said. I was suddenly cold.

I opened the door and stepped inside to the residual warmth of the stove, which had been banked for the night, and darkness, stumbling against a coal hod near the door, which scraped on the floor. I caught my breath, heard a surprised exclamation, a shuffle, and then suddenly there was Shin emerging from the pantry with a lamp. She'd been waiting for me. She reached into her pocket and took out a piece of folded paper, and then raised her finger to her lips, a warning.

Almost in answer came the scream.

FIFTEEN

It came from the foyer.

"What was that?" I rushed to the kitchen door.

Shin grabbed my arm as I passed her. "Miss, wait—"

I brushed her off and kept going.

When I got to the stairs, the scream seemed still to echo into the domed ceiling. The moonlight cast a dim glow upon my aunt, crumpled lifelessly at the bottom.

I dropped to my knees beside her. Her head was positioned oddly, her hip at a sickening turn. Her cheek was still warm. "Aunt Florence."

Something fell from her hand onto the floor, rolling to a stop at my foot. I grabbed it without thinking, and shook her. "Aunt. Wake up, please."

Her head rolled drunkenly to the side, too loose, grotesque.

"She's dead," I said dully to Shin, but she hadn't followed me. I was alone.

Someone turned on the light. My aunt stared into nothing. Her mouth gaped open.

Goldie, in her nightgown, stopped halfway down the stairs. Her hand went to her mouth. My uncle, still dressed, the gold buttons on his vest glinting, misbuttoned, raced past Goldie and knelt on the other side of his wife.

My uncle looked to Mr. Au and the cook, who were blinking blearily in the hall. Then he looked at me. "May, what have you done?"

"She must have been sleepwalking again—"

Uncle Jonny rose and backed away with a horrified expression. Again, he asked, "What have you done?"

Still, I was too shocked to understand. "She was like this when I came in."

My uncle said grimly, "Mr. Au, it's time to make the call."

The butler went to the telephone. The cook shrieked quietly into her hands.

"I didn't want to believe it. Even all those times when you upset her. Oh, I didn't want to believe it. And now you've killed her!" Goldie's voice held the edge of hysteria.

"What? No. No. Of course I didn't. I found her this way. She was already here. I heard her scream. Shin—" I looked frantically around for the maid, who was nowhere to be seen. "Where's Shin?"

Mr. Au spoke quietly into the phone. He hung up the receiver and said, "They are on their way."

"We took you in. We've given you everything, and this is how you've repaid us!" Goldie cried.

"I didn't do this!" I protested.

"Mr. Au, if you please." Uncle Jonny said.

The butler came to me, and the two of them took my arms and propelled me up the stairs, to my bedroom. I was too shocked to fight them. I didn't believe it was happening.

I stumbled into the room. My uncle closed the door hard behind me; I heard the rattle of keys, the turn in the lock. I was numb and stupid. My aunt's death, the accusations . . . I could only stand there in darkness. Finally, I pushed on the bedroom light, flinching at the brightness, then was vaguely surprised that I was still in my coat and hat, still dressed, boots on. Slowly, I began to come back to myself.

It was only then that I realized I was still holding the thing that had dropped from my aunt's hand. It was a gold button.

I stared at it, and then, suddenly, I knew where I'd seen it before. My uncle's vest, misbuttoned, but no, it hadn't been. It had gaped across his stomach, the button not in the wrong buttonhole, but missing. This button here, the one in my palm.

The button that had fallen from my aunt's hand.

As the hours passed, the house became even more eerily silent. Dawn, and then day, and again that sense of isolation and abandonment, only this time it was worse because there truly was an absence; the breathing of the house seemed to have changed. I was cold, and now afraid. It was all a mistake. This was not happening. Shin would explain that I was with her, that it was impossible for me to have pushed my aunt down the stairs. And then . . . then there was the button from my uncle's vest. I tried to remember everything Aunt Florence had ever said to me. Her words seemed ominous now, warnings I should have listened to. Was it madness, really, or had I only believed what I'd been told? How could my uncle's vest button have been in her hand when she fell—unless she'd grabbed it as she was falling?

Unless he'd pushed her?

I didn't know what I was waiting for. The police? My uncle? Where was Shin? The bedroom sparkled and shone in the light, beautiful and cold and empty, like the prison I'd drawn at Coppa's.

I was so attuned to every sound and movement that the shuffling at my door made me start, though it was hardly perceptible. I turned to see that someone had slid a piece of folded paper beneath my door.

It was only then that I remembered Shin had taken a folded paper from her pocket when in the kitchen. Had this been why she'd been waiting? Had it been this same paper?

I knew it before I picked it up, though I had not seen its color in the kitchen, in the lamplight. Cheap paper of pale blue. Yes, I knew it, though my mind refused to believe it. Here in this place it was a thing discordant, a slip back into time, into a boardinghouse room, Mama with piles of lace and pantaloons, sewing away while I studied French conjugations. *"I should be helping you, Mama." "You can help me better by learning French. Now, again—"*

It was much worn and creased, as if it had been carried in a pocket for months. I knew, as I picked it up, that I would unfold it to see the address on the bottom, *Central Shirtwaist Factory, Brooklyn, NY*. I'd seen such paper many times before, with the items given my mother typewritten on the page, a signature beneath, *16 pantaloons, 43 yds lace trim* on one side.

On the other, my mother's writing, broken, hurried, dated only days before she died.

Florence—

I have waited some time for your apology, even as I knew it would not come, and I have understood as well why it has not. But I have grown tired of waiting, and I have received some news which says that for me, time has run out. I am dying.

I wish to believe that this news does not please you, that you do not find it comforting to know that I am to receive still more punishment, or to know how I have suffered, and how your niece has suffered because of your cruelty and your jealousy. I wish to believe, as I have always believed, that there is something fine and good in you, and that the years have softened you, and that you feel the regret that I feel. I can only say again that I am sorry Charles chose me over you, Flossie, and had I been able to keep from loving him, I would have, but then I would not have my darling daughter, my May, and she is worth everything. I know you will think it too, when you meet her.

I worried, when you married Jonathan, that you had found a man so like yourself that, instead of making you the better person I believe you could be, he might make you a worser one. At the time, you praised his cleverness, and I know too well how you turn cleverness to your advantage. I hope I am wrong about him. I console myself by remembering that you can love a good man—you too loved Charles, after all.

Yes, I know—you thought me a fool for believing in Charles. But it seems that of the two of us, I was the one who knew him best. He was an honorable man; I understood that when he decided not to involve his family in scandal, and I trusted him to keep his promise to leave an inheritance to his daughter, illegitimate though she was. He died two months ago. His family will obey his request to bequeath May, as long as we continue to adhere to my promise to Charles that we never contact them in any way.

So you see, your niece will soon have a fortune. When I last looked into Sullivan Building, two years ago, the business was not doing well. Bad luck, or bad investments? Perhaps if you are kind, May will help you. But you must promise me this, Flossie. You must take her in and treat her as your own. You must make up to me all these years of suffering we have endured because of your schemes. I will never tell her that you are the source of all our troubles. I will never tell her how you spread lies about me to Charles's family so they forced him to abandon me. I will not tell her that you sold our family home in Newport without telling me and then left me in the cold with nothing because you were so jealous that Charles preferred me. I will not do this because you are all May has left. She will need family. I desire only that you be there for her.

My heart is tired, and the doctor says it will soon fail. I can no longer work such long hours. I've done my best to keep this from May, but soon I fear I will be gone. Bring her to you, and love her as you could not love me. This is all I ask, Flossie, and if you care at all for my forgiveness, or if the possibility of atonement eases your fear of God's judgment, I give you the chance for it now.

Charlotte.

I stared unseeing at the letter, letting my mother's words, her voice, the truth, settle. My father had left me an inheritance. My father. *Charles.* I had come to San Francisco with an anticipated fortune.

My father had not betrayed my mother, as I believed. She had released him to his family and promised never to contact him if he would provide for me in the end. He had kept his promise, as she had kept hers. She had never even told me his name, knowing as she must that I would not be able to resist searching him out. *Charles.* Charles who? The names raced through my head—Astor, Vanderbilt, Belmont, others. Where was there a recently deceased Charles? I could think of none. I was too distracted by the most fantastic part of it.

I had a fortune.

My aunt was dead. My uncle had a business that suffered "bad luck" or "bad investments," an expensive mistress, and, according to Dante LaRosa, was involved in city corruption. My cousin was smoking opium and had not paid whatever she owed to China Joe.

Stephen Oelrichs's words sneaked back. *"You're in over your head. Learn to swim. Or drown."* What was it Dante had said? *"I'm still trying to figure out where you belong."* I was in the middle of something, but what exactly?

I heard my aunt's laudanum-drunk voice in my ear. *"You must listen. It will be soon. Soon, the papers—"*

The papers. What papers? The papers concerning my father's will? My inheritance? She'd been trying to warn me and now she was dead and my uncle's vest button had rolled from her hand. My uncle and my cousin needed my money—I had seen the evidence without understanding. The foyer mirror disappearing and never returning. Sold? Pawned? The angel on the hallway table? All the empty, unfinished rooms. Everything placed in the front rooms for show. And all this time their feigned generosity. No one had ever told me I was not a poor relation. They meant to steal from me and keep me believing I was beholden to them. *"Soon,"* my aunt said. *When?* How much money did I have? Was it in their hands yet? How much had they spent?

Shin had known all this. She'd known I was looking for this letter. Where was she now?

Too many unanswered questions, too many dawning realizations, and all of it too late—far too late. They were accusing me of murder. Still, I did not really believe that the accusation would stand. Still, I believed that I could win.

But I had no idea just how oblivious I'd been, or for how long.

I heard the horses and the carriage, but I could see nothing but dark shapes through the fog. Voices in the foyer rose into the angel-hosted dome. When my door burst open without a knock, I turned from the window to see a group of people standing at my open door. Dr. Browne and Uncle Jonny, along with a man and a woman in dark coats and hats. Goldie too, and next to her—

"Ellis?" I breathed.

"I've brought some people to take care of you, May," Uncle Jonny said in a careful, soothing tone.

Dr. Browne stepped forward. "These good people are going to take you with them, Miss Kimble. For a rest."

"A rest?"

He smiled. "I think you'll find everything to your liking. Blessington is well known for its beneficial treatments."

I looked at my uncle. "What is this?"

"I've agreed with Dr. Browne. You'll do as we say in this, May."

"I don't understand."

"You see?" said Goldie to the man I didn't know. "She doesn't see what she's done. Didn't you say that was a symptom, Doctor, to be unaware of one's own behavior?"

"Indeed." Dr. Browne nodded sagely.

"She's killed my mother." The tears in Goldie's eyes were ones I'd never seen for her mother before now. Only impatience. They were so obviously false and she was so obviously playacting that I would have laughed had it not been so dire.

"That's not true," I said. "You know it's not. She was at the bottom of the stairs when I came home. I had nothing to do with it! Ask your father what happened. Why did she have your vest button in her hand, Uncle Jonny? Where's Shin? She—"

"Shin? You won't need a maid at Blessington." Uncle Jonny shook his head sadly.

"You see? She's so mad she thinks she must have someone to do her hair." Goldie reached for Ellis's hand, grasping it hard—*his hand*—a bewildering intimacy; as far as I knew, they'd never even met. "She made me a laughingstock. The very first day, she insisted on going round the Horn like a . . . a *loose* woman! Thanks to her, I've been gossiped about, written about in the paper"—she choked as if the words were too distressing to say—"and she nearly made Mr. Farge insane, the way she followed him around. Didn't she, Ellis?"

Ellis. Ellis nodded. "I tried to dissuade her. I could not."

"She knew of our attachment, and still she tried to come between us." Goldie patted her eyes delicately with her handkerchief.

"What attachment? I did no such thing." I realized then the true extent of my danger. I saw my aunt again, reaching for me. *"You must go, May."* My poor aunt. Her headaches had started a few months before I'd arrived, Goldie said. *With the arrival of my mother's letter.* They'd doped her with laudanum. They'd made her insane. I wondered if Aunt Florence had even written the letter that had summoned me to San Francisco. Perhaps Goldie had done so, or my uncle. I would not know the difference; I'd never seen my aunt's handwriting. And now she was dead. I knew I could say nothing more of Shin. Not now. Not here. She would be in danger if I did. I needed a lawyer. "I think I would like to speak to Stephen Oelrichs."

As if this were a fair game. As if I had any chance at all against them.

"Stephen?" Goldie blinked. "Whatever for?"

Uncle Jonny sighed. "Enough of this. It's all in the order signed by Judge Gerard. The papers are all correct."

"Order?" I asked. "What order?"

No one answered.

"No," I said, and then more loudly. "No! I'm not going anywhere."

"Please, May." My uncle truly looked pained.

"I'm not the least bit mad!" I appealed to the man and the woman. "They plan to steal from me. My fortune—I have a great deal of money. My father left me . . . My father is . . . Charles . . . I don't know his name, but they do . . ." I trailed off at their sorrowful expressions, at their frank disbelief and impatience, at Dr. Browne sadly shaking his head, and though I knew I was only making it worse, I could not stop.

"I have proof. My mother wrote a letter. I have it right here, on the dressing table—" I started toward it.

The dark-coated man held out his hand to me. "Now, now, miss. Do as your uncle says. We don't want to have to confine you."

"That imaginary letter again." Goldie sighed. "It's become a—what does one call it?"

"An idée fixe," Dr. Browne provided.

"Please don't distress yourself so, May," Uncle Jonny said.

The nameless couple each took one of my arms, tightly, pinching. I fought them, but they clung as if they'd hooked into my skin. Goldie gave Dr. Browne my coat, and he followed me as the couple dragged me from the room. I set my heels, but they pulled me, flailing and half falling, down the stairs. At the bottom, Dr. Browne held out my coat, and they released me to put it on. I ran for the door.

My custodian was on me before I'd gone three steps. She shoved me against the hall table, sending the salvers scattering and the telephone skidding. Glass shattered on the floor.

"That's enough, *miss*."

She slapped me across the face. I gasped in pain and shock, and she jerked me again to my feet and thrust me into my coat. "Let's go."

Goldie, Ellis, and my uncle stood at the top of the stairs. Each of them wore the same expression. Polite interest, now not even the pretense of sorrow. I could have been anyone, no one, as I was dragged away.

PART TWO:

LESSONS

BLESSINGTON HOME FOR THE INCURABLY INSANE

SAN FRANCISCO, NOVEMBER 1904

SIXTEEN

We did not go far, that was all I knew. The leather curtains on the carriage windows were drawn so I could not see out, the thin lines of daylight peeking from the edges lent a coppery gloom. My captors sat, silent and stone-faced, on either side of me.

The carriage stopped, and the light escaping the curtains dimmed. Before the driver opened the door, my custodians had grabbed my arms again, but when I stumbled from the carriage into a dank and dim porte cochere, there was no place to run. They were closing the wooden gate that had been opened to admit us. Brick walls enclosed the other three sides. Before me was a rounded stoop of shallow stairs, also brick, and a heavy wooden door scarcely illuminated by a gas lamp turned very low.

The door opened; a tall and well-proportioned woman with flaw-lessly upswept chestnut hair stood waiting. She smiled reassuringly and said, "Hello, miss. Don't be frightened, but hurry now, before you let the heat out. It's chilly today."

I was too stunned to be frightened or anything else. A none-too-gentle push up those stairs, and we followed the woman into a narrow hall redolent with the long-trapped odors of stewed mutton and fish and acrid soap. Steam billowed from an open door—a laundry room bustling with the hazy shapes of women. On the other side, a kitchen with great stoves and blackened kettles. The door slammed shut behind us, the bolt jammed home with a solid click.

I heard moaning, someone singing "Cockles and mussels, alive, alive, oh!"—just that one line, over and over again, and someone else shouting "Ha! Ha!" and a constant and rhythmic *clank clank clank*, metal hitting metal, murmured voices. We passed a great room where women wearing gray, shift-like gowns gathered on settees and chairs, another with long tables and benches, and then a line of closed doors. Nurses passed with only a cursory glance at me. The combined smells of urine, sweat, unwashed bodies, and carbolic soap stank so unpleasantly that I wanted to pinch shut my nose.

At one of the doors, the chestnut-haired woman paused and knocked. At the grunted answer from beyond, she ushered us into an office before a ruddy-faced man with light brown hair. He was in his shirtsleeves. His eyes were small; when he peered at me I had the impression of shortsightedness, proved correct when he took up his glasses and settled them on the bridge of a bulbous nose.

"Miss Kimble is it?" His brief smile raised my hopes that here was someone who might listen to me. "Welcome to Blessington."

The man who'd brought me took a sheaf of folded papers from his suitcoat pocket. He handed them to the man at the desk. "I believe everything is in order, Dr. Madison."

"Hmm." Dr. Madison barely glanced at the papers before he set them aside and looked again at me. "Do you know who you are?"

"May Kimble," I said without hesitation.

"Where are you from?"

"Originally from New York. But I've been in San Francisco for some months now, living with my relatives." Now was my chance. Surely he would see by my answers that I was not the least insane.

"The Sullivans."

I nodded. "I don't belong here. I've been most grievously betrayed."

"I'm told that you suffer from dementia, Miss Kimble, and that you pushed your aunt down the stairs."

"I don't know who told you that—"

"Your mother suffered from dementia as well, did she not? And your aunt?"

I struggled to answer carefully and calmly. "My aunt suffered from laudanum. My—"

"You came to San Francisco to serve as a companion to your cousin?"

"A companion?"

"Was that not your understanding?"

"I've never heard such a thing. I was to be one of the family, as my mother had just died. I did not know that I'd inherited a fortune from my father. That was kept from me. Deliberately. This is all a cruel plan to relieve me of my inheritance."

He'd been listening politely, but now his eyes glazed. "Of course." To the two who'd brought me, he said, "Thank you. You may leave her to me and to Mrs. Donaghan. Tell Mr. Sullivan that everything is as expected."

The two left. The chestnut-haired woman closed the door behind them. I was glad they were gone. I said, "I don't belong here. You must see that. I didn't kill my aunt. They want my money. They're lying about everything. Please, Doctor."

He tapped the papers my captor had given him. "We'll take good care of you here, Miss Kimble. You've been lucky that your uncle cares so greatly for you. Otherwise, you might be in police custody even now, and then . . . who can say what might happen to you?"

Anxiously, I said, "I had nothing to do with my aunt's death. They've planned all this from the start. They want my money. Please. You must believe me." That was sympathy in the doctor's eyes, wasn't it? It moved me to greater urgency. "If you allow me to speak to a lawyer, it will all be made clear."

He smiled and rose. "Let's not think of that just now, shall we? Now, we must focus on making you well." He gestured to the woman waiting. "This is Blessington's matron, Mrs. Donaghan. She will show you to your room."

Mrs. Donaghan touched my arm. "Come along now, Miss Kimble."

"Dr. Madison, please. You can't think I belong here. My father was of New York society. My uncle knows—"

"Miss Kimble," ordered the matron.

"Go with Mrs. Donaghan, Miss Kimble," the doctor advised.

"No!" I pulled away from the matron. "No. I tell you, I don't belong here! They're lying about everything!"

Mrs. Donaghan exhaled heavily. "Miss Kimble, 'tis best if you come along nicely."

I tried to calm myself. "I am not insane."

"Of course you're not," said Mrs. Donaghan soothingly, and though I heard the condescension in it, and knew I was being placated, I was so desperate for someone to believe me that I grasped at her words. "But we'll talk about that later, miss. You come along now."

"I don't want to go." I knew I sounded like a child. I couldn't help it.

"Must I call the attendants?" Dr. Madison asked.

Mrs. Donaghan looked at me. "Well, Miss Kimble? What will it be?"

I heard the steel in her voice, and I saw the determination in Dr. Madison's expression, and there seemed to be no other choice. I was not helping my case. No doubt I looked as mad as my uncle had claimed. "I'll go."

Mrs. Donaghan became brightly cheerful again. "That's the way. You'll get along just fine, miss. I can tell. I can always tell."

It would be all right. I could manage a night here. I had not slept for nearly two days. I was exhausted and weepy. Tomorrow, I would start the battle again, well rested. A night would not kill me.

She led me down the hall, and motioned for me to precede her up dark painted stairs. On the next floor, she said, "To your right, dearie." The dimly lit hall ended at a dormitory with at least ten beds, most of them holding women in various states of undress. Some stared blankly into space. One stared out the barred window. One woman banged her head against the wall. Another sobbed helplessly. Still another sat on the floor, shouting, "Look out! Look out, I tell you!"

A woman sitting on her bed, braiding her hair into a dozen tiny braids, drawled, "Shut up, Millie."

Millie snapped back, "They'll take you first, you stupid whore!" and then spat on the carpet, which was muddied and frayed and curling at the edges, before she launched back into her shouting.

I stepped back. Mrs. Donaghan pushed me forward. The stench made me gag: stale urine, damp and mildew, the stinking rot of fabric, and again unwashed skin and hair, a miasma of close breath and sweat. The floor sucked at the soles of my boots.

"Wait—" I clutched at the doorframe. "This isn't . . . this is not . . . You can't mean to put me in here?"

The nurse, a large woman with green eyes, who sat at a small table by the door, looked up from her cards and laughed. "Oh no, missy, we got a nice plush room for you down the hall. All the a-coot-trah-mints."

"Be kind, O'Rourke," said Mrs. Donaghan mildly. "How are things today?"

"Not bad." She nodded toward the woman on the floor. "Millie shut up for an hour."

"Ah, that's good."

"But Costa's late again. She was supposed to be up here ten minutes ago."

"I'll find her as soon as I get this one settled," Mrs. Donaghan said. "This is May Kimble. Dementia. Murdered her aunt."

"What? No!" I burst out.

They both ignored me.

Just then, a petite, dark-eyed nurse came hurrying into the room, smoothing her skirt and plumping her dark hair.

"You're late, Nurse Costa," Mrs. Donaghan warned.

"There was a fight in the toilet. We need to have another discussion about the Third Ward." The newcomer narrowed her eyes at me. "Who's this?"

"May Kimble. Dementia and murder," O'Rourke said casually. Then, to Mrs. Donaghan, "Eight is open."

Mrs. Donaghan frowned at Costa, but said nothing more about her late arrival. The matron led me to one of the beds in two parallel rows. This one—not mine, I would not believe it—was against the far wall, between two others, and some distance from the window, so the stink of perpetual damp gathered with that of everything else.

"Here you go, Miss Kimble," she said, not unkindly. She turned to go.

I grabbed at her. "You can't leave me here." They were all looking at me. The woman on the floor spat again on the carpet and picked at her teeth. The stench dizzied with its foulness. "You don't know who I am. I'm a . . . a—" *What was my father's name?* "I don't belong here—"

"So you've said." Mrs. Donaghan gently unpried my hands from her arm.

"Please. Any other place. Please."

"Now, dearie, I don't want to have to strap you down. Be good, won't you?"

One of the others laughed. The woman on the floor began to chant, "Strap 'er down, strap 'er down," and the others started in as well, laughing and cackling, taunting. I backed up against the bed, uncertain, afraid, in the middle of a nightmare from which I couldn't wake, and Mrs. Donaghan left.

I sat on the edge of the bed. The thin mattress sagged beneath me, and I caught a whiff of it, unwashed sheets, a rank damp I did not want to explore any further.

A woman with loose and tangled red hair crawled to the grate by a nearly nonexistent fire, huddled into a ball beside it, and began to sob so loudly and brokenly that her entire body shook.

The spitting, cursing woman—Millie—shouted, "What you got to cry about, bitch? I'll show you what to cry about!"

The nurse at the door kept playing cards.

I understood why that woman curled into a ball because I wanted to do the same, to close my eyes and wish away the last few hours, the last few days. I wanted to take it all back, to pretend I'd never followed Goldie, that I'd never heard my aunt's warnings, or Dante LaRosa's, that I hadn't read my mother's letter. *I take it all back. I want it the way it was. Make it the way it was.*

My eyes watered from the stench; I unbuttoned my coat and fumbled in my skirt pocket for my handkerchief. Instead I felt the button from my uncle's vest. I drew it out, rolling it in my fingers. I wondered how exactly it had come about. An accident? Had she grabbed at him and he tried to save her? Or was it something else? *Something else.* I pressed the button hard, imprinting it into my fingers, the reminder of my life, of who I was, taking solace from its materiality as I'd once taken solace from my drawings—gone now, in Ellis Farge's office. *No don't think of that.* I had bigger questions now than Ellis and Goldie and what their connection might mean.

A girl came over to me, barely a girl, skeletal, with dark hair so tightly braided it slanted her brown eyes. She stood too close, her shapeless gray skirt brushing mine. "Pretty," she said, plucking at the jet trim on my coat. Then, "Pretty," again, plucking harder. "Pretty." Digging her nails beneath it, trying to rip it loose. I slapped away her hand instinctively. The button fell onto the mattress.

She grabbed her hand in shock, then screamed. "She hit me! She hit me!"

Nurse Costa moved more quickly than I expected. She was stronger than she looked too; she pushed the girl away and then twisted my arm hard enough to bring tears. "That's not how we play here." She released me when she caught sight of the button. "What's this? Gold, is it?"

"It's mine," I managed.

Costa ignored that, picked up the button and dropped it into her apron pocket. "Go on now. Keep your hands to yourself."

She bustled away.

Again, the woman on the floor spat. She shouted, "Look out! Strap 'er down! Look out!" over and over again until some of the others began to throw pillows and shoes at her. She ignored them all, and soon there was a pile of things scattered about the floor. Nurse Costa kept playing cards. The woman near the fire only rocked and moaned, and another woman cawed like a crow at irregular intervals, each time making me jump.

I could not stay here. I could not spend another moment here.

But then another nurse came in—long-faced Gould. She was not unpleasant, like Costa, but wearily efficient as she divested me of my clothing. She had obviously done this many times before. She took my burgundy skirt and striped waist, my yellow ribboned combination, stripping me in front of the others before giving me a coarse, stinking nightgown. Prior to bed, I was told to use the toilet, which was so incredibly loathsome that I could not bear to stay longer than it took to relieve myself. The room was airless, the only window high and painted shut. The floorboards warped from frequent flooding but not frequent cleaning.

"You'll get used to it," Gould told me in a tired voice, but her expression made me doubt it.

The nurses made the rounds with a bitter-tasting sleeping draught. I was going to refuse it until I thought it might be better to be drugged into an oblivious sleep, and I swallowed it without argument.

The medicine made me feel drunk and stupid, but at least then I cared nothing about the condition of the bed and the sheets. They didn't turn off the light, and I had to bury my face in the ill-smelling pillow, and the noise continued, not just in this room, but from every corner of the asylum. It reverberated through the walls, rumbled through the floor. How could one sleep with such restless noise, such a burning light?

But despite all that, I must have, because at one point I was shaken brutally awake. I blinked and stared blearily up into a face that was inches from mine, a grimacing, distorted face—the red-haired woman who'd been sobbing by the fire.

"Get out," she snapped. "You're in my bed."

I could not make my thoughts cohere.

"You're in my bed! Get out of my bed!"

"Calm down, Josie," said the nurse wearily from what sounded like a far distance.

But then Josie's hands were around my throat, squeezing, strangling. I tried to pry them loose, but I was drugged and she was preternaturally strong. I could make no sound. I could not shove her off. I kicked and flailed and she did not budge and I could not breathe. The room began to go black around the edges.

I heard a *snap!* then a scream. Suddenly the vise around my throat was gone, and Josie was cowering, the nurse beating viciously upon her head and shoulders with a leather strap. Josie put up her hands to ward off the blows, whining, "I'm sorry. I'm sorry. I won't do it again. I won't—"

Another blow smacked against Josie's lower back. She screamed and rolled on the floor. Other patients murmured and twisted in their beds.

Costa blew a whistle, and minutes later Gould and O'Rourke came in, looking resigned.

"Looks like it's the hoses for you again," sighed O'Rourke as they plucked Josie off the floor—literally plucked her, as if she weighed nothing, when I'd been unable to budge her. The bruises on my throat burned.

"Go back to sleep now, all of you," ordered Costa as they took a whimpering Josie out.

No, none of this could be real. I hugged myself, trying to still my shaking. I was not here.

But I could not make myself believe that, and even the chloral could not help me find my way out of this nightmare.

SEVENTEEN

Josie was brought back hours later, soaking wet and shivering. They strapped her to the bed, where she keened softly until the relentless ringing of bells at five thirty, when the world outside was only a swampy miasma of dark.

I was groggy and stupid. There was no dawn here. There would never be dawn. We were yanked to our feet, the beds stripped of their filthy sheets so we could not crawl back in between them. We were given shapeless gray dresses to wear, not much different than our nightgowns. By then I was so used to the fetor that I could not tell if they too reeked, but I recoiled at obviously stained underwear until the nurse—one I hadn't seen before, whom the others called Findley, shrugged and said, "Dr. Madison won't like that," and called to the other nurse to make a note in my file. I could not afford for the doctor to think poorly of me. I relented with gritted teeth.

I went with the others downstairs, to the room with the long tables I'd seen on my arrival. They and the benches flanking them were scarred, but there were pictures on the wall, framed paintings of peaceful land-scapes and placid waters. No one spoke. The silence was punctuated only by the clank of spoons on bowls of lumpy, tasteless oatmeal, and the shuffling of inmates being led in and out.

The bells rang again. Gould, who, besides her long face was skinny and pale, with ropy arms, took me to my examination. "Dr. Scopes for you today."

"Who's Dr. Scopes?"

"The assistant to the super." Then she offered a helpful "He likes for you to be nice."

My spirits rose at the thought of someone different. Someone who might understand. She took me to an office with only an examination table and sparsely filled bookshelves. Dr. Scopes was younger than Dr. Madison, bearded and handsome, with tired and compassionate blue eyes.

I sat on the edge of the table as he glanced over a folder. "May Kimble," he read, and then said, as if he'd asked the question thousands of times, "Can you tell me why you're here, Miss Kimble?"

How exactly did one *sound* sane? I drew myself up straight and answered him plainly. "The reason I was sent here are lies, Dr. Scopes."

He inhaled deeply. "I see."

The wrong thing, then. I tried again. "That is, my uncle believes I am mad, but I can assure you that is not the case. I have been wrongly accused of murder."

He scrawled something.

"I have an inheritance. I believe my uncle had me committed so that he might take it for himself."

"What has that to do with murder, Miss Kimble?"

"My aunt tried to warn me. I believe my uncle killed her for it." I spoke urgently, taking his questions as interest, an opportunity.

But Dr. Scopes's expression did not change; he only set the open folder on a nearby desk. His hands moved over my face, my jaw, brushed the bruises on my throat above my collar. When I flinched, he said, "Nurse Costa says that you got into a fight with another patient last night. Are these bruises from then?"

"I got into a—? It wasn't like that. Josie attacked me."

"For what reason?"

"She claimed I was in her bed."

"Why were you in her bed?"

"I wasn't in her bed. Or if I was, I didn't know it. I took the bed Mrs. Donaghan gave me."

"I also understand that you hit another patient earlier in the evening."

I stared at him in bewilderment, and then I remembered the girl picking at the trim on my coat. "She was trying to pull my coat apart."

"And the correct response was to hit her?"

"I—I wasn't thinking. I was distraught."

"As you were when you took the wrong bed?"

"I wasn't in the wrong bed."

"As distraught as you were when they had to forcibly remove you from your uncle's home?"

"You don't understand. They were . . . It was all a lie. All of it. I didn't touch my aunt. My uncle is trying to steal my money. If you would just listen to me—"

"Miss Kimble, you know none of that is true. Your uncle cares very much for you. He brought you to San Francisco, when you had nowhere else to go. Isn't that right?"

"Yes, but—"

"Even when there were rumors of insanity in your family. Your aunt was so afflicted. Your mother too, I understand."

"Mama was *not* afflicted," I insisted. "I don't know why everyone keeps saying that."

"I believe there was some long-ago incident? A—" Dr. Scopes glanced briefly at the open folder. "A dispute of some kind, where your mother's inappropriate behavior caused her fiancé to break their engagement? Your uncle says it was bad enough that her own family refused to have anything to do with her."

I did not know what to say to that. I didn't know the full story, only what was in my mother's letter, but I did not believe for one moment that my uncle was telling the complete truth. "I never saw any evidence that my mother was insane."

"But would you know it if you saw it?" Dr. Scopes asked. "Given your own tendencies toward inappropriate thoughts."

"I don't have inappropriate thoughts." I couldn't soften the edge of desperation in my voice. This was all going so wrong. "I don't know what you mean."

"No? Did you not just say to me that your uncle killed your aunt and accused you of murdering her so that he could steal your money? Your uncle, who wants only the best for you? Who has sent you to Blessington to guarantee you get the very best care?"

"He wants me out of the way," I tried.

"And what of your inappropriate thoughts about"—again, a glance at the folder—"Mr. Farge?"

My stomach lurched.

"He claims you followed him and urged him to immoral behavior. He says you pursued him at all hours, that you even skipped church to bedevil him."

"No." I could not make my voice louder than a whisper.

Dr. Scopes's expression softened. "You see, Miss Kimble? There are reasons you're at Blessington. But we cannot help you unless you try to remove these absurd fancies from your head."

How he turned everything. Even to my own ears I sounded a lunatic.

As I was led back to my bed, my panic grew with every step, as did the fear I had not yet truly let myself feel. But I was terrified now. Terrified of the doctors, of myself, of the way they made me question my thoughts. How long might it be before I began to believe them? How long before this mirage turned real? Once in the ward, I crept behind the curtains, pressing my face to the window so the chill might sear through my fogged brain. The only view was a hedge next to a brick wall. Numbly I stared at a bed of dead flowers between the hedge and the building.

"Come away from there, Kimble," Gould called.

I stepped into the chaos of the room and the noisomeness that the window had cleared for the briefest of moments. Josie rocked by the fireplace again. Millie spat repeatedly on the carpet. The dark-haired girl who'd torn at my coat watched me with a wide, unblinking stare that made my flesh crawl.

Nurse Costa was back at the door. She'd taken the button, the proof that my uncle had been with my aunt in her last moments. I was not foolish enough to believe it was proof of anything now. Only my uncle knew what it meant. Only he and I. But it was a reminder that I was not delusional, a reminder that what I'd seen was real, and without it, what might I start to believe about what had happened? What might I become? I'd seen how easily my thoughts and words could be twisted. I could trust no one. I had to have that button. The nurse would surely give it back to me if I asked nicely.

I stood before her.

She didn't look up from her cards. "Go back to your bed."

I didn't move.

She slapped a card down. "Are you deaf? I told you to go back to bed."

"I wanted to thank you for saving me from Josie."

Now she looked up. I saw no recognition in her eyes. "What?"

No doubt such things were frequent enough to forget.

"When she tried to strangle me."

The nurse returned to her game. "You're welcome. Go back to bed."

"I would like my button back please."

"What button?"

"The gold button you took from me. It was on the bed, remember? It was mine, but you took it."

"It's my job to take all possible weapons." She spoke it as a much-recited rule.

"How could it have been a weapon?"

"Why, it could've choked someone."

"I assure you I had no intention—"

"You could've shoved it down someone's throat. Or even your own."

"I would never do such a thing."

She set down the deck. "Go back to your bed."

I held my ground. Without that button, I might truly go insane. "I will. When you give me the button."

The bells rang. Stiff, staccato chimes, so loud it sounded as if the bell tower were right above our heads. The other women in the ward responded like animals in a zoo, on their feet, lining up at the door.

The look in Costa's eyes should have warned me. I should have gone to stand in that line. I should have forgotten about the button. Instead, I stayed put, and Costa called, "Gould! Miss Kimble here is asking for special treatment."

"Special treatment? No. I just want—"

"She's new, Costa," Gould said mildly as she came up beside me.

"Then it's better she learn quickly," Costa said with a sneer. "The filth that came out of her mouth! She needs a lesson."

"Maybe just a warning this time," Gould suggested.

"Are you questioning me?" Costa's dark eyes hardened. I felt the silent struggle between them, and then Costa's triumph when Gould looked away. "I thought not. Go on now. I'll send O'Rourke."

I was wary when Gould led me from the room, but I didn't yet know enough to be panicked. The other women filed downstairs. The gamy smell of boiled beef mixed with all the other scents of the place in a sickening mélange, and still my stomach growled with hunger.

"It's time for lunch, isn't it?" I asked.

"You'll get your meal." Gould's words were cloaked in a deep weariness.

She stopped before the door to the toilet. I said, "I don't need to use it, thank you."

She ignored me and pushed it open, escorting me inside. I gagged at the stench emanating from the wood, rotted in places around the toilets lining one wall. Porcelain sinks were corroded. Paper bits adhered to the floor. Something had splashed onto the walls and stained them. Someone had vomited recently and missed the toilet.

"I really do not need to use this," I insisted.

At the far side of the room, beneath the window, was a chair. I'd assumed it was for a nurse waiting for a patient, and so I was surprised when Gould pulled me over to it. "Sit down," she demanded.

The chair too was filthy and stained. "I'd rather not."

At that moment, the door opened again and Costa came inside with O'Rourke, who carried a tray.

"Go on to the dining room," Costa instructed Gould with a grim smile.

It was all I could do not to beg Gould to stay, especially when she gave me a quick, sympathetic glance. But she fled.

"Sit down," Costa snapped.

"No, I—"

She shoved me hard to the damp, slimy floor. I caught myself with my hands, and drew away in disgust. "Oh dear God. Is there a towel—"

Costa yanked me up by the hair. I cried out, and she twisted harder until tears blurred my eyes, until I had no choice but to sit into the chair, and then I saw the straps. Leather straps that she buckled around my throat and my breasts and my hips, my shins.

"I don't understand. What are you doing?"

Costa gestured to O'Rourke, who strapped the tray across the arm-rests. It held a hank of stringy boiled beef, a wedge of bread, a glass of water. There were no utensils. "Lunch time. Eat up."

I stared at them both in horror. My appetite died abruptly. "I'm not hungry."

"No?" Costa asked. "Not even a little bit of bread?" She tore off a piece and waved it before my mouth. Then, deliberately, she dropped it to the floor. "Oh, dear. Well." She picked it up. "Waste not, want not." She shoved it against my lips. I clenched my jaw. She shoved harder, grinding my lips against my teeth until I tasted blood. "Open up!" She sighed and gave O'Rourke a sorry shake of her head. "Shall I get the wedge?"

O'Rourke rolled her eyes and crossed her beefy arms over her chest, but she didn't argue, and I realized that whatever it was that had forced Gould to follow Costa's orders had struck the other nurse as well. She would not help me. Costa leaned over and grabbed my jaw, pinching until I could not resist. Tears streamed down my cheeks as she shoved that soiled bread into my mouth. When I spat it out again, she repeated it. Once, twice, a third time, until I could only swallow, and then she stood back in triumph.

"Eat it all," Costa commanded. "You'll stay here until you do."

"Don't bother throwing it to the floor," advised O'Rourke. "She'll only do it again."

I believed her. The bread lodged in my chest; I felt it as a diseased thing trying to claw its way back up, and the nurses had no sooner left me alone in that nauseatingly wretched room than I threw it up again, along with everything I'd eaten at breakfast, all over myself. It ran down my front, pooled in my lap. I tried to wipe it away with my already begrimed hands. I wanted the water, but when I drank it I only vomited again. The meat glistened in the half light, the bread mocked me.

A patient came in to use the toilet. She cocked her head like a dog at me, lifted her skirts, and when she was done, she came and grabbed the meat from my tray. She tore it apart with her bare hands, shoved half of it into her mouth and threw the other half back on my tray before she went away laughing.

I don't know how long I was there. The window darkened. The gaslight burned steadily and low. No one else came. No nurse to check on me. My bladder became full, then overfull, and I held it until I could not. The mess on my hands dried and stiffened. The bells rang out the schedule. I did not know what it was, what they meant. I gagged and cried and tugged at the straps and then I did nothing but sit and stare and moan in pure helplessness, and then, finally, I closed my eyes. I pretended I was not here. I was in a quiet room, my dining room of dark walls and pale floors. I pretended I was drawing.

Finally, O'Rourke peeked in. "What? Still not eating?"

"I'm sorry," I whispered. "I'm sorry. I'll be good."

She stood before me and crossed her arms over her apron. "Is that so? Why don't you show me then? Eat it, and I'll take you back to the ward."

I was desperate by then. The offer seemed a miracle. I reached for the bread.

She slapped it from my hands. It rolled across the floor, coming to rest against the base of a toilet. "The meat. I want you to eat the meat."

My stomach roiled. "I can't."

"Then I guess you'll stay." She turned to go.

"Why are you this way? No one can be so mean. Why do you let Nurse Costa tell you what to do?"

It was the wrong thing to say.

O'Rourke turned back. Again the crossed arms. Again the waiting. This time, her eyes were stony. Whatever compassion I might have seen in her before was gone.

The meat was cold and greasy and quivery in my soiled fingers. I pulled off a piece. The gristle caught; finally I had to tear it with my teeth. My gorge rose; I would not be able to swallow this, I knew I could not, and there was vomit and filth on my fingers and still I pressed it into my mouth—I could no longer see; I was crying, no, I was sobbing.

Nausea rushed so violently through me I could not get it past my lips. I vomited everything all over the tray, and O'Rourke watched me until I was dry heaving and then she bent until her face was even with mine. Only then did I see any hint of emotion in her eyes, though it wasn't sympathy. It was relief. Relief that it was over, that she'd done her job, that we could dispense with this.

"You going to be a good girl now, Kimble?"

I nodded fervently.

She unstrapped me, making a face the whole time, as if I were so disgusting she could not bear to touch me. Then she prodded me into the hall. By then the stench had permeated my skin, the inside of my nostrils. I thought I would never be rid of it. I shook as she led me, not to the ward again, but down the stairs, past others who stared at me as if I were a walking disease, to a room I hadn't seen before, lined with rubber-sheeted mattresses, some of which held women wrapped shroud-like in water-soaked sheets. Two men in raincoats and rubber boots sloshed pails of water over the women. There were three empty baths with limp and swollen leather straps. Coils of dripping hoses hung on the walls. The tiled floor was pocked with drains.

O'Rourke took me to a chair in an empty corner and called over one of the men. "She stinks."

My mind was gone; I was nowhere. I was no one. I scarcely knew what was happening when he uncoiled a hose, when he pointed the nozzle at me. I was completely unprepared for the force of freezing water that blasted me from the chair. Pain shot through my arm, my head hit the chair leg, but the chair was bolted to the floor and did not move, and then I was drowning, gasping for air through a gush of water, wishing I were dead.

When they took me back to the ward, I could no longer feel any part of myself. They gave me a draught of chloral, which went to work quickly on my cramping, empty stomach. O'Rourke said, "Be good now, Kimble," and I clutched those words as tightly as I could. *Be good. Be good.* Yes, I would be very, very good.

EIGHTEEN

I did whatever was asked of me without argument. The days ran into each other. The cursed light burned all night long, but sleep could not come soon enough for me, and I welcomed the chloral, though I did not take it in the daytime because I was too afraid. I saw what the bored lunatics did to the women in drugged stupors. Picking at their hair, slapping them in a game of *Who can slap them hard enough to make them shout?* The nurses standing guard were lazy and pretended to be oblivious, but they took notes constantly, and when they were roused from their inertia, they had heavy hands and many weapons at their disposal. Long fingernails, leather straps, slaps. The corners of the metal beds were sharp. All of us had bruises.

The nurses rotated shifts throughout the wards, and so we knew them all, and we knew who were the kinder ones. Gould, Findley. O'Rourke sometimes, though none of them could be relied upon when Costa was there. After the asylum matron, Mrs. Donaghan, Costa was next in charge. Her poison infected them all to one degree or another, but the attitudes of the nurses originated from a more base instinct. In their eyes, we'd lost our humanity along with our minds. Those of us who could not be cajoled, corralled, or otherwise controlled were seen as animals. Whatever compassion the nurses once had was stripped away by the sheer relentlessness of our insanity.

Only ten days ago, I'd been living in luxury. My sheets had been soft and scented. My clothes fine, perfectly fitted. The food of the best quality. But it had all been a lie. Everything financed in anticipation of my inheritance, which was no doubt in the hands of my relatives now. I wondered if they'd already replaced the things they'd sold—the hall mirror, the angel worshipped by all its little fawns. Was my money even now furnishing all those empty rooms? I tried not to think of it. It only made everything worse.

I fell into the schedule dictated by the relentless and despised asylum bells. Each time I met with Dr. Scopes or Dr. Madison, I tried to act completely sane, but the strain made me seem otherwise, and I knew the doctors saw that too. It seemed a conundrum without a solution. I tried to be polite and pleasant, to not constantly harp on my family's perfidy, because each time I did, the doctors only sighed and muttered variations of *You must put such thoughts from your head.* Each time, I believed the truth must matter. Each time, I left more desperate than before. Each time, my desperation threatened to drown me when they called a nurse to escort me back to the stinking ward.

Then, one morning at breakfast, Mrs. Donaghan, whom I hadn't seen since I arrived, came to where I huddled over the grayest oatmeal imaginable—I had no idea how they got it such a foul color. "It's a good day for you, Miss Kimble. You've been assigned."

"Assigned to what?" I asked.

"To your regular ward. Come with me."

I had thought the dormitory was my regular ward, but it was hard to imagine that any place could be worse, and so I did not argue. I followed Mrs. Donaghan up another flight of stairs to the third floor, another large room, but this time with only six beds. The nurse's table at the door was unoccupied. The room still smelled of unwashed bodies— mine included; I had not bathed since the horror with the hoses—but it wasn't so bad as the other. The curtains at the windows were open, allowing sunlight to spill across a scratched and worn wooden floor, illuminating dust and stray hairs. The view was still the brick wall, but here the top of the wall boasted a cast-iron railing with dark arrows pointing up to a gray sky. The hearth was guarded by a needlepointed fire screen of meticulously detailed pansies bursting with color. My hungry eyes devoured it.

The room was empty.

"Where is everyone?" I asked.

"This will be your bed." Mrs. Donaghan took me to one against the far wall.

I looked cautiously around. Unlike the other ward, here there were bits of personality. Above one bed was pinned a collage of calling cards, above another a woven heart bedecked with dried flowers. Each had a rag rug beside it. Books and magazines were stacked neatly on tables.

"The schedule will be a bit different here," Mrs. Donaghan informed me crisply. "Dr. Madison believes that some work will be beneficial to you."

"Work," I echoed, uncertain.

"It's quite an honor, you know. It shows that he trusts you to be a good girl."

I thought of what awaited me if I wasn't. "I am good."

Mrs. Donaghan smiled. "Now come with me."

I followed her downstairs, to the laundry room I had glimpsed on my arrival. When Mrs. Donaghan opened the door, clouds of choking carbolic steam boiled out. Inside were large kettles and wringers, sweating women stirring and lifting and ironing.

I am good, I told myself, and I kept saying it when Mrs. Donaghan introduced me to the head laundress, and told me I was to stay here in this hot, wet place with the sting of soap in my nose, red faced and watery eyed as all the others. The laundress looked me up and down and harrumphed. "You look strong enough, and it don't take much thinkin'."

She gave me a full-length apron and a kerchief to tie back my hair. Then she set me to shaking out sheets and pillowcases, undergarments, skirts, and nightgowns to hang for drying. It was mindless, and though my shoulders and my back soon began to ache, it was better than the boredom and fear of the ward.

Piles of filthy and stinking laundry rested at the far wall. All the clothes were tossed in the same pots, even those horribly soiled with urine and vomit and feces. The very dress I was wearing had been in those pots, my underwear, my stockings. Then they went to rinse, and after that they came to the wringers in wheeled baskets, which is when they came to me.

But here there was no need to watch for malicious madwomen, sudden pinches, a slap for no reason except that one looked slappable. I might have forgotten that these women working alongside me were mad, but for the fact that suddenly one of the women at the wash kettles plunged her bare arm into the boiling water. Her screams of pain and terror stopped us all in our tracks until two nurses hauled her away, and the head laundress shouted, "There's nothin' more to see! Back to work!"

It was like a contagion. Soon after, one of the women wringing clothes swooned. Another at the ironing boards began to mutter, and they moved her to folding clothes, away from heat and danger. I began to fear that madness spread through the steam, and if I breathed too deeply, it would gain hold. I tried to laugh at the fancy; it was becoming harder and harder to do, and I found myself taking the shallowest of breaths.

The best part of the job was the monotony of it. As I grew used to the job and the days passed, I allowed my mind to drift, to think of Goldie's glowing face, her inclusiveness, her confidences. My uncle's affection. I had wanted so to belong to them that even now I could not decide what had been true and what had only been lies meant to bind me more deeply. I tried to remember each moment, to gauge a sincerity I had no means of measuring. Had Blessington always been my fate, or had there been a moment when I might have said something or done something to change it?

That was the question that bedeviled me. *Was there anything I could have done?*

My new ward was different from the other in one major respect: here the inmates had learned to be docile. I went to the laundry each day and worked myself into exhaustion, then returned, eyes burning, hands chapped, to the ward. The window there was my salvation. From it I watched the groundskeeper work, and the women walk in the strip of lawn. Sometimes the women were accompanied by nurses and sometimes they were alone. I wondered why they were allowed there, and the rest of us were not.

"Who are they?" I asked my bed neighbor, matronly Elizabeth Kennedy.

"Those're from the First Ward." Mrs. Kennedy had been put into Blessington by her two sons after her daughter had been killed by an automobile. Or at least, that was the story. Mrs. Kennedy spent hours every day on her knees, muttering prayers. "They do whatever they like."

"How do they manage that?"

Mrs. Kennedy shrugged. "They're good."

How good did one have to be to gain that freedom? It took some time for the hierarchy of Blessington to make sense to me, but then I understood that—like society—there was something unspoken that put women into the first tier, and behavior was only part of it. First Ward women also got the best in the dining halls. Milk, when there was any. Eggs too—I could smell them from where I sat, and the longing for a shirred egg made my mouth water. Now and again, I spotted a carrot or some vegetable other than stewed cabbage on a plate. Money, perhaps? Was someone paying more for their upkeep?

No one seemed to know the answers, and I knew better than to ask the nurses or the doctors. I was focused on being good, and being good meant not asking questions of those in authority. Being good meant not seeming the least bit discontented.

It was not that easy, however. Boredom was my greatest enemy, and there was no outlet for it. I could not draw. Pencils were not allowed in the event that I might poke out my own or someone else's eyes. There was nothing else to do but worry and think and pick at the past until it seemed I really might go mad.

I lifted pillowcases and undergarments and shook them out, but I saw my aunt's face in clouds of steam, and I fantasized about what I would do when I put this place behind me, how I would take my revenge. I dreamed of burning down the house at Nob Hill, of those cupid-and-coat-of-arms-decorated pillars crumbling. I imagined beheading every one of those porcelain angels and sending their head-less corpses rolling down the marble stairs and into the crushed white stone of the drive. Some nights I rocked myself to sleep with visions of the Sullivans living on the streets in rags, begging for scraps, while I swept past imperiously and pretended not to know them. Other times, I imagined my uncle behind bars. I said nothing to the doctors of these fantasies, of course.

I stopped keeping track of time. Better not to know how it was passing. Better not to think of them spending more of my inheritance with every hour. Better to abide, to wait. If I was good enough, reason-able enough, they would see I was not insane, and they would have no choice but to let me go. The irony was that the only way to prove that I did not belong here was to do whatever I could to fit in. I set myself to that, and each day, when I saw the approving smiles and heard "That's a good girl, Miss Kimble," and realized they trusted me to behave, I knew I was getting closer. Soon, it had to be soon.

The sad Christmas decorations of limp sprigs of mistletoe and shedding pine boughs gave way to Valentine's Day hearts with crumpled lace and then to Easter chicks and cross-eyed cartoon rabbits before I finally understood the true extent of the Sullivans' treachery.

Dr. Madison listened to my lungs and heart with his stethoscope during one of the daily exams, then stepped away with a smile. "Very good, Miss Kimble. I must say I am impressed at how well you're getting along at Blessington. The nurses have all given you excellent reports."

I took a deep breath. I did not want to seem too eager. "I do feel much better."

He tapped my shoulder with a father's pride. "The atmosphere here favors you. You are blooming, as we hoped."

"Do you think I might be allowed to go home soon?" I was glad that he no longer had the stethoscope pressed to my chest, where he would hear how my heart raced.

"Do you not like it here?"

"Oh yes. It's only . . . patients do go home when they're well, don't they?"

"That's what you think you are? Well?"

"Am I not?" I smiled brightly at him.

"You are much better. But not, I think, fully cured. You may get dressed now."

I jumped from the examination table. "When do you think I might be? I mean, how long do you think it will be? As I'm making such progress."

He opened the curtains. Cold sunlight filtered into the room. Dr. Madison cleared his throat. "How long? Well, as to that, it's hard to say. The mind works at its own pace, Miss Kimble. It would be up to your guardian, I think."

"My guardian? What guardian? I'm of age. I don't need a guardian."

"Apparently the judge felt otherwise. Your uncle was appointed such."

My uncle. "When?"

"Now, Miss Kimble, no need to be upset—"

I struggled to calm myself. "I'm not upset, Doctor. I'd just like to know when, exactly, my uncle made himself my guardian."

"Why, I believe it was when you were brought to us."

It took a moment for that to sink in. When I was committed. My inheritance had become available, my aunt—my only champion—had been killed, and my uncle had been given power over my person and my money. *"Soon, the papers . . ."* Suddenly I understood something that I must already have known somewhere deep inside, had I allowed myself to think it. My uncle had planned this carefully. Truth had nothing to do with anything, the truth was whatever the Sullivans wished it to be, and I had been a fool not to understand their reach.

It didn't matter how good I was, or how sane I appeared. I was never getting out of Blessington.

NINETEEN

There was only one way for me to survive, and that was to be clever, to be smart. I must not surrender to despair. As in those weeks after Mama's death, before my aunt's letter had arrived, I had only myself to depend on. But this was not the same. I had an inheritance now, that is, I did if it hadn't all been spent. I had means. This time, I was not aimless and grief-stricken and afraid. I was furious.

One morning I woke to a strange bustle. The maids—many of them inmates too weak-minded to care about doing such menial chores, who usually moved with the languid placidity and dumb wonderment of cattle—were being prodded by excited nurses to work more quickly. The muffs and straitjackets and straps normally slung about the room were hung neatly, wooden wedges for the administering of medicine to clenched jaws were stacked, shelves made orderly, floors scrubbed. The windows were opened to let in a cool, wet breeze, banishing the perpetual effluvia that I had stopped noticing until it was gone.

"What's happening?" I asked Nurse Findley.

"Best if you keep to yourself, Kimble," she counseled.

The bells rang; we were taken to the dining room for the midday meal. When I entered the room, I was surprised to see a black-suited man and two women with notebooks standing against the wall, watching and noting. Dr. Madison was there as well, looking very serious.

"The commissioners," whispered blond Sarah Grimm—another inmate in my ward, in Blessington because she'd tried to kill her brother. She'd told me that the voices had ordered her to do it, but at Blessington the voices were quiet. She guessed there was no one here they wished for her to kill. A blessing, I supposed.

"What commissioners?" I whispered back.

"From the Lunacy Commission. They have to check on everything. If we don't pass we get shut down."

Prayers were said—this was usually skipped over. Everyone was clearly on their best behavior; when one woman began to sing a filthy song, a nurse soothed her kindly and removed her from the room instead of thwacking her on the back of the head. Usually the meat was of the cheapest cuts, the vegetables whatever hadn't sold at market, the broths watery, but today the soup was thick and hearty, and the butter was not rancid. But I was distracted by the commissioners, and what that meant. I had not known there was anyone to whom I could appeal, or anyone who supervised this terrible place beyond Dr. Madison. It was something to know that there was a higher power here. It seemed an opportunity.

It was the single time in my experience there that we were not urged to swallow our meal in haste. Finally we were given the signal to rise, and the maids swept in to clear the dishes away. Table by table, we stood for inspection; then, we were led to our various activities for the day, where we were treated like human beings for once as the commissioners made their tour.

I tried to think of ways to gain their attention, but the nurses watched us carefully; there was no chance, and then the commissioners were gone. Clearly, there were regulations that Blessington pretended to follow, and the money that could have made this place marginally pleasant was going somewhere else.

I was thinking hard about how I might use that information as we were led up the stairs to our wards. I heard the commotion on the next floor before I saw it. Footsteps racing down the hall, shouting. Nurse Gould saw us and called, "Findley, come here! We need you!"

Findley rushed over, forgetting to give us an order in her hurry. Several of the women rushed with her. I wanted to see what was happening, and so I went too.

The scene inside was appalling. Josie again, her red hair falling into her face as she strangled O'Rourke. O'Rourke tore at Josie's hair, but I remembered the woman's strength and my own throat constricted in response. The veins popped in O'Rourke's face and her eyes bulged. Gould grappled with Josie, but she could not be budged. O'Rourke flailed soundlessly. The other patients watched in fascinated horror.

It was not that I liked O'Rourke—in her way, she was the worst of them, since you never knew which O'Rourke you were going to get. But watching this was no pleasure. Gould tried again to pry Josie's hands loose. O'Rourke had gone bright red.

The patients, including those who'd come to watch with me, began to cheer.

Findley shouted, "Shut up! Shut up, the lot of you! You all standing there at the door—get back in line!"

One of the patients echoed, "Shut up, shut up, shut up," and the others took up the cry, a low and haunting chant. *Shut up shut up shut up.*

I could not stand it. I turned to go back, but before I got to the stairs, a door down the hall opened. Dr. Scopes came out, adjusting his suitcoat, running a hand through his hair to smooth it.

"Doctor! She's going to kill her. The nurse! You must go—" I motioned toward the room.

He frowned and broke into a run. In that moment before the door closed, I caught a glimpse of inside. A private room. A bed. And on that bed, Nurse Costa, pinning up her long, dark hair.

When O'Rourke appeared in the ward the next morning, she wore a necklace of bruises. The whites of her eyes were red, and the skin around them was black. She looked horrible and her voice was raspy and faint, and she was in a very bad temper. I stayed near the window and well out of her way, and when Costa came to relieve her, she was so solicitous toward the nurse that all I could see was her guilt, that mussed bed, and Dr. Scopes adjusting his jacket—and the two of them together while Josie's sinewy hands gripped O'Rourke's throat.

Mrs. Kennedy was on her knees already, offering up promises to God as surety for her daughter's ascension to heaven. "I will do only good works, my Lord. I will turn my sons' eyes to you. I will bend every woman here to service in your name. A church I will build, my Lord. I will perform whatever sacrifices you demand—" She choked, either on the words or on God's horror at her offer. Or perhaps it was just the cascara they gave her daily, because the choking turned into farting, and suddenly she was bent over, clutching her stomach, and a terrible smell wafted through the room.

"Oh God, she's shitting herself," Sarah moaned, burying her face in her pillow.

Mrs. Kennedy had collapsed onto the floor, groaning and gripping her stomach. Her nightgown dripped with diarrhea. Costa hurried over with O'Rourke, and I turned away. This wasn't the first time this had happened, not with Mrs. Kennedy nor with others, and I closed my eyes and resigned myself to the stink that would sicken the rest of us all through the night.

O'Rourke took Mrs. Kennedy away to bathe. One of the feeble-minded maids came in to "scrub" the floor. All she had was a cloth and a bucket of already gray water. She wiped in rhythmic circular motions for fifteen minutes, and ended up only creating a scrim of filth.

The poisonous stench lingered, choking. I pressed my face to the windowpane, wishing I could inhale fresh air through the glass.

"Come away from there, Kimble," said Costa from where she sat near the door, idly reading a magazine.

"I can't breathe," I complained.

"Everyone else is breathing just fine. Get into bed."

I glanced around. The others studiously avoided looking at me. I should have done as Costa said. No one else seemed to care. But I could not. Perhaps it was my disappointment over being unable to talk to the commissioners, or perhaps it was the brutality I witnessed every day. Or perhaps it was something else entirely. All I knew was that I hated Costa. I was tired of being stupid. I was tired of being used. I was tired of being a victim. I reached through the bars—a wide enough opening for my fingers only—to the window clasp.

"Kimble!"

I unlatched it. I heard the shush of Costa's skirts, the *clap clap clap* of her boots. I pushed the window open, and gulped the cold, damp air, and then I turned to face the nurse, who held a leather strap.

"Close that this instant!" she demanded.

"Why wasn't Dr. Scopes on his rounds yesterday?" I asked.

She stuttered to a stop. "What?"

"When O'Rourke was being nearly strangled to death. Where was he?"

Costa frowned. Her mean little dark eyes squinted.

"You don't know?" I lowered my voice. "I think you do. In fact, I know you do. I saw him coming out of the bedroom across the hall. I imagine the commissioners would like to know that, wouldn't they? O'Rourke might like to know it too, given that she was nearly killed."

Costa stared at me, but she was disconcerted, and I heard it even through her threat, which did not have its usual force. "You'd best watch yourself, Miss Kimble."

I smiled.

"No one will believe a word you say," she said quietly. "You're a lunatic."

"Maybe," I said. "Or maybe not."

It was a gamble. I was surprised when it worked, when she considered me briefly and then retreated to the table. She hung the strap on the hook and sat down, turning back to her magazine.

I took a deep breath of air and left the window open when I went to bed.

Be clever, I told myself. *Think like Goldie. Think like Uncle Jonny.* What had happened with Costa gave me confidence.

The next time I saw her, she raised her eyes warily, and I said, "I'd like my button back, please."

She said nothing, but the button was on my pillow within the hour. I squirreled it away; I kept it with me from that moment on, and my fortunes changed. I watched the way the head laundress, Mrs. Thompson, favored quiet, delicate, and somewhat stupid Cynthia Letterer, who toiled over the wringers until the laundress put her to the less onerous work of folding. I watched when Thompson pressed too close to Cynthia, when she ran her hand over Cynthia's hip, and then later took her into the supply closet.

Two days later, when Thompson asked me to take a turn on the wringers, I said casually, "I don't think so," and then, at her infuriated expression, "I wonder if Mrs. Letterer's husband would like to know how she's being handled by the laundress."

Again, I was surprised when it worked, and Thompson stepped away.

I spent hours at the window, watching the yard, and noted the special relationship one of the groundskeepers had with a young assistant. I watched them go surreptitiously behind a shrub near the wall, and then emerge later, both smiling. Some of the nurses liked the boy too, and some of the inmates—the women from the special First Ward—preferred another groundskeeper with blond hair and a winning smile. O'Rourke constantly and surreptitiously tucked things into her pockets. Findley bribed patients into behaving with sugar, which was strictly forbidden.

Now, suddenly, I understood that my revenge against the Sullivans would have nothing to do with burning down the house on Nob Hill or sending porcelain angels to hell. I understood that the power I held was far more destructive than that.

Secrets.

I knew then how I would destroy them if I ever got out of Blessington. I would give Dante LaRosa the information he wanted. I would tell him everything I knew. Then there was Shin, who could not only help me clear my name of murder and madness, but who also must be privy to other Sullivan confidences. I set it all out in an elegant list in my head: *What I Will Do, by May Kimble:*

1) *Prove that I did not kill my aunt*
2) *Take back my inheritance*
3) *Use the Sullivans' secrets to destroy them*
4) *Find out who my father is*

And the most important piece of all, the key to everything:

5) *Enlist Shin and Dante LaRosa to help me*

In the asylum I honed my skills. I prepared. I worked toward planning my revenge with a zeal and a talent that surprised me. But then, I'd been trained in treachery by the best.

And so I listened when Sarah Grimm's comments about Dr. Scopes became more and more descriptive. Not only did she let him undress her, but he had suckled her. He had put his fingers into her. She hoped for more. True? Not true? Oh, but the truth didn't matter, did it? When Dr. Scopes asked me to lift my skirts for an examination, I said, "I didn't know doctors were allowed to make love to their patients. Or to their nurses. When do the commissioners visit again? I think they'd like to know."

I noted how he grappled with my words. "You must not allow yourself to believe such delusions, Miss Kimble."

"Sarah has a love bite on her breast. Here." I pointed to a spot on my own. "I am not imagining that, I think. I might point it out to Nurse Costa. Do you think she would be angry?"

It was that gem that won me the private room. It was small and bare, but it was mine. The bed was bolted to the floor. The window was too high up to see through, the panes small and round and thick, but it let in the light, and when the sun drew reflections and patterns upon the floor, I would start at the reminder that there was still something beautiful in the world. Most importantly, the smells here were my own.

For weeks, I changed my circumstance in this fashion. Clothing was regularly donated to the asylum, I discovered. Most of it went to the nurses. I managed to win some things for myself, including a nearly new nightgown in soft pink. I began to be allowed into the room where the best-behaved women whiled away their hours reading or talking or playing games. From there, the grounds were not so hard to gain, and I was allowed an hour every day to walk the circular path through the grass, to glimpse the garden that visitors were told was for the use of the inmates, but which was kept for Mrs. Donaghan only. Sometimes I saw her out there, clipping or digging in the cool sun. I watched her exchanges with the favored groundskeeper, the bags and small packages tucked into her apron pockets. It took me weeks of watching to connect those packages to certain patients. Mrs. Donaghan was taking bribes to get patients forbidden items from outside the asylum.

And so I asked for a few hours alone in her garden. She was agreeable enough, rather easily persuaded, in fact. She even, bless her, got me the sketchbook and the pencils I requested, and so, for the first time since I'd set foot in this hell, I found myself at peace among a bounty of flowers, alone and surrounded by scents and the quiet buzzing of insects that drowned out the asylum noises beyond.

The day she brought me the sketchbook, I stared at the curling, pink-edged petals of a yellow rose and the urge to create surged as it always had, undiminished, blazing to life as if it had been waiting. I clutched the pencil and turned to the first page in the sketchbook and began to draw. The sheer relief of it made me want to cry. As long as I had this, I knew, I could bear anything. I could bear this place forever.

Yes, I could bear this.

The echo of my thought startled me. The weight of the future it contained frightened me more than anything else that had happened at Blessington. I looked up from the page, past the heavy rose bobbling now in the breeze. I had found a way to *be* here. I had found a way to survive, and that was the first step to acceptance.

But I did not want to accept this. I could not. My fear was too great that I might become complacent, one of the many women treading this endless circular path and finding it pleasant, commenting upon the good stew on the days the commissioners were here, reading and chatting and pretending this was all some society social hour with a hostess who made a truly terrible tea.

Belonging, just as I'd always wanted.

Not here. *Please don't let it be here.*

I stared at my hand clutching that pencil, awareness and regret chasing one another. I did not want to give up drawing, yet I knew what would happen if I did not. It would save me, just as it always had. It would make everything all right, but in the end, that would numb any necessity or desire I had to get out of this place. It would give the Sullivans exactly what they wanted. It would destroy me.

I scratched out the lines of the room I had begun to draw. I banished it from my memory. Then I tossed the pencil to the ground. I shoved the sketchbook beneath the bench, and even as my heart ached at releasing it, I wished for rain to soak it, to cover it in mildew and remove its temptation.

I would make my life bearable here, because I had to, but I would never accept it, and I vowed not to draw another thing until I was out of this place. One day, I would be free, and when that day came, I would do what I could to take back what was mine. I would make them pay for what they'd done to me.

In the meantime, I was the seed, biding its time, waiting for the soil to warm and soften, stretching my roots, reaching for the sun.

I did not expect the earth to move itself for me. But when it did, I was ready.

PART THREE:

RETRIBUTION

SAN FRANCISCO, APRIL 18, 1906

EARLY MORNING

TWENTY

I was already awake when the roar thundered from a sky blued with encroaching dawn, a howling from nowhere, from everywhere. I struggled to my elbows as the walls began to shake. The bed rocked as if it were desperately trying to escape the bolts anchoring it to the floor. A train—no, something—had hit the building, or no—what was this?

The floor rose and fell in disorienting, nauseating waves. The room bucked and jerked; I grabbed the sides of the bed to keep from being thrown. The ceiling split with a thunderous crack. I looked up, too stunned to be afraid, and someone's bare leg thrust through amid a rain of plaster dust. The building lurched, my stomach lurching with it, and the ceiling snapped shut again with a rumbling groan, severing the foot, which fell onto me with a hard thump, spurting a spray of wet into my face. Blood.

I screamed and lunged from the bed just as the floor upended and tossed me down. I dug my fingers into the floor, trying to claw into the wood, to anchor myself. The building twisted and moaned and shook me loose again. Nothing steady, nothing fixed. The disembodied foot danced across the floor as if it were alive. The thick round panes of my little window smashed, one after another, shards jumping and skittering. The ceiling rattled, plaster fell in chunks, raising choking clouds of dust. I was going to die. We were all going to die, and it was going to hurt. Terrified, I dragged myself beneath the bed.

Then the shaking stopped. Barely long enough to catch my breath, to think, *It's over*, to hear the screams and the wails coming from beyond the door, before it started again, more violently than before.

A terrible grinding filled my ears, vibrating into my skull, and then there was no more floor, nothing beneath at all, only a pitch into absence and darkness. I grabbed for something, anything, but I was falling and all I could think was *No. Please. Not now, after all this. Not yet.*

I don't know how long it was before I opened my eyes to dust and grit and gloom. I wasn't dead after all, but trapped. The foot, thankfully, had fallen into its own hell. The bottom of my bed was only a breath from my face; the heavy metal frame pinned me in place. I flexed my fingers, dislodging rubble, trying to pull loose, failing. I could not tell where I was in the world, or even if the world still existed. I could not even tell if I was hurt.

Sounds came to me in fractured bursts: muffled groaning, faraway sobbing, brick and stone crashing, someone shouting, "Watch out!" A horse screaming.

"Over here!" someone called from a distance.

I raised my hips. The bed did not budge. Trapped, yes. Buried alive. With growing panic I punched at the frame with my one free hand, and then again. Nothing.

"Help! I'm here! Help!" Desperate effort made me cough, and then I couldn't stop hacking—eyes watering, throat stinging, so much dust. When the spasms finally subsided, I twisted, or tried to. As if in response, the world trembled once more, the ruins shaking, a quiet roar now, but no less terrifying. I closed my eyes, once again expecting both pain and death. More stones cracked and broke and fell, brick and plaster and wood, a distant explosion, a panicked cry, but the earth was merciful this time, and it was just enough to unsettle the rubble, enough to free my other arm and shift the bedframe. I could ease from beneath it, but I couldn't get past the beam that had crushed it. No amount of prying or digging, no matter how frenzied, moved me an inch. The quiet was deadly. I could hardly breathe, my lungs full of dust, my nostrils and my mouth caked with it.

"Help!" I rasped again, breaking on a sob of frustration and fear. "Please! I'm here! Help!"

I heard someone vomiting, very close, and then a man called, "Did you hear something?"

I scrabbled more urgently. "Here! I'm right here!"

Now the crunch of footsteps settling debris, the scraping slide of things dragged aside. The crack of light widened, and then widened again, just as had the ceiling in my room. This time there was no foot punching through, but instead a man peering down, the sky behind him. The brightness blinded briefly before I made out his rough and craggy features.

"You all right, miss?" He looked over his shoulder, gesturing, calling, "Come here now! Hurry! I got a woman!"

Slowly, they managed to pull me free, and I was out of my tomb and into the morning. My head throbbed, my back and my hips ached. I coughed so violently and painfully I thought I might split my lungs.

I had no time even to thank them as another man called and they went hurrying off to help, one of them pausing only long enough to glance at my forehead and say, "You'd best find a doctor."

Gingerly, I touched my forehead. My fingers came away covered with blood. The severed foot, I thought, but no, this was my own blood trickling down my cheek. I choked on filthy mucus that I spat into the wreckage as I stumbled forward, my bare feet tender, gray with dust. The entire side of Blessington where my room had been had collapsed upon itself, four stories now only crushed brick, broken glass, twisted metal, splintered wood. The wall that had surrounded the asylum lay in pieces, the iron railing mangled. I stared at what was left. A half-formed building, exposed rooms, jagged bits of flooring and plaster hanging. Impossible to imagine that it had ever been anything to fear.

Everyone looked as I felt; we were like ghosts haunting the aftermath of a tragedy. A woman huddled in a blanket. A man in underwear and a tattered coat blinked as if he'd just awakened—one of the groundskeepers. The silence was eerie, a city gone mute when before it had sung joyfully with activity. The only human sounds were the grunts of the rescuers, the cries for help, others hacking and sneezing in the dust.

I expected someone to call out, *There you are, miss. Come now,* but no one spoke any such thing. It occurred to me then that no one was watching; there was no one to call me back. No one yet had grasped who I was. But at some point they would.

I pressed for the reassuring lump in the waistband of my drawers beneath my nightgown. Yes, there it was, secured in the pocket I'd forced into the seam. My uncle's vest button. What was left of my confusion vanished with the sharp reminder of my purpose. This was not how I'd imagined things to happen, but I was no longer the fool I'd been. I would not miss an opportunity when it presented itself. I had to get as far from Blessington as I could, as quickly as I could, as unobtrusively as I could.

A burst pipe spilled water into a gurgling course over loosened cobblestone, creating a sudden stream in the center of a city street. The water stung the cuts on my feet, but I did not rush my step, not yet, though I wished to run.

Once again, the earth beneath my feet shrugged. I steadied myself against sudden vertigo—no wall, nothing to grab on to. It was soon over, and other patients emerged from the rubble, injured and bleeding, one of them crying, "She's dead! I saw her die! Oh God, save us!" I did not slow to discover who was dead, because now attendants were coming to themselves, chasing after bewildered patients and tying them with sheets and straitjackets and leather belts to whatever secure thing they could find.

I ignored the pain of my injured feet and the gash in my forehead and kept walking, losing myself in the people massing in the streets, moving with them away from Blessington. Thankfully I was no longer wearing inmate gray, but my pink nightgown. Only a nurse or another patient would recognize me as belonging to the asylum, but that was enough. I didn't want to call attention to myself. *Do not look at me. Do not see me. I am no one.*

A ghost. Smoke and dust and shadow. Nothing substantial until I chose to be, and when I did, no one would ever underestimate me again.

TWENTY-ONE

I t was no longer a city I recognized. The street before me had cracked into great fissures running helter-skelter, the sidewalks bordering it broken into slabs like candy brittle. Rail tracks twisted. Horses lay dead in the streets, downed by falling walls or bricks. A woman stood crying before a house that had shifted off its foundation and tilted into the one next door. The exterior wall of another had crumbled away, leaving it exposed like a dollhouse, and the man inside rushed about picking up shattered dishes. The fronds of the palm in the yard below wore a chair and a crocheted throw.

Keep walking. Don't stop. I bowed my head against any curious glances, but everyone was too dazed to care who I was. No one would be looking for me yet. They would think me dead until they didn't find my body in the ruins.

Now, I was only one of hundreds of others coming into the morning, another woman wearing a pale nightgown, having awakened to a nightmare. All of us dazed, most half-clothed, or bizarrely dressed in bits and pieces grabbed in haste. One man had on a woman's skirt as he worked to free someone in the debris. Another wore a nightshirt and heavy work boots. Some still wore the gowns and evening wear that said they'd not yet been to bed. All staring in disbelief at the chaos, at streets frozen in mid undulation, their cobblestones popping, alleys blocked by rubble, houses that were only piles of matchsticks or sliding into sinkholes or with folded walls looking flimsy as paper. Windows shaken free of glass, leaning telegraph poles, and electric wires hanging loose or snaking and hissing and sparking on the ground. A church spire was only metal scaffolding. Grass on a hillside slid apart in great patches like pieces of carpet. My nose and lungs itched at the hovering cloud of dust and the increasingly pervasive stink of gas and oil.

People combed desperately through the rubble, tossing aside brick and stone and wood. The eerie silence continued, punctuated by cries for help and rumbling and crashing, now and then an explosion. Even the sobbing and the groaning had a muffled, strangely quiet aspect. People paced the ruins. "My husband is dead!" "Where is my daughter? Have you seen her?" "Anna! Anna! Where are you?" They spoke in low, quick voices, spooked by the silence. Horses stomped nervously and whinnied. Dogs slunk about, jumpy and cowering and snappish. Rats scampered in confusion.

It took me a long time to work my way through the jigsaw of wreckage. The morning advanced, the sun undisturbed, the relentless press of time unaffected. Blood from my forehead dripped down my cheek and onto my dusty shoulder, but I hardly felt the gash. I had been lucky. Dead bodies lay in the street where people had dragged them from the ruins. Here, a leg protruded from a pile of rubble. There, a man sat on a heap of brick, sobbing over a dead woman half-buried at his feet.

The ground shifted, wakeful still. More than one person screamed. I stopped, my heart pounding. The earth breathed beneath my filthy, bloody feet, turning in its sleep, no longer something I could trust. I walked quietly, lightly, careful not to disturb, flinching at every sound, pausing to wait for the reaction, the restless waking, the roar, then relieved again when it was only a shudder.

I passed a crowd gathered to watch smoke rise from the streets below. "Fire," said one man. I caught the eye of another driving a produce wagon, though I didn't mean to, and he frowned and stopped. He called, "You should be in the hospital. Get in. I'll take you."

It was then I noticed there were others in the wagon as well, all hurt. The wagon would put greater distance between me and the asylum more quickly, so I didn't protest, though I had no intention of going to any hospital—it was no place to hide—and who was to say one was still standing, anyway?

I climbed into the back, among baskets of carrots and cabbages and other wounded. It was only then I realized how much I hurt. The bottoms of my feet were shredded. I ached all over. The wagon slowed as the streets became mobbed with those escaping the city, people lugging personal treasures, framed pictures, carpetbags, men pulling playwagons loaded with children and possessions, hauling trunks that scraped and thudded relentlessly over the cobblestones. One woman had a parrot on her shoulder and carried a birdcage that held two kittens. A boy shuffled along holding a chromolithograph over his head. No one spoke, everyone was gray faced, and no one was running, but only walking in a steady, onward flow, and I had the sense that they too felt that the world was restless, that a wrong step could wake it again.

Soldiers—where had they come from so quickly?—were everywhere, directing digging men. The produce wagon stopped, and a soldier peered over the side at us.

"They need a hospital," said the produce man.

"Mechanics' Pavilion," the soldier said. "Hurry up now."

Mechanics' Pavilion. No, that could not be right. It wasn't a hospital. I had been there skating with Goldie. There would be people there I knew.

But that was another life. No one would be skating today.

The entrance of the Pavilion was cordoned off by police. Crowds pushed to get inside. One of the officers hauled me from the wagon and passed me to a nurse. I'd been off my feet long enough by then that they throbbed, no longer numb from shock and walking. They moved me and the others so quickly I had no time to argue or to thank the produce man, and he was gone.

Inside, the huge building was filled with people, men and women holding crying babies, children whining at their feet. Near the entrance were operating tables surrounded by doctors and nurses, all of them full. I had to turn away at the sight of a badly mangled woman held down by her husband as the doctor brought a bone saw to her leg.

The nurse hurried me past. Mattresses and cots and blankets crowded the floors. Damaged and destroyed hospitals had apparently rushed staff and supplies to whatever large buildings were still standing, but I was surprised at how quickly it had been organized, though honestly I was so shaken that my notion of time could not be counted upon.

It stank of blood and coffee and carbolic. Everywhere were people searching for someone. Thankfully, it was too chaotic for anyone to care who I was. A nurse directed me to a mattress, stitched up the gash on my forehead, and cleaned and bandaged my feet. The high, vaulted ceiling echoed with the buzz of talk and groaning and cries of pain. I stared up at it uneasily, remembering how Blessington had fallen upon me, discomforted by being again inside, twitchy. I would have fled if not for the fact that my feet hurt so much I didn't think I could. I was impatient now. It was time to begin putting my plans in motion.

Two men passed carrying a makeshift coffin of a wicker basket. They went behind the seats ringing the main floor; the Pavilion was serving as a morgue too. It wasn't until then that I wondered if the earthquake may have made my plans moot. Were the plans I'd spent so long scheming in the asylum only to be shiny, pretty useless things?

I had made them assuming nothing would have changed in the time I was gone. Who lay now in the morgue beyond? Was anyone I knew on those operating tables? Shin? LaRosa? Downtown was a shambles, what of Nob Hill? What of the Monkey Block? Had God given me my escape only to take away the reason I'd wanted it? Had he taken retribution for me?

I hoped not. I didn't want the Sullivans dead in the earthquake. I didn't want them dead at all. I wanted them to suffer, as I had suffered. An earthquake wasn't enough.

As if in answer to my thoughts, the building seized, the ground rumbled and rolled. The vaulted ceiling shook, wooden struts groaned. I stumbled to my feet, forgetting pain in panicked terror, and rushed to the door along with many others. Police gathered to block the way and push us back.

"Stay where you are!" a doctor shouted. "Do not move! Stay where you are!"

The shock eased, but everyone was jumpy. I limped back to the mattress. A nun brought coffee, blessedly hot, and bread. My forehead and my feet stung, and I was exhausted by panic and fear, but I knew I could not rest here. There were too many people; someone might recognize me, and while I knew I might not be thinking clearly, I believed I must find some place to hide until I could locate my allies—if they were still alive, and if they were still my allies. If they weren't alive, if they refused to help me . . . *No, I wouldn't consider that.*

I glanced at my poor bandaged feet and winced at the thought of walking, but I had no choice. First I needed shoes.

Then I heard something change within the cocoon of sound and motion all around me, a low and almost imperceptible rustle at first, then carried whispers, a rush of excitement, or panic, or both. Nurses and doctors and everyone who could lift a hand were pulling mattresses and carrying patients toward the rear entrance of the Pavilion.

Then the whispers formed voice. *Fire.*

Time to go. I hobbled toward the seats ringing the pavilion floor, toward the makeshift morgue. There were still people moving among the corpses, but the hurry now was for the living. I tried not to look at the mangled dead too closely, to feel nothing at the stilled children, the man missing an arm and a part of his skull, the woman who was only half there. I found a young man still wearing his boots. I unlaced them and took them off, ignoring his crushed shins and the blood matting his trousers. I shoved my feet into the boots, lacing them again as tightly as I could. They were too big, but the bandages on my feet helped, and they would do.

The rush to doors intensified; the panic of the crowd grew electric, and now I smelled the smoke. I took the man's coat from him, not noticing until I had it on that blood stained the back, but it was more decent than only my nightgown. Someone shouted, "Hurry!" and men came running now to carry out the dead.

There was no more time. I clomped in my heavy boots to where the others were herded out into waiting automobiles and ambulances and wagons and whatever could be corralled. Once I was outside, it was an easy matter to disappear again into the crowd and the pandemonium.

Across the street, the facade of city hall's elegant dome had peeled away, leaving only the metalwork structure. I stared at it in shock, remembering the awe with which my cousin had pointed out the pride of San Francisco and Sullivan Building. *"This is what Papa does,"* she'd said, grabbing my arm. *"Look at how lovely it is! Papa says it's what all buildings in the future will aspire to."*

It had been imposing, and beautiful. What had taken decades to build was now only a spectacular wreck of broken pillars and piles of powdery stone. The ground shook again to the accompaniment of screams and gasps. Another pillar from city hall toppled, smashing, spewing debris from its interior.

A steady exodus spilled from rising pillars of smoke. Most headed toward the waterfront and the ferry to Oakland, away from the city. Others stood watching the fire grow south of Market Street, where there were mostly poor shanties and ramshackle wooden buildings. Firefighters raced with their engines and muscled horses while others worked relentlessly, looking for survivors. Smoke grayed the air. A tangle of warped rails, fallen trolley poles, and drooping wires choked the streets. Posters from *Carmen*, which had apparently played at the Opera House last night, lay trampled and torn.

I was caught in the moving crowd, pressed on all sides, borne along without volition.

My feet hurt even with bandages and shoes. I stopped dead at a sudden, deafening blast, and a manhole cover shot fifty feet into the air, with it a fusillade of paving stones and dirt. The horse standing near shied, upsetting its cart, spilling kegs of wine, which ruptured and poured into the hole, so the stink of sewage mixed noxiously with the tang of wine.

"Get out of here!" shouted a soldier. "Go on! Over there!"

I went to where he directed me. Men scrambled over fallen walls, trying to pull survivors from the ruins in a cloud of smoke and heat. Screams from inside the rubble: "Help!" "Don't let me burn alive!" and "Please, get me out!" Rescuers swore and worked feverishly, then fell back as the boards caught in the intense heat and the screams that followed from those caught within—dear God, such a terrible sound, one that vibrated into my skull until the flames took it and it dissipated in smoke. I spun away, my eyes stinging. The cries were swallowed by the sound of sucking air and crackling boards and plaster and paper. The heat was stifling; cinders fell like rain, one burning its way into the wool of my jacket until I beat it away.

After that I walked without regard for my feet or the smoke or my throbbing head. The city was no longer mine but a place I didn't know. I had no idea where I was going, only that I must keep on, get away, stay hidden, find a place to rest, to think. I was mad with thirst; the next time I came across a broken water main, I knelt with others to drink. Though the water was dirty and tasted foul, it was water, and I was grateful for it.

Finally, I stopped at the edge of a large crowd filling a square surrounded with buildings. It took a moment before I saw something familiar in the piles of gathered trunks and bags and people sitting on the grass to watch the billowing gray smoke beyond as they might watch a fireworks program or a grand parade. The genteel grass lawns, the hedges and the benches, mobbed. The pillar with the statue Victory stretched into the sky, glinting in smoldering sunlight, the blocky white pedestal nearly hidden by the masses.

Union Square.

I remembered my uncle and his mistress walking that circled path. Goldie pulling me back behind the pedestal. *"Is she wearing any new jewelry? Can you see?"* So long ago. Hard to think it had been my life. Now the square felt entirely different, alien and yet oddly safe and companionable, as thronged as it was. We were all survivors of a disaster, and the wonder of it, the disbelief that it had happened, that it was still happening, was evident in the voices of those all around me as they recounted their stories of this morning.

"I was on my way home from the night watch and the road just rose up under me. Thought I was drunk at first, but I hadn't had a drop. Not a drop."

"I got up to start the stove and I heard this terrible sound and then the stove jumped like it'd come alive."

"The pigeons would not quiet. Did you notice that? They would not quiet. I wonder if they knew?"

"I thought it was a train off the tracks—"

"—a tornado—"

"—I never heard a sound like that."

On and on, people repeating themselves with fervor, as if repetition might make it more real. I was exhausted. There were more explosions, someone said they were setting off dynamite to stop the fires. It only added to the nightmarishness. The sun lowered, turning the sky a weird greasy orange, and the smell was sickly and hot and sweetly cloying. A death smell. A roasting smell. When I remembered what must be roasting, I wanted to be sick.

Some of the people in the square had army tents. A relief wagon at the edge of the square offered soup and water. I had not been hungry, especially now, with the smell, though I was still thirsty. But there were so many people. Someone might recognize me.

I could not bring myself to care just then. I got some water and collapsed in the grass like the others, and there I slept until the wee hours of the night, when the St. Francis Hotel and the other buildings around Union Square caught fire, and we were ordered to flee into streets, where the pavement was so hot the cobbles popped. Shattered glass and brick flew from all sides. My lungs burned. My ears rang with gunshots, explosions, and a hundred different shatterings and rumblings and crashings, and the roaring, gasping suck of the fire-fueled wind, and all there was to do was keep going through the restless night, moving blind and purposeless into the weird, dusky copper darkness, until finally I was on a street too quiet to be alive. I was so tired and bleary I could no longer feel any part of myself, and I had no idea where I was.

The throbbing pulse of the city had stilled. Shadows huddled in corners, men and women and children sleeping, or trying to. Now and again a scampering rat. A group of people wrapped in blankets and carpets slept on the sidewalk before a house that dipped and sagged. A rosebush twined about its porch, and how red those roses glowed in the strange bronze light. I'd never seen such a vibrant color. It did not look real. I was mesmerized by them, such beauty in the desolation, such an otherworldly hue.

I stared at them for a long time.

TWENTY-TWO

O n your feet!"
I jerked awake to the shout and a sharp jab in my shoulder.

A soldier, young and angry, with another very tired-looking soldier behind him, prodded me again with the bayonet fixed at the end of his rifle. "I said, get up!"

I stared at him, disoriented. There had been no bells to wake me, I was not in Blessington, there were no roses; all these things came to me before I remembered, though I had no idea really where I was. An alcove of some kind, slumped in a filthy corner that stank of old beer.

Slowly, I rose.

He gestured with the rifle to a broken window. The still intact part read **SHOEMAC**. "All saloons are closed. Liquor is forbidden. Looters are to be shot on sight."

"I wasn't looting anything," I protested. "I didn't know this was a saloon."

"How'd the window get broken?"

"The earthquake? I don't know. I was only sleeping—"

He backed away, aimed his rifle at my chest, and said, "Empty your pockets."

I resisted the urge to feel for the gold button. "I was only sleeping," I protested again. A shouted, "Hold! No looting!" came from across the street. The soldier training his gun on me jumped, the other turned to look.

"I said hold!" Again, the shout across the street. Another shout, and a shot shattered the quiet.

I cried out, but I wasn't hurt, the shot wasn't for me, not from my soldier's gun. By the time it registered, the two questioning me had run to their comrade and the man who'd been looting, now lying sprawled and lifeless. People ran, more shots rang out, the soldiers, everyone, panicking.

I too ran. Someone shouted behind me; I braced myself for a shot that didn't come, and didn't relax until I'd turned the corner, but even then I hurried on, my feet aching, my heart racing.

The city was misery and ruin. Groups gathered in the middle of streets, sitting around stoves that had been dragged from houses, or makeshift ones made of brick and metal. The yellow-gray pall of smoke made it hard to see anything past a half block, and the fires still raged. *Find Shin. Find Dante LaRosa.* Yes, but how exactly was I to do that in this chaos? I needed someplace safe to sit and think and plan my next steps.

Explosions from dynamite shuddered the air, the crashing of walls its accompanying thunder. When I came upon a bread line, I waited, too hungry and thirsty now to care if I met someone I knew. I must look like everyone else anyway—dust covered, filthy, unrecognizable. After two hours of standing, drinking hot coffee and water passed out by a man making his way down the line, I took the box they offered, and then hurried off alone to eat whatever was inside.

I found a place behind a pile of rubble, and sat on the tumbled brick near a fallen chimney. The afternoon was advanced by then, the day grimy and unseasonably hot, or maybe it was just the heat of the fires. Soot and ash and dirt itched, and the wool coat was now far too warm, but I kept it on as protection against hot cinders and wind-spun sparks. Nearby, a man sat on the curb of a broken sidewalk, reading a newspaper as if it were perfectly normal to be doing such a thing in the middle of devastation. I could see the headline from where I sat: Earthquake and Fire: San Francisco in Ruins.

Well, I hardly needed a newspaper to tell me that, but I wondered where he'd got it and where I could find one myself. I was hungry for news, for something to show me how to proceed. The man folded the paper again and stood, caught sight of me watching, and before I could look away, came over and handed it to me. "I'm finished."

I took it eagerly. The newspaper was a combined effort of the *Examiner* and the *Call* and the *Chronicle*.

But not the *Bulletin*. Why not? What had happened to it? Where was Dante?

No Hope Left for Safety of Any Buildings.

Whole City Is Ablaze.

At Least 500 Are Dead.

Who was dead? Which of those five hundred were those I knew?

I was so lost in my questions that I didn't notice the man who stood in front of me until his shadow crossed the page. He was as grimy as I was, wearing a ratty gray sweater and sagging trousers.

"Hello?" I said politely.

"I'll take that," he said.

"Oh, but I'm still reading it—"

"Not that." He gestured to the box I'd been given in the bread line. "That."

At first I was confused. "The line is right over there. They're giving it away for free. All you have to do is wait."

"Now why should I do that, when you've done it for me?" A quick flex of his fingers. "Hand it over."

I did not know how to make it more clear. Again, I tried to explain. "No, no, really. You needn't steal it. They're giving them away to everyone—"

The knife was in his hand before I could blink. "Give it to me."

I should hand the box over. I could stand in the line again. It was only time, and what else had I to do? I could explain it to them if they recognized me. *Just give it to him.*

But I was tired and hot and hungry. I had escaped an asylum, being buried alive, and fire, and suddenly I was angry. Brutally, furiously, inescapably angry that anyone might try to take advantage of me again.

Before I had a chance to think, to even know what I was doing, I kicked, connecting with his knee. He let out a grunt of surprise and went down, and I hurled myself at him, kicking him again in his crotch. He screamed and curled up, clutching himself. The knife clattered to the ground. I kicked it away. It slid beneath a pile of nearby rubble.

"Go stand in the goddamned line like everyone else," I snarled as I picked up the newspaper and the relief box and walked away.

I had perhaps terribly injured a man for a box of Postum and a few slices of bread. I could not bring myself to feel bad about it, or even anything but awed at the way sheer rage had taken over. Perhaps it had been stupid; he could just as easily have turned on me. I shoved the dry cereal into my mouth. Nothing was as it should be now, the world upended.

I tried to squint through the smoke, to see something beyond the ghostly masts of telephone poles or looming shadows of crumbling buildings, but I could not. Impossible to tell where the fire was, whether Nob Hill had survived, or if, even now, my relatives sat in their garden among my uncle's angels, drinking champagne and watching the city burn. Had they replaced that gilded mirror with my money, and was it even now shattered into a thousand pieces? Impossible to know if the mansion there had survived the earthquake, or if any of them had, if any of the things and people I'd known still existed, and what I should do if they didn't—or even what I should do if they did. *Think.*

All around me, people went about their business, women talking and visiting, men looking restless and ill at ease, as if they'd no idea what to do with themselves. The smoke, the explosions, and the damage made nothing normal, but the thing was not yet at an end, either, and so there was no way to go on into the future because who knew what the future would be? We were all suspended. A holiday that wasn't a holiday, but uncomfortable and anxious, with dread in every look and word and gesture.

I moved as everyone moved, with no other direction but away from the encroaching fire. At night I lay awake, staring at the simmering bronze-black sky edged with sickly green. The glowing clouds above split to show a glimpse of starry sky, orange against a dazzled greenish black, and it was so beautiful and terrible that for a moment I could not breathe for the sheer majesty of it. Strange, that destruction should hold its own kind of splendor. It nudged something in me, long dormant, but I was exhausted and everything in me said to ignore it and to rest, and I could not remember the last time I'd done that, or if I had, it was in another time entirely, and perhaps this truly was all a dream, and when I woke I would still be in Blessington, waiting for the bells to ring in the dawn.

Three days of this, of booming all night long, of waking to a sun barely visible through the pall of smoke, which pulsed a sickly pink and then a ghastly purplish red and then gray yellow. When the sun did break through—not often—it was a bright red disk.

Chinatown on fire. North Beach. The concussion of explosions wracked the air. When buildings did appear through gaps in the smoke, their windows were lurid like the eyes and leering mouths of jack-o'-lanterns, glowing from the inside until they burst into flame and then nothing. I sat with others on the slopes of Telegraph Hill, among the shanties and homes built nearly one on top of the other. Men kept kegs of wine ready to dump over their roofs to douse any embers, along with rugs to soak in wine to protect their walls. Refugees had made shelters of blankets and lean-tos out of trunks and whatever could be found. The wind picked up, sending plucked feathers, bits of paper and trash, more cinders and sparking bits of debris that people stamped out wherever they fell, and again came that raging, sucking sound, a howl like a storm. The air was muggy and hot and heavy but not still, a swirling, scorching wind, sometimes strong enough to knock people back. My lungs burned with the effort of breathing it. My eyes watered and stung.

The flames took hours to burn themselves out. Nothing could be seen but for roiling clouds and the red advance of fire. The residual heat from the coals rose. Like sitting at the edge of Vesuvius must have felt, I thought. Heat and wind and poisonous smoke.

We watched the destruction as if it were an entertainment. Someone began to sing an aria, sad and mournful, an elegy, and people all around quieted to listen. If I'd been told that I was witnessing the end of the world, I would have believed it.

Then it began to rain.

The morning brought with it a scene of such destruction that it was hard to fathom. Nothing but wasteland spreading below, blackened streets where soot and ash had become greasy mud, everything smelling of smoke and rain and sewage, a tannic, noxious mix. Gray and cold except where the still smoldering embers cast a stinking fog over the ruins.

But it was, at last, over. The fires were done, leaving behind a smoking, gasping wreck. I was wet through and through and shivering as I made my way to the nearest soup kitchen set up in the middle of the street, where they gave me hot coffee and porridge. The woman looked me up and down with such sympathy that I wanted to cry. "Are you alone, dearie?"

I nodded.

"Have you a place to stay?"

"Not yet," I told her.

"They're setting up relief camps everywhere. They'll have clothes for you, and supplies. Someone to check that bandage for you. You'll look for one, won't you?"

I said I would, and took my meal to a counter they'd set up, where people stood and ate quickly so others could take their places. I kept my head down. It was over, yes, which meant that soon the chaos would give way to authority, and authorities would be asking names and trying to determine where someone belonged, and people who had left would be returning to see to their property. The city would go on. The question was, Where would I be within it?

I did not have to continue with the plans I'd made. I had only this bloodied wool coat and nightgown, my button and these boots with their melted soles. I could do as that woman at the soup kitchen had suggested. Find a camp. Get a tent, some clothes, some food. I could hope that Blessington had burned to the ground, obliterating all those corpses, or those who had been buried, like me, in the debris—I shuddered, thinking of those screaming as the flames took them—and that everyone believed me dead and that no one was looking for me. Change my name, leave the city, become someone else and start my life over again.

But the thought of letting the Sullivans get away with their schemes, of letting them muddy my name with murder and madness, spend my money and cheat me as my aunt had once cheated my mother by selling the family home and spreading rumors that caused my father to leave her . . . No, I could not do it. I could not do it and live with myself. My mother had believed in the ultimate goodness of my father, and in the end, she had hoped that my aunt would repent and help me. Perhaps Aunt Florence had done that; I wanted to believe she had. But I was not going to waste my life suffering as my mother had done, and trust that somehow, some way, the world might right itself. The Sullivans had tried to destroy me.

I was going to take the fact that I was still alive, despite false accusations and Blessington and earthquake and fire, to mean that the world wanted my help in meting out justice.

The best plans I had for that were the ones I'd made in Blessington. But where were Dante LaRosa and Shin now? The *Bulletin* building on Kearny Street was in pieces. My original plan had been to find Shin first because she knew what had really happened that night, and she could clear my name. I knew from the newspaper that most of the Chinese were in a relief camp at Hunters Point. It was as good a place to search for Shin as any, but it was too far away; there were no cable cars now to take me anywhere, no bicycles, and too many military lines to cross. Yet I had to get there somehow.

Until the ruins cooled, no one was allowed back into the city without a pass, not even to examine their own property. The streets were full of militia and police and exhausted firemen sleeping off their exertion in the drizzling rain. Men walking were commandeered to help clear the streets. The city was a stranger. No clang of cable cars and calls of peddlers and newsboys. Instead the slow thud of carts and wagons and now and again the horn of an automobile speeding off with supplies. The crash of rubble and trash tossed aside or thrown into wagons. No birds but for crows picking among the ruins beside the rats, and pet canaries and parakeets and cockatiels that had been loosed from their cages to escape the fires, dashing bits of color flitting confusedly about the telephone poles and lighting upon the sagging network of tangled wires dangling to the street.

Every saloon had been closed. The selling of liquor was forbidden. Broadsheets bearing proclamations by Mayor Schmitz were posted everywhere, promising no risk of famine and asking citizens to comply with regulations. There was to be no lighting of fires in houses or fireplaces. Water was scarce; what there was must be boiled and should not be used for anything but cooking and drinking. Looters would be shot, as would anyone caught entering a deserted building.

The city had become as dangerous as the asylum. Men crawled through the wreckage, looking for valuables. I slept with my hand curled around the gold button. As many soldiers as there were, they could not be everywhere, and at night there was little keeping the denizens of Barbary Coast to their usual haunts, nothing preventing anyone from taking what they wanted. I found a twisted bit of metal about as long as a dagger amid the debris and tucked it into my coat pocket for a weapon. The next thing to do was to find different clothes. Many San Franciscans had left their homes with only what they wore, and so when Relief began handing out clothing and shoes, I wasn't the only one standing in line.

When I reached the front, the woman glanced me over and picked up a skirt from a rapidly dwindling pile. "You're so tall. This will be short on you, but—"

"What about those?" I asked, pointing to the trousers, the men's clothes.

She didn't argue. There was so little to choose from, and the supply of men's clothing was greater. She handed me a pair of trousers, a shirt, a pair of boots and some thick socks, as well as a woman's combination, and I was grateful for all of it, especially because the clothes were the perfect disguise, and more comfortable than anything I'd ever before worn.

I threw out the ruined boots with the melted soles. I transferred my uncle's vest button—my good luck charm, my talisman—into my trouser pocket. I kept the coat. Someday I might find the water to wash out the bloodstains, and it was well made and thick. But the nightgown and underwear I took to a man standing over a fire in a half-destroyed, blackened ash can and asked him to burn them for me.

I chose a man because I knew he would not question why I would destroy perfectly good clothing, and I was right; he didn't. I walked away before he could catch a whiff of the stink that would undoubtedly rise from the burning rags.

I felt safer dressed as a man, though no one mistook me for one, at least not after an initial glance. My walk, perhaps, or maybe my face was too feminine to hide. I wished otherwise; it might have been easier if they had, because joining a cleanup crew could buy a man a pass, and without a pass, it was impossible to move about the city.

During the day, I scouted the location of the soldiers, then, when twilight came, with its smoky greenish light, I set out. It was easy enough to hide behind the twisted ruins, to take advantage of the lack of streetlamps. At night, I managed to travel farther; I avoided soldiers and police and took on what I imagined was a confident walk, quite different than what I felt, because I was well aware of how many in the shadows had bad intentions, and as a woman alone, I was vulnerable. In the dark it was easier to be mistaken for a man. I kept my hand on my twisted bit of metal. But most only glanced at me without inter-est, their faces ghoulishly illuminated from the glow of ash can fires or street-improvised cookstoves.

I'd grown used to the hot, smoky, sickly stink of the city, a smell that had not belonged to it before. I'd grown used to the bodies laid out in makeshift morgues set up in vacant lots. In certain places, the sounds of gravediggers' shoveling was constant, impossible to distinguish from the digging of those shoveling wreckage, which often contained human remains.

I turned a corner to see a horse waiting while a man knelt over the body of a woman lying in the street. Another scavenger. It was too common a sight now to raise any distress. But a horse . . . a way to get quickly to the relief camp at Hunters Point, and hopefully to Shin. *A horse.*

The old May would never have risked it. But I was no longer the old May, and I no longer cared for anything except what I needed. Just now, it was that horse. The woman on the ground was dead and beyond helping anyway. I didn't know if the man had been the one to kill her. He worked over her quickly, yanking rings from her fingers, bracelets from her wrists. When he reached for her hatpin, I pulled the metal rod from my pocket and hoped that he could not see clearly in the dark. Then I cleared my throat, lowered my voice, and said, "Looting's against the law. Did you kill her too?"

The man jerked and swung around to face me. "Who are you?"

My mouth was dry from nerves, and it roughened my words perfectly. "Get away from her. Go on. Give me the horse, and I won't call the militia."

He was on his feet.

"They'll shoot without asking questions. Don't think those rings will help you then." I waved the metal at him and hoped he wouldn't call my bluff, because I wouldn't call for a soldier or a policeman even to save my life. I could not risk being found. "I'll tell him you killed her too. Go on. Get out of here."

He raced off. The rings and the bracelets were undoubtedly worth more than the horse. I stepped over to the woman. She was indeed dead, but someone else would come upon her soon, and the last thing I wanted was anything to do with the authorities.

The horse was half-starved and swaybacked and too weary to give me any trouble when I mounted it, which was good, because my experience was limited to a neighbor's cart horse that I'd played upon, surreptitiously, as a girl. At a nudge, it plodded on down the street. I might get to the Chinese relief camp before morning with the horse, and my healing feet were grateful for the respite. But I'd only been on the animal's back for a quarter hour, maybe less, when someone called out, "Halt!"

The problem with riding was that one could not really hide in shadows or burrow about like a rat.

One of the militiamen came from a doorway where I hadn't seen him. "You there! Where'd you get that horse?"

"It's mine," I said.

"We need him for cleanup work," he told me. "I'm requisitioning him in the name of the US Army."

Desperation made me momentarily stupid. I opened my mouth to argue with him. I considered spurring the horse to a run. But I wasn't certain it could run, or would, and the soldier fingered his gun as if he knew I might try, and in the end, I dismounted and handed him the reins.

"Wait a minute." He stepped back to grab something, which he threw to me. I caught it clumsily. It was a tin, but in the darkness I couldn't see what it contained. "Enjoy. Now get back to where you came from, before I arrest you for not having a pass."

I tucked the tin into my pocket and walked until I found a pile of bricks to lean against, and went to sleep, given that my plan to get to the relief camp was not happening—not tonight, and not in the near future. It was too difficult. My plan would have to wait. I wanted to cry with frustration. But one good thing came from it. When I woke, I discovered that the soldier had given me a tin of tobacco, which was nearly as good as gold.

I traded some of the tobacco to an Italian man for two cans of peaches, a loaf of bread, a bottle of wine, and a sausage. I gave the wine to a doctor who cleaned my stitches and rewrapped my feet. I gave the peaches to a woman in trade for coffee and a blanket. I ate half the sausage and the bread and traded the rest for cans of tomatoes, which I traded again. It was a simple truth that someone always wanted whatever you had, and in this way, I survived until they relaxed military restrictions in the city, five days later.

TWENTY-THREE

Restrictions were no sooner loosened than San Francisco filled with people, not only those with property or business in town, but tourists from unburned parts of the city or from Oakland or other areas, drawn by disaster like flies to a corpse. They were everywhere, gawking. They hired opportunistic guides to fill their ears with details, the more grisly the better. They bought mementos of burned bits and shattered relics. In such a circus, rumors mushroomed, sometimes spored by nothing more than a casual question or supposition, so I didn't know if it was true when I heard that they had set up a relief camp at Nob Hill for those rebuilding. I still did not know if any of my relatives were alive. But if they were, and there was a relief camp on Nob Hill, it was where they would be. That house had been the showcase of their wealth. They would not abandon it, even in ruins.

I went in search of a newspaper to find the truth. They were all free, at least for now, and when I saw a copy of the *Bulletin* for the first time since the disaster, I was almost embarrassed at the extent of my excitement. I didn't know if he was still there, I told myself as I looked for the society page—who knew if there would even be a society page? I drifted over ads for the stores on Fillmore that had not been touched by the fire, and those that had temporarily moved to new locations, and announcements of shipments due in a few weeks. When I saw the column, I was half-afraid to see if it was still his.

The Rich Are Just Like Us!

The latest disaster has made all classes equal. The rich have no more than the poor, and stagger about the relief camp on Nob Hill in filthy boots and stinking clothes like the veriest beggar on the street, most of them clad by today's most popular of designers, the Red Cross.

Mrs. James Sheldon wears overalls and a flannel shirt, and Miss Bessie Osmoss treads through the mud to the soup kitchen where today's banquet consists of canned soup and Postum, and the decorations are stockings and unmentionables hanging on the many laundry lines stretched from tent post to tent post. After dinner, instead of dancing, the best of San Francisco society sit around campfires like their hallowed grandfathers, who pried from the earth the fortunes that built their houses, which are now only piles of rubble. The earth giveth, and the earth taketh away . . .

While some toil at cleaning up the city, others toil at love. The city reports an astonishing rise in the application for marriage licenses, and one cannot turn a corner without stumbling upon a new engagement announcement. Disaster is the best aphrodisiac! Some are so anxious to tie the knot that they will not be waiting for churches to be rebuilt, as they fear it will take longer than nine months . . .

The writer was indeed Alphonse Bandersnitch, though I would have known it even without his byline. I recognized his style, his sarcasm. He was still alive. Until that moment, I didn't know how afraid I'd been that it was otherwise. I thought of him sitting beside me that first time at Coppa's, smoking his cigarette, his dark eyes that seemed to miss nothing as he took me in. *"You're no coward, Miss Kimble."* And then, later at the Anderson soiree. *"I find you puzzling . . . Nothing about you makes sense, unless . . ."* He'd never finished the sentence. I'd never known what he meant. Now I wondered if Dante LaRosa had suspected that I was caught in the Sullivan game not as a player but as a victim.

But perhaps that was wishful thinking. *Be clever,* I reminded myself. I did not know yet whether Dante LaRosa was a friend, and first there was the camp on Nob Hill.

It would be dangerous for me to go there; I knew that. Goldie would recognize me in any garb. But Shin had been with the Sullivans when I'd seen her last. Could she be there still? Surely it was worth a visit to see.

Truthfully, Shin was as much an excuse to go as a reason. I wanted to see the people who had destroyed me. I wanted to revel in their suffering. I needed Shin, yes, but what were the chances that she would still be working for them now, after all this?

A visit to Nob Hill, and then . . . Dante LaRosa, whether or not I found Shin. My plans put into motion at last. Excitement, anticipation, and fear powered my steps as I made my way to my old neighborhood. The landscape was wind- and fog-swept, black, here and there a copse of singed trees and hedges that had somehow eluded the fire. But the mostly destroyed world showed signs of regrowth among the relief lines and soup kitchens and ramshackle huts erected wherever there was space. Signs of burned wood read RESTRANT or HOT COFFEE AND SANWICHES, DONUTS—obviously no one cared much about spelling— and one said, BROWN'S CAFÉ: CHEER UP! HAVE A CUP OF COFFEE AND REST. WE ARE IN THIS TOGETHER. Work crews labored, soldiers shouted orders, and exhausted and starved-looking horses dragged wagons piled high with refuse or building supplies.

The most direct way to Nob Hill was through Chinatown. It had been strictly forbidden to go there until now, so I hadn't explored it, and I was surprised at its condition. It looked as if it hadn't been touched by work crews. The streets were so filled with wreckage that I had to pick my way through. Pools of stagnant water filthy with silt and ash created perilous potholes. It stank, too, and not of its usual fragrant mixture of fish and incense and sandalwood, but of rot and corruption—bodies still in the debris.

Also, there were few Chinese there. I didn't know whether they had not been allowed back into the city, or whether they'd decided not to come, but the people crowding and digging through the detritus did not look as if they belonged there. Women in shirtwaists and skirts and some in their Sunday best, hatted and cloaked. Men in suits. I was surrounded by white men and women, many who looked to be the kind of people I might have known in society. It was not safe for me to be here.

I drew back as much as I could into the crowds, trying to decipher what I saw. I thought at first they were digging for bodies. But then I realized they were pillaging. People attacked the piles with shovels and rakes. They were too busy to look at or notice me, too focused on digging. Every block was the same. Everyone furiously shoveling and picking while armed guards looked on, now and again calling out things like, "Try over there! No one's been at that yet!"

The few Chinese who wandered through the streets looked helpless and dazed. Some stood to watch those brazenly looting what had been their homes and businesses. People carried off sacks and baskets of melted bronze and chinaware, and no one stopped them. Only a few days ago, such looters would have been shot.

One young woman scrabbled through a mound, tossing aside bits of rubbish. Her skirt was filthy with soot and ash halfway up its length. She dragged something loose, calling out, "Look, Elsie, look!" She held up a scorched plate.

The woman above her on the mound squealed with excitement. "Oh, lucky you!"

"I can get three dollars for that, don't you think?"

"I'd say so. It's the burned bits that are worth the most."

Behind me, someone called out, "Behold, the Stinking Catacombs of Vice!"

I turned at the horrified gasps and titters to see a group of people snaking their way through the devastation. A tour led by a dirty-faced young man, who gestured dramatically, his voice loud enough to carry through the grasping of the looters.

"The most notorious of the tunnels were just over there. You can see them if you look closely—be careful, miss, not too close! I can't guarantee your safety. No one knows what's left down there, but that was once a secret entrance to the Subterranean Hellholes. The Underground City branched out for blocks and blocks. We still don't know the reach or the depth of them. Some say it went at least three stories down. Now, if you'll come this way, I'll show you what was once the most Notorious Opium Den in Chinatown."

His voice faded as he led the group down another junked corridor that must once have been a street. It was hard to tell.

The place was a mess, and not only that, but crowded, and I hurried through. It was impossible not to think of the last time I'd been here—the gambling house, the opium den—impossible to look at the blocks I passed and not wonder where the place had been. How far up the hill had I come from Coppa's? Halfway through Chinatown, perhaps. There had been a store on the corner, with silk robes in the windows and embroidered slippers, and next door to that, bins of long beans and big white rounds of some unfamiliar vegetable and gnarled knobs of pungent roots tumbled in a basket.

None of it was there now. I had found Chinatown frightening and foreign, but also interesting, and its absence made me melancholy, and I wondered what Goldie would do now that her opium procurer was gone, and again, did it matter? What had changed in the time I'd been in Blessington? Secrets only mattered if they were still poisonous.

Please let them still matter.

I kept walking.

Nob Hill had been transformed beyond recognition. The only buildings still standing were James Flood's mansion and the Fairmont Hotel. Flood's brownstone had been gutted; it was only a skeleton with empty sockets for windows. The Fairmont—which had not been finished when I'd been sent away—loomed in the near distance, its pillars unwarped and its windows glassless, the only obvious effects of the fire the scorching across its facade, stretching black silhouettes of flame. The fire had transformed marble into lime and melted steel and iron into bizarre shapes. Runnels of liquified glass and lead sash weights dripped over sills and pooled in hollows. Granite blocks had turned into boulders, their outer layers crumbling and gritty. A bright green parrot, the only spot of color in a fog of black and white and gray, perched on what remained of a stone gate, squawking raucously. Everything scorched and crumbled, and now the rounded peaks of army tents crowded the ruins, looking no different than any relief camp in any part of the city. Women and children crowded near communal tent kitchens. A line of wooden latrines—a far cry from baths with delft sinks and marble-like commodes—and wash lines were humiliatingly out in the open. How far the rich had come down in the world, that everyone could see their unmentionables. In the middle of the camp, someone had erected a flagpole, and the American flag rippled contentedly over all. *The earth giveth, and the earth taketh away.* I bit back a smile.

I stayed to the outskirts. I walked casually, my hands in my pockets, trying to blend in, and no one seemed to look twice at me. When I thought I saw someone I recognized, I moved quickly away, or slowed to walk behind someone else. I saw no sign of my uncle or my cousin. The camp was larger than I'd imagined, and more crowded. Obviously the only way to find them would be to walk through, and I was not that stupid. If Shin was here, there was no good way to find her.

A blasting horn from an automobile behind me made me start and jump out of the street. The car bounced jerkily over the cracked road, no doubt on important business. Automobiles all over the city had been hired or requisitioned by the military and the government, and this one too held soldiers, and a man I recognized, though I'd only seen him once, at the Palace Hotel. But he loomed large in my mind, so often had he been mentioned. I could not forget him. Abe Ruef.

The car pulled to the side of the road. Abe Ruef got out. He crossed the street, and hailed someone, who emerged from a corridor between tents.

My uncle.

That distinctive hair, that red gold that splintered in the sun, though it was disheveled and unoiled—and his ragged jacket was so uncharacteristic that it took me a moment to convince myself it was really Uncle Jonny. I dodged out of sight behind a decapitated lion guarding a broken stairway, but I could see them if I leaned just so. I watched the two of them talk.

My uncle gestured to someone behind him, and brazenly, in public view, Mrs. Dennehy joined them, clad in a plain skirt and shirtwaist, with diamonds around her throat and that diamond on her finger throwing reflections on the side of the nearby tent. She twined her arm through my uncle's, proprietary as she'd been that day in Union Square while my aunt, half-mad, poisoned by laudanum, suffered in her dark room. Now, the three of them smiled and laughed—worry-free, unchanged by events, untouched—and my resentment and anger churned so hot I broke into a sweat.

They spoke for a few more minutes, then Abe Ruef returned to the car, and the soldiers drove him away. My uncle and Mrs. Dennehy disappeared. I sat by the headless lion and tried to calm myself.

Now I knew my uncle was alive, as was his mistress. There, at least, was something to focus on. If my uncle existed, there was a way to clear my name and get back my money. There was a way to punish the man who was truly responsible for my aunt's death. I rubbed the gold button in my pocket. It had truly brought me luck. What of Goldie, then?

I could not leave after that. I stayed out of sight and watched people move about the perimeter of the camp. At the asylum, I had grown adept at waiting, and I did that now. I watched as the sun set, and the oil lamps and lanterns began to light, and women gathered at the communal kitchens. When it became dark enough that I knew they could not see me outside the perimeter of lamplight, I moved farther up the stairs, hoping for a broader view, and was rewarded with a full sight of the kitchen, women crowded about a stove. The flash of blond hair glowing golden struck me with its familiarity, bringing with it a mix of emotion I hadn't expected. Anger, yes, but also a wounded, bewildered pain. Why I should still feel that, after so long, after everything she'd done to me? To think that I had ever trusted her at all or ever wanted to be her friend . . .

Goldie wore men's overalls with a shirtwaist. She lifted a sloshing bucket, set it outside the tent flap, and called for someone. There was something about the way she called, her posture, her imperiousness, something that told me just who I would see, and I was right. Shin, who came to grab the bucket of water and took it away.

Shin. Thank God.

Shin, alive, and still with the Sullivans. I had hoped for that, but now I wondered what exactly it meant. I saw none of the other servants, not Au or Nick or Petey. How, after everything, after helping me, could Shin still work for them? Not only that, what did it mean in terms of helping me again?

I was puzzling over that, as well as how I might meet with her, when a shadow approached Goldie, and then resolved itself in the light, and I realized I was looking at Ellis Farge.

I had not forgotten him, of course, or his role in my commitment, but I'd thought him just one of Goldie's pawns. I'd never expected to see him again. More than Ellis himself, I mourned the opportunity that had been a lie, and the part he'd played in letting me believe such a thing could be possible for a woman. I'd wondered what he'd done with all my sketchbooks. Thrown them in the fire, I imagined. How readily I'd believed him when he'd said I had talent. Now, the thought of him raised only humiliation, and I could not bear to think of his false admiration, the flattery I hadn't seen through, and that evening at Coppa's . . . my God, that evening, when I'd drawn on the wall and shown them all the extent of my dilettantism. I was glad that Ellis had smeared it. If the restaurant was still standing, I hoped it had been wiped away.

I had not expected to see him now with Goldie, in this camp. She'd said there was an attachment between them, I remembered. Had that been true? What kind of an attachment?

Now, they spoke briefly, and then he left her again, and I put him from my mind. He was not the problem I had just now. My problem was getting to Shin.

The camp took on the look of Mark Twain's mining camp story. Glowing tents, soft talk, campfires. Carefully I made my way to the line of latrines. The stench was nothing compared to the asylum, and it was easy enough to wait there—at some point, everyone must use them. All

I had to do was stay out of the way. The shadows behind the temporary buildings were dense; I waited where I could see up the line. The camp grew quieter and quieter. I grew more and more anxious. It would be dangerous now to make my way back to town. I would have to find a place here to spend the night, and hope that I would not be caught, but it would be worth it if I could talk to Shin.

The night grew cold; I drew my coat more closely about me. She wasn't going to come. She'd used a pail instead. I should find a place to sleep among the ruins. But then, a shadow approached, a hurried walk I thought I recognized. I waited until I was certain, and then I stepped out. She started with a gasp that echoed in the space between us. I saw confusion in her eyes reflected in lamplight, and then recognition, and then . . . fear.

"No," she whispered. "You cannot be here."

"I need to speak to you."

She shook her head. Again, she said, "You cannot be here."

"Just a word—"

"You must go!"

My aunt's words. The echo shook me, and turned my desperation into anger. "I can't go! Don't you understand? I'm tired of warnings and demands. I've risked a great deal to find you, Shin. I want the truth, for once, and I think you know it. I deserve to know it. Please. I need your help."

I'd surprised her, I saw. She looked furtively about. "I cannot be gone long or they will wonder. Can you meet me tomorrow?"

I couldn't hide my relief. "Wherever you say. Whenever you wish."

"In the morning. The first thing. I am supposed to be in the relief lines, but they can be very long."

I understood. They would not question her if she were gone for some time. "Where?"

"The Fairmont." She put her hand on the latrine door—it seemed to glow in the darkness. But before I'd taken two steps, she cautioned,

"Do not be seen. They cannot allow you to be dead, but they don't wish you alive, either."

I frowned. "What?"

Shin said, "Tomorrow morning. Be careful, Miss May."

Now all I needed was a place to wait for morning. If I was to meet Shin at the Fairmont, why not there? In the darkness it loomed, an ominous shadow. I crept into a lower-story window when a cadet's back was turned, and into the vestibule of the Fairmont Hotel. It smelled of plaster and wood and smoke, newness tainted by fire and fallen stone. There, hidden well away, and feeling strangely at peace, I slept.

When morning came, the daylight highlighted the worst of the damage, lath and plaster fallen from walls and ceilings, construction scaffolding broken and teetering. The hallway felt narrow and confining; I remembered the severed foot and my own burial with a dizzy panic, and hurried into the broader vestibule. Marble pillars gave the illusion of vastness, and one could imagine that it would be elegant when it was finished, the damage repaired, the exposed brick plastered over. It had held very well in the earthquake, but it was dark and shadowed and huge, and I wondered where Shin had thought to meet me, and decided that the vestibule was the most obvious place.

I sat on the unfinished stairs, staring at the brick wall, trying to ignore my stomach grumbling. It wasn't long before I saw Shin's familiar dark and shining hair.

She said again, by way of greeting, "You should not be here."

"I needed to find you. You helped me before—"

"You don't understand. It is impossible."

"You know I didn't kill my aunt. You know they're stealing my money. You tried to warn me, and I wasn't paying attention. But I need you now. I'm going to take my money back. I'm going to clear my name—"

"How?"

"We'll go to the police. You'll tell them what you know."

She laughed. "You think the police will listen to me?"

"Why not? You know I was in the kitchen when she died. You're my only witness."

"Then you might as well plead guilty. It is the same thing."

I was taken aback by her insistence. "I don't understand."

"Look at me." She gestured, shortly, impatiently. "Look at what I am, Miss May. No one here believes a Chinaman. You will be putting yourself in your uncle's hands once more. Is that what you wish? Better to be dead."

I remembered now something Goldie had said about Chinese lies, about the police not trusting them. I had not questioned my cousin, but coming as it did now from Shin's mouth, I found it ludicrous that I had so simply accepted that a whole race could be liars. And yet, Shin was right—I'd been naive to think she could save me. I had seen only that she was my ally. I'd been too blind to understand that because she was Chinese, it wouldn't matter. Neither did I want to admit it now. I was too desperate; I'd pinned my hopes of clearing my name on her.

"But you know I didn't kill my aunt." I pulled the button from my pocket and held it out to her. "I found this in her hand. My uncle's vest button."

Shin glanced at it briefly. "Yes. They fought. I heard them."

"You heard? Then we *must* go to the police—"

"The police will not help you! He knows the police! Why don't you understand?" She quieted. "I am dead if we go to the police. He can't afford for you to be dead, but you will be locked away. This time forever."

"What do you mean, 'he can't afford for me to be dead'? You said that last night."

"The asylum burned, along with the papers. There is no record of who was there and who was not."

I had no idea why that was relevant. What did it matter if there was no record? The Sullivans knew I was there. "You're speaking in riddles."

"Your money. If you are dead, it must be returned."

"To whom?"

Shin shrugged. "Whoever gave it to you."

I struggled to understand. "You're saying that if I'm dead, my inheritance has to go back to my father's family?"

"Yes."

I grappled with that, with the sheer—I didn't know what to call it.

"No one can say if you are dead or alive, and so . . ." Shin trailed off.

And so this netherworld was exactly where I should stay if I wanted to be safe. But safety was not what I wanted, was it? I wanted justice. I wanted back what was mine. I wanted revenge.

I asked, "Why are you still with the Sullivans? You know what they are. You know what they did. Why do you still work for them?"

She glanced away uncomfortably.

I studied her the way I'd studied Costa and O'Rourke, the same way I'd studied Mrs. Donaghan. Everyone did things for a reason. Everyone wanted something. "It's not because you like the job too much to leave it. If that was so, you wouldn't have risked it to help me."

She said nothing.

I said, "Where are the rest of them? Mr. Au? Petey? Nick? The cook?"

She shrugged. "When the earthquake came, they ran. They didn't return."

"But you did." That was the key. "You have no fondness for Goldie, and if you cared for my aunt, well, she's dead, so she's not the reason, either. It's not lack of opportunity. Everyone needs a maid; you could get a job in another house easily. The others left. You stayed. Why?"

She turned her gaze slowly to me; some emotion I couldn't read flickered within it.

"It's because you have to." I knew when I said it that I was right. My uncle held Shin imprisoned in some way. I didn't know how and it didn't matter then. If I destroyed him, then she was free. She had been my ally; I wanted her to be one again. So I simply said, "Help me, and we'll destroy my uncle together. You'll be free. Is that what you want?"

Shin laughed shortly and shook her head.

"Why not?" I asked. "What aren't you telling me?"

I don't know what she heard in my voice. I don't know why she gave me the look she did. Grave, testing.

I said, "By all rights, I should be dead. I escaped an asylum and an earthquake and a fire. I promise I can help you."

"Maybe," she said slowly. "Maybe you can do it."

"I can. Tell me what I must do."

I did not expect what she said next, nor the chill it sent through me.

"We must see China Joe."

TWENTY-FOUR

China Joe. That disturbing face, the sense of danger, the fear that had sent me running. I remembered my cousin, sleepy and languid and anxious when I'd returned from the opium den. "Does Goldie still go to him?"

Shin did not look surprised that I knew. "She did. But there have been no ships and no opium. She suffers."

It did not pain me to know that. I had meant to use Goldie's secret against her, but I did not like the thought of China Joe, and I liked less the thought of paying him a visit. "We can do this without seeing him, surely? Why do we need him? What has he to do with you?"

"He has to do with everything in San Francisco. He knows everything about everybody."

I truly did not like the sound of that.

Again, that small smile. "Miss Sullivan needs opium. Mr. Sullivan needs property. Who do they go to?"

"You're saying that China Joe knows secrets about my uncle as well."

"Mr. Sullivan wanted Chinatown gone, and China Joe with it. There is a reason for that. There are many things that do not get done without China Joe, Miss May."

I sighed. "Very well. Do you know where to find him?"

Shin nodded. "Yes. But we cannot go now. I must get back."

"Tomorrow then. Can you go tomorrow?"

"Yes," she said.

But I was impatient; now that there was something to be done, I wanted to get started. I felt I had waited forever. I did not want to wait another day.

"Do not stay on Nob Hill," she warned. "It is too dangerous for you."

"No, I won't." I was nervous enough in the Fairmont.

"Meet me in Chinatown," she said.

"There is no Chinatown," I said grimly.

"The burned-out trolleys—did you see them?"

There had been a line of them along Pacific Avenue, nothing but twisted metal now. I nodded.

"Meet me there tomorrow morning. At eleven." She left with a final warning: "Do not be caught here, Miss May."

I needed no more warnings. The moment I could, I sneaked from the Fairmont, and left Nob Hill far behind me. I would be happy never to return.

I decided to look for Dante after the visit with China Joe. Better to have all the information in my hands when I met with Dante, to present him with a story he could not resist, and so I spent a sleepless night wondering about Shin's connection with Goldie's opium procurer, and both dreading and anticipating what I might learn.

The next day, I waited for what seemed endless hours at the wrecked cable cars. The collapsed roof of one, still bearing its clanging bell, tilted over what were left of wheels and a piece of painted side. The ones linked to it were only wheels and the metal rails that held them together, bits of flooring. I leaned against the standing brick wall of a hollowed building, rolling the gold button in my pocket between my fingers, staring up into the bright overcast beginning to show now through a lazy fog.

"Miss."

When Shin arrived, she looked as tense and strained as I felt. It was not reassuring. We spoke little as we walked down the hill and into Chinatown with its trophy hunters gleefully pulling teacups from still warm embers and men exclaiming over bits of cracked jade and soldiers watching as they leaned idly on their rifles. We passed a charred telephone pole bearing an order for every able-bodied man and woman to serve on work crews—an unbelievable irony, given that not only did Chinatown provide most of the domestics and low-wage workers in San Francisco, but also because the many whites here were digging not to clean up or to help rebuild this part of the city, but to steal whatever they could from it. I felt uncomfortable and ashamed. I could not look at Shin.

We went a twisted route, through a break in a wall, down a passageway made of other broken walls, this way and that, until it seemed some secret route like those rumored to lead to subterranean grottoes in Chinatown—*Dens of Vice and Degradation!* The earthquake had given the lie to those stories, though the tour guides still found them irresistible. Before long Shin stopped where a street had partially fallen in, creating a cavern beneath. Rugs had been strung up to turn the shallow cave into a shelter. Shin stepped carefully down a slide of gravel and refuse, and I followed, slipping as stones rolled beneath my boots. There, where a carpet flapped before a makeshift entrance, sat a man I recognized from the opium den, the one with the scarf, who had called for Joe. Shin spoke to him in Chinese. He only grunted a reply. She gestured for me to come with her and dodged beneath the carpet.

Inside, a candle spilled a wavering light. It smelled of dirt and stone, smoke and damp. The small space clung to the ash and destruction of Chinatown; the air was gray with it. The corner held a tumble of blankets and clothing, but the walls were lined with stacks of items, some scorched, others cracked, obviously relics retrieved from the ruins, and again I thought of all those people carting off their baskets of melted bronzes and blackened china. Then I saw that these items were marked with price tags. Souvenirs for sale. Obviously China Joe meant to compete with other San Franciscans in profiting from Chinatown's destruction.

A wooden box, a pull wagon, and a chair served as the only furniture in the cramped space. Sitting on the chair was China Joe, looking impatient.

He listened as Shin spoke to him, again in Chinese. Then he held up his hand, stopping her midword, and looked at me. The candlelight made his already high cheekbones sharp, and buried his dark eyes. He considered me in a way that made me shiver. "Goldilocks's cousin, hmmm?"

I nodded, momentarily stripped of the ability to speak.

A half smile. "Ah yes. You ran from me before I could give you what you needed. Poor frightened little hen."

That he remembered me was unnerving.

"Chen Shin says you have something to offer me. She says we will all help one another, yes?"

I glanced at Shin, who nodded. I had no idea what I could offer him, but I said, "I hope so. Yes, I think so."

"Tell me what you want, little hen."

"Remember who you are." "The Sullivans have stolen from me, and I want back what's mine."

"Ah," Joe said. "Yes, I see."

It was only when he reached for it that I saw the book beside him. It was large and fully stuffed. He pulled it into his lap and opened it.

The pages had pockets, each pocket full of papers, or photographs, or letters—I could not tell exactly. He leafed through it until he found what he wanted, and then he set it in the bed of the wagon between us. He gestured for me to look before he sat back again.

I glanced at Shin, who watched without expression, and then I looked down at the book. The pocket on the page had Chinese characters in black ink. They meant nothing to me, of course, and no one bothered to elucidate. The pocket bulged with papers. When I looked at him in question, he put out his hand as if to say, *Go ahead.*

I reached for the corner of one of the papers shoved within it and pulled it loose. It was the size of a check, a bit smaller, and written in English. *I, Goldie Sullivan, do promise to pay China Joe twenty dollars.* It was dated and signed by both her and, I assumed, Joe. It was not the only one. There were dozens, all for different amounts. Some higher, some lower. I did not need to look at all of them to know that it was a great amount of money.

It was more debt than I could possibly have imagined. "This is for opium?"

"So many secrets," he said softly. "Not just opium, little hen. Gambling. She loves to gamble, your Goldilocks."

The story of Goldie's engagement returned to me. Stephen Oelrichs, taking her to Ingleside, teaching her to gamble. His words to me at the Anderson soiree. *"Stay away from China Joe."*

The paper between my fingers smelled of sandalwood and tobacco smoke. It was crisp and thin. A blocky, inked red stamp took up one corner—again, Chinese symbols.

I took a deep breath and pushed it back into its pocket. I closed the book, nauseated. "And my uncle?"

Again, Joe flipped through the book. This time when he set it before me, the papers inside were not IOUs, but invoices bearing my uncle's signature, as well as a ledger showing dollar amounts, names, and accounts. "I don't understand. What are these?"

"Evidence of graft, bribes."

"Corruption," Dante LaRosa had said.

"Sullivan Building wrote many false invoices to build city hall," China Joe went on. "They exchanged cheap materials for those the city paid for, and bribed those in charge to look the other way. Where did the money go, little hen, hmmm? Now, people see that walls promised to be solid brick were filled with sand and trash. The great pillars were only shells. Now they ask questions. They want to know who to blame."

I'd seen how the elegant facade had slid from its metal structure like melting chocolate. The walls had been pulverized. Years to build and the pride of San Francisco, and it was a sandcastle of a structure that had trapped several in its collapse—there had been a hospital and an asylum in its basement. It was the building the newspapers and everyone else pointed to when they spoke of needing new codes and updated standards for rebuilding. City hall was a disaster. My uncle's fault, and China Joe had the proof of it.

Joe watched me with an expression I could not read. Amusement, perhaps, or perhaps he was only watching to see the moment when I put it all together. This time, when he turned the pages of the book and handed it back to me, I was afraid to take it.

I feared the name on the pocket was my own.

I was right to be afraid. The pocket was full of newspaper clippings. The society page, every time I'd been mentioned. The notice of my arrival in San Francisco. The drunken frivolity at the Cliff House. The picture of me in the bathing suit. Then, after that, the articles of my madness, the accusations of murder, my commitment to Blessington.

He reached for one of the papers in the pocket and pulled it out, holding it until I took it between numb fingers. His gaze ordered me to read it.

I glanced down. It was the Classifieds section of the *San Francisco Call.*

Found: Italian boy, 3 years old, from Union St.

To ANYONE at the ST. FRANCIS HOTEL, SF, who knows anything about my son, Robert Fletcher. Please notify Mrs. Francis Fletcher, Valencia Hotel, Los Angeles.

Just like every other day. Advertisements like this had been running since the earthquake. Lost children, missing relatives, requests for information. I had no idea what it had to do with me, but when I looked up at him in question, he nodded for me to keep reading.

Found: Green parrot. Says "Hurry sailor" constantly. Please claim.

Seeking information about BLESSINGTON HOME FOR THE INCURABLY INSANE, regarding certain patients from the facility. Please contact David Emerson, Private Detective, temporarily at West 1922.

I stopped, hoping I'd misread, but I knew I had not. I understood what Joe meant by showing me this. The Sullivans had hired a private detective to look for me. China Joe would make certain the man found me unless I did what he wanted—whatever it was. Had Shin known this? Had she brought me here only to cross me?

Joe's gaze was slow, sweeping; his little smile made me think of rosy light, a heavy sweet smoke, and the languorous drawl in Goldie's voice. His had not been a benign smile then, and it was less so now. Beside me, Shin shifted from one foot to the other. She said something quickly, but he did not answer. To me, he said, "It is simply information, Miss Kimble. Information I believe you should know."

My instincts told me otherwise. I could barely get out the words as I asked him, "What do you want from me?"

He sighed. "I have worked very hard to make my kingdom, Miss Kimble. It has taken years of planning and special . . . shall we say, negotiations? And now, I find—we find, my friends and I—that after all the favors we have done, all the allies we have made, we are betrayed by those who owe us the most."

"I see." Actually, I had no idea what he was talking about, but I understood secrets, and I listened.

"They wish to take Chinatown from us. They wish to move it to Hunters Point. Do you know of these plans?"

"I'm not surprised."

"Then I think you will not be surprised to know who is at the center of these plans."

"My uncle."

Again, that slow, considering look. Again, a frisson of unease down my spine. "You help me stop them, Miss Kimble, and I will help you with your . . . difficult . . . relatives. Perhaps also I can help you—or not—with this Mr. Emerson."

Again, I understood. China Joe had me neatly trapped.

He went on. "And I give Shin what she asks for."

I was confused. "What she asks for? I'm confused."

"She is my eyes and ears on the Sullivans," he said. "If we keep Chinatown, Chen Shin's debt to me will be paid. She will have her liberty. You will do this for me. Agreed?"

"You still haven't told me what I need to do."

Joe reached for a wooden box on the wagon. It was small and inlaid with leaves of a lighter wood. He opened it and took out a cigarette, which he lit. Joe drew heavily, held it, and opened his mouth, releasing the smoke in a ring. He looked so pleased at its perfection that for a moment he seemed a child, or would have, if child's play had held such threat. "I need a reporter to remind the city what they owe us and what they would lose if they choose to go against us. You know one, I think. At the *Bulletin*. He is a good friend of yours."

How easily it came together. So much so that I was suspicious. Shin had said he knew everything. Even my own intentions, it seemed. "He's hardly a good friend."

Joe said, "You convince him to help me keep Chinatown safe from the city schemers and Jonathan Sullivan."

I had no idea what he meant or how he expected a society reporter to help him accomplish that. But before I could ask, he went on, "You get me that, I give you the proof you want, and I give Chen Shin what she wants. If you do not—" A shrug. He looked at Shin, such a cold look. "Shin stays in my employ; your cousin finds out what happens when I don't get paid, and you . . ." He didn't have to say it. *David Emerson.*

Shin's expression was desperate, pleading. This was the freedom she'd wanted. From my uncle, yes, but from something worse. Until this moment I'd not realized how tightly she was bound, or that it was not my uncle who held her, but China Joe.

China Joe said, "Send him to me. I will be waiting."

With a flick of his hand, we were dismissed.

I was glad to go. Shin seemed equally so. Neither of us said anything until Shin paused a few blocks later and said, "I must leave you here."

But I wasn't ready to let her go. I could not forget the way he'd looked at her. "What did he mean when he said that Goldie would find out what happens when he doesn't get paid?" I asked softly.

Shin hesitated.

"Tell me." I struggled for the right words, not wanting to offend. "How did this happen, Shin? What debt do you owe him? Why must you do as China Joe says?" Then, as I sensed her discomfort, "No, never mind. You don't need to tell me. It's none of my concern."

"I was brought here five years ago." Shin stared at the men digging for bronze in the rubble. "In China, my parents were very poor. I had a brother and two sisters, both younger than me. When a man came looking to buy children, they sold me to him."

"They sold you?"

"It was the way things were."

"Yes, but . . . your parents sold you?"

"They could not feed me. What else were they to do? He told them I would have a better life, that there were good jobs in America, and that if I was a good worker, I could send money back to my family. Many girls from my village were sold. I was not unhappy to leave. He made America sound like a blessing. He was a kind man, who gave gifts to my parents. He said he would be a second father to me." Again, a small smile, this time caustic. "He brought us here on a ship—me and ten other girls. When the immigration men stopped us and tried to send us back, men stepped forward to claim us as their wives."

I stared at her in horror. "Wives? How old were you?"

She didn't answer, but I could guess by her face. She couldn't be older than eighteen, which meant she would have been thirteen when they'd brought her here. "Those 'husbands' sold us to be whores. I bit mine and ran away—he was old and lame, and I outran him easily. I hid for days, until one of China Joe's boys found me."

Alone, in a strange city, sold to a stranger, and then to another, and meant for prostitution, probably in the worst parts of town, the alleys of Chinatown, the warrens of the Barbary Coast. Places I knew about because everyone knew, places carefully avoided, ignored, only mentioned obliquely, *"Oh, never go there!"*

Shin looked at me. "He paid my debt and put me to work as his spy. Yes, I owe him."

I didn't know what to say.

"I have been his eyes and ears for a long time, but I want to leave San Francisco. He has refused to let me go. I tried once." She held up her hand, fingers splayed to showcase that terrible missing finger. "This is what he did. What do you think he would do if I tried again?"

"He cut off your *finger*?" I could hardly speak it.

She fisted her hand. Her expression told me better than words what she'd endured, the things I could not know. "He has people everywhere. But he needs what you have, a connection to a reporter. He asked me to bring you to him if you appeared again. I did not want to, because I was afraid for you, but . . . you are different now."

I laughed shortly. "Yes, you could say that."

"You must not disappoint him, Miss May." Her eyes said what she did not. *Or me.*

Her words weighed heavily. I heard in them her disillusionment, and a bitter pragmatism. She hoped I could do this, but she would not allow herself to believe I could. It had been one thing when it was only me depending on my success. It was something else to be responsible for someone else's future as well.

"Be careful. China Joe is not the only dangerous man. Mr. Sullivan is too. He could make me disappear. And you . . ." Shin trailed off, but she didn't need to finish the sentence. I knew very well what would happen if Joe exposed me to my uncle's private investigator.

But it was time now to play the game I'd schemed in the asylum. It was time to make the next move. "I'll convince Dante to help. And when I win back my inheritance, if the Sullivans haven't spent it all, I'll give you some money so you can—"

"I don't want your money, Miss May," she said, raising her chin, and I knew that I should not have offered it.

The sounds of the city faded. Shin and I seemed to stand in a vast plain of silence.

Very quietly, she said, "Your aunt meant to cheat you too, at first, when your mother sent the letter, but then she changed her mind when your mother died. She felt guilty, I think. She talked often of her sister, and the past."

I thought of how worn and creased my mother's letter had been. As if it had been read and reread. As if Aunt Florence had worried over it.

"She threatened to tell you everything. Mr. Sullivan told me to give her the laudanum and wrote the letter inviting you here. Then he made me give her more and more, but I could not bear to watch her stumble and she was so confused. The less I gave her, the more she wanted to tell you. They argued all the time. I was afraid. I knew you were looking for the letter, and so I decided to give it to you. That night, I waited, but—"

"The night she died."

Shin nodded. "I must get back."

"Yes, they mustn't become suspicious." When she turned to go, I said, "I'll do whatever I must to help you leave San Francisco, Shin, I promise it."

"I'm glad you're free, Miss May," she said.

"Not yet." I tried, not very successfully, to smile. "But soon, I hope we both will be."

TWENTY-FIVE

The *Bulletin* had set up temporary headquarters on the roof of the Merchants' icehouse, but the last thing I was going to do was march into a den of reporters all looking for a story. Nearby was a cluster of tents and a still-standing fence where children played with their dog. Beyond, a relief wagon handed out eggs and water to those standing in line. I went to join them, just one more woman waiting for her portion. I didn't take my eyes from the icehouse.

Several men came and went, none of them Dante. I worried that I might not recognize him, but I hadn't yet made it to the front of the line when he stepped out, and I knew him immediately. His walk, the way he held himself, that palpable charisma that I'd noted that first time I'd met him. I'd thought I was prepared for the sight of him, but I wasn't. All I could think about was the last time I'd seen him, at Coppa's, my juvenile drawing in response to his challenge—so embarrassing.

That, coupled with what he must know about my imprisonment at Blessington, suffused me with sudden panic and humiliation.

But he was key to both my plans and China Joe's. I gripped the vest button in my pocket, steeling myself, and stepped from the relief line. By then, Dante was striding away; I ran after him, not allowing myself to think. I did not call after him. The last thing I wanted to do was bring attention to us both. When I reached him, I fell into step beside him. He lost his stride, looked at me in puzzlement, a double take, then stopped completely.

"Hello," I said through the tightness in my throat.

"Well, well, if it isn't May Kimble." That he'd been mucking about the city was obvious. His shirt was gray with dust and ash and open at the throat to show both his long underwear and the start of the hair on his chest. Healing blisters reddened his cheekbones, dark shadows of sleeplessness marked beneath his eyes, and his beard shadow was heavy.

"I wasn't certain you would remember me."

"I'm not likely to forget the woman who made Ellis Farge an artist."

I must not have heard him correctly. "What?"

His dark gaze swept me. "You're a mess."

"You don't look much better."

He glanced about, and then he took my arm, gently at first, as if afraid I might bolt, and my heart sank, because I recognized the care in it, the kind of care one took with a madwoman, and when he tightened his hold, I knew it was a mistake to have come upon him this way. He was going to turn me in to the authorities.

"Come with me," he said quietly.

I pulled back. "No. I'm not going anywhere. I'm sorry. I've obviously made a mistake—"

"I just want to talk to you, May," he said earnestly. "But not here. There are too many people. You'll be safe, I promise."

"Safe from whom?"

"I'm assuming you sought me out for a reason—ah, I'm right, I see. You can trust me. I swear it. Come on." He pulled me with him to the narrow stairs of what was now only side walls of mostly collapsed brick and burned frontage. Up those stairs, and then into a corner against a soot-blackened wall that partially shielded us from the street. I was grateful for that at least. All around us, the sounds of rebuilding were a constant music, clanging, hammering, sawing, shouts and wagons and horses. No one was going to overhear our conversation. It was only then that I noted how neatly he'd trapped me. I was in the corner, and though he was not the least bit threatening, he stood before me in a loose stance, one I was certain was deceptive. He could easily stop me should I try to bolt.

Dante looked at my forehead and said, "It's a bit Frankensteinian, but it makes you even more interesting. You're going to have quite a scar."

Gingerly, I touched the stitches. "A building fell on me."

"Ah. No doubt the reason for your release."

"I will say that it was rather unexpected."

"Is it true? What they said about you?"

"You're the reporter," I answered. "What do you think?"

Slowly, thoughtfully, he said, "I think you know something about the Sullivans that they're desperate to keep secret. I think you have the answers to questions I've been asking for a long time."

"You're wasting your talents being a society reporter," I said. I met his gaze. "I need your help."

"All right."

I frowned. "Just like that? You know where I've been and you don't even know why I want your help."

"I don't care. I've worried about you. I've wondered . . . too many things. Whatever they did to you, you didn't deserve."

The words pleased me, but I'd been fooled by words before. "How can you say that? You hardly know me."

He shrugged. "I know you well enough. I'd been watching you for months before we met, remember. You aren't mad. Easily manipulated, maybe. Foolish, yes. But not mad. Out with it, May. We're friends, remember? Tell me what you want me to do."

So I told him. To his credit, he took no notes, but only listened. When I got to the part about following Goldie to China Joe's, he whistled low and patted his pockets, searching. "Christ, I need a cigarette."

"I hope that doesn't mean you're afraid of China Joe."

"I don't like the sound of that."

I told him about my meeting in Chinatown. By then we were sitting on the ash- and rubble-strewn floor.

"China Joe wants me to help him keep Chinatown," Dante said when I finished. "How exactly?"

"He said something about needing a reporter to remind the city what it owes the Chinese. I'm not sure what he means."

"Hmmm." Dante mused. "He means that for all the city complains about the Chinese, we can't exist without them. Imagine it . . . the Chinese are driven out, and with them go most if not all of San Francisco's servants, as well as all the men willing to work for low wages. Entire industries would be crippled—cigars, boots, men's clothing . . . The landlords would find the rents they can charge for their Chinatown properties cut in half; white tenants won't pay those prices, and they won't be quiet about it, either. Most of the gambling halls close down, prostitution, opium dens . . ."

"You can't tell me that wouldn't be a good thing."

"Except revenues from vice run the city. They're all in on the graft. The board of supervisors—your uncle included—the police, the commissioners . . . The Chinese who run Chinatown are more powerful than the city wants to admit; they've got their hands in everything. And that's not even to mention China itself. There'll be no more silk imports for society dresses, not to mention opium. San Francisco would fall to its knees without Chinese investment."

"China Joe knew what he was talking about when he suggested you, then," I said with a smile. "You're very well informed."

Dante waved that away. "I wouldn't be any kind of reporter if I didn't know this."

"Once you write the articles China Joe wants, he'll help me. He has the proof I need to ruin Goldie and my uncle." I heard the chill in my voice, and I saw Dante note it, his stilled attention.

"What about Farge?"

I frowned. "What about him?"

He rose and held out his hand for me. "Come on. I want to show you something." I let him pull me to my feet, but halted as he started off, and he paused and looked back. "What is it?"

"I probably shouldn't be seen with you."

"Why not?"

"The advertisement. The detective. I can't risk being noticed."

He frowned. "No one knows who I am, remember? Thanks to Alphonse Bandersnitch."

"Ellis knows who you are. And don't be so modest. You draw attention. You know you do."

He looked genuinely puzzled, and then he grinned. "Maybe it's only that I draw your attention."

"Dante," I said patiently, "I've escaped an asylum. I've been accused of murder. I'm in hiding. My family is searching for me. I cannot be recognized."

"You don't look like yourself. You look like you've been through a disaster, honestly. Here." He took the hat from his head and tossed it to me. "Put this on and tuck your braid under it. Swagger a bit. Pretend you're a man. I've got a reporter's pass to keep us from being inducted into a work crew. Now come on, it's important."

I did as he suggested, put on the hat, shoved my braid beneath it, and followed him back into the street. I was mystified as to what he wanted to show me, and why now, this minute. He gave me no clue, but walked quickly. We were stopped twice for work crews, and Dante offered his pass with an ease that told me he was asked often, took firm hold of my arm when they looked askance at me, and said, "My fellow reporter, Mr. Hardy," and then led me away before the officer had a chance to question us.

"Mr. Hardy?" I asked.

"A good name, don't you think? You've proved to be a hardy soul."

As if to belie his words, I nearly tripped over the edge of twisted steel poking from a cascade of fallen brick. "Where are we going?"

"Not much farther now." All the humor left his face, his full lips pressed tightly together. "It was just completed, so of course they worked hard to save it. It should rightfully have burned to the ground."

I frowned in confusion. "What should have burned?"

"This." He stopped as we turned the corner.

There before us was a building I'd never before seen. It was obviously new, three stories, stone and brick, with stairs rising to a pedestaled front. Like the Fairmont, it showed earthquake and fire damage, cracked stairs and pillars, soot from flames staining the stone, and several windows missing glass.

I turned to Dante. "What is this?"

"The new Parson Library for the Arts." His expression was strange, wary and hesitant. I had the sense that, although he'd felt it necessary to come here, he regretted it. "It was built while you were away."

Uncertain what reaction he hoped for, I said, "It's very nice."

"Let's go inside," he said grimly.

"That might be difficult." I gestured to the two soldiers guarding the door.

Dante started up the stairs. I followed him, still curious, but with increasing tightness in my chest, fed by his wariness or regret or whatever it was.

At the door, he pulled his pass from his pocket. "Reporter for the *Bulletin*. My associate is an illustrator. We're doing a story about the library. Since it's one of the most notable surviving buildings."

The soldiers glanced at his pass. One of them opened the door. "We'll have to search you when you come out," he informed us.

Dante nodded. He stepped back to usher me before him. I gave him a curious glance, but he only offered a small, sad smile, as mysterious as everything else about this.

The foyer was marble, the light sconces on the walls dark, which wasn't unusual; there was no city light. On either side of the foyer, stairs led to a second story. Another set of wooden doors were before us, light leaking from beneath. I went to them, hearing our footsteps echo forebodingly into the stairway.

I opened the door and went inside.

The room reached the full three stories, with mezzanines at every level. Wooden flat files and bookcases lined the walls, though there were no books—either they'd been taken to save from the fire or they hadn't yet been shelved. In the center, a squared pillar rose to spread into an arched ceiling. Desks were positioned all around it.

I knew every detail of this room, every single line, though I'd never stepped foot in it before.

"You could put in a few statues."

"The books are the decoration. Imagine their colors. Calfskin bindings and morocco and gold-leaf—"

"All with uncut pages, no doubt. What's the point of a book if no one reads it? Are there any paper covers on those shelves?"

The memory of Goldie's voice, mine, as we looked over the drawing in my sketchbook, that same drawing reproduced here in marble and stone, wood and glass. The only thing missing was my signature. *"They are so beautiful you must claim them as your own."*

I could not breathe. I put out my hand, thinking to touch it, but it was not paper.

"It's yours, isn't it?" Dante asked quietly.

Mine, yes. My imagination somehow made real. My throat was so tight I could only nod. This was impossible. How could it be?

As if he'd read my mind, Dante inclined his head toward a bronze plaque on the wall.

Designed by Ellis Farge, 1905.

Shock first, then disbelief and pain. Ellis's flattery, his admiration, my gratitude at the chance to learn, and all the time, this was what he'd intended. Stealing what was mine. Everything I had been through, everything I had borne, and yet this . . . this was the worst of it. He'd taken something no one had ever touched, because how could they? How safe and certain and unreachable I'd thought it, my mind and my history, and yet, how easily he'd stolen it, and how much more it was than simply a design. My solace and my hopes. Everything. More than he could possibly know. Furious tears blurred my vision.

Dante took my arm, steady and solid, and my rage gathered and hardened, no longer a hot burning, but icy and growing more frigid every moment, a rallying force, a foundation. My family had begun my destruction; if Ellis meant with this to finish it, he had done exactly the opposite. My voice did not sound like mine when I said, "I've made him an artist, you said. This is what you meant."

Dante nodded. "I suspected it, but I wasn't certain until now. Over the past year, he's reinvented himself. He's doing interiors. They're different from anything he's done before. Because they're yours. Tell me how he's doing it."

"My sketchbooks."

Dante frowned, not understanding.

"I had sketchbooks. A dozen at least. He asked to see them. I wanted his opinion."

"He still has them." It was not a question.

"Well, I don't. So . . . He told me once that it was a pity I was a woman."

"A pity for you. Not for him."

"He stole my drawings." No wonder Goldie had been so insistent that I show them to him. Her words that night in my bedroom as the Blessington attendants waited to take me away echoed painfully. *"She knew of our attachment, and . . . tried to come between us."*

I remembered Ellis in the camp at Nob Hill, coming to speak to Goldie in the communal kitchen.

Goldie had entangled Ellis in her plot against me because they were together. Yet I'd thought she hadn't even known him. In the asylum, I'd dismissed Ellis as a pawn. Everything made sense now, except—"But why? Why did he need them? He's an architect himself. They say he's a genius."

"Yes, that's what they say." Dante's voice dripped sarcasm.

"You hate him," I remembered. "He hated you too. I knew it even at Coppa's. Why?"

"I don't like him because he's a liar. Because he's weak. Because he pretends to be something he's not, and he doesn't care who he hurts to get what he wants. He's a hophead, you know."

It was hardly a surprise, given what I knew about Goldie. Their *attachment.* The way they'd kept it so quiet. But of course Dante would know that about them.

"When he first came to San Francisco, everyone loved him," Dante explained. "That was six years ago, maybe seven. He was already well regarded in Philadelphia, and John McKay had seen one of his buildings there and hired him to build the Yeller Block here. Farge came out and stayed. I have to admit that he was worth praising. But then he smoked away his talent and his buildings became disasters. Have you ever seen the Hartford? It looked like an Egyptian nightmare, with all these corridors and tiny rooms. You expected to come upon a secret entrance guarded by a mummy. The earthquake is the best thing that could have happened to it. I wrote the review of the reception for its opening, and I reported what everyone was saying. He never forgave me for it."

I remembered the drawing of the building framed on Ellis's wall, my own comment that it seemed a prison.

Dante went on quietly. "I didn't mean to destroy him. That wasn't my intention. But that's what he thought."

"What happened?"

"He wrote a letter to the paper attacking me. Older told me to apologize. I did but not in the way Farge wanted. I think I said something like, 'People can of course discern the truth for themselves.'"

I couldn't help smiling.

"Yes, you see? The damage was done. He lost commissions. I don't know how many. Farge wasn't my main focus, then or now. I saw him at Coppa's, he was drinking and depressed and nasty; if I knew he was there I tried to stay away. Edith—I think it was Edith—told me to make amends because he was making everyone miserable and she was afraid he might try to hurt himself."

I thought of that day at the baths, when I'd first met him, his agitation and desperation. Now I understood. He had lost his way, and he was afraid. I had trusted my uncle and Goldie when they said he was talented and important. That he was coasting on his reputation, I hadn't considered, even when I saw his work. Nor did it occur to me to suspect what was so obviously true in retrospect: Goldie had seen that my work could save Ellis, and she had managed to make certain it would. Her *"These are perfect!"* when she'd first looked at my drawings, the compliment I'd taken it for, so ominous it seemed now, and then the way Ellis began to appear. His return from Del Monte that Linette had commented upon at the Cliff House, his weird presence at Sutro's, so out of place. How had I not seen?

"I didn't understand at first." Dante sighed. "But then I did. That day—do you remember?—when everyone was drawing on the walls? I saw it then. Your talent and what Farge wanted from you. It explained everything, because otherwise you weren't his type."

"No. My cousin is, however."

Dante looked sympathetic. "They married while you were away."

That surprised me, though it explained his presence in the Nob Hill relief camp. "I didn't know. Well, they deserve each other. You were right when you said I was easily manipulated. I had no idea they had any relationship at all."

"No one did. Well, some of us did. It had been going on for some months. I don't know where they met—maybe China Joe's, but you could see them circling one another at events if you watched them. I wanted to see how it would develop before I wrote about it. It must be true love."

"She can control him," I said. "Better than she could Stephen Oelrichs."

"Oelrichs. Now that was interesting too."

I took a deep breath. "Goldie has ambitions."

"I guess it's up to us to make sure they're foiled. And Farge's too. When do I see China Joe?"

"As soon as possible. Shin will take you to him. He's expecting you. You look nervous. He's actually very reasonable. If I can beard him in his den, you certainly can."

Dante laughed. "I'm not so pleasing as you. Nor as persuasive."

I was not expecting the compliment, and it flustered me. "If I were that persuasive, I would have been able to convince everyone that I didn't kill my aunt."

His smile faded. "You're playing a rigged game, May. Your uncle has the police in his pocket. There was nothing you could have done. Not then. You didn't have enough information. But now . . ."

"Now what?"

"Now, you do."

"Their secrets, you mean."

He shook his head. "You've always had those. But no one's going to listen to May Kimble. Especially when she's a lunatic poor relation."

"That hasn't changed."

"Oh, but it has. You're not May Kimble, are you? Or at least, not only that." When I frowned, he continued, "Your inheritance. Your father. The telegraph is up again. It shouldn't be difficult to discover what rich man died in New York City—when did your father die?"

"Mama made it sound recent. Just before she died, I think."

Dante took out his notebook and scrawled something. "You said his name was Charles, right? I'll send a telegram to a friend of mine at the *New York World*. He'll check the obits. If your father is as important as your mother said he was, he'll be mentioned there."

"It seems so . . . easy."

"If you know the right people, it is. It will take a couple of days. Once we have your real name, we'll find a lawyer here to handle it."

To think that in a matter of days I might have the answer I'd been waiting for my whole life felt impossible. But Dante seemed to think it nothing. I wanted to believe him. "Now it's getting late, and I'm hungry. Where are you staying?"

The change in subject momentarily jostled my thoughts. "Staying? Around. Here and there."

"Here and there," he repeated. "You know it's dangerous, don't you? There are robberies and murders every night even with the soldiers about."

"Believe me, I know. I'm safe enough." I pulled out the metal rod and showed it to him.

Dante's eyes darkened. "Someone with more skill is just as likely to turn that on you, May. For God's sake. You'll be safer staying with me."

"Staying with you? You must be mad. What will people say?"

"Says the woman who set the tongue of every gossip in the city wagging."

"That was not my fault."

"We're in the middle of a *disaster*, or haven't you noticed? No one cares except those up on Nob Hill, and I'm the only one watching them.

Not only that, we can plan better if we're together. And I have an idea for Farge that I think you'll want to hear."

"What idea?"

"Oh no," he wagged his finger playfully. "Not until we have something to eat. Let's go."

I looked again at the library, my vision made real, beautiful yes, but a terrible betrayal. I would never be able to come here again, I knew. Goldie and my uncle had been cruel and avaricious, but their greed was not so personal as Ellis's. Not so intimate. And yet, I knew also, in a way I had not known before, that its very intimacy made me stronger. I would not forgive him this, and this time, I was not helpless, and I was not alone.

TWENTY-SIX

Dante took me to the west side of Telegraph Hill, where he stopped at a cluster of small wooden houses that had been saved from the fire. One of them was a single-story house with a flat roof and narrow, slatted stairs that led to the front door. The windows were cracked and busted from the earthquake, and plaster had fallen from the walls in places to show the lath beneath. Other than that, it seemed mostly undamaged. A small front room fitted with a secondhand settee, a desk, and piles of books was to the right. To the left, a kitchen and a table with two chairs. At the rear were two bedrooms.

"I share it," he said. "But Bobby's to Oakland for a few days."

"Bobby?"

"My cousin." He motioned to one of the closed doors leading to the bedrooms. "You can stay in his room. He won't care. But you might. He drinks too much and he's a slob."

Gingerly, I opened the door. The curtains were drawn. I saw a bed, a chair, lumpy shadows. It smelled sour, of dirty clothes and unwashed skin and yes—what was that? Spilled beer?

"I try not to go in there," he said.

I closed the door again. He was in the kitchen. The stove had been pulled out into the street like every other in San Francisco, leaving only the cobwebbed, greasy wall behind it. Dante pulled things from a cupboard to set on the table: a half a loaf of bread, two tins of sardines and one of tomatoes, and—

"Where did you get wine? No one's allowed to sell liquor."

"They never said we couldn't drink it." He set the bottle down with a victorious thump. "I know the right people. Papa Gennaro down the street. I helped him save his place." He shoved up his sleeve and held out his arm to show smooth olive skin. "Burned all the hair off my arms doing it too. Sit down."

I took off his hat and put it on the desk, and then I took one of the chairs at the table.

"All the glasses broke in the earthquake. We'll have to be bohemians and drink from the bottle. I know society girls don't do such things, but . . ."

He pulled the cork and handed the wine to me, and I raised the bottle in a toast and took a gulp. I hadn't tasted wine in so long that it burned its way down my throat, but it was a long and luxurious burn, and I closed my eyes to celebrate it and sighed. "Oh, that is lovely. It's been so long—" I broke off, humiliated at unexpected tears. I dabbed at them with the edge of my sleeve, trying to be surreptitious, but when I looked up, Dante was watching me. I felt strangely, horribly vulnerable; I had to turn away.

Gently he took the bottle from my hand and took a gulp himself. Then, softly, "What was it like?"

I didn't pretend not to know what he meant. "It was all right." I blinked and tried to swallow the memory. "Fine, once I found my way."

"What way was that?"

My attempted smile was a failure. "Secrets."

"Ah," he said. "Just as brave as I remember."

It made me teary all over again, and he gave me back the wine. He opened the sardines, then tore off a piece of bread. He put a chunk of the oily fish on the bread with his fingers and handed it to me with a care and concern that made me laugh with embarrassment. "I'm sorry. I just . . ."

"You don't have to tell me," he offered, but it was his grace in relieving me of the obligation to say it that released me so I could describe that first horrible night when I'd been nearly strangled, and then the wretchedness of the toilet and the hoses and then finally the way I'd learned to *be* there, and he listened and made no comment, and my words spilled in a torrent I could not control, and when it was done, I felt as if I'd emptied an ugliness from inside me that I hadn't known was there. I would not forget it, but the poison was somehow gone. I had not realized until then how sick I'd been with it.

He opened the tomatoes. He had two spoons, and he gave me one, and we ate contentedly from the can until we finished them.

He took the notebook from his pocket, along with the pencil, and laid it on the table with a quiet deliberation I didn't understand. And then suddenly I did. Suddenly I knew that he'd heard something in my story that I'd forgotten. He took out a precious cigarette, got to his feet, and said, "I'm going for a smoke," and went outside, leaving me there. I stared at that notebook, the page with *Charles* written on it and then the dates I'd given him. I pulled it toward me. The stink of sardines was in my nose, their salty oil on my fingers. The wine was almost gone. I took another gulp and picked up the pencil, and turned the page. The imprint of the words Dante had written pressed through. He'd left the door open; the smoke of his cigarette drifted inside.

I rolled the pencil in my fingers. I had banished my talent. I had glimpsed beauty with a gnawing longing and let it go untouched and unheralded. I had gathered it for only the briefest of moments and determinedly ignored the ache it left behind, and after a time, not so long, the urge to capture such things had died from lack of nourishment. What if it meant to punish me by staying away? But there again, that touch, the familiar way the pencil settled into my hand, and the images I'd suppressed roused: the light from the thick panes of my windows reflected on the floor, the tea rose in Mrs. Donaghan's garden, the orange smoke clouds against a starry sky, and the red roses in the alien light, those garishly gorgeous roses. At first tentative, waiting, hopeful. *Now?* Waiting for my *no*, as I had said *no* a dozen times, a hundred, in the past year, and there too, that prick of fear, the warning of complacency that meant defeat and acceptance.

But I was free of Blessington now. I was no longer a prisoner. I'd denied my talent and my comfort to save myself then, and I knew instinctively that to use it would save me now. The earth had set me free. The city was at my feet. I forgot where I was and that I had not touched a pencil in months.

When I was finished, I let the pencil drop. The drawing was smudged, pressed hard into cheap paper to make it show, the edge of my hand smeared black. It was not my best drawing. The imprint of Dante's words—*Charles*, the dates—made a palimpsest of my rose-bedecked bier, which blazoned richly in pencil, nearly glowing with release and with joy. I had not been defeated, the drawing said. I had not lost myself.

For the first time since the earthquake, I slept deeply, without waking at every noise, without being on the alert for any possible attack. I'd burrowed into Bobby's blankets, which were musty and stinking of sweat, but I was warm for the first time in days, and when I woke, the sun was fully up and I smelled coffee.

When I stepped from the bedroom, there was Dante, again in shirtsleeves and sitting at the kitchen table, drinking from a tin mug and writing furiously in his notebook. He glanced up with a smile. "At least you don't snore."

"Does Bobby?"

"When he's been drinking. Which is all the time." He gestured to another tin mug on the table. "I brought you some coffee from next door. It might not be hot. And there's no sugar, and no milk unless you've got children, which I don't, so—"

"I don't care." I picked up the mug and took a deep and grateful sip. It was lukewarm, but it was coffee. I'd had it from the relief wagons, but somehow it was better gifted by a friend. "What are you writing?"

"Notes from last night. You do want me to tell your story? I wasn't mistaken about that? You want me to help you ruin the Sullivans?" His eyes glittered; he was afraid I would say no.

"Yes. Soon. But the Chinatown articles first. Then we'll have the evidence of my uncle's corruption and Goldie's gambling that China Joe promised, and that will give you more than just my word." I sat down next to him. "Today, we're going to see him."

"Your servant, milady. I'll send that telegram to my friend too. In the meantime, about Farge . . ." He grabbed the rest of the bread from last night, and set it before me for breakfast. "We'll need Shin for my plan. Do you think she'll help?"

"Help how?"

"You said Farge has your sketchbooks."

"If they didn't burn. Everything on Nob Hill did. The last place I saw them was at his office, but—"

"The Monkey Block is still standing," Dante said.

I had avoided the area completely, afraid to come upon anyone I knew, and also because the memories of Ellis's office, of Coppa's, were not ones I wished to revisit. "It's still there?"

Dante nodded. "They saved the whole block. Coppa's too."

"How lucky for Ellis." I could not keep the bitterness from my voice.

"Luck follows him everywhere." Dante's voice was equally caustic. "Time for it to run out. What do you say we steal those sketchbooks back?"

I only looked at him.

"What? He'll be lost without them. Tell me what happens when he can't fulfill any of his contracts because his idea source is gone. He'll be ruined."

Of course it appealed greatly to my hunger for revenge, which felt boundless. An appropriate justice, to destroy Ellis with his own weakness. Still . . . "How exactly do you intend to steal them back?"

"It will be easy. Or it should be. If they're in his office, we simply walk in and take them."

"Don't tell me they don't know you there."

"They do, but I'm not doing the walking in. You are."

"Dante! They'll recognize me. I worked with him for weeks."

"They won't recognize you like this." He gestured to my attire. "They know a woman, not trousers and a flannel shirt. We'll give you an old jacket of mine, and you can keep my hat. We'll smudge you up a little, and there you are, Mack Kimble, errand boy. They'll see what they expect to see."

I would have argued with him about that if I hadn't already known that he'd been invisible at every entertainment I'd attended. I couldn't believe I'd never noticed him, given his magnetism, but then, I had been busy trying to fit in, and the truth was that, even when I tried, I couldn't remember the face of any servant beyond the ones at the Sullivan house. Dante was right; I simply hadn't seen whomever I'd thought unimportant.

"If that's the case, maybe we should put you in a dress and let you do the stealing."

He grinned and scraped his hand along his jaw, freshly shaved, but still beard shadowed. "We'd need plaster to disguise this."

"What do we need Shin for?"

"To keep watch up on Nob Hill, to keep Farge from setting out for his office before we're done. Will she do that, do you think?"

"I think she'll do whatever she must to be free."

He tapped his fingers restlessly on the table. "Good. Finish up then, let's talk to China Joe and see what he has in mind for me."

"You're nervous." It was surprising and amusing. He was always so confident.

"You weren't, when you paid him a visit?" Dante asked. "You know he runs one of the tongs in Chinatown."

I remembered Goldie's theory that Shin had lost her finger in some fight as a tong—gang—girl. The real story was so much more horrible. But then, so was the story of my aunt at the bottom of the stairs, and the terrible destruction wrought by the corruption involved in the building of city hall and my own incarceration in Blessington.

"How is a Chinese gang different from the board of supervisors? They're all the same. It's only the color of his skin that makes us think China Joe more dangerous. They're all dangerous. Every one of them."

"San Francisco is a viper pit of corruption." Dante rose. "Let's go."

I shoved the rest of the bread into my mouth and gulped the coffee, and then we were off.

Shin waited at the burned-out trolleys, and when she saw Dante walking beside me, her relief was palpable.

"You must be Shin," he said.

Breathlessly she said to me, "He will help us?"

"I will," Dante said. "Unless China Joe wants me to murder someone. I draw the line at that."

"He has men to do that for him."

It was not the most reassuring thing she could have said.

She led us again through the wrack of Chinatown while Dante explained our plan to steal my sketchbooks back from Ellis, and her part in it.

When he was finished, she said, "I told you not to show him the drawings."

"I thought it was because you knew I would embarrass myself. Did you know what Goldie intended?"

Shin shook her head. "I only knew that she wanted him to see them, so I knew it must be bad for you."

I snorted. "It was all too good to be true. I knew it, I just . . . didn't believe it."

We arrived to find China Joe sitting serenely behind his wagon-desk. He looked as if he had nothing better to do than wait for us.

"Dante LaRosa," I introduced. "Writer for the *Bulletin*."

Any hint of Dante's nervousness was gone. There again, that self-assuredness that I found so compelling. "I understand that you're looking for a reporter."

Joe smiled. "And you, Alphonse Bandersnitch, are looking for the story to raise your position."

Dante looked momentarily surprised. "Your spies have been busy."

"In my business, it is good to know what people want," China Joe said. "One might say it is my only business—to make everyone happy."

The next morning, the first of four articles—each increasingly threatening—in the *Bulletin* was small, not on the society page, and not by Alphonse Bandersnitch, but prominently placed where the well-to-do merchants and city leaders would be sure to find it.

Chinatown Rumblings

It is rumored that the city plans to move the Chinese to Hunters Point. Authorities claim the move would be most beneficial to the Chinese, who would be safe and protected there, living in a happy society together. Those who oppose the plan point out that Hunters Point is next to slaughterhouses and mud flats, which are hardly salubrious for anyone, and note that the current location of Chinatown, in the middle of downtown, easily accessible, protected from wind, has been coveted for years by rich real estate interests. And of course, it is even more desirable now that the fire has burned away all the dangerous germs.

Chinese leaders assure this reporter that they will fight for their property rights, and say that the landlords of Chinatown will lose a great deal of income if the Chinese are forced to leave. They threaten that China can and will be pressured to stop trade with San Francisco over this matter, and that Chinese merchants will take their money elsewhere. Portland, Tacoma, and Seattle have indicated that they are anxious to reap the known benefits of Chinese investment. The Chinese consulate has confirmed that it is considering a move to Oakland, as there would be no reason for it to stay in San Francisco without a Chinese population to attend.

The Chinese currently own thirty-five lots in Chinatown, and white landlords with substantial investment in the area have also vowed to fight the move. The future of San Francisco's Chinese population will be decided by city authorities in the coming weeks.

TWENTY-SEVEN

That morning, I braided my hair tightly and pinned it close to my skull. I wore an old and shabby bowler of Dante's, as well as his worn jacket, which was too big, but it easily hid what curves there were of my figure, and as my legs were long, I did look remarkably like a boy.

Dante looked me over critically. "Those stitches need to come out, but we'll leave them in for now. They help your disguise. Try not to walk like a woman—no swaying. Swagger."

"Like this?" I took a few steps across the room.

He winced. "Can you drop your voice an octave?"

"Like this?" I tried.

"I guess that's the best we can hope for."

I caught a glimpse of myself in the cracked mirror in Bobby's bedroom, and I looked nothing like May Kimble. The only thing that gave me away was the slenderness of my face and my jaw, and if I lowered my chin just so . . . Well, I wouldn't be there for long.

"My guess is that no one else knows the significance of those sketchbooks," Dante told me as we walked to the Montgomery Block. "So if you come asking for them, they won't question that he's sent you. Just don't act nervous."

Shin had promised to do her best to keep Ellis occupied.

"I'm not nervous. I'm furious," I said.

"That won't serve, either. You're a messenger boy. You're bored, and you're tired of tromping around ruins, and Mr. Farge better give you that nickel he promised because you need a beer and a smoke."

"I have a whole story, I see."

Dante chuckled. "Just remember it. It will keep you in character. Like an actor."

"You'll be waiting right outside?"

"Looking longingly through Coppa's window, waiting for the day he clears the smoke damage and reopens. But I'll come running if anything happens. Do you still have your metal rod?"

"Do you think I'll need it?" I asked in surprise.

"One never knows. Just be prepared, all right?"

"All right."

Even having been told that the Monkey Block was still standing, I somehow didn't expect to see it there, amid a plain of desolation, with people going in and out as if it were just another day at the office. The memories it brought held a gentle despair. Coppa's, with its cigarette smoke–infused room, the red walls with their animated illustrations, the plates of spaghetti and the wine spilling as it was poured, and everyone crowding around. Blythe and Edith Jackson and Wenceslas and Gelett . . . What did they think about me now, if they thought about me at all? I'd been briefly one of them. Surely gossip had kept me alive for a time, but now I suspected I was not even a ghost at Coppa's, my drawing on the wall ruined, no doubt drawn over. Nothing of me left. The thought saddened me more than I expected.

Now, the windows of the restaurant were dark. At the corner, still out of sight, Dante touched my arm. "Be careful. Remember, run if it goes wrong. I'll be waiting."

"Wish me luck." I tugged at the canvas bag at my shoulder and took a deep breath.

I went to the door that I had so naively entered over a year ago. But that girl was gone now. I gripped the button in my pocket, reminding myself of everything that had happened, everything I'd vowed to do.

I went up the stairs, my mouth dry with nerves, reminding myself to look like some messenger boy on business and hoping no one looked too closely. It was dim inside. Like the rest of the city, there was no gas or electricity here. Light came from whatever studio doors were open, or oil lamps. I tried not to think of what I would do if the sketchbooks weren't there.

They had to be there. The thought of Ellis carefully copying them, my creation turned to his hand, that plaque on the library wall bearing his name instead of mine . . . Anger cleared my head. Beyond the windowed door of Farge & Partners moved shadows. Inside, an assistant I didn't know spoke to two dark-suited men hovering about the desk. I paid them little attention. When the assistant glanced at me, I lowered my voice and tilted my head down, not meeting his eyes. "I'm here to pick up Mr. Farge's sketchbooks. He's asked for them."

The assistant barely looked at me. He nodded and called, "Robinson!" When a tall young man appeared, the assistant said, "Mr. Farge needs his sketchbooks. Take the boy back to get them."

My heart raced as Robinson led me down the hall. The place was busy; I met no one's eye and no one looked twice at me, a nobody, as Dante had been at the balls where I had not seen him. He'd been right; I was invisible. The door to Ellis's office was locked, but Robinson took a key from his pocket and opened it, ushering me into a room so familiar with its smells of paper and ink and Ellis that it momentarily knocked me back. I had leaned over that desk with him, looking at plans. I had discussed the Hartford standing right there. And all the time, he'd been scheming with Goldie. All that time, he'd been meaning to rob me, not just of my freedom and my dignity, but of my talent.

"There." Robinson pointed to a bookcase where my sketchbooks were neatly shelved. "Do you need some help?"

"No, thanks." I tried to growl the words. I opened the canvas bag and shoved the books inside while Robinson stood by and watched. The familiar feel of their covers, their weight . . . I had missed them. Once I had them all, Robinson led me out of the office and locked it behind him.

"Good day," he said.

I hurried back to the door. The assistant was still talking to the men; no one looked at me or seemed to note my departure. It was all I could do not to race down those stairs. *"You're a messenger boy. You're bored and you need a beer and a smoke."*

I did not relax until I was out of the building. It was done. It was done, and they were in my hands again, and the thought of what Ellis would do now that his inspiration was gone . . . I couldn't help smiling— a smile that faded when I saw Dante running panicked toward the door.

"He's on his way," he said when he reached me. "He's just down the block."

The bag full of books beat against my hip as I raced with Dante around the corner of the building. There, we stopped.

"Did you get them?" he asked.

"Yes. What's he doing here? Shin was supposed to keep him—"

"She tried. She sent a boy to warn me, but he was only steps ahead of Farge. At least you got out of there in time. Come on." Dante started off.

I didn't move.

"Come on. Do you want him to see us?"

"He can't see through a building." My heart was racing again, excitement and apprehension both. "I want to see what he does."

294

"This is exactly how murderers and thieves get caught," Dante protested.

I peeked around the corner. No Ellis yet. "By standing behind buildings?"

"By watching the scene of the crime. It happens often enough that it's almost a cliché."

I glanced over my shoulder at him. "I'm not a murderer."

"No, but you're being an idiot and it's going to be how he finds us."

"Don't tell me that you don't want to see Ellis's reaction when he finds the books gone."

Dante hesitated.

"Come, now. You know you do. But if you truly don't, then go ahead and leave." I shrugged the bag from my shoulder and handed it to him. "Take these with you. I'll meet you at the house later."

He took the bag and slung it over his shoulder, but he didn't move.

"They destroyed me, Dante." The soft danger of my fury was impossible to harness, and I made no attempt to do so. I said it again, more quietly, "They destroyed me. Ellis stole my . . . he stole *me*. I have to see him. I have to know."

"Know what?"

"If this will destroy him too."

Dante's expression was both tender and pained. "The things you say sometimes . . . It breaks my heart."

The words and his gaze caught me and held; suddenly and unexpectedly, I wanted to step into his arms. So disconcerting . . . I lost what I'd been about to say; I lost my focus. Just then, Ellis came into view. I backed up quickly from the corner, cracking my head into Dante's chin. "Ouch! Sorry."

He swore quietly. "What if he stays in there for hours?"

"He won't."

"Why do you say that?"

"Because I wouldn't."

And in fact, we waited only another few minutes—long enough for Ellis to reach his office, to discover his treasure trove gone, to question Robinson, the assistant—before Ellis came rushing again from the building. He stood helplessly at the entrance, looking wildly about. I smelled the stink of his desperation from where I stood, and I understood it; I knew exactly how he must feel. But Ellis had made a choice, and he had not cared that it crushed me when he made it, and so when he sank back against the building and buried his face in his hands, I turned to Dante, who watched over my shoulder.

"Seen enough?" he asked.

"It will never be enough," I told him.

"Don't worry," he assured me. "His hell has only just begun."

When we arrived back at the house, having stopped at one of the relief lines for our portion of eggs and canned meat, bread and coffee and canned peas, Dante emptied the bag of my sketchbooks. "Do you mind if I look at them?"

The urge to deny him came first, that lingering fear that the drawings were juvenilia, or worse, that I was talentless and deluded. But my library had been built, and Dante had already told me he knew I had talent, and so I nodded, and went to the stove set among the rocks outside to cook a meal.

When I came back, bearing eggs scrambled with potted meat, he was still looking through them. He didn't look up until I set a plate before him.

"No wonder Farge used these. They're beautiful."

I let myself bask in the pleasure of his praise. Again, I felt the urge that had overtaken me at the Monkey Block. I ignored it. It was only the tension and excitement of stealing the sketchbooks. "That one was inspired by hollyhocks in our back alley. They grew along the fence. The narrow windows are the slats, and the curtains and the stucco—"

"Yes, I can see it."

"My mother showed me that when you turned the flowers upside down they looked like ladies in ball gowns. We used to dance them along the railing. She said it would be my life one day." I hadn't thought about that in a long time. *"You'll be like these ladies, but it won't be pretend. You'll be wearing a ball gown, and you'll dance all night, and have such fun . . ."*

It had been like that, hadn't it? I had danced all night. I had worn ball gowns, and yet—"But when it was mine, I didn't like it."

"Hmmm." He motioned to a chair. "Here, sit down. Let me get to those stitches."

I did as he asked. He pulled out a pocketknife and lit a match, blackening the edge to sterilize it while I watched unseeingly, thinking instead of suppers distinguished by endless talk of nothing, teas and receptions and parties shimmering with illusion, so much emptiness. "I'd been raised to be a lady in society, but when I actually became that lady, it was boring. It was all so—"

"Stupid," he offered, leaning in. I felt the warmth of his breath as he touched my cheek. "At least you see it, unlike most of them. That picture you drew at Coppa's said pretty well what you think of it all. Sit very still. I don't want to take out an eye."

I would have jerked back in surprise if he had not held me firm. "You saw that? Ellis didn't."

He was deft and quick; the knife pressed gently, I heard the faint snap of the stitch and forced myself not to make a face at the strange sense of the thread pulling through my skin. "Farge is an idiot. Haven't I said that before? Anyway, you're in the wrong crowd. You should be with the Hoffmans and the McKays. That set at least tries to make the world better, with all their charity work. Some of it's misguided, but at least they make an attempt."

My aunt had once done the same, Goldie had told me. How my cousin had objected when I'd thought to do some charity work myself.

How my uncle had objected. Now I understood that they wanted to keep me close and isolated, where they could manipulate both me and society as they wished.

"I met Mrs. Hoffman once. At the Cliff House."

Another press and pull. His fingers were warm and sure, his hand cupped my cheek. I'd not felt such tenderness in so very long that it was mesmerizing. He plucked another stitch. "Don't tell me it was that time you were with Belden and the others."

"It was. Why?"

"Because you were drunk. I'm sure you made a fine impression."

"It was less tedious with champagne."

"That's why Ned Greenway makes a fortune selling it. There." Dante sat back with a satisfied expression. "At least you don't look sewn together now."

I touched the wound, a puffy ridge, but smooth now without the roughness of the stitches. "Thank you. I had no idea you had so many talents."

"That's me. A veritable treasure trove." He smiled, such an engaging, beautiful smile, one so real, one that asked nothing of me, and suddenly I felt unbalanced, as if the ground had shifted beneath my feet.

Hastily, embarrassed for no reason I could say, I looked away. "You should eat before it gets cold."

"Oh yes." He picked up his fork. But I could see his thoughts grow distant, and he kept looking at my sketchbook as if something there troubled him. I waited until I couldn't stand it any longer, and then I said, "What's wrong?"

He blinked. "Nothing's wrong."

"Why are you looking at my drawing that way?"

"I'm just thinking . . . What did you intend to do with these?"

There it was, the question that had plagued me, asked so directly that there was no way to avoid my own uncertainty, or the fact that these drawings held my entire history: who I thought I was and who I meant to be, a future I had only just begun to consider before Blessington buried it—or so I thought. At Dante's question, the possibility teased again.

"All of San Francisco has to be rebuilt," Dante went on. "The interior architects that are here can't possibly handle the work. Farge will be useless now without these, of course, and that means everyone will be looking for people like you. Maybe . . ." Dante trailed off tentatively. "I don't know if that's something you might want, but if you do . . . maybe I could help you make it happen."

"But I'm a woman."

"Needs must. Desperate people make choices they might not otherwise. People want their houses built now. Offer your services. See who takes you up."

"I—I don't think I'm ready for that."

"Aren't you?" He gestured to the books. "You're more than ready. You're just afraid. Think about it, May. Look—" He turned the pages quickly, stopping at the drawing of the library. "Farge didn't change a single line. Not one. If he thought they were good enough to call them his, why can't the person who really drew them?"

Again, that flicker of hope, or desire—along with fear. "I don't know—"

"You have a gift. It would be a sin to waste it."

His belief was tantalizing. Still . . .

"Let's do this: let's run an advert in the *Bulletin*. We'll print one of these drawings to show them what you can do—what do you want to call your firm?"

"If I did that, the Sullivans would know I'm alive," I protested.

Dante met my gaze. "They'll know that anyway, when I write the articles. They'll know it when you take your inheritance back. How long do you mean to hide?"

"Until we can publish my story, until I have my inheritance, I can't risk that they'll find me. They've hired a private detective. If I publish an advertisement, they'll know exactly where I am."

"We'll ask that inquiries be sent to the *Bulletin* offices."

"Then Ellis will know it has something to do with you, and he knows where to find you, doesn't he? He knows who Alphonse Bandersnitch really is."

"I can manage Ellis Farge."

"But he belongs to the Sullivans now, and you don't know them as I do."

"No, I know them better. Wasn't I the one to tell you? They're not as clever as we are together. They won't find you here."

"No," I insisted. "Not yet."

His jaw tightened. "All right. As you like."

I tried to make him understand. "If they find me this time, I'll disappear."

"You won't disappear. I won't let you. I'll look for you. I'll have the whole city looking for you."

How intent he looked, how devoted. I should not feel so warmed by his concern. "At least someone would be out there searching this time. I could bear it better, knowing someone was trying to find me."

For a moment, he was quiet. Then, hoarsely, he said, "I'm sorry, May. I'm so very sorry. For all of it."

"It's not your fault."

"I'm sorry anyway. I wish I'd been able to stop it. I would have done anything if I'd realized."

The words raised in me a longing I didn't expect, again that need to be close to him, to touch him. No one had truly cared about me since my mother had died, and in that moment the loneliness I'd borne since her death, the loneliness I'd told myself Goldie and my uncle had assuaged, swept through me so strongly that I rose and stepped away. I could not be still. I could not look at him; I was afraid I would cry if I did.

TWENTY-EIGHT

A week later, when I next met Shin, she rolled up her sleeve to show me the bruises on her wrist, but her voice was triumphant. "No opium since the earthquake, and she has bad nightmares. Now, she is worse than ever."

I was horrified. "She hurt you?"

"She suffers. She does not know her own strength." Shin rebuttoned the cuff and gave me a small and wicked smile. "It is all right, Miss May. It is worth it to see her this way. Mr. Sullivan does not care about his daughter's problems these days. The Chinese are unhappy. They have asked for a meeting with the governor and he has granted it because of the stories in the newspaper. Mr. Ruef is worried about the meeting because he has no power with the governor, and he is not listening to Mr. Sullivan, and so Mr. Sullivan is not listening to his daughter's complaints."

Dante's articles were working. I imagined my uncle watching his grand plans for Chinatown slipping away. It was satisfying, but it wasn't enough. Not nearly enough. "What about Mr. Farge?"

"He is . . . sad. Upset. Nothing pleases him. They fight all the time."

"Good," I said.

"Miss May, there is something else," Shin said urgently. "Mr. Sullivan had a visitor last night. Mr. Oelrichs."

"Mr.—Stephen Oelrichs? You mean Goldie's ex-fiancé? Why would he come to see Uncle Jonny? He didn't see Goldie?"

Shin looked grim. "He saw your uncle. They spoke quietly, then they fought. They were both very angry."

That was puzzling, and troubling too. I had thought Stephen Oelrichs wanted nothing to do with the Sullivans, so why would he come to Nob Hill to argue with my uncle?

Of course, I'd been gone a long time. Perhaps things had changed. Perhaps Oelrichs and my uncle had business together.

"Did you hear anything they said?"

"No. But Mr. Sullivan was not himself the rest of the day."

"I see. Well." I took a deep breath. "I'll see if Dante knows anything about it. Be careful, Shin. Please. And . . . don't let Goldie touch you. She hasn't the right."

"It is almost over. I am doing my part, Miss May. I trust you to do yours."

Again, my responsibility and obligation pressed. Things were going according to plan, and I should be content, but the scene Shin had described between my uncle and Stephen Oelrichs disturbed me. I didn't understand it, and it seemed important, something I should know. I rolled my uncle's vest button between my fingers as I walked back to Dante's house.

I'd only gone a few blocks when a bright blue canary flew past my shoulder, so close I could have touched it. A sign, if I chose to see it that way, because I started from my thoughts and turned to see the man behind me. There were men everywhere, of course, but this one stepped casually—too casually—aside to study a half-standing brick wall. There were a hundred half-standing brick walls just like it, and the way this man studied it was strangely intense. I could not see his face; his hat shadowed it.

No one could possibly recognize me. It was just a man with a predilection for brick walls. But my gooseflesh told me otherwise, and I knew now to pay attention to my instincts, no matter how silly they seemed.

I turned back again, pretending not to see him, but now I was aware of him. I tried to give him no hint that I knew I was being followed, but at the next corner I turned abruptly, and then at the next. My excursions throughout the city in those days after the fire had given me a rat's sense of safety. The moment I found a fallen chimney, I crawled into it and waited.

The man *had* been following me. I wasn't wrong about that. He turned the corner onto the street where I was, hesitated, searched, and then turned away again. I did not move. I curled in that cramped and uncomfortable position for the rest of the day. When twilight came, I crept from the chimney and made a circuitous way back to Dante's house. It took more than an hour, and I came to the back door, where I waited another fifteen minutes to make certain I had not been followed before I went inside.

The door opened into Dante's bedroom—the bed neatly made, clothes hanging on hooks in the walls, boots encrusted with mud and ash, a tilting dresser cracked up the side, scattered with an overfull ashtray and hairbrushes and shaving things, and throughout the scent of cigarette smoke and Dante's soap, which I would have recognized anywhere.

From the other room came the clacking of the typewriter. I closed the door softly behind me and leaned against it, catching my breath, trying to calm my pulse and my fear. I was safe. He had said he would let nothing happen to me. He would not let them take me away again.

He would look for me . . . In some part of my mind it seemed impossible that I might trust him, or anyone, to do those things, but the truth was that I did. He had seen what I'd put in that drawing at Coppa's. He'd recognized *me* in that library. He understood what no one else did.

The clacking stopped abruptly, and then he was in the bedroom doorway. "Where the hell have you been?" he snapped, and I saw the worry in his face, the way his thick hair stood on end as if he'd raked his hand through it a dozen times. "I was just getting ready to go looking for you."

"Someone was following me."

He took two strides to the door and pulled me into his arms, and I fell against his chest with relief. "Are they still?"

"I think I lost them. I know I did."

He locked the door. "Who was it?"

"Some man . . . I don't know who he was."

Dante pulled me closer and rested his chin on my hair. His hands went to my back, soothing—I was trembling, I realized. "You can't go out again, May. Not alone. Not until this is resolved."

I pulled back. "I can't not go out. Who knows when it will be over?"

His hands came to my face, his thumbs at my jaw, caressing, rubbing. "What's this all over your face?"

I reached up to feel. "I don't know. Soot? I hid in a chimney."

"A chimney?"

"All day. It was very uncomfortable."

He stilled. "You hid in a chimney all day."

"I didn't want to be found."

He laughed. Short, at first, in disbelief, and then in real amusement. "What a survivor you are, May Kimble. You'll still be among the ruins when the world ends. You don't need me; you don't need anyone."

I gripped his wrists, keeping his hands on my face. "Don't say that."

"But it's true. You have a remarkable—"

"I don't want to be among the ruins when the world ends. I'm . . . I'm so very, very tired of . . . being alone." The last words slipped out before I knew I would say them.

Dante's smile died. In his eyes I saw an emotion I did not want to escape.

He whispered, "May," and then he kissed me. It was as if I'd been waiting always for this kiss, and when he started to draw away, I pulled him closer. I put my arms around his neck and opened my mouth to him, and he made a sound deep in his throat that dropped into my stomach and pulled at my every nerve so I was like those houses during the fire, glowing from the inside out until they burst.

Disaster is the best aphrodisiac, he'd written. The knowledge that everything could change in a heartbeat, that a mother could die on the way home from picking up piecework, or a whole life could be upended by a word, by a lie, by the earth waking, or a spark catching from a fallen chimney. After what I'd been through, how did one stop at a kiss? Who knew what tomorrow would bring, if it came at all?

Whatever it was, the uncertain future, the city in ruins, the fact that I'd felt Dante belonged to me months before I knew him . . . I don't know which it was. Perhaps all of those things. What I do know is that I wanted him. I was starving for him. I had his shirt open and my hands on his skin, my fingers in the hair on his chest, and it was not enough. When he shoved my own shirt from my shoulders, I pressed my breasts to him and it was not enough. His tongue on mine was not enough. I fumbled at the buttons of his trousers, and then we were at his bed, and it wasn't until then that he paused, that he drew away and looked at me in question, and I knew he would stop if I said no, enough, and I heard my mother's voice in my head as she warned me away from the boys in the neighborhood. *"You must always watch yourself, May. There are expectations for you. You don't want to be known as that kind of girl . . ."*

"I'm a modern woman," I breathed.

Dante lifted a brow and gave me a look that turned me inside out. "That you are."

"Please don't stop. I don't want you to stop."

His expression softened, so unbearably sweet and wondering, with that hunger too that matched my own. "I'll be careful. I promise you."

After that, we did not slow, and though it hurt when he first eased into me, it was a pain I welcomed, and one soon swept away as the pleasure mounted along with my desire, and then, at last, it was enough. Then, at last, I had what I didn't know I was looking for: the antidote to my loneliness, which shriveled and withered away. Until that moment, I hadn't realized how much of me it had been.

It wasn't until long after, when we were physically exhausted but unable to sleep, that I said, "I've changed my mind. I want you to run the advertisement. Choose a sketch you like and we'll have inquiries sent to the *Bulletin* office, as you said. I'll call my firm the Brooklyn Company."

He'd been tracing circles on my shoulder, but now he paused. "What of your family? What about this private detective?"

"You were right, what you said before. It's time. In Blessington, I knew I had enough of their secrets to destroy them. All I needed then was you and Shin. China Joe has the evidence, and I'm done running. I want them to know I'm alive. I don't need to have my money to show the city what they are or what I am."

A long pause, but I felt the tension in him, and I knew it for excitement and not apprehension. "Are you certain?"

"Yes. Maybe nothing will happen, but . . ."

He kissed my hair. "My dear girl, have you forgotten where you are? This is San Francisco. Anything can happen here."

Long after he'd fallen into sleep, I lay awake, thinking of possibilities, until dawn broke and with it the bustle of the city waking. The world had opened for me at last. I had allies. I had my sketchbooks.

All I needed was my inheritance. We had not yet received an answer to Dante's telegram to New York about my father, though he checked every day. I was growing more anxious, but he'd assured me it would come. His fellow reporter was thorough, and once we knew who my family was in New York and contacted them, once they were told what happened and we contacted an attorney with all the information, Stephen Oelrichs perhaps, as he'd once—

With a start, I remembered my conversation with Shin.

I shoved Dante, who moaned and grumbled and squinted against the morning before he opened his eyes to peer at me. Then he threw his arm over his face and said, "Generally I prefer something gentler. Coffee. Perhaps a kiss."

"I'd forgotten—I meant to tell you. Yesterday morning I went to see Shin."

He sighed. "What time is it?"

"Early yet."

"I don't have to be at the paper until eight." His hand went to my hip. "I can think of something better to do than talking about Shin."

I brushed my lips against his rough cheek. "Dante, Shin said Stephen Oelrichs was at the camp to talk to my uncle. That they argued."

"Oelrichs?" He sounded as surprised as I had been.

"I hadn't thought they even socialized. Has something changed since I've been away?"

"Changed how?"

Ellis and Goldie in the kitchen tent at the camp, her golden hair in the lamplight. *All of Nob Hill forced to hobnob together.* "Come now, put on your Alphonse Bandersnitch hat for a moment. Has Goldie's marriage to Ellis made a difference socially? Have they moved into a different tier? Has Ned Greenway invited them to join the Cotillion Club?"

"You think *Farge* could get her in?" Dante snorted.

"If he's so famous now—"

"No. He's been invited to the Bohemian Club, but that's a different thing altogether."

"The Sullivans are still in the Sporting set?"

"And never the twain shall meet—unless they have business together," he confirmed. "But that's not likely with the Sullivans, especially after Goldie jilted him."

I was quiet.

Dante frowned. "What aren't you telling me?"

"It wasn't Goldie who jilted Stephen Oelrichs. It was the other way around. He found out she was gambling and probably about the opium too, and he jilted her. But he let everyone think that *she* broke the engagement. He was trying to protect her, but Goldie thinks he did it to humiliate her. She hates him. And Dante . . . At the Anderson soiree, Oelrichs told me to be careful of the Sullivans, and he warned me about China Joe."

"Why?"

"I don't know. He told me that I was in over my head. I think he was afraid for me."

Dante went thoughtful. "I wonder what it means?"

"Maybe that he wanted to help me?"

"Do you never suspect anyone of ulterior motives?" he asked. "That's what got you into trouble, you know."

Tartly I said, "Mr. Oelrichs jilted Goldie *and* warned me against the Sullivans. I can't help but think that it's possible his motives aren't in conflict with mine. But it's strange that he would be arguing with my uncle, and I don't like it. I want to know why."

"I'll see what I can find out today." He rolled to face me. "But not yet. First there's the little matter of a rude awakening . . ."

I was, of course, happy to make it up to him.

TWENTY-NINE

S tay here today, please. Can you do that for me?" Dante said. "I'll be back before long. I want to see if there's an answer from New York about your father, and check on this Oelrichs business, and I don't want to worry where you are."

I promised I wouldn't leave. I sat on the stoop with one of my sketchbooks. Dante had taken one with him to the *Bulletin*. I knew he meant to put the advert in the newspaper today, and I had trouble settling. But the morning felt fresh and new, even with its familiar scent of salt and wet ash and smoke. Perhaps my life was not turning out exactly as Mama had hoped, or as I dreamed, but it was turning into something rather more interesting.

I drew in the foggy air until my hands were too cold, and then I went inside and put the sketchbook away and wondered if standing in the relief line for today's provisions would be breaking my word to

Dante. Before I could decide, there was a knock on the doorjamb, a "Hello?" at the open door that made me jump.

I turned to see a man standing there. He wore a dark heavy coat, and a hat with its brim pulled low, and he held a folded newspaper.

It was the same man who had followed me yesterday.

My instinct was to run. But he blocked the door, and I didn't think I could get to the back without him catching me.

"Miss Kimble?" he asked. "May Kimble?"

I'd been found. I'd been caught. Too late. My uncle had won after all. Still, I tried. "N-no. No, I'm afraid you—"

"I'm David Emerson." The man reached into his pocket and took out a card, stepping inside to offer it to me. "I've been hired by—"

"I know," I murmured.

"—Mr. Stephen Oelrichs, to find Miss May Kimble, of the New York Van Berckyls."

The words did not register at first. I was too busy trying to find a way out, to wonder how fast I could run, if he would follow, if I could push past him, but then what he'd said landed hard in my panicked brain.

"*Stephen Oelrichs?*"

Mr. Emerson nodded. "He's been looking for you, miss. He asked me to tell you that he personally guarantees your safety."

I stared at him, speechless.

"You're the daughter of Charles Van Berckyl, of the New York family, are you not? Friends of Mr. Oelrichs?"

"The daughter of Charles Van Berckyl." I repeated the name woodenly. The name I'd been waiting my whole life to hear, and to hear it now, so unexpectedly, from such an unexpected source . . . I could not fathom that this was me. It had nothing to do with me.

"Yes. Might I take you to Mr. Oelrichs, Miss Kimble? He is most anxious to speak with you."

"Stay here," Dante had said. I did not know if I could trust Stephen Oelrichs. Except that he'd tried to warn me. He'd been arguing with my uncle. Why? Emerson said Oelrichs was a friend of my father's family. *The New York Van Berckyls. The daughter of Charles Van Berckyl.* My father, who had left me an inheritance, but who had allowed me and my mother to live in poverty and hardship. The man with whom I'd been angry most of my life.

"Do you never suspect anyone of ulterior motives? That's what got you into trouble, you know."

The button in my pocket was again in my fingers, turning and turning. Mr. Emerson waited for my answer with a pleasant expectancy, the card still proffered.

I plucked it from him and perused it quickly. "Thank you, Mr. Emerson, but I expect Mr. Oelrichs can wait a bit longer for my visit."

"But Miss Kimble—"

"Tell Mr. Oelrichs that I'll call on him later this afternoon. I'll bring a friend."

"This is a private matter, I'm afraid."

A private matter. My family had wanted nothing to do with me. My inheritance was predicated on accepting those terms. According to Shin, they wished only to know whether I was dead or alive. This did not involve the Sullivans, or the police.

"It is *my* private matter," I told him with my haughtiest manner. "I am not Mr. Oelrichs's chattel, nor his relation, and I am not obliged to answer his summons. Tell him I'll visit him at his home this afternoon, with a friend. Thank you, Mr. Emerson. That is all."

The man looked flustered, but, as inconsequential as I looked in my trousers and my shirt, dirty and sweating and not at all the lady I was supposed to be, I had learned such a manner well, and I knew how to use it.

Mr. Emerson sighed. "Very well, Miss Kimble. I will give Mr. Oelrichs your message."

When he left, the courage and hauteur that had sustained me collapsed. I sank into a chair and tried to swallow a hysterical urge to laugh—or to cry. I did not know what to think. Van Berckyl. The name should have meant everything to me, and yet, I could not find my center; I did not know how to feel about it.

I heard Dante before I saw him, bounding up the short front stairs and through the still-open door. A paper—a telegram—fluttered in his hand, and excitement animated his every move. The moment he saw me, he burst out breathlessly, "It came, May. It's here—the answer. Your father is Charles Van Berckyl."

"I know," I said.

He stopped short. His hand dropped to his side. His surprise was almost comical. "You know?"

I nodded.

"How in the hell do you know that?"

"He found me," I said. "Mr. Emerson. The private detective. He found me."

More surprise. "He came here?"

"After you left. The Sullivans didn't hire him. Stephen Oelrichs did."

Silence. I could almost hear his mind spinning. "What?"

"You'd best sit down."

I waited until he had, and then I told him about Emerson's visit. He handed me the telegram. "This was waiting at the office."

I looked down at the paper. *Charles Van Berckyl fits dates STOP Died mining accident NV STOP Age 50 STOP.*

Charles Van Berckyl. The name felt alien. "It doesn't change anything. I'm still me."

Dante said, "But you're not. Do you know what being a Van Berckyl will mean to San Francisco society? A *New York* Van Berckyl?"

I didn't like the way he said it with such wonder. "Of course I do. They're one of the Four Hundred families, just as Mama always said."

"A pedigree that goes back to the Dutch founders of New York City. You've just been put into the Hoffman/McKay set—do you realize that? No one can touch you."

"My parents weren't married—"

"It doesn't matter. They'll fall over themselves to accept you. You're as good as royalty. A bastard Van Berckyl—I couldn't write a better story if I came up with it myself. Still, I don't understand why Oelrichs is involved, and I don't trust anyone but myself when it comes to you. I'm going with you to see him."

It was what I'd hoped. "I told him I was bringing a friend." I took his hand, nestling my cold fingers in his warm ones. "I admit I'll feel better going to see Stephen Oelrichs if you're with me. He's a lawyer; perhaps he can help me get my inheritance back. And clear my name."

Dante laughed. "You really don't understand, do you? Once San Francisco society learns who you are, there won't be anything for you to fear. They'd rather fling themselves into the ocean than accuse a Van Berckyl of murder—you can quote me on that. We'll find out what Oelrichs wants, but whatever it is, I promise I'll keep you as safe as I can. And that means splashing this news all over the *Bulletin*. By the day after tomorrow, everyone in San Francisco will know exactly who you really are. No one will dare to touch you with scurrilous rumors. Even I wouldn't dare."

"You? I don't believe it."

"I'd be run out of town."

He was smiling. But there was something of regret in his relief and joy that checked my own, and I found myself wishing that David Emerson had not found me.

The oldest families in San Francisco, and the old money, as Goldie had once told me, were not on Nob Hill. First, they'd built on Rincon Hill, and then had spread elsewhere, many—like the Oelrichs—to Van Ness. The fire had reached Van Ness but had not crossed it, and even with the evident earthquake damage—the cracked and broken boulevard, ruptured watermains, crumbled chimneys—the residential parts had a peaceful, settled look with their shade trees and their stately homes with pillars and turrets and little of the ostentatiousness of Nob Hill.

The Oelrichs home had a genteel and reassuring solidity, no doubt accented by the fact that, from the outside, the only earthquake damage it seemed to have suffered was broken cornices, an off-balance turret already surrounded with scaffolding, and a tumbled stair, of which pieces had been carefully and neatly stacked beside it.

Stephen Oelrichs's study too, unlike my uncle's, had the deep, luxurious textures of old money. Worn, rich leathers and expensive carpets that looked as if they had been in place, exactly this way, for a hundred years, though San Francisco had not even existed as a city that long. An oil portrait of his father, whom Oelrichs looked very like, hung above a mantelpiece. Shelves of books, not a paper cover among them, and ones whose pages I was certain had all been cut, lined one wall. The room had the feel of having been lived in, of things purchased for beauty and utility instead of show, and with none of the frenzy that had marred my uncle's rooms.

Which is to say that I felt comfortable, though I was acutely aware of how little I looked as if I belonged there. I was, after all, dressed in men's clothing. Stephen Oelrichs did not seem the least taken aback by that, though he was obviously discomfited by Dante when I introduced him as a reporter for the *Bulletin*.

"I hope you aren't here in a professional capacity, Mr. LaRosa."

"I'm here as Miss Kimble's friend," Dante said easily, but firmly. "And to make sure she's well treated, given that it seems to have been a problem in the past."

"Indeed. Miss Kimble. Might I call you May? I feel we are to know one another quite well."

"Are we?" I sat, as did Dante, when Oelrichs motioned to the facing chairs. "You appear to have weathered the earthquake well."

"We've cleaned up quite a bit. Fortunately the house is sturdily built, but for the servants' quarters in the back, which were badly damaged. Our troubles are slight compared to the rest of the city. I'd despaired of finding you in this chaos. I've been looking for you for weeks. Also, I feel I must offer my sincere apologies that I did not act on my first impulse."

"What impulse was that?"

He smiled, that same charming smile he'd offered when I'd first met him at the Cliff House, smoothly assured. I remembered Goldie's tension as she'd sat beside me, the set of her mouth. "The impulse to tell you to run screaming from the Sullivans."

"I believe you wished me luck. And then, later, you told me to learn to swim."

"Too little too late, I'm afraid. All I can say is that I didn't know that you were a Van Berckyl until very recently."

"Perhaps you could tell us how you know now," Dante put in.

Stephen Oelrichs went to his desk and rifled through the papers there until he found what he was looking for. "Shortly after the earthquake, I received this."

He handed it to me. It was a letter from a Peter Van Berckyl in New York City.

"Peter is a good friend of mine," Stephen explained. "We went to school together, and he was my companion on my grand tour. As you can see there, Peter wrote to me inquiring about an inheritance received by an illegitimate daughter of his late cousin, Charles Van Berckyl. Charles was a bit of a black sheep. He kept his distance from the family. Went out west shortly after a scandal involving, well, your mother, I believe, which is where he died. Apparently, he never forgave his family for forcing him to abandon her."

It was some consolation to know that she had mattered to him. My mother had called him honorable, and I supposed I would never know the entire story, or why she could so easily forgive him for leaving us. I didn't think I could, but it was good to know that I agreed with my father on one thing: his sentiments regarding his family. *My* family. Really it was remarkable, given my bloodlines, that I'd turned out at all well.

"In any event, the daughter—you—had been given this inheritance on the condition that she never contact the family, but he said they'd received word that she'd gone to San Francisco, and that they were concerned that she may have perished in the disaster, and—" He waved at the paper in my hand as if he did not wish to say the rest.

I glanced down at the letter, easily finding what he must be referring to. *It is a rather substantial amount of money, and if she is dead, we should not like it to be lost, but returned to us, as the original agreement states.*

Just as Shin had said. It was impossible not to laugh at my family's . . . well, I would be generous and call it *practicality*.

Stephen made a face. "Peter is a good man. I can't vouch for the rest of his family. I do know they've endured their share of scandals over the years, and so . . ."

"And so you agreed to look for me?"

"Yes. It's been difficult, of course, given the circumstances. Mr. Emerson had learned little. You'd simply disappeared. I did go to speak to your uncle. Knowing as I do of Jonathan Sullivan's unsavory business dealings, I was reluctant to involve him, but I felt I had no choice by that point. I was disturbed as to how unconcerned he seemed to be about you. He said your name had not appeared on any lists, and so you could not be presumed dead without investigation—"

"Because if I were dead, the money would have to go back," I said.

"—and when I asked about the money, he told me it was none of my concern and accused me of harassing Goldie and informed me that I would be very sorry if I did not leave them alone. I was suspicious, but I felt I should be cautious before I contacted Peter. I knew so little of what had happened, you see. So many city records burned, and there was the fact of . . . well . . ."

"Blessington," I said.

"Yes. Blessington." The play of emotions across his face was wonderful to see. He hid nothing; he would have been easy prey for Goldie, and I was grateful that he had escaped her.

"You wanted to be certain I wasn't insane."

"Your uncle had appointed himself your guardian."

Dante said, "You'll pardon me, Oelrichs, but why should Miss Kimble trust you—especially as a representative of a family who wishes to have nothing to do with her? Why are you involved at all?"

Oelrichs sighed deeply and sat on the edge of his desk. "I've told you. Peter Van Berckyl is a friend."

"There's more to it," Dante noted.

"Let's just say I feel sorry for anyone attached to the Sullivans."

"And yet you almost became attached to them yourself."

Stephen Oelrichs colored and glanced away. "Yes. A momentary madness. Miss Sullivan is quite beautiful. And she can be charming."

"She said you taught her to gamble," I informed him. "And then jilted her when she grew to like it."

He was obviously taken aback. "That's what she said?"

"She also said that you took every opportunity to shame and humiliate her."

"Ah. I'm sorry she thinks so."

"Is there any merit to it?"

His finely arched brows—a perfect foil for Goldie's, dark where hers were gold, what a perfect couple they would have made—came together in a thoughtful frown. "It was only a matter of time before I realized that your cousin cared little for me, but wished only to move in a—forgive me—better class of society. Also, she needed money. I did not teach her how to gamble, May. She was already very proficient when I met her. I knew she visited China Joe. I have no idea how she became involved with him. He's no one to toy with, you know."

I thought of the folder full of IOUs. Shin's missing finger. That menacing smile. *"If you do not . . . Your cousin finds out what happens when I don't get paid."* I tried to feel nothing. Goldie had set her own fate. That she didn't realize it should not be my concern.

Oelrichs went on, "Anyway, she wished to marry me, and she was ruthless about how she went about it."

"Ruthless how?"

Again, he colored. I thought of Goldie's seductive smiles that had so beguiled me. "Never mind. I think I know."

He cleared his throat. "Yes, well. When I realized it, I was appalled at my own stupidity. And yes, I'll admit that there have been times when I have sometimes added to the gossip about her. I was angry, you see."

"Are you still angry? Is that the reason you're helping me now?"

"What if I am?"

"Goldie manipulated me to make all of society believe me a lunatic." I remembered my desperation when I'd realized how they'd used just enough truth that everything I said or did only made things worse. "I thought I'd never be able to make anyone understand, and now here you are, and . . . and maybe I don't need to explain how easily she made me a fool."

"No," Oelrichs said with a smile that was both embarrassed and compassionate. "No, you don't need to explain."

"My uncle named himself my guardian the moment my money became available. He killed my aunt when she tried to warn me, and then he blamed me for it. I have a witness to prove it. Now I want my inheritance back, Mr. Oelrichs. I want to clear my name. And I want to punish the Sullivans for what they did to me. Will you help?"

Stephen Oelrichs seemed surprised that I would ask. "Of course I will. You're a Van Berckyl. You belong to us. We protect our own."

And so that afternoon I learned the true significance of my mother's words, *"Never give Them a reason to think you don't belong."* She was not only talking about etiquette and manners, but about something more amorphous, an entire state of being, membership in a tribe of which I was now a part, simply by virtue of the right name. *"You're a Van Berckyl."*

But again, I could not ignore the frisson of discomfort through my relief, or the echo of my cousin's reassurance more than a year ago, which turned out not to be reassurance at all, but something else entirely. *"You belong to us."*

Dante and I sat on the stoop. The paint of the little house had blistered in the fire, and I picked at it while he wrote feverishly in his notebook. The sun was setting, the fog of his cigarette smoke became tinged with the gold-gray light of sunset, and the evening breeze tickled the loose hairs dangling from my braid and made me shiver. The view was not beautiful, nor was the sunset. It was desolate and hostile, and it stank of smoke and sewage and an oily harbor sea. And yet, I thought I would keep this memory for the rest of my life. The day I took hold of my identity and my destiny.

One would think the world would be colored differently. Or that I would feel it so. But everything felt the same. I had a father—he was dead. I had a family—which didn't want me. I had a fortune—not quite yet. Nothing had changed and yet everything had, and the truth was the life that had felt so new that morning was already sliding away from me, borne on a breeze sweeping out to sea, dissolving in the mist. I wanted desperately to clasp and hold this moment, breathing in the foul smoke of Dante's cigarette, listening to his pencil scrape irritatingly across the page.

Tomorrow I would become the guest of Stephen Oelrichs and his mother until I could settle my affairs. They had insisted I stay with them tonight, but I had begged off, saying I needed to collect my things, which consisted precisely of what I wore and the metal rod in my pocket and my sketchbooks. Once Stephen—yes, Stephen now—had contacted my family in New York and had the papers drawn, we would go to the bank. Then, money in hand, I would be free to be anything I wanted. I would no longer be a poor relation. I would no longer be dependent on anyone.

It was time to start the life my mother had promised me.

Dante glanced up from writing. His hair had fallen into his face, and he pushed it away. "You'll be glad to get away from this shack, I imagine."

"I've rather got used to it."

He laughed. "A few days with a maid and a cook, and you won't miss this time at all."

I put my chin in my hand and stared out at the horizon, the fog bank rolling in, obscuring the line of color. "You know that's not true."

"In no time I'll be watching you at balls and entertainments and you won't even notice me."

"That won't happen. I know who you are now. You won't be able to hide from me."

He, too, stared off at the incoming fog. "You'll have all kinds of new friends among that set. You'll be too busy with them to think much about me."

"I've already lived that life, you know. I doubt I'll find it any more amusing now."

"Yes, well, you felt you didn't belong to the Sporting set, and you were right, you didn't. You're at the top of the ladder now. It might be different this time."

"Maybe. Anyway, you won't be watching me. You won't be the society reporter after this." I tapped his notebook. "Older will move you to a different beat and you won't be attending society balls."

"Here's to that, at long last."

But there was nothing to toast with, and I think that neither of us felt much like toasting, despite the successes of the day. Melancholy rolled in with the fog, a missing for something not yet gone, and I thought he felt it too, and then I knew he did when he set his pencil down on the stair, where it rolled to the dirt below, and he braced his arms behind his back. I leaned against his shoulder, and we sat like that for a long time, watching the fog and darkness sweep over the hill and the campfires flare to life, one after another, until it got too cold to stay, and we went inside.

We spoke no more of it as we went to bed. Even as we made love, I felt a tentativeness that had not been there before, an ambiguity we could not touch or address. What would happen was impossible to know. We'd found in one another a haven in disaster; together we'd gained what we each wanted. But how to make those wants fit together, and whether we should even try . . . The world was too new, as yet unformed and grasping. We hardly knew it, and so the question hovered between us unspoken, cautioning that we make no promises: What now?

What now?

I was to be at the Oelrichs house by noon, but when I woke the next morning, Dante was nowhere to be seen. He had promised to go with me, but as the hours passed and he made no appearance, it was clear that I was going to have to go alone.

There were pencils everywhere, in all stages of wear, and so on the margin of a copy of the *Bulletin*, I wrote: *Off to Stephen's, thank you for everything. See you soon!*—too little, too glib, but anything more would be too much, and I could not think of what else to say. I left it where he would see it, and told myself it was not goodbye. We still had plans. There was still the story that he was writing about the Sullivans, which we hoped would be the thing to destroy them once and for all. There was still the bank and my taking back my inheritance and settling things with China Joe and Shin. But those reassurances didn't make me feel any better as I packed up my things and closed the door behind me and contemplated the long walk to the Oelrichses' on my own.

The sketchbooks were heavy; by the time I arrived, I was tired and sweating, and annoyed with Dante for disappearing. Stephen was not there, but his mother, Rose, was, and she welcomed me as if I were a long-lost daughter. She reminded me of my own mother, actually, not because her rather distracted manner and vaguely affectionate smiles and her flurry of powder-scented, brief embraces were like my mother's, but because of her simple acceptance. She seemed to belong to another world, one more genteel, mannered, and gracious than I'd seen before, and one that bore no resemblance to the one I'd entered with Goldie and my uncle, and it did not take long before Mrs. Oelrichs made me realize that this world could never include the Sullivans.

My second day there, Mrs. Oelrichs came to me where I wandered aimlessly about the library. "This just came for you, my dear."

When I saw Dante's handwriting, I nearly ran to the door to catch him, but Mrs. Oelrichs said it had only been a messenger. Dante had sent a copy of the latest *Bulletin* with a note:

> Here it is, the last of the Chinatown articles. I'll visit China Joe and finish things there—no need for you to step your pretty foot into Chinatown again. The Sullivan article will be published soon, I promise. And so . . . I guess you won't be drinking at Coppa's with degenerate society reporters anymore. Good for you—you deserve the very best and I could not be happier. Dante.

That was all. I felt his sincerity and his affection, but . . . but what? I was disappointed. I wanted more, but I couldn't say what. The article was excellent: in-depth, well researched, and clearly written. He had been wonderful as Alphonse Bandersnitch, but it was obvious that news was his real talent, and that he loved it was even more so. I could barely contain my pride. It had all turned out so well.

This was the second time in my life that I had everything I wanted, everything I'd dreamed about. And just as then, I was dissatisfied.

Mrs. Oelrichs was kind, and Stephen was kind, but I was impatient and tense and restless. The loneliness I'd thought I'd banished returned with a vengeance. I was unused to doing nothing. The change from struggling to survive in a destroyed city to the luxury of a mostly undamaged manor was jarring. I waited for something to worry about, for something to do. I wondered about Goldie and Ellis and hoped that Joe had truly given Shin the freedom he'd promised. I wondered what was happening with the advertisement Dante had placed for me in the *Bulletin*, because I'd heard nothing. I supposed no one had responded and told myself I shouldn't feel disappointed. Why should I have expected anything? But I was haunted by the existence of that library, the plaque with Ellis's name. I sent Dante a message, hoping for good news. I received no response, not a word. I wondered if I'd been gullible again, if Dante had only used me, but I couldn't make myself believe it this time. He was simply afraid to tell me the advertisement was a failure when he'd been so encouraging.

All I could do was wait. Before I'd come to San Francisco, I'd never had a dull moment. I'd been busy working or helping Mama. The life I'd actually been living had spun the hours of the day so fast they blurred. I had my sketchbooks, but even drawing now could not make enough hours pass quickly. Not only that, but I found myself drawing a different world in my sketchbooks now, other rooms, not those rich with ornament and luxury, but those inspired by gray-pallored streets, smoke- and fog-smothered sunsets, and a kitchen where I drank wine with a man who was nothing as I'd imagined him.

And I longed for something more with an intensity that surprised me.

Stephen and I were ushered into the house quickly and shown directly to the large study, which had been converted into a banking office, something many of the city's banking executives had done. The leading banks had opened soon after the fire in whatever rooms or buildings could be procured, even with their vaults too hot to open and their records burned. As large as San Francisco was, most bankers knew their own customers, and by collaborating with the US Mint, they had worked to get the city up and running again.

Mr. Johnson was an easy man, Stephen added. Or he would be now that he'd seen the papers demanding the return of my accounts.

Johnson was tall and thick, but he had a grace that belied such a tree trunk of a man. His dark hair was graying; delicate spectacles perched on a face too broad for them. He welcomed us with a sober handshake for Stephen and a perusal of me that was not unkind.

"You're Miss Kimble, then?" he asked as Stephen and I settled in two armchairs. "You're the young woman all this fuss is about?"

"Rather an important fuss to me," I said.

"Indeed." He seated himself behind the desk and picked up the papers that Stephen had sent over the day before. "Such curious happenings. But I assure you, Miss Kimble, that all was in order. All the papers were correct. The guardianship—"

"Nonexistent now, and fraudulently obtained," Stephen put in.

"I'm certain Mr. Sullivan meant only the best for his niece. I am very glad that you are fully recovered and able to take control of your account, Miss Kimble. It is a great deal of money."

"You've seen the papers from my father's people, Mr. Johnson?"

"Oh yes. Charles Van Berckyl. Very impressive. I assume you intend to keep your account with us? This bank has served the very best families of San Francisco."

"I imagine that depends on how helpful you are," I said.

Mr. Johnson looked surprised.

I said firmly, "You do understand that any monies drawn from this account from this point on will be approved only by me?"

"Of course." Mr. Johnson slid papers toward me. "Here are the checks Mr. Sullivan has written and the bills he's approved for payment. I assume you wish to honor them."

"No."

Mr. Johnson pushed his spectacles farther up his nose, as if they might aid his hearing. "No?"

"No," I affirmed. "I will be paying nothing more for the Sullivans."

"But Miss Kimble, there are several outstanding accounts—"

"Those are not my concern. I still haven't decided, in fact, if I mean to sue my uncle for what he's already spent. I would appreciate it if you could please provide me with a history of the transactions."

Mr. Johnson looked to Stephen, who merely smiled and gave a slight nod.

Johnson said, "Perhaps you don't understand that they have few funds of their own. I had assumed, given that you are Mr. Sullivan's niece, you would continue to support the family."

"You assumed wrong. I want nothing to do with them. Can I trust you to obey my instructions in this, Mr. Johnson, or will I be better served by another bank after all?"

He looked shocked. "No. No, no, of course not! A Van Berckyl! Absolutely unthinkable."

"You have had a long relationship with my uncle."

"Long, yes, but hardly exclusive. In fact, if that association troubles you, I would be happy to suggest that Mr. Sullivan find another bank for his business."

"Why, I think that would be a wonderful idea. Thank you for suggesting it, Mr. Johnson. I should like that very much. I know I will feel much more comfortable if my uncle is nowhere near my money."

"Consider it done." Mr. Johnson wrote hastily on a piece of paper. "I'll inform Mr. Sullivan by the morning."

"I'd prefer it done by the end of today," I said.

He bobbed his head. "Absolutely. End of today."

I smiled. "Very well, Mr. Johnson. The account stays here for now. And just so you know, in the event that anyone asks, not only will I have nothing to do with the Sullivans, I will not do business with anyone who does. Is that clear?"

Mr. Johnson straightened, and I saw in his face a respect that I had not seen when we first came into this study. "Completely, Miss Kimble. Completely."

"Now," I said with satisfaction, "I would like to make a small withdrawal . . ."

THIRTY

Sullivan Scandal: Debt, Theft, and Murder!

Jonathan Sullivan Accused of Murdering His Wife.

Sullivan Heiress Well Known in Chinatown Opium and Gambling Halls.

Graft, Corruption, and Lies.

The headlines were on everyone's lips, as was the name of the reporter who'd written the story—Dante LaRosa.

The *Bulletin* sold so many copies it had to go back to press.

For a week, it was all anyone spoke about.

But then, well . . . the main witness to Florence Sullivan's murder was a Chinese maid, and it was rumored that Florence Sullivan was a laudanum addict. No doubt she fell.

As for Goldie Sullivan, it was unfortunate, but she was not the first woman in society to have a love of gambling, or opium, for that matter. Her debt was regrettable, but it wasn't as if she owed money to anyone *respectable*, and Chinamen had their own ways of dealing with such things, and it was really no concern of anyone else's.

And who could blame Ellis Farge's business for declining after such a shock? It was not at all surprising that he could not work and talked of retiring for a few months to the country. Those rumors that he'd stolen another interior architect's ideas . . . What harm was done, really? His clients were satisfied, and could anyone even remember the other man's name?

As for the accusations that Jonathan Sullivan plotted to keep the Chinese out of Chinatown and buy up the land himself . . . It was one thing when it was only the Chinese nattering on about it, but when it was China threatening to stop trade, and the white landowners of Chinatown saying that they didn't want to lose their lucrative Chinese renters, and the threat of millions of Chinese business dollars moving elsewhere, well . . . The Chinese had won that battle, and all was as it should be. It was time to move past it and get San Francisco back on her feet.

Surely too the concerns over city hall and Sullivan Building's crimes in its construction were overstated. So much hullabaloo when no one had actually died in its collapse! Everyone had escaped, and not that many people had been badly injured. And all that about the board of supervisors and Ruef and the mayor involved with the denizens of the underworld in city graft . . . What mattered now was vision and rebuilding. How could the city prosper if it was tangled up in indictments and arrests and trials? No one cared about corruption.

And wasn't it astonishing that a *Van Berckyl* had landed in San Francisco? It was proof indeed that San Francisco had no reason to feel inferior to New York City. The highest echelons of society were right here. As for the difficulties of May Kimble's arrival and all that nonsense about insanity and inheritances—she had come at a trying time for her family. It had been such a terrible misunderstanding. Best that the parties agree to put it aside.

San Francisco herself, after all, was the main concern.

Two weeks after the article was published, I received a postcard. On a photograph of palm trees lining a street, someone had drawn a girl smiling. The figure was crudely drawn, but she had long black hair, and beneath the picture's caption—*Palm Drive, West Adams St., Los Angeles CAL*—were written two Chinese characters. I could not read them, but I understood the message.

Shin was free.

The Benefit for the Rebuilding of San Francisco was the event of the year. It was held in a great circus tent erected in the ruins of Market Street, ironically with a perfect view of the majestic destruction of city hall. Everyone who could buy a ticket was there, with all proceeds going to the rebuilding fund, or to whichever millionaires ran such things. The point was not the money. The point was to be seen. It was to be my first major appearance since I'd been discovered to be a Van Berckyl—an *illegitimate* one, which was made clear by my relatives in New York, who asked me quite politely by letter to abide by the terms of my mother's agreement, lest I face legal action (very litigious people, my relatives) and on *no account* use the Van Berckyl name. It didn't matter what I called myself; San Franciscans still insisted on referring to me as "May Kimble, our own Van Berckyl." Despite their claim to care nothing for New York's opinion, or for the snobbery of the old wealth in New York, or for New York's claims to superiority, the coup of having a member of a real New York Four Hundred family in society's midst, bastard or not, was a source of pride and excitement.

The hypocrisy was astounding, and I chafed at it. These people had been more than willing to throw me to oblivion a year before. I dressed anxiously for the benefit and wondered why I even bothered to care what they thought. I'd bought one of the ready-made gowns that were just coming in to the temporarily relocated department stores. Mrs. Oelrichs had been kind enough to lend me her seamstress, who had done her best to turn the gown into something befitting my position.

It was pale bronze, with darker embroidery all over the bodice that left off in a fringe at the hips, and quite the most beautiful thing I'd ever owned. I felt like a queen in it, which was good, because I knew who had been invited to the benefit. All of society, as it was, after all, a benefit meant to raise money.

It would be the first time I'd see the Sullivans face-to-face since they'd put me away.

"You seem nervous," Stephen said as he helped me and his mother from his automobile. "You don't need to be. Remember who you are."

My mother's words again. How odd they sounded coming from his mouth, and yet here I was, at another ball, another assault on society. How well I remembered my first night in San Francisco, how the memory returned now, the hundreds of glowing candles, the gleam upon the torso of the bacchante in the middle of the ballroom. The champagne. The way I'd stumbled from the room and into a labyrinth of secrets and lies.

No more of those. No more.

The tent was decorated lavishly. Mrs. Oelrichs and Mrs. Hoffman had been on the planning committee, and I had heard Mrs. Oelrichs complain about the scarcity of supplies for decoration, but they had done themselves proud. The makeshift ballroom was festooned with gold bunting, transformed into a glittering forest of bare branches draping from oil lamps suspended from the canvas ceiling, along with pearl-like beads dripping to look like rain.

At the far end, a small orchestra played. Ned Greenway, whom I'd never met, but who was impossible not to recognize, given Dante's description—and it was true how much he looked like my imaginary society reporter—stood laughing with a young lady near a champagne fountain, supplied by Greenway himself. There were some benefits to being a champagne salesman. How, with the relief efforts still going on, they had managed oysters and pâté, I had no idea. I had no appetite for any of it, in any case. It was as boring as any other society event, and the thought of a lifetime of this brought a fluttering desperation. I was not going to live like this. *There must be something else.* Once again, I thought of the classified advertisement Dante and I had placed, of which I'd still heard nothing.

I would think of it after tonight. Tonight, I had one more thing to do.

I looked around the room for someone I might recognize, aware of how many gazes turned back to me, of the quiet talk—not mocking or disparaging this time, but admiring. I had to admit that I did enjoy the power of it as I heard—or thought I did—*Van Berckyl*, whispered over and over again. I could probably call them hypocrites and spit in their faces and they would still smile back at me and ask if they could fetch me a lemonade.

In spite of the fact that I had been to society parties many times with Goldie, there were many people here I didn't know. A different set entirely. I struggled to keep both my composure and my smile. Stephen brought me some champagne and then went to speak with a friend of his. I saw Thomas O'Keefe standing with Linette Wall near the orchestra, both staring at me as if they could not quite believe their eyes, and I remembered our drunken afternoon at the Cliff House so very long ago.

My nerves tumbled in my stomach. I sipped the champagne, which tasted sour.

"Miss Kimble," said a familiar voice at my shoulder.

I wanted to cry with relief. I turned to Dante with a smile. "I thought you wouldn't come."

"You sent me a ticket. How could I resist?"

"I expected you would be tired of balls."

He tugged at his formal collar. "I am, but you pleaded so prettily."

I didn't bother to disguise my pleasure at his words. "Well, thank God for that. I don't know another soul."

"Of course you do." He leaned close to whisper, the warmth of his breath once more against my ear. "There's Angel Martin—the one in the peach satin, an old gown, but who can blame her when there's so little to be had? And over there is Mrs. Lassiter—no, not her, the one by the champagne where the bunting looks ready to fall. That's an old gown too. She wore it to the Christmas ball last year. I think it's a theme, actually. No one's in anything new. Except you. Very becoming. Still . . . City of Paris."

"How silly of me. I should have thought to telegram Mr. Worth in Paris."

He took a sip of his champagne. "He'd fall over backward to oblige you."

"I'm glad you came."

His gaze was so warm it made me want to whisk him off to someplace private. "You mean to beard the lion in its den. I wouldn't miss such a show."

"I thought, because the article had so little effect—"

"I'm sorry it didn't do what you hoped for," he said. "But Older's moved me to the waterfront beat, so . . ."

"You must be happy."

"I don't know. I find I rather miss all the gossip."

"There should be plenty tonight," I told him dryly. "Enough for a lifetime."

"I'm leaving that for the new reporter who's taken over Bandersnitch. He's here somewhere." Then he said quietly, "I would have come even without the show, you know. Just because you asked me. I've missed you. I'm sorry I—"

He stopped. I followed his gaze, and when I saw what he was looking at, everything I'd been about to say, or hoped he would say, fell away. There was my uncle Jonny, returned to his sartorial splendor, his red hair gleaming, with Mrs. Dennehy on his arm. Behind him was Goldie, resplendent in green, with emeralds about her throat, and Ellis, and at the sight of them the rage I thought I'd mastered returned. How happy they looked. Goldie's smile, Ellis's gracious nod, my uncle shaking hands, everyone welcoming them. Nothing had ruined them. Not my taking away the money. Not the gossip, not Dante's articles. They had not even been tainted.

"Astonishing," Dante whispered.

I said nothing. I could only watch, mesmerized, as they came into the ballroom and took their champagne. Goldie talking with Linette, laughing with Thomas. All just like that night so very long ago, when Goldie had gripped my arm and said, *"We shall have so much fun!"* And Ellis, self-assured, his hand on her elbow a light touch. And my treacherous uncle. *"You're part of the family now."* Untarnished. Bright as the flames that had devoured the city. San Francisco still welcomed them. Everything they'd done, and nothing had touched them.

Yet.

I saw when they noted me. Goldie's smile froze, and she whispered something to Ellis, who licked his lips and never lost—not even for a moment—his self-assurance. My uncle, turning at Goldie's mouthed, "Papa."

Uncle Jonny looked toward me. The welcome and pleasure that came into his expression—had I not known him, I would not have thought it an act. Even now, it raised a flutter of longing.

But I knew better.

"They're coming over," Dante said, laughing beneath his breath. "Christ, what nerve."

I had known this was what they would do. I had known it because once I had seen Goldie poring over Dante's society columns. I had seen the way she'd cried over losing Stephen Oelrichs, not in sorrow, as I'd thought then, but in anger and frustration. I'd heard her resentment of Mrs. Hoffman, and her longing to be invited to the Cotillion Club. Goldie had not bothered to discover what I wanted from my life, but I knew very well what she wanted from hers, and I wondered, had I the power to take it from her? Were the lessons I'd learned from my mother enough? Was *I* enough?

I stood my ground as they came over. Goldie with her glittering smile, Ellis looking certain he would be forgiven. My uncle with his assured and knowing glance, penetrating, believing, and Mrs. Dennehy with a smile of welcome that made me sorry that she must be included in this, but not very sorry, because she had to know, on some level. She had to realize.

Everyone was watching. I took another sip of champagne.

Dante stiffened beside me as Goldie—first, of course, always first— hurried to me, holding her arms out for an embrace. Oh, that smile— one could not see the serpent behind it. How happy she looked. As if I'd just granted her greatest wish. "May! Oh, May, how glad I am to see you! We were all so worried!"

I waited until the precise moment before she would gather me close, and then I looked her in the eye and turned sharply and quite deliberately, and then, as if I did not see her at all, I walked away.

The Sullivans did not stay long after that. They couldn't, because no one would speak to them. Once I'd cut them, so did Mrs. Hoffman. Ned Greenway looked through them. Mrs. Oelrichs's expression became wax. Stephen kept talking to his friend as if Ellis Farge had not tapped him on the shoulder. One by one, San Francisco, who prided herself on following her own drummer, followed a Van Berckyl from New York City.

I had my revenge after all. I had ruined them, not with the proof of their own misdeeds, but because of who I was.

Dante and I stood outside beneath a settling mist. Behind us the lights burned, before us was the dark ghost of the city. My hand went into the pocket of my gown, unerringly to the button, which I rolled between my fingers. I said quietly, "I bought Goldie's IOUs from China Joe."

"You did?"

"She had no idea of her danger. She still doesn't."

"I'd say it was kind of you, but somehow I doubt that's your motivation." He spoke lightly, but I felt how closely he watched me.

"She doesn't know enough to be afraid of China Joe, but she'll wonder what I mean by it. She'll be uncertain."

"Uncertainty is what keeps people up at night," Dante said wryly.

"I know." I remembered those days in Brooklyn after my mother's death, my fear of the future. "I don't want Joe to hurt her, and I don't want her dead, but is it terrible to want her unsettled? Maybe to suffer . . . just a bit more?"

"I'm the wrong one to ask. I'd throw her off the docks if it made you happy."

I pulled my uncle's button from my pocket and held it out for him to see.

"What's that?"

"The button I found in my aunt's hand after she was killed. From my uncle's vest."

"You've kept it all this time?"

"I didn't want to forget," I told him. "I never wanted to forget what they'd done to me, and now . . ." I let it go. It dropped onto the street, rolling into invisibility. Had I been asked, I would have said it was not a burden, that I'd scarcely felt it. Now I knew that wasn't true. It was a relief to release it.

"How does it feel?" Dante asked.

"Good. Good, but . . ."

"But now what?" he finished.

"It's all I've thought about for so long. And now that it's done, I can want so much more. I can think about other things." I put my hand on his arm and turned to him. "Dante—"

"Before you say anything more, you should see this." He reached inside his suitcoat and pulled out a pocket folder, which he handed to me.

"What is it?" I undid the string clasp and opened it. Inside were letters of inquiry to the Brooklyn Company, in care of the *Bulletin*. Dozens of them.

"They've overtaken our mail. Older's ordered me to tell you to start redirecting them or we'll throw them out."

The first I saw was a missive from a Mrs. Elliot Longmire, who wrote:

> *I'm no good with finding something peaceful for the eye, and have a bad hand at decorating. I thought your parlor was the most calming thing I ever saw, and it makes me think that you might be the one to design the crypt for my father, who loved peace above all. I have no eye for beauty, but I don't want my father spinning in his grave for all eternity because I've put him into some grotesque. He was a lovely man in life, but I just know he would haunt me. I know you must get dozens of requests a day, but if you could find it in your heart to provide me with taste, when I have none, why, I'd pay any expense.*

I stared at it, suddenly breathless.

Dante said, "Look at this one." He leaned over my shoulder, shuffling through until he found it, and pulled it out for me to read.

I was very impressed with your design and I think you might know the perfect thing for my wife, Sukie, who is a cripple who dreams her days away, and I would much appreciate you making her a beautiful place to spend her hours. I have the money to get her whatever she needs.

I said, "Are they all like this?"

"Not all of them. Some are from the likes of those in there—" He gave a sidelong glance behind us, into the crowded tent. "But it's not just the rich who want beauty in their lives. Though, now that you are rich, I guess no one can expect you to do anything more than toil away at small talk."

"I'm not very good at small talk," I said, staring down at the letter. *A beautiful place to spend her hours . . .*

"No, you're too clever for it."

"I can't believe it worked," I mused. "I mean, I hoped, but . . . After your article came out, Mrs. Oelrichs asked to look at my drawings. She'd donated money to help build the Parson Library for the Arts and she was horrified by what Ellis did. She's asked me to design her a new parlor. She particularly likes bright colors, she said, and no one wants to oblige her. Everyone is too serious."

"Big globe lights," he suggested. "Geometrics mixed with paisley."

"You have terrible taste," I said.

"I'm better with gowns," he joked.

"I imagine that will come in handy on the waterfront beat." I wrapped the cords around the portfolio and handed it back to him. "Will you hold this for me until we leave? I've nowhere to put it."

He took it obediently and tucked it back into his coat. "So you'll take it up, then?"

Oh, that possibility . . . The flare it lit within me, the joy it raised . . .

"Someone once told me that I had a gift, and it would be a sin to waste it."

"Whoever said that was a genius."

"Or perhaps it's only that he knows me very well."

His smile became strangely shy. "Maybe he'd like to know you even better. I know it's not really acceptable. Not for someone of your set, and I've tried to stay away, and we could be friends, if that's all you want, but I thought, if you have time in between all your society commitments for a drink or . . . I don't know . . . a walk or something . . ."

"What you're suggesting is scandalous, Mr. LaRosa," I teased in my most snobbish voice, and then I laughed. I couldn't help it; I couldn't contain my happiness. "Where shall we go first? The horse races? I've never been. Or perhaps we could spend a few months together at Del Monte—I hear it's beautiful. We could start with Sundays at Coppa's, don't you think?"

He grinned. "I have a feeling San Francisco has no idea what having a Van Berckyl in its midst really means."

"A *Kimble*," I corrected. "It's about time a truly modern woman stirred things up a bit, don't you think? Life is short. No need for it to be boring too."

Beyond, the orchestra played and the crowd talked, and their laughter carried on the wisping cigarette smoke twining about the beads falling like rain, and gathered in the flickering light of the lamps that seemed to set the gold bunting afire. Fire and smoke and rain. Where we stood, the fog thickened, enveloping us in its embrace.

"Shall we go back inside?" Dante asked.

"I suppose we must," I said.

I took his arm, and stepped into the ballroom, and like the city herself, was remade.

ACKNOWLEDGMENTS

Many, many thanks are due to my agent, Danielle Egan-Miller, as well as Ellie Roth and Mariana Fisher and the rest of the team at Browne & Miller, for helping me work my way through this project, from inception onward. I could not have done this one without you, Danielle. Also eternal thanks to the editors who guided my steps: Jodi Warshaw, whose faith inspires confidence and who intrinsically understands the bones of a story, and Heather Lazare, whose suggestions I never doubt will make the book better, and who I trust completely to help me work things through and make the right decisions, which is a gift. To everyone at Lake Union Publishing—you are, as always, wonderful to work with, and I value your efforts more than you can possibly know. So many things go into making a book shine, from copyediting to cover design to artist to interior design to marketing and promotion and sales—thank you to all of you for your work on *A Splendid Ruin*.

Again, to my partner in friendship and writing lo these many years, Kristin Hannah, who keeps me from jumping off bridges and driving into traffic (metaphorically), I cannot express the depths of my love and gratitude; you know how I feel. To Suzanne Selfors, thank you for walks and tea and toast and hanging out and honesty and compassion. To Jena MacPherson, Melinda McRae, Liz Osborne, and Sharon Thomas, for being my sounding board for far too long, thank you, thank you.

I've been privileged to walk this path with many other talented authors who have become dear friends and who have generously provided advice, commiseration, celebration, and support through many brunches, lunches, teas, cocktails, dinners, and retreats over the years. There are too many to list, but you know who you are. I could not have asked for better companions on this journey. Thank you.

To my huge and beautiful family—my anchor in every storm—I love you.

Finally, to my husband, Kany, and my wise, beautiful, and courageous daughters, Maggie and Cleo: the center holds because of you.

ABOUT THE AUTHOR

Photo © 2012 CMC Levine

Megan Chance is the critically acclaimed, award-winning author of twenty novels, including *Bone River*, *Inamorata*, *The Spiritualist*, and *An Inconvenient Wife*. She holds a BA from Western Washington University. She and her husband live in the Pacific Northwest, with their two grown daughters nearby. For more information, visit www.meganchance.com.